"I'm not nervous, just anxious," she said tartly. "I need to get back to my shop."

"Yeah, and I need to get my life back."

By the time the music changed to another slow song, she was tingling in places she'd forgotten existed, and she nearly melted into his arms. Grateful for the crowd forming on the dance floor, she said nothing, just clung to the strong arms enfolding her while she pretended none of this was happening. She ought to pull away, but it had been so long . . .

He smelled of the hotel soap he'd used to shower this morning. He hadn't shaved, and his beard stubble grated her cheek as he leaned down to her. She had to stop this, knew she had to stop it, but a little voice in her head kept whispering it was just one more song.

Muttering a curse, Adrian caught Faith's elbow and dragged her into the darkness towering speakers. Without explanation, her against him, lungs with jus

She'd never before . . .

By Patricia Rice:

PAPER MOON
DENIM AND LACE
WAYWARD ANGEL
GARDEN OF DREAMS*
BLUE CLOUDS*
VOLCANO*
IMPOSSIBLE DREAMS*
NOBODY'S ANGEL*

Published by The Ballantine Publishing Group

NOBODY'S ANGEL

Patricia Rice

IVY BOOKS • NEW YORK

This book contains an excerpt from the forthcoming book by Patricia Rice. This excerpt has been set for this edition only and may not reflect the final content of the forthcoming edition.

An Ivy Book
Published by the Ballantine Publishing Group
Copyright © 2000 by Rice Enterprises, Inc.
Excerpt from forthcoming book copyright © 2001 by Rice Enterprises, Inc.

www.randomhouse.com/BB/

Library of Congress Catalog Card Number: 00-191737

ISBN 0-449-00602-6

Manufactured in the United States of America

First edition: December 2000

10 9 8 7 6 5 4 3 2 1

All characters are fictional.
The traffic, *however, is regrettably real.*

NOBODY'S ANGEL

❧ ONE ❧

After all the vengeful years of plotting and planning, and weeks of searching, he thought he'd found her.

Adrian's stomach rumbled as he ordered a beer. In his haste to get here after work, he hadn't stopped to eat. He couldn't eat. His stomach had twisted in knots so tight he wasn't certain if the beer would pass through.

His hand crushed the bottle the waiter brought, but his gaze never left the stage. The shaved-head waiter shoved his tip in his pocket and sauntered off. To Adrian, the kid looked too young to work in a bar, but he wasn't in any position to report him. He sank lower in the cracked vinyl seat of the booth and tried drinking the beer, barely noticing the taste. He hadn't touched the stuff in years, but in these last few weeks of hunting his prey he'd guzzled enough to dull any desire to drown in it.

The noise level in the barroom had already reached rocket-launch proportions. Tearing his gaze from the unlit platform of the stage, Adrian scanned the almost all male crowd, gauging it as he had learned to do from these last years in confinement with repressed male hostility.

The red and blue bar lights illuminated the smoky haze just enough for him to catch glimpses of weather-seasoned faces. This wasn't any polite yuppie hangout where the constant murmur of networking laced through the entertainment. This was a very large, noisy, drinking, brawling, pickup crowd. How the hell had Miss La-de-da wound up here?

She was a "Miss" now, he remembered. Before, she'd been *Mrs.* S.O.B.

1

For the most part, the crowd left him alone. Herd instinct warned them to steer clear of loners, and his naturally brown coloring marked him as alien in their all-white world. He knew how to overcome the obstacle of his mother's Hispanic origins when he wanted, but he wasn't in the mood for that game anymore. He had only one purpose here—to find the woman who had ruined his life and return the favor.

Adrian cracked a peanut shell between tense fingers and sought the stage again. The band was moving about, setting up instruments. The last singer had left to a chorus of boos and catcalls. The audience didn't care for melancholy love songs, it seemed.

He hadn't even known Tony's wife could sing. Hell, what he knew about her could fit in a thimble. If it hadn't been for the conniving old reporter, Headley, he could have spent the rest of his life searching for her.

Or he could have bought a gun on the street and rapped a few skulls until he got what he wanted.

First time around, he would try the peaceful approach. He wasn't in a hurry to spend any more time behind bars. The black hole of the last four years had already sucked him dry.

The audience stirred restlessly. The tinny noise from the jukebox didn't provide sufficient vibration to animate more than a tapping toe or two. Two couples in the booth across from him erupted in a name-calling argument. The burly bouncer edged his way through the throng at the horse-shoe bar in their direction.

Adrian shifted uncomfortably in his seat. He was out of his territory. Hell, he was out of his state, violating parole. No one knew him here, but he had no wish to be identified later.

The band began tuning up. The crowd's roar lessened perceptibly and all eyes turned toward the stage. Obviously, she wasn't a newcomer.

He propped his snakeskin boots on the far seat and sipped from his bottle. Those boots had caused him some ribbing years ago, back in Charlotte, in the good ol' days. But boots were the order of the day here in Knoxville, in this end of town. Maybe he should have a hat, too.

He couldn't afford one.

He didn't go down that depressing trail. He'd been broke before. He knew how to persevere against all odds. Hope was what mattered. As long as he had a smidgen of hope to cling to, he would survive.

Hope came in the form of Faith this time. Faith Hope.

Adrian snorted at the incongruous appellation. He assumed it was a stage name. He'd known her as Faith Nicholls back in the days of yore. Even that name hadn't fit. Faith Dollars might have made sense. Faith Fatbucks. Faith Moneybags. Her kind didn't deal in nickels and dimes.

Curiosity curled the edges of his mind as the spotlight blinked on. Maybe the beer was working on his empty stomach. He threw another peanut in his mouth and wrapped his fingers around the neck of the bottle. What the hell was Faith Moneybags doing in a dive like this?

Headley had broken the story that culminated in his arrest all those years ago. The old reporter had felt responsible or guilty enough to keep in touch ever since. Headley had been the one to tell him Ms. Moneybags walked out on her S.O.B. of a husband long before the trial. Adrian hadn't known that at the time. Nicholls hadn't said a word, and once the shit hit, he had been too busy trying to save his own hide to care what his partner's wife did.

The spotlight changed colors and Adrian popped another peanut as his gut clenched. Would he recognize her after all this time? Last time he'd seen her, she'd looked like the proper SouthPark matron she was—her flaxen hair smoothed into a chignon, her red suit screaming "designer," her nails neatly buffed and polished as she swore on a Bible to tell the truth, the whole truth, and nothing but the truth.

She'd lied.

As the band struck a fast chord with a heavy bass beat, he recognized the tune. The crowd roared, probably more in gratitude at not having to make more small talk than in appreciation for the music. If that was her signature song, it wasn't very original.

Adrian had his doubts that he had the right woman, but

Headley had sworn she was in Knoxville and that he'd heard reports she'd been singing in bars. That meant some of Headley's drunken cronies had seen someone who looked like her, but if she used the name Faith—

The cymbals crashed, the guitar hit a screeching crescendo, and the spotlight burned red.

Adrian nearly crushed the bottle neck as Faith Hope strolled on stage, belting out the familiar country refrain.

He didn't hear the song. He strained to see the Stepford Wife he knew behind the white leather miniskirt, sequined vest, bouncing blond locks, and red knee-high boots. Only the red silk shirt hinted at the woman he wanted to see. He didn't recognize her, but he'd never really met Faith Nicholls. He'd seen her in the office occasionally, saw her once at the trial. This couldn't be her.

Disappointment washed over him as the singer crooned a song of love, her blond shoulder-length hair swinging with the beat. She already had toes tapping and heels stomping. She didn't look any older than the damned waiter.

How in hell did that enormous voice exist in such a delicate package?

Adrian would have ripped the cap off the bottle with his teeth if the waiter hadn't already removed it. His blood simmered and settled in his groin as he studied the slender bundle of energy on the stage. She probably wasn't being deliberately seductive. She'd covered nearly every inch of her but the long legs, and she wore boots to deemphasize them.

He'd considered banging the first willing female he found as soon as the prison gates opened, but life had gotten in the way. That had been a mistake. As Faith Hope's voice lowered into a sultry refrain, he practically sizzled in his own juices.

It couldn't be her. Nothing he had seen of Faith Nicholls had ever caused him to so much as blink an eyelash, and not just because she'd been his partner's wife. He didn't like dainty blondes. People shorter than him made him feel like a gangly youth.

But the woman on stage was an irresistible ball of fire. She shouted, she crooned, she laughed and sweet-talked her way into the hearts of every damned man in the place. And she wasn't that great a singer.

Adrian scowled as even that realization didn't cool his lust. He wasn't a musician, but he recognized most of the songs because he'd grown up with them blaring out of the radio. She had most of the words right and didn't mangle the notes badly enough to jar, but a skilled vocalist, she was not. She captured the audience by sheer passion alone.

He watched in awe as she not only silenced the testosterone-laden crowd with the haunting refrains of "Blue Bayou," but had them weeping in their beer for lost loves and lost places as her voice broke on the chorus. Without missing a beat, she swung into a rocking version of "Rocky Top," and the crowd stampeded to the dance floor, with or without partners. The woman might not be a musical genius, but she knew her audience.

He couldn't tolerate the doubt any longer. This couldn't be Faith Nicholls. Every cell in his brain screamed the impossibility. Respectable society matrons did not descend to stinking, smoky dives to sing for truck drivers and hog farmers. But he couldn't bear hitting another dead end either. It had to be her. He didn't know where else to look, and the rest of his life depended on finding her.

Leaving the bottle on the table, Adrian edged around the foot-stomping crowd on the floor. Sticking to the shadows outside the circle of light, he leaned against a massive, vibrating amplifier at stage edge and watched her from a few yards away.

She was all sparkle and light, flashing sequins, flying golden hair, and shimmering stockings over tanned legs. She stroked the microphone and crooned to it in a way that probably aroused every prick in the place. It certainly did wonders for his own.

Wryly, Adrian noted she had a run in her stocking that snaked a thin trail over a leg so shapely a man's hand could mold it like clay. He wanted to cling to that small evidence of imperfection, prove to his straining groin that she was a woman just like any other, and no goddess capable of restoring his life with the wave of a wand.

But if she was Faith Nicholls, she had that power.

Normally, Faith wouldn't have noticed a stranger standing in the darkness. She tried not to see any of the men avidly following her every move. She hated the stares and concentrated on the words and the music. But the intensity of the stranger's gaze drew her like a magnet. Alone in a crowd, he collected shadows.

Did she know him? Was that why he was staring at her? She swung to the other side of the stage, away from him, but the spotlight only allowed so much leeway. She preferred not being recognized, but had always known the chance was out there.

Damn, why didn't he at least move? Out of the corner of her eye she caught the coiled tension in muscled arms folded tightly over a wide chest, giving the lie to his casual pose against the amp. Had he worn a cowboy hat or a workshirt or anything normal, she might disregard him entirely, but in black long-sleeve shirt and jeans, he was a silhouette of sharp, hard edges. He wasn't the usual city-soft Friday-night cowboy. She caught a glimpse of silver at his ear and the swing of coal-dark hair slicked back in a long ponytail. He had "Danger" imprinted on his forehead as clearly as any flashing road sign.

A beer bottle crashed somewhere in the rear of the bar, jarring her back to attention. On weekend nights the place could explode like a powder keg if not controlled. She could see Egghead elbowing his way to the shouting combatants, and she eased into a lighter song. The man in the shadows didn't break a smile at the sexual innuendoes and puns that had the rest of the audience howling.

She'd break after the next song and hope the stranger would leave. The regulars here treated her with respect and had a habit of removing hecklers without Egghead's help. But the stranger wasn't heckling. Maybe no one noticed him but her.

She shivered as the altercation in the rear escalated. She needed to concentrate on the music, soothe the savage beasts, give her audience the kick they came for, not obsess over lethal strangers. Keeping the bar from igniting into warfare was in her job description.

Even the stranger turned at the sharp report of gunfire. A woman screamed, men shouted, and the crowd broke in two directions at once.

It only took seconds, too fast to follow entirely. The dancers on the floor surged toward the stage as the crowd at the bar retreated from the brawl onto the dance floor. Someone took a dive over the sound and light booth, tilting it precariously. Beer spilled, amplifiers crashed, and the house lights shorted out just as a mass of bodies rammed into the plywood stage.

Faith tripped on a wire in the dark and started to tumble into the sweat-and-beer stench of the crowd.

Muscle-taut arms caught her by the waist and hauled her out of the melee with no more effort than a shopper heaving a bag of flour into a cart.

She gasped as she sailed over sprawling bodies and swinging fists into the relative safety of the harbor at stage right, sheltered by heavy equipment. The instant the hard arms released her, she gulped a deep breath.

"Some party you throw here," a whiskey-velvet voice spoke through the dark.

She knew that voice, but she couldn't place it. The mellow drawl shivered down her spine, reminding her of ages past, better left behind her. Though she searched for the memory, it eluded her. Maybe, in the chaos of the moment, she imagined its self-assurance.

"We hand out balloons to everyone still standing when the lights come on," she answered lightly, trying to ignore the electric vibrations emanating from his proximity.

"Faith, hey, you all right?" the drummer called from the stage.

"I'm fine, Tommy. I don't know about the mike. Maybe Artie ought to unplug the amps before the electricity returns. They may short the place out again."

"Hell, let's electrocute a few of the assholes first," the bass guitarist replied from the edge of the stage near them. "Where you at, Faith? Want me to get you outta here?"

"Go pull the plug, Artie, and stick your finger in the socket."

Tommy hooted, and ungrudgingly, Artie apparently stood up and sauntered back to the sound and light booth.

"Speak softly and carry a big whip," the stranger quipped dryly from behind her, nearly startling her to death. He was as still and silent as any phantom until he had a notion to make his presence known.

"They're good guys; they just don't think it's macho to give up." Faith didn't turn around to look at him. Intuition told her it would be as dangerous as gazing at Medusa, even through the veil of darkness. "I appreciate your help, but I'll be all right now. They'll have the lights back shortly."

"It has to be you," he whispered.

Startled, she froze.

He hesitated. Even though she couldn't see him, she knew he wanted to say more.

To her surprise, he didn't.

As the lights flickered on, she turned, and he was gone.

❧ TWO ❧

Faith lightly brushed her fingertips over the silver-blue luminescence of an antique bowl before she returned it to its case. Against the backdrop of black velvet, artfully lit to resemble the moonlight it was named for, the clair-de-lune porcelain possessed a power to mystify and attract as no other piece in here could.

Carefully lowering the crystal lid of the case, she turned with dust rag in hand to contemplate the contents of her gallery. Had she riches enough, she still wouldn't collect more clair-de-lune pieces, although she'd dearly love to find a contemporary work that stirred her equally. She had an artist's appreciation of the beautiful, but not the collector's urge to acquire more. The one piece she owned satisfied her need for that particular slice of heaven.

She often scouted the catalogs, hoping to discover the same brilliance as the antique bowl in a contemporary artist, but so far she had acquired only the one modern example, and she didn't know who had made it. She'd left the unknown artist's vase packed in the boxes of her old life. She didn't need the physical reminder of all those wasted years, and she couldn't sell the vase without knowing its origins.

She specialized in high-temperature glazed stoneware, a stronger form of the earthenware made since the 1700s in this part of the country. She might love the elegance of the translucent porcelain few Americans created with success, but the sheer joy and practicality of the vivid stoneware appealed to another side of her nature. The ability to create heaven from earth had always fascinated her.

Carefully, she dusted her one Lucie Rie, an exquisite jade-green bowl balanced impossibly on a slender pedestal. People were beginning to recognize that pottery could be an art form, not just a practical place to put food or flowers. The artists in these hills deserved recognition for their talents, and the prices on the more contemporary works of unknowns were well within the budgets of many of her customers. She displayed them as carefully as the expensive Rie porcelain.

She lifted her latest acquisition. The cracked glaze known as "crazing" would have been considered a flaw in dinnerware, but as art it added an exotic patina to the Chinese red that would draw every eye in the room. She marveled that a flaw caused by cooling a glaze too rapidly could produce such drama when done deliberately.

As she finished dusting and unlocked the door to open the shop for business, Faith turned on the display lights and admired the total effect. Artie had helped her with the wiring, but she'd had to hire a professional to choose just the right lights for each setting. She might have an appreciation for art, but she knew she had no talent.

Still, she was proud of what she'd accomplished in four short years. When doubts crowded the back of her mind, she swept them away by standing here as she was doing now, knowing she was gradually filling the empty well of her life with something good and decent. She might not be in New York City or Miami, making a big splash, but she was introducing the area to fine porcelain and stoneware and providing an outlet for local artists. She was determined to like the person she was turning herself into.

The overhead chime rang, and Faith swung out of her trance. A visitor arriving just after she opened could mean only one of two things: a convention was in town and she'd have a busy day—or trouble.

She recognized trouble as soon as Annie walked in the door, her thin face screwed up in her perpetual frown of worry.

"Faith, do you have a minute?" she whispered, as if the shop were a museum.

Annie was one of those people Faith couldn't convince that art was for everyone and not just the wealthy. She supposed she understood the mindset. If one spent one's life scraping up coins for groceries, art was a ludicrous waste of time and money. But Faith's love of beauty mourned the bleakness of a life without art.

"What's the matter, Annie? Surely the roof isn't leaking again. It didn't rain last night, did it?"

Before Annie could reply, Faith's breath caught in her throat as a lean shadow materialized outside the shop's plate-glass window. Him.

A pulse pounded at her temple as she tore her gaze from the window and back to the waif of a woman before her. An observer would never know Annie was the director of a shelter for the homeless and not one of its occupants. Faith started nervously at the ringing door chime but concentrated on Annie.

"We had a woman with three children come in last night," Annie whispered, darting an anxious glance at the man strolling through the doorway. "I'm sorry, you have customers. Call me when you can, will you?"

Faith didn't want Annie to leave. She knew the man in black presently perusing the Rie piece was the man from last night. She was already picking up his high intensity vibrations.

She caught Annie's wrist and steered her toward the counter. "There aren't enough beds?" she asked, keeping her voice low. She liked separating the various parts of her life. A customer didn't need to know of her involvement with the homeless shelter or the bar.

Annie heaved a massive sigh. "Not enough beds, not enough privacy, not enough clothes. The baby is still in diapers." She hesitated, cast a glance at the customer, and continued hurriedly. "I think she belongs in the battered women's shelter, but she hasn't said a thing, and I can't make her go.

Faith, the kids are all *girls*. You know how many men we have in there. If only we could afford—"

Faith patted her hand. "I know, we need another building. Let me see what we can do about the beds and clothes first. The building fund will have to wait a little longer."

"Bless you," Annie said with obvious relief. Darting a glance at the lean, dark man now gazing at a consignment of contemporary Navajo pottery Faith had taken as an experiment, Annie hurried away.

The rush of cool fall breeze as the door opened and closed was all that stirred the palpable tension left behind after Annie's departure.

Faith reached for her telephone.

"Don't." He stretched over the counter and closed his fingers over her own, holding the receiver pinned in its cradle. She hadn't heard him move.

Shaking, she clenched the hard plastic and dared to look up.

The impact of deep brown eyes framed in heavy black lashes nearly undid her. The physical contact of their hands was no longer tolerable as she floundered under the intensity of his stare. She jerked her hand from beneath his and awkwardly balled it into a fist.

"You." She spoke first, breaking the stretching silence. "How did you find me?"

"Artie has a major crush on you," he said dryly, returning his hands to the pockets of his trousers. They hung loosely on his narrow hips, as if designed for a better-fed man.

"Artie is twenty-three and has a crush on any woman who refuses him." She spoke neutrally, grateful for the barrier of the counter as she tried to probe the stranger's vague familiarity. With Cherokee-straight black hair, naturally tan skin, and a lean physique accentuated by muscle rolling tautly beneath black cotton shirtsleeves, he didn't look like anyone she should know. Taut creases cut either side of his unsmiling mouth, and a sharp beak of a nose emphasized his uncompromising appearance. He held himself with an air of authority that terrified her.

He said nothing, only stared as if he could see beneath her skin. Nervously, Faith brushed her loose hair back from her face and wished she'd put a barrette in it. "Artie shouldn't have told you where to find me."

"He had a lot of beers, and I'm told I have a persuasive tongue."

Oh, yeah, that he did, but it was his voice rather than his words that stroked and wrapped around her like loving fingers. He would put a preacher to shame with a voice like that. Put him in a pin-striped suit and silk shirt and tie and stick him before a courtroom—

Faith gasped and stepped back, eyes widening. "You!" she exclaimed for the second time, for a different reason.

"We've established that." He bent his head slightly in acknowledgment. Sunlight shot a gleam off the silver of his earring. He still didn't smile.

She'd seen him with an expensively styled haircut, in a tailored suit, with a gold watch on his wrist. He'd looked like a pirate—a corporate one.

Ridiculous. She shut her eyes against the image. She hadn't known him as any more than a shadow of Tony back then. "What do you want?" she demanded.

"Your husband's books."

She heard the grating harshness behind his innocuous words. "He's dead," she reminded him. "I thought they'd locked you away."

"Time off for good behavior." The voice dripped satire. "Not difficult to do in a minimum security prison. And since I'm not married and couldn't be granted conjugal visits, I had lots of incentive."

Faith's eyes shot open as soon as the vision of this man, naked, having sex, appeared in her overactive imagination. She hadn't thought about sex in years, had given it up for Lent and forgotten to pick it up again. This man exuded a sexual aura that hummed through all her senses.

She saw the mockery in the depths of those dark eyes. "I have nothing of Tony's, wanted nothing. The court kept his papers."

"Not the ones I want." Adrian studied her, studied the pale skin with only the merest of cosmetics to dress it, the gray eyes staring at him with widened fear and bone-deep wariness. He contemplated the best method of pushing her buttons until he got what he needed without resorting to violence.

She wasn't what he expected. She was taller than he'd thought, and wore her hair loose like a girl's, straight and slightly turned under where it brushed her shoulders. She had skin as smooth and translucent as the fabulous porcelain she protected in her glass cases. Porcelain should be touched to be admired. He wanted to stroke her in the same way he'd stroke that clair-de-lune piece behind her. Both were magnificent.

He jerked his mind back from the impossible. She hadn't responded to him, but she couldn't have lived with a lawyer like Tony without learning the lesson of keeping silent. He hadn't expected her to be cooperative. He hadn't expected her to be this fragile either. She looked as if she'd fracture at the slightest touch. He had the pieces of enough shattered lives in his hands.

"You sent Headley the pages copied from the bankbook and the canceled checks," he reminded her. "You have to know where the rest of them are."

"If I'd known that, I would have turned them over to the court and watched Tony fry in hell." Her dry tone matched his own, with an undercurrent of bitterness.

"You *had* them," he insisted, "or you couldn't have copied them to send to a reporter. Tony's dead now. You don't need to protect him or anyone else. I just want to clear what remains of my name, and try to turn my life around."

She gifted him with a look of scorn that should have scorched the shirt off his back. "You think those books will *clear* your name? I was there. You filed the wills. You filed the trusts. It was your name on the documents, on the bank accounts, on the fax transfers. I'll admit, I never believed Tony was innocent, but he was smart enough not to get caught."

"Except by his wife. Where did you find those papers?" he demanded. He was too angry to argue her accusations. He'd argued them four years ago, without success, because he'd done every damned thing she'd just accused him of. What he couldn't prove, however, was his arrogant ignorance.

Unbelievably, in the face of his fury, the delicate figurine of a woman on the other side of the counter relaxed and smiled enigmatically. Taking a seat on the high stool of her work counter, she pulled out a stack of invoices. "I found them in the same place I found the canceled checks written to Tony's girlfriend. At the time, I was more interested in Sandra than the accounting records. The records were just icing on the cake when Headley figured out what they meant."

He didn't believe this. Couldn't. She had to be lying, just as she'd lied at the trial. "Who are you protecting?" he growled irritably, trying to regain his cool but not succeeding. The ice queen he remembered from the courtroom was rapidly replacing the open child he'd encountered when he entered the shop minutes ago.

"I'm not protecting anyone," she replied with much more composure than he possessed right now. "All I had were those copies stuffed in his wall safe. Knowing Tony, I'd say he kept them as a kind of insurance against anything you might pull, or a means of getting rid of you should you become inconvenient. I just played his card a little earlier than he anticipated."

No, this couldn't be happening. For four years he'd built an airtight case based on the evidence he knew those records would produce. He'd figured out the whole rotten scheme, made lists of every client Tony had robbed, obtained all the transcripts, all the copies, written dozens of letters of inquiry. All he needed was the hard evidence linking Tony to the missing money—

Adrian's eyes narrowed as "money" rang in his head just as his gaze hit the clair-de-lune bowl mounted in its case behind the counter, probably protected by a dozen security alarms.

"*You* took the money," he whispered. He'd considered it, but had not really believed—until now. Why? Had he really trusted that look of pure innocence in the eyes of the wronged wife, even as she sat there lying through her pearly white teeth?

"You would have let those old ladies and children starve so you could keep living like a damned queen after Tony cut off your money faucet."

His accusation wiped away her smile. She looked at him as if he were lower than the carpet beneath his feet. Frigging hell, she could stare a man into icy perdition.

"As far as I'm aware, Tony and his tart absconded with everything. I signed my share of the law office and all of its assets over to the court to repay what they could. The lawyers' legal fund paid the rest. You have the wrong woman, Mr. Raphael. If I were you, I'd find Sandra. Now, if you don't mind, that's the end of our discussion. Please leave."

She didn't even resort to the obvious threat: "Or I'll call the police." If the police found out he was here, they'd book him for violation of parole and heave him behind bars.

Battening down his rage, Adrian calmly looked her up and down. While she'd talked, he succeeded in reading her calendar. He knew her schedule, and tomorrow's suited his need for retribution. She wasn't off the hook yet. "I am guilty of greed, Mrs. Nicholls, but I am not guilty of theft, or even perjury. Sandra Shaw was Tony's girlfriend long before you became his trophy wife. She's living in a trailer park in Florida now, struggling to support their three kids. You're the one with a priceless porcelain on your wall. I've given you the opportunity to do the right thing. Now, I'll do it the hard way."

Without waiting for a reply, he turned on his boot heel and stalked out.

The fury in his velvet voice hung in the air long after the door slammed closed.

Sandra didn't have the money?

Frozen breathless, Faith had to remind herself to breathe as Adrian's angry accusations settled into the astonishment of revelation.

She'd spent the last four years without a life, hating a

woman she didn't know, and Sandra didn't have Tony's ill-gotten gains?

Where the hell were they, then?

❧ THREE ❦

Four and a half years earlier

Carrying a shopping bag containing Tony's favorite delicacies from the gourmet deli in one hand, a packet of information from the adoption agency in the other, Faith strolled up her front walk beneath the towering willow oaks, admiring the spill of pink azalea blossoms across the aging brick cottage. She loved this house in the comfortable old Charlotte neighborhood of Dilworth where she knew everyone and everyone knew her. Her parents' constant traveling had never allowed that kind of stability in her youth.

Tony was talking about selling and buying one of those formidable million-dollar mansions over in Myers Park, but she was resisting. The two of them didn't need that kind of extravagance, even if Tony listened to her and acted on the packet in her hand.

Juggling bag and envelope, she opened the weathered copper mailbox—one of her prouder acquisitions, if she said so herself. She'd scoured the antiques stores for weeks looking for the perfect one. That had been back in the days when she was still working at Tony's office and their budget had been tight. She'd finally found what she wanted under the rubble of iron in a junk store and carefully bumped out the dents herself. Tony had wanted everything brand new and expensive, but she was used to living cheaply and hated debt. After the first few of their sophisticated neighbors admired the box, he'd reluctantly admitted she had taste.

Now that she didn't have to work, she handled all the details of their home life, while Tony concentrated on building a bigger and better law practice. She was proud that he helped so many widows and orphans with the legal burdens of estate management, along with his usual cases. Tony was a good lawyer. She shouldn't complain about his traveling and long hours. She just wasn't used to having so much time on her hands. She needed something of her own.

She needed children, but she couldn't have them.

She wouldn't dwell on the pain. The envelope from the adoption agency explained things more clearly than she could. Once Tony understood how it worked, he'd be more comfortable with the idea.

If only she could make him understand that she needed to be needed, that she had something to offer beyond adorning his home. She didn't make a good ornament.

Pushing aside a fleeting resentment, she unlocked the door and flipped through the stack of catalogs in her hand as she headed for the kitchen with her shopping bag. Setting the risotto and spiced lamb in the refrigerator, she frowned at a priority mail envelope from the travel agency. They usually sent travel itineraries to the office. She hoped Tony didn't need this today.

Or could this be Tony's surprise for their anniversary? Could he finally be taking her on the cruise she wanted?

Lips twitching upward in anticipation, Faith debated opening the envelope. She always opened the mail. That was her job. Tony would be upset with the agency, though, if this was supposed to be a surprise and they'd mailed it here instead of the office. Tony loved to surprise her on birthdays and anniversaries and holidays, and he always had the perfect gift. It had to be the cruise tickets.

She'd best check the envelope and return the tickets for proper mailing. She'd have a hard time keeping a secret, but Tony was impatient with incompetence, and she didn't want the ladies at the agency to lose their jobs. He'd said he would be out of town next week, so she wouldn't have to hide her knowledge long.

In the study, she removed the ticket packets from the envelope, deposited the mail on the desk, and glanced at the printed travel schedule inside the top packet. Her smile broadened as she read Tony's name on the itinerary and recognized the cruise line brochure. She'd always dreamed of visiting the Caribbean, but they'd never had money in the early days, and now Tony never had time.

Dreaming of the naughty lingerie she'd wear to thank him for taking time from his hectic schedule just to please her, she flipped open the second packet.

In disbelief, she stared at a name that wasn't her own. And an identical cruise brochure.

The Present

Faith hurried down the Sunday morning sidewalk, skirting winos still sleeping in doorways, swinging her sacks of supplies, singing softly to herself in the crisp fall air. The past was past. She had a new life now, one she loved. She adored autumn. Even though this was the first crisp day they'd had this September, she could almost smell the leaves burning, and she was eager to head for the hills.

They'd had a great time at the bar last night, and she'd put Adrian Raphael and his accusations completely out of her mind. After the Friday night fracas, the police had patrolled the crowd more than usual, but she'd sung a song about policemen every time one entered, and the crowd laughed at her warnings and tolerated them without complaint. Faith had been grateful for the presence of the men in blue. She figured they'd kept Adrian from returning.

She didn't want to think about Adrian Raphael and waste a perfectly lovely Sunday. After she dropped off the supplies with Annie, she planned on touring a new pottery she'd heard about. She needed to take some time out of her schedule to visit the wealth of potteries down in Seagrove, but she only had part-time help to mind the gallery during the week, and the band was booked on the weekends for months. Maybe she could close up for a few days for the big November auction.

She shoved her shoulder against the shelter door and hauled in her heavy sacks as it creaked open. A few snores greeted her from the room to one side, but the laughter of children drifting from upstairs warmed her heart—until she consciously shut the mental doors barring access to that vulnerable organ.

An eight-year-old boy with a head of tight curls she remembered from her last visit darted down the hallway to warn Annie of her arrival. One of the workers from the soup kitchen wandered out to give her a hand. Faith wasn't truly comfortable with any of the occupants or workers of the shelter, but then, she wasn't entirely comfortable with herself some days.

She smiled at the children poking and prodding each other on the stair steps. More arrived as if responding to some unseen telegraph signal. She'd tried buying them with candy on her first few visits here, until she realized books were as highly prized as candy. Now she brought a little of both. They were seldom the same children from one visit to the next, but somehow they always seemed to know who she was.

Recognizing one of the older ones, she handed up a Wal-Mart sack on her way toward Annie's office. The child knew what to do, and Faith could hear the muffled shrieks and giggles as the loot was distributed. The kids tried to be quiet so as not to disturb the sleepers in the room below, but kids had too much energy at this hour.

Annie appeared at the back of the hall just as the giggles of the children escalated and grumbles emerged from the room of sleepers.

Breezing past Annie, Faith dumped the last sack in the chair with the others. Annie's office looked a lot like its occupant—dumpy, disheveled, tired, and overworked.

Pulling her raveled cardigan together, Annie peered into the sacks. "Faith, you're a lifesaver. Your parents should have called you Charity."

"That's what they called my sister." Faith removed an overlarge cable-knit sweater from one sack and jerked it on over the thin hair of Annie's head. "If I hadn't seen my father's birth certificate, I'd swear they'd made up the name of Hope, too. Unrepentant hippies."

Annie's head popped out as she wriggled her arms into the sweater. "I wasn't cold," she protested.

"You make me cold just looking at you." Faith shivered inside her thermal-lined denim jacket. It was colder inside the drafty building than outside in the sun. "How are the girls and their mother doing?" She'd intended the sweater for the mother, but knowing Annie, that's where it would end up anyway.

"They're doing okay. That man has a way with kids. Is he a cop?" Annie asked bluntly.

Startled, Faith stopped unpacking the bags. "What man?"

"That man who calls himself Quinn. Didn't you send him? I saw him in your shop yesterday, and I didn't figure it was coincidence that he showed up here last night. He's hardly inconspicuous, so if he's undercover, he has problems."

"Quinn?" Faith desperately searched her memory for the name, but she knew in her heart who it had to be. She wasn't normally prone to anger, but he'd had her temper cooking twice now, and this time he wasn't even in the room. "What does he look like?" she asked, striving for rationality and not a hysterical fit.

Annie gave her a queer look. "The Highlander, maybe?" she suggested. "Are you telling me you don't know this guy? That I could be letting some pedophile up there with those kids?"

"What did he tell you?"

Annie glanced toward the ceiling. "That he's just out of prison, doesn't have a place to stay, and he's washing dishes at O'Riley's until he can manage a deposit on a place of his own. I didn't believe his story because I'd seen him in your place. He isn't exactly the type we get in here."

No, Faith didn't imagine he was. Even with the long hair and earring, Adrian Raphael was too well put-together, too visibly solid and powerful to be among the world's lost and confused. Still, the court would have fined him everything he owned. He was probably broke.

She didn't think it was coincidence that he showed up here. He could have overheard her conversation with Annie and checked the nearest shelters. Annie wasn't hard to find.

"The man you saw in my shop was no cop," she warned. How much more should she tell Annie? Should she go upstairs, verify it was Raphael, and have him thrown out on his rear?

What could he want with the homeless shelter? Any possibility she considered didn't sound healthy to her well-being.

"Good morning, Mrs. Nicholls," the smooth baritone abruptly interrupted before she could organize her thoughts. "Easing your guilt with a little charity this morning?"

Damn him. Double damn him. The grating tone of innocence didn't set her off so much as the use of that hated name. Ignoring Annie's startled reaction, Faith swung around to confront the monster. His physical presence struck her in the face as her nose nearly brushed his flannel-shirted chest. She hurriedly stepped back.

"My name is *Hope*. And I suggest you leave now." Which was a ridiculous threat given her head was at his chin level and, despite his leanness, he could probably break her in two.

"Hope?" Amusement and disbelief curled his lips. "Faith *Hope*, and this is your charity?"

She'd heard every form of the joke from the moment she was born and had no patience with it now. "*Charity* is my sister." She stepped farther back, out of the danger of his solidity. "This is Annie, my friend. I told you before, I have nothing to say to you. Leave me alone."

"I just took doughnuts to Joe at the station. Should I call him?" Annie asked with concern.

"I really don't think Mister . . ." Faith watched in triumph as he flinched over the hesitation before she chose his fake name. ". . . *Quinn*, will want that, will he?" She might not know a lot about law, but she could guess a parolee shouldn't be out of state. "I think Mr. Quinn will leave quietly."

"And leave you to sprinkle your largesse like bread crumbs while you live off the lives of widows and orphans?" he threw back brashly. "Perhaps your friends would like to know about the source of your benevolence, Ms. *Hope*."

"What I own, I earned. I owe no one any explanation."

"Earned? I'll admit, living with Tony deserved combat pay, at the very least, but not at the expense of the innocent."

Slack-jawed, Annie eased toward her desk. Annie had been her first friend in the city when she'd desperately needed a friend. She didn't want to see that relationship shattered by this vile man's wild accusations. Let the police have him. She glared at him and did nothing to stop Annie's progress toward the phone.

"Mr. Quinn! Mr. Quinn, will you play with me now?"

A pigtailed toddler in a threadbare pinafore threw her tiny arms around Adrian's leg. Tears sprung to Faith's eyes at the sight, even as she backed from the scene.

Adrian crouched and chucked the toddler under the chin. "Why don't you let Sissy read you one of the new books?"

" 'Cause I wanta play with *you*," the little girl entreated.

Throat closing up, Faith gripped her handbag and nodded curtly at Annie. "I have to go. I'll talk with you later."

Brushing past the lean man with the child clinging to his leg, Faith hastened down the hallway and out the door to the street.

She heard his unhurried stride on the pavement behind her as she turned the corner toward her car. Searching frantically through her purse for her keys, she walked a little faster. She didn't want to talk to him. She didn't want to be reminded of who she'd been and who she'd never be. She just wanted to be left alone to make what she could of what was left.

A street kid leaned against the driver's side door of her car. She didn't need the hassle right now. She stayed on the curb and aimed for the passenger side.

"Hey, lady, where ya goin'? I just wanted a ride is all."

Maybe that was all he wanted, but the knit cap and the gang tattoos warned that he was more trouble than she had time for. She shoved her key into the door lock.

"Hey, look lady, I don' mean no trouble." He ran around the bright turquoise hood as she jerked the door open.

Faith climbed into the car and tried to shut the door, but the kid grabbed it.

A stealthy form clouded the window, and the kid miraculously released his grip. Faith slammed the door as her would-be assailant suddenly hovered a foot above ground.

"She's with me," the deep voice said with none of its usual smoothness.

Through the window, she could see a long-fingered brown hand wrapped in the kid's shirt, holding him clear of the ground. Faith hastily climbed over the stick shift and hit the driver's seat with key in hand. She just wanted out of here.

A silvered flash in the passenger window halted her before she could turn the key. The kid had a *knife*.

Before she could open her mouth to scream or even think of doing anything heroic, the silver weapon arced harmlessly down the street.

The kid howled in pain as long fingers bent his thin wrist backward.

Faith could only watch as the young tough hit the street running, holding his wrist protectively against his chest. She didn't see much point in arguing as the passenger door opened and Adrian folded himself into the seat beside her.

"I'd rather not wait for the police to investigate the altercation," he said politely.

And they would. The station was just down the block and the army of eyes and ears around her would have passed the word by now. All she had to do was refuse to turn the car on and she could be rid of him without a fight. They'd revoke his parole and lock him up for another year or two.

Or she could pull away from the curb and drive peacefully away. Wondering if she needed her head examined, Faith switched on the ignition with shaking hand. She could feel the lethal violence emanating from Raphael's tense fists, but he'd used them to help her. In her book, one good turn deserved another. If he really wanted to physically harm her, he'd had plenty of opportunity already.

He breathed a quiet sigh of relief as the car rumbled from

the curb and picked up momentum as a pair of patrolmen turned the corner.

"I don't know what you want with me." Faith guided the car toward the main thoroughfare out of town. "I left Tony before your trial. I can promise you he didn't give me any papers to hide, and I never saw the money, never suspected it existed until Headley explained those papers to me."

Adrian gave the cracked plastic dash of the shabby VW a wry look. "Keep it up. You just might convince me. Where did you find this thing? Mexico?"

"Actually, yes. My parents live down there. It's not as old as it looks." Stiffly, she stared at the road ahead. The man beside her filled the small car until she couldn't breathe. She opened the window, but the breeze didn't diminish his overpowering presence. He wasn't wearing aftershave or any scent beyond whatever male pheromones drew her like a moth to a flame. Why had she never noticed him when he was working with Tony?

Because she'd never seen anyone but Tony. Blind, stupid—

"Why did you run back there?" he asked with open curiosity.

"Because thugs with knives scare me?"

Long brown fingers gestured impatiently. "Not then. You *should* have run then. Back at the shelter. You could have had me routed but you crumpled."

Her hands tightened on the wheel. "Where am I taking you?"

"Wherever you're going. We need to talk."

She didn't want to talk. She didn't trust him and he was ruining her beautiful, carefree day. Stubbornly, she sat silent as she steered onto the wide open road toward the mountains.

He tolerated the silence for a while, admiring the scenery but not relaxing, if his crossed arms were any indication. When they were sufficiently far out of town, he prodded her again. "This is the perfect opportunity to clear the air."

"I don't think we have anything to clear. That part of my life is over, done, kaput, *finito*. I don't need your problems."

"Tony did a job on you, too, huh?" Awkwardly, he adjusted

the uncomfortable position of his long legs as he swiveled to watch her. "Why didn't you ever have kids of your own?"

"None of your damned business." The pain curled inside her, a spiked ball that gored her vital organs. "I'm heading into the mountains for the day. You'll be bored silly."

"If I wasn't bored silly staring at four walls and butt ugly men, I won't be bored in the fresh air and freedom of the mountains."

Faith winced at the dry whiskey of his voice. It really did have a magic quality that wrapped an air of trust and security around him, even though she knew he was a lying, conniving thief. A *dangerous* conniving thief. Even worse, a *lawyer*.

"You're not afraid I'll leave you stranded on a mountaintop?" she asked boldly.

"Not now that I'm warned of the possibility." Humor sparkled through the dryness. "You're not at all what I expected."

"Disappointed?" she taunted, hitting the gas. "Thought I'd be another of Tony's tarts?"

"Sounds like a frozen pizza dessert—Tony's Tarts, with lemon cream marinara sauce—yum yum."

A grin tugged at the corner of Faith's mouth before she caught it and remembered just exactly who she was dealing with here. "Most amusing, but you'll remember I lived with charm and wit for eight years. I'm not fooled by appearances any longer."

"Eight years?" Astounded, he stared at her. "You endured that lying bastard for *eight years*? Are you a saint or just stupid?" He waved his hand hastily. "Forget I said that. He must have married you out of the cradle."

"There you go again. It comes as naturally as breathing for you, doesn't it? It still won't do you any good. I don't have any papers, and I don't have the money, so you can't charm me out of them."

"All right, let's say I buy that for now. We can have a refreshing trip through the autumn hills and figure out what Tony might have done with them. Or we can drop the topic, enjoy the day, and get to know each other. Right now, I'm about ready to opt for that last. I can always track you down again tomorrow and continue the argument."

Faith shot him a doubting look. "I just told you, I lived with a con artist. I know better than to believe one now."

He leaned forward to admire the spectacular view of the mountains ahead. She might survive this trip if he would leave her alone. Concentrating on the traffic and the road, she pretended he was a tourist.

He waited until they'd reached the dangerous passage through the mountains before he tried again. "Why did you run from the shelter? You looked as if you'd been gut-punched. You have some strange kind of phobia about kids? Are you allergic to them? Is that why Tony kept Sandra on the side, to produce miniature Nichollses?"

Struck broadside, Faith considered ripping the steering wheel from the dash and pounding it over his ponytailed head, but the semis roaring around them discouraged it. She'd forgotten how irritating, demanding, self-centered, and just plain ornery men could be.

"I can't have kids," she said bluntly, hoping to put him in his place. "We waited years until Tony was earning enough to support children, and then I couldn't have them."

Adrian stared at her in disbelief. "Of course you couldn't. Tony had a vasectomy while he was still in school, right after Sandra had the twins."

The VW shot straight for the side of the road.

❧ FOUR ❧

"Faith, give it up, willya? We've tried and we can't have kids, so just let it be. It's not that I'd have time for them anyway."

"But *I* would," Faith argued timidly. She didn't want to send him on a tirade, but she wanted this desperately. "I have enough time for both of us, Tony. If only—"

He flung the papers he'd been holding at his desk. "They'd be nothing but a hassle. You wouldn't have time for our social engagements, and we'd have to come up with money for private schools and save for college and we'd be stuck in this dump for the rest of our lives." He used his best wheedling tone as he leaned back against the desk edge and caressed her cheek. "We'll buy one of those places in Myers Park where we can live with the movers and shakers, and you'll have plenty of things to do. You're good with the country club biddies."

She didn't understand his attitude, and wondered if she wasn't making hers clear either. She moved away from his tempting touch and tried to be practical. "Neither of us went to private schools, and you worked your way through college. We turned out all right. And I don't need to live in Myers Park. I love this house."

Tony's handsome face lost its smile. "We've tried, honey, and we can't have kids. Let's not make a production of it, okay?"

She knew she was treading dangerous ground here, and

29

she did so carefully. "The doctor says we could go to a specialist, find out why—" His dark look cut her off. "Maybe we could adopt?" she asked hopefully.

"I don't want anyone else's bastards," he answered tightly, then gave her his best smile. "I need you at home, honey, and I don't want you hurt anymore by these so-called doctors. Take some more painting classes. You can auction your oils off for the charity fund again. They made a big impression last time."

He walked out, leaving her holding back tears. Tony never told her no. Why, on the one thing that meant so much to her, wouldn't he listen? The doctor had told him that he wasn't at fault, so it couldn't be male pride.

She decided he must love her too much to accuse her of being only half a woman.

The Present

"Do you think, if this is a business trip, the business could pay for a new tire?" Perched glumly on the guardrail, Faith contemplated her flattened front tire without commenting on the declaration that had driven her off the road. "Where does one put 'tire' on a tax return?"

She behaved as if there were no more between them than bad memories. Interesting perspective, Adrian thought. Leaning against the rail, he crossed his arms and tried not to watch too obviously for police cars. Considering her questions rhetorical, he, too, avoided the painful and stuck to a more relevant topic. "I can't believe you drive in these mountains without a spare. I'm taking back any kind thoughts I had of your intelligence."

"Those were almost *new* tires," she protested, shivering as another semi roared by not two feet from their noses. "New tires don't normally go flat. And if they did, I couldn't change them anyway."

Well, that little bit of illogic almost made sense. "You do realize the state police are more likely to get here before Triple A, don't you?"

She shot him a scornful look that should have withered his insides but made them do a merry jig instead. She wasn't more than a hank of hair and bundle of bones, but he could feel the energy boiling out of her. If he didn't watch out, she'd heave him over the guardrail and straight down the mountain. He glanced over his shoulder to verify the distance. The interstate had been carved from a steep cliff. It was a *long* way down. He blessed guardrails and lightweight VW bugs and cursed his flapping tongue.

"You have been locked away a long time, haven't you?" Faith said, interrupting his reverie with sarcasm. "The tunnel should have given you some clue. We're not in Tennessee anymore. We're in Encee."

"Encee? N.C." Adrian rolled his eyes at the abbreviation as several semis flew by at once, shaking the rail. The road had almost no shoulders. Either one of them could murder the other with a single shove. "Obviously, my mind hasn't been sufficiently stimulated in a while," he reflected out loud, striving for similar disinterest. "Or I was watching the scenery." Some scenery. She wore a tight knit yellow sweater thing under her jacket, and it took every ounce of his strength to keep his eyes straight ahead. Four years of abstinence wreaked havoc with his concentration.

"If you're still worried, you could hide in the bushes, and I could call one of the guys to come get you," she suggested helpfully.

He didn't have to see the gleam in her eye over that one. "You'd like that, wouldn't you? No guilty pangs over leaving a half-starved man without a coat on the mountain for untold nights?"

"All you'd have to do is stick your thumb out," she replied dismissively. "Here comes the sheriff. And a wrecker."

Adrian regarded her suspiciously as the sheriff pulled up, blue lights circling. She hadn't offered a single comment about the cause of their accident since they'd hit the rail. He'd learned his lesson. He wasn't tiptoeing within a mile of that subject again. He didn't care if Tony had done a number on his wife. He had more important concerns than feeling sorry for a woman who put herself first.

"Little mishap, folks?" the sheriff asked, strolling up as the wrecker maneuvered into place.

Adrian had had quite enough of police mentality these last years. He firmly shut his mouth.

"I tried to miss a squirrel," Faith answered with false calm.

Adrian breathed a sigh of relief. For once, he was grateful for her facile tongue, even if it reminded him to be especially wary of her insouciant pose.

"I bent the fender and flattened the tire. Quinn's already yelled at me for not carrying a spare."

Adrian prayed the sheriff wouldn't ask for his license, too, as Faith produced hers for inspection. Renewing a license from behind bars wasn't an easy trick.

Cynically, Adrian watched Faith do her Southern belle flirt with both the sheriff and the tow truck driver as they discussed the best means of towing the damaged beetle. He'd only seen the sexy side of her on stage; she'd certainly never tried it on him. Maybe she had the good sense not to wave a meaty bone before a starving dog. Or she disliked him too much even to try.

He didn't care what she thought of him. He'd had several conversations with Tony's mistress over the years, and he was satisfied that Sandra didn't have a clue where Tony stashed the money. Sandra not only didn't know anything about Tony's accounting records, she thought accounting records were checkbooks. He didn't think Ms. Faith Hope quite that stupid.

A plane crash in Brazil had ended his partner's fantasy that he would live forever, and Tony had taken any record of his hidden funds with him. Which meant Faith was the only hope he had left. He didn't find the play on words the least bit funny.

"The sheriff says he can drop us off at the pottery."

Reluctantly, Adrian forced himself to meet Faith's gaze. She oozed defiance from every silken pore. He contemplated riding with the tow truck driver, but he never could resist a challenge.

Without a word, he pushed away from the guardrail and followed her to the patrol car. Without waiting for permission, he climbed in the front seat. Let *her* ride in the back like a criminal for a while.

"Surliness doesn't become you," she whispered mockingly as she climbed in while the sheriff directed the wrecker onto the busy highway.

He wasn't used to being taunted by women. Hell, at this point he wasn't used to women. "So, sue me," was the only reply he could summon as the sheriff approached.

Faith chattered about her gallery as the sheriff drove them to the next exit and down a narrow two-lane toward the pottery. Adrian hadn't picked her for a chatterer, but she seemed to be able to turn on different personalities at will. Insane people were supposed to be particularly cunning, and capable of adopting different personas. Maybe insanity hid her knowledge of Tony's activities.

Maybe she was protecting him from the sheriff's questions.

That notion didn't go down well.

As the patrol car turned down a gravel drive with a familiar name on the mailbox, Adrian smiled in satisfaction. For a change, *he* was in the driver's seat, figuratively, at least.

"Thank you for your help, Sheriff," he said gravely as the car stopped beside a sprawling, ramshackle farmhouse.

"Wondered if you had a tongue." The older man eyed him speculatively. "Relation of Juan?" He nodded toward the house.

"*Sí.*" Affably, as if he hadn't shocked the woman in the backseat into silence, Adrian stepped from the car and opened the door for her.

They waved the sheriff off before Adrian jerked his head toward the shed behind the house. "He'll be back there."

Addled with disbelief, Faith followed in his footsteps like a puppy dog. Why would a hotshot Charlotte lawyer know a backwoods potter? Or know his way around the place? How had he known she was coming here? Without her car, she had no good means of escape should Adrian try to hold her hostage. Was this some kind of trap?

She couldn't believe her cheerful Sunday outing had become such an unmitigated disaster. But then, she couldn't believe she'd allowed him to stay in the car in the first place.

She refused even to consider the blunt statement that had sent her careening into the railing. To consider it would mean thinking about its effect on her past and present and future, and she didn't dare shake her precarious existence by changing an inkling of the plans she'd laid out upon a foundation she had thought secure. The creep was probably lying.

"Hola, Juan, que tal?" Adrian called into the shadows of the shed.

He spoke Spanish. None of Tony's friends spoke Spanish. They waved a little French over a wine list occasionally, but Spanish was for maids and construction workers.

A volley of rapid-fire insults rattled from the back of the shed before a wiry, brown-skinned man emerged, wiping his clay-coated hands on a rag. Seeing Faith, he nodded cautiously and elbowed Adrian's arm.

"You worry your mama, *muchacho*," he greeted Adrian, before turning to her. *"Buenas dias, señorita."*

"Como esta usted?" Faith replied politely in her best high school accent. Traveling with her parents, she'd picked up a lot more of the language, but lost it for lack of practice.

Still, the potter beamed approval at her poor attempt. "I am fine, thank you. I see Quinn has finally learned some sense in his choice of ladies."

Quinn? His name really was Quinn? She ignored the insinuating flattery for what it was but turned a questioning gaze to her nemesis.

"Faith Hope." Adrian lifted a doubting eyebrow over her name in retaliation. "My cousin, Juan Martinez. Faith has a shop that sells pottery. She's here to see if any of your worthless pieces rate her attention."

Faith couldn't follow the exchange of Spanish insults resulting from that remark as she wandered after the men into the shed.

She'd been inside enough potteries, large and small, to recognize the slate wedging bench for kneading clay into elasticity, the wheels for spinning round pieces, the various shaping tools, chucks, and boards, and the clay trough itself. She'd played with some of them as a child but never had the "feel" for clay that genuine artists did. She could only wholeheartedly admire their results.

A work light shone over a bench containing a series of rounded, handleless mugs in their raw, unfired state. The "handles" hung in narrow cylinders from the bench, waiting to be shaped. Even as he carried on in a swift spate of Spanish, Juan moistened his hands and intuitively began pulling and working one of the narrow cylinders onto a wet mug. Attaching it to a prepared knob of clay on the rim, he casually shaped it with his hands until the clay cylinder flattened and curved into a decorative S. It always amazed her how an experienced potter could make this difficult process seem effortless without ripping the cup rim, cracking the handle, or watching the whole thing slump indecorously onto the floor.

Despite Juan's obvious experience, Faith was disappointed that he seemed only interested in commonplace kitchenware. True, the rounded base of the mug and the delicate S handle showed skill, and possibly his glazing process would add a uniqueness she might sell, but she approached every new pottery with the awe-filled excitement of a child at Christmas, hoping that this time she'd find the perfect piece. She supposed it was more profitable to make kitchenware, but she ached to find a contemporary counterpart of her clair-de-lune porcelain, or a piece of brilliance like the vase Tony had given her.

"Juan keeps his stuff back here." Adrian started toward a door at the back. "Let him finish the mugs, and I'll show you around."

"Why didn't you tell me you had a cousin who makes stoneware?" she hissed as they skirted the benches and wheels.

Adrian threw open a door and flipped on the light switch. "I didn't realize you were interested in local artisans. He makes the stoneware for tourists, but he dabbles in porcelain as well."

Faith held her breath as she gazed around the shelves of finished pottery.

A quick glance didn't reveal anything, but the shelves were crowded and the overhead glare of fluorescent lighting didn't help. She started with the corner on her right, looking for saleable pieces as well as the flash of brilliance she craved.

The heavy, dense stoneware with its duller glazes was interspersed occasionally with a few fanciful animal figurines of translucent, hand-painted porcelain. The bright traditional cobalt, orange, and yellow of Mexican earthenware mixed with a few contemporary experiments in forest greens and earth browns. Juan apparently preferred experimenting in all forms rather than specializing in a few. She could understand that.

She cradled a wide bowl glazed in a blue-green mist that almost matched her memory of the brilliant vase now locked in her storage shed. The color didn't have the same translucence, and the design lacked the surety paired with an almost mystical irreverence of form that her vase possessed, but still—there was something.

"The color is extraordinary," she commented, holding the bowl up to the light.

"Not clair de lune," Adrian said dryly, appearing at her shoulder.

"Well, now I see how you know about pottery. Was your cousin attempting to create clair de lune? I don't think it's possible with the glazes available today, and in today's kilns."

"Juan copies everything. He should spend more time creating his own." Dismissively, Adrian strolled along the shelves, picking up one piece after another, discarding them all.

"One can learn by copying, and in this case the result is better than anything I've found recently. He has an interesting sense of design."

"The tourists want Indian pots." Juan grunted with annoyance as he strode through the doorway. "You can't sell decorative bowls like that. If they want fancy glass, they buy it at the mall."

"People have to be taught art appreciation," she replied. "They're more receptive when the economy is good and they're told art is an investment that can increase in value. That's what I try to get across in my gallery." Faith handed him the blue-green bowl. "I'd like to buy this outright. If you're interested, I could try to sell the animal figurines on consignment. Some people collect animal figures, but I don't know how willing they are to pay art prices, and your work deserves the recognition of a good price."

Juan looked at his cousin. "You're the negotiator. Negotiate."

Faith opened her mouth to protest, then closed it again. She wanted the bowl. She just didn't want to argue with a dangerous male animal over it. She watched Adrian's reaction suspiciously.

He shoved his hands into his pockets and contemplated the bowl, but his casual appearance didn't fool her. Beneath that long ponytail lurked the mind of a shark.

"I can draw up a consignment contract, no problem." He shrugged. "The lady knows gallery prices better than I do. Judging from what she has in that shop of hers, anything she sells them for will bring a whole lot more than you're making in Asheville. Name her a healthy price on the bowl. She'll sell it for twice as much in the city, and you'll have some cash in your pocket."

Faith couldn't believe it was that easy. "I have a standard consignment contract in my case." She nodded toward the slim leather bag she'd left by the door. "Don't overestimate my abilities to obtain high prices. The higher they are, the longer it takes to sell, and you're a newcomer to the market."

"Come inside, eat with us, and we'll talk money after we're full." Juan lifted the bowl from her hands and carried it to the shop to wrap in bubble plastic. "I've not been able to duplicate this color since I made it. It's a rare piece."

Faith smiled. The negotiation had begun, just a little more subtly than most. "I don't want to impose. I need to call the garage and see if my car is ready. We had a little trouble on the way over."

She nearly jumped from her shoes as Adrian clapped a

hand on her shoulder. "I would give my left foot for some of Isabel's enchiladas. We'll stay."

As if he had anything to say about it. She remembered what it had been like obeying a man's whims all the time. Moving out from under his presumptuous hold, Faith yanked her cell phone out of the case. The phone wasn't an extravagance but a healthy business expense, given the capricious hours of the artists with whom she dealt. Consulting the business card the driver had given her, she punched in the numbers. She had better things to do than listen to the cousins exchange family stories. She really didn't want to know that much about Adrian Quinn Raphael.

She paled as the voice on the other end of the line answered her inquiry. "You don't understand—" she protested into the receiver.

Adrian caught her shoulder again and steered her toward the door as she hung up, disbelieving. "I could have told you," he whispered in her ear, "but you wouldn't have listened. They don't stock anything but tires for American-made trucks up here. You'll have to wait until tomorrow."

Tomorrow? She stared at him in dismay. Surely he wasn't saying she'd have to spend the night here?

The look of challenge in Adrian's dark eyes verified her worst fears.

Chin tilting, she stalked away from him. Nope. Not in a thousand million years. She'd learned to survive on her own. Men made it easy to be weak, but she knew better than to trust or rely on their support now.

She was getting the hell out of here if she had to walk home.

First, she wanted that bowl.

❧ FIVE ❧

Four and a half years earlier

In disbelief, Faith stared at the cruise ticket bearing the name of Sandra Shaw. Tony never took so much as a secretary on trips, and he never scheduled conferences in the Caribbean. He was extremely tight with money on things like that. It was one of the reasons they'd never gone anywhere for vacation unless it involved a business meeting that he could write off. He'd explained that business meetings out of the country were not as easily tax deductible.

There had to be some mistake. Perhaps someone had mixed up names. She picked up the phone and dialed the travel agency. To her shock, they readily verified the dates and credit card and names. Sitting at Tony's desk, she stared at the tickets in bewilderment. They had to be hers. Nothing else made any sense. The date corresponded with their anniversary. St. Thomas had been her destination of choice. Tony would have to straighten it out.

She dialed the office, but Tony was out. Tony was always out.

The depression that nagged her more and more often these days threatened to swamp her now. She had a wonderful home, a loving husband, but resentment built day after day, until sometimes she couldn't deal with it. Sometimes it was easier to let things slide.

This wasn't one of those times. Deciding action was better than letting resentment tumble her into misery, she pulled out the telephone directory. There had to be some logical explanation for the stranger's name on the tickets. Who was she, anyway? Perhaps the agency had sent her own ticket to Sandra Shaw.

There were dozens of Shaws in Charlotte alone. Half a dozen or so used the initials S. Tony even had an old friend named Shaw, but he was male and, as far as she knew, still lived in that small country town where Tony had grown up.

The beautiful spring day faded to twilight and her gourmet meal went forgotten. Tony didn't come home to eat it.

How many nights did Tony not come home?

Biting her bottom lip to keep from screaming in fury or weeping hysterically, especially when this still could be a product of overactive imagination or resentment, Faith dug in the desk drawer until she found the combination to Tony's safe. He'd never tried to hide it from her. They had no secrets from each other. Or so she'd thought.

She had always respected his privacy. Tonight, privacy could go to hell. She was just angry and depressed enough to believe anything.

Pulling back a designer print from the wall, she spun the lock until the door opened. Removing the stacks of papers inside, she sat down and began to read.

By midnight her eyes were too blurry with tears to discern the payees on any more of the canceled checks in the bank account she hadn't known Tony possessed. Even through her blind fury and despair she could recognize her husband's signature.

For years she had fought loneliness, unhappiness, and resentment. She'd dearly loved Tony, and, convinced that her bitterness over her infertility had warped her thinking, she'd never blamed him for her inability to cope. She had even tried counseling.

Staring now at the proof of Tony's perfidy, rage crashed through her foolish, lovestruck bubble, washing away eager, obedient Faith and replacing her with a savagely determined woman. Tony had thought her loving obedience meant stupidity. He was about to find out how damned wrong he was.

The Present

"Faith?" An elbow nudged her ribs. "Care to join us?"

Furiously reliving the anger and sheer disbelief that had molded her hard-won independence, Faith jerked back to the moment. Following Juan and Adrian toward the farmhouse, she glared at the man beside her as if he were the cause of all the trouble that had begun that horrible spring day. How dare he come here and shake loose all those ancient horrors?

Deep brown eyes looked at her with what could almost pass for concern. He had disgustingly long lashes, but what could she expect from a man with hair longer than her own?

She forced a brittle smile. "I would rather be getting on with my life than staying here," she said.

Adrian's proximity reminded her all too uncomfortably of how barren her life was of close human contact. She hadn't been brought up that way. Her family had been given to hugging and kissing on any and every occasion. Tony hadn't been averse to hugs and kisses and more when he was home. But for four years now she'd lived in a world where an occasional handshake passed as a close encounter with humankind. She'd wanted it that way, but she was seeing the downside now.

Adrian casually wrapped his arm around her waist and tugged her into a kitchen steaming with mouth-watering scents. Just that common touch ripped open a longing so deep and wide inside her that Faith nearly wept from the shock of it. She'd been managing so well until this man came along. She didn't dare trust herself with any more fast-talking lawyers, and a dangerous ex-con with an agenda was a time bomb waiting to go off.

Why couldn't he be someone else? A sexy artist not looking for a long-term relationship maybe. Someone who would expect nothing of her and would demand nothing in return.

Adrian Raphael wasn't that man.

She eased away from his casual gesture and smiled blankly

at the rounded, rosy woman stirring pans of mysterious ingredients at the stove.

She would have a rental car delivered.

Lounging in Isabel's porch swing after dinner, replenished with good food for the first time in years, Adrian narrowed his eyes and watched the woman he desperately needed to do his bidding. She had glazed up as solid as one of her china figurines when she'd discovered rental cars couldn't be delivered this far into the hills. Her gray eyes went blank and she yanked her bouncy hair into a tight knot. He could scarcely believe this was the same woman he'd seen on stage, shouting and singing and worming her way into the hearts of men. Despite the casual attire, this was the woman he'd seen in the courtroom. She looked as if she could shatter at a loud noise.

He might be a desperate man clinging to a crumbling cliff of sanity, but his mama had brought him up better than this. Faith Hope wasn't a dummy. He had her trapped, and she knew it. He could keep her for days, or force her into a car and back to Charlotte. He could even seduce her, and the temptation to do that was so overwhelming that he glued himself to his chair rather than get up and hold out his hand to her.

He didn't think she was totally unaware of the charged vibrations bouncing like balls of electricity between them. He might be out of practice, but she was an easy target. A soft touch, a whispered word, a hot kiss . . .

Hell, he could speculate until his pants popped, but he'd never know because he wouldn't try. He wanted her body, yeah, but she'd cut out his liver if he used her that way. And his mama would cut off more vital parts should she hear about it.

She wouldn't hear about it, a tiny voice nagged in his head. He was a desperate man, and Faith Hope was a deceitful devil in angel's disguise. And it was for his family's own good that he needed what she possessed.

He'd rather have her warm and flushed beneath him than sitting here like a lifeless doll, as she was now.

With a growl of disgust, Adrian shoved aside the swing and stalked into the house. He didn't know what the hell Juan and Isabel thought they were doing, leaving him alone with a woman like Faith. They should know better.

When he marched back out with the keys to his cousin's truck clenched in his fist, he found her wandering through the wildflowers by the drive, heading toward the road. She didn't have the bowl or her briefcase in her hands, so he figured it was only a preliminary inspection, but she was already contemplating escape.

"What'll you give me if I take you home tonight?" he challenged as he caught up with her.

She didn't look startled, didn't look at him at all, just kept on walking. "I don't need you. I don't need any man to get where I want to go."

He didn't want to hear the note of vulnerability behind her angry declaration. He had to maintain control of the situation until he had what he wanted. That meant he had to keep control of her, in whatever way it took.

He was a man who had made bold choices in the past. Some of them had been the wrong choices, but he'd done what he had to do and lived with the result. His choices now were obvious. He could use force, or he could use sex, or he could appeal to her better instincts. He'd seen her at the homeless shelter and knew she possessed compassion. She just wasn't inclined to apply it to a man she feared. So, he had to take away her fear if he wanted her cooperation. He'd save force as a last ditch method. That left sex as his fallback position.

"Juan is letting me borrow his rattletrap truck. I won't swear it will make it over the mountain, but if it does, he can drive your mobile garbage can up to the city when it's ready and we'll exchange them. Go find your things. I'll get the truck."

She shot him a look of suspicion but didn't waste time questioning. Swinging around, she strode toward the house. A piece of silken hair slipped from its knot and curled around her nape. Adrian stayed one step behind and watched it bounce in rhythm with her sway. Yeah, this was definitely the best course to take. He was much better at persuasion than force, and the results could be very interesting.

Maybe he needed to get sex off his mind first so he could focus better on the task ahead.

As if she heard his thoughts, Faith swung around on the bottom step and glared at him with just enough warning to remind him that she carried a phone in her case and could call the police anytime she wished.

They would definitely need to develop a level of trust before he could have his way with her, in whatever form he imagined.

Uncomfortably aware of his lack of a current driver's license, Adrian stayed well within the bounds of the speed limit all the way back to the city, enraging the semi drivers barreling down the mountain behind him. The semis should have scared the shit out of him, but the woman beside him had already done that.

If he intended to control this situation, he needed to hold Ms. Faith Hope Nicholls firmly within his limited circle of power. Leaving her without a means of transportation was a good start.

"I don't know Knoxville," he said innocently enough as they reached the outer lights of the city. "You'll have to tell me how to find your place." He hadn't had time to track down her home, as he had the shelter. She wasn't in the phone book, and he hadn't followed her from the bar, though tempted to do it. That had been next on his list.

She threw him a shrewd look but must have realized it wouldn't be difficult for him to find her. Sinking back in the patched upholstery, she returned to staring out the windshield. "Take the next exit."

Her directions led him to a deteriorating mansion in the city's inner streets. The sign out front advertising a vacancy gave evidence that the old house had been converted to apartments.

"You'd be safer with me at the shelter than in there," he said derisively. In the dark interior of the truck cab, he felt a protective urge toward the slim woman clutching her bubble-wrapped bowl. He couldn't undo decades of upbringing in one night. He wouldn't let his damned sisters go into a place like that.

"I've never had any trouble," she said quietly, opening the door.

He didn't like it when she got quiet. He hadn't analyzed that reaction yet, but he threw open his door and leaped out of the truck. He really hadn't intended to follow her in, but he jammed his hands in his pockets and trailed her up the broken sidewalk, through the fallen gate.

"If you can afford that expensive shop, surely you can afford better than this." He tested her, still not believing her story. He'd spent four years building this woman into a selfish society bitch. He couldn't blow away four years.

"I don't need much." She shrugged as she removed her keys from her purse. "I rented this when I first arrived, and everything I earned went into the business. When the store started making money, I put the profits into a more expensive location instead of moving. Works for me."

Adrian noted the sagging porch steps and couldn't adjust his thinking fast enough to reply.

"You needn't follow me in." Scorn lingered beneath the otherwise calm of her voice as she inserted a key in the outer door. "I'm perfectly safe."

"Just because I spent a few years in jail doesn't mean I've forgotten what my mama taught me." Reaching over her head, he shoved open the door as she unlocked it, verifying that no danger lurked in the foyer.

Her resistance made him even more determined to follow. Sensing that, she stepped inside and strode toward the battered staircase. As he closed the door, darkness enveloped them, broken only by the electricity they were generating as he followed her up.

She'd been his partner's wife, an expensively lacquered socialite accustomed to finger bowls and imported china, a woman who would perjure herself to protect her wealth, and she was climbing a battered staircase to a room not much better than his prison cell.

She had sunk to his depths now, and he was more aware of her than he'd been of any woman in his life.

❧ SIX ❧

Faith unlocked her apartment door, excessively aware of the tightly wound tension of the man behind her. Adrian Raphael was anything but a relaxed companion. She had the unsettling feeling that he was always balanced on the edge and that in some way she was responsible.

He didn't take his leave as the door opened. If he thought she was inviting him in, he was highly mistaken. "Thank you for bringing me home," she murmured with her best boarding school manners. The year her parents had gone to Ecuador and left her at the fancy school had been an enlightening experience.

"Check to make certain the room's safe," he said gruffly, standing in the shadows of the hall where she couldn't read his eyes.

He must have grown up in a rough world. Opening the door wider and flipping on the overhead light, Faith searched the interior. She didn't have much, but she liked quality. She'd found a bargain in the wide designer-tapestried sleeper sofa some client of the interior decorator's had rejected. The jewel colors picked up the ruby red and cobalt blue of the antique glass she'd carefully shelved over the old bay window. A contemporary glass kitchen table accompanied by chrome and cobalt chairs she'd found on sale in a gallery completed the essentials. She had a small office and library in a back room, but she couldn't imagine any thief finding room to hide in there, or in the ancient bathroom with its huge claw-footed tub. She liked the old musty building with its high ceilings

47

and fading grandeur. She turned to see if her companion was satisfied that the room was safe.

He seemed transfixed by the everydayness of the interior, but he snapped back quickly. "The shelter closes at ten, I'd better be going."

"It's almost ten now." Alarm clattered briefly through her veins. Did that mean she should invite him in? He'd brought her home, probably given up a comfortable bed with his family in exchange for the noisy cot room at the shelter. She'd been selfish—

Faith stopped that guilt track instantly. Tony had manipulated her that way. She wouldn't feel guilty about anything any man chose to do ever again. Adrian had chosen to go with her today so he could harass her more. Where he would sleep was his problem.

He shrugged. "I can sleep in the truck if they won't let me in. One thing jail teaches you is to sleep wherever and whenever you can. Lock the door behind you." He examined the dead bolt. "It's a good lock, but you shouldn't be living here."

Faith stared after him in amazement. He hadn't argued, hadn't blamed her for his discomfort, had merely accepted his responsibility for his predicament, already formed a solution, and acted on it. Damn, where were all the rest of the men in the world like that?

Probably in jail, she snorted, shutting the door and carefully bolting it. Men like that tended to think they were the only human beings on the face of the earth. That led to sticky results when the rest of the world intervened.

She unwrapped her bowl and admired it beneath the glare of the overhead light. Adrian Raphael's cousin had talent. Perhaps she could help him focus it a little more?

Dropping her case with its signed legal documents and a bankbook considerably lightened by her purchase, she undressed and showered and wrapped herself in her velour bathrobe. She told herself she should go to bed early, but restlessness grated on her nerves, and she knew sleep wouldn't come easily.

Thinking a rehash of the day's events might straighten out her thought processes, Faith pulled out her journal. When her pen wouldn't settle on the paper, she realized Adrian Raphael had an unsettling effect she didn't wish to analyze for the sake of her journal.

She started to flip the pages to the day she'd actually walked out on Tony, but her gaze caught on a tear-blotted page toward the beginning, and her hand hovered there. The knowledge Adrian had given her of Tony's vasectomy wrenched at something vital inside her. She didn't want to grasp it yet, feared it would rip her already scarred insides into more shreds.

Tony had never loved her back. Tony had never loved anyone but Tony. Faith doubted he'd even loved his mistress or the children she'd had by him. But to know he'd deliberately *lied* over something so immensely vital to her soul . . .

Feeling sick, she threw the journal aside. Examining the past only helped if it led her to decisions for the future. She'd made that decision. She would stick with it. She wanted to experience life on her own from now on, explore all the possibilities she'd been denied while she had tried to please others. She was doing precisely what she wanted to do, and the gut-twisting knife Adrian had plunged into her today wouldn't change any of that. She'd heal.

She hadn't thought she'd heal from Tony's deception, but she had. Quite rapidly. She smiled in satisfaction at that thought as she opened the sofa bed. She really did have a backbone when it came down to the crunch. It was only in the little everyday things that she was wishy-washy—like, should she suffer the agony of another man in her life now that she could possibly have a baby?

Pushing her grocery cart briskly through the supermarket the next evening, Faith froze at the sight of a man with a straight black ponytail, hovering over the meat counter. He wore jeans with his flannel shirt today, faded jeans that had probably once fit like a second skin. Now, they draped almost loosely over his muscled thighs as he reached over the counter and examined a single slice of ham. That's when she noticed he held a shiny new frying pan in his other hand.

Something about the image of a lonely man furnishing his life with a frying pan and ham twisted her admittedly weak heartstrings. He'd once been a highly paid attorney, dressed in suits that probably cost more than the truck his cousin loaned him, dined in fancy restaurants, probably with lovely young things on his arm. How dangerous could such a man be without his trappings of wealth?

She could avoid him. He was concentrating on his next meal. If he'd been sleeping on the streets and in shelters since he left prison, he was probably enjoying the freedom of his cousin's truck. He wasn't her responsibility.

She had to remember he was here to harass her for information she didn't have, that he believed her capable of robbing widows and orphans. She didn't know why she had to remind herself of that. Just because he'd treated her politely last night didn't mean he wasn't dangerous.

He turned and saw her just as she'd made up her mind to escape down another aisle. He didn't smile often, but he flashed a white grin now at the sight of her. Something about the shimmer of a silver earring against dark skin should have repelled her, but it drew her forward instead. Maybe she was one of those ninnyhammers drawn to dangerous men.

"I put the truck to good use today," he said, waving his frying pan as Faith pushed her cart closer. "Moved someone across town and picked up a nice stack of cash, made a deposit on a furnished room."

"That's stupid," she said automatically, not filtering her thoughts before they spouted from her mouth. She never used to say things like that. Astonished at herself, she waited for him to flinch or strike back, but his grin broadened. She shrugged. "You need to go back to North Carolina before they start looking for you."

"My next meeting with the parole officer isn't for two weeks. I can catch a bus down to Charlotte then." His grin disappeared as he fixed her with a dark gaze. "I'm not giving up."

She knew she should be afraid of the intensity behind his

eyes. He was an intelligent man, capable of going after what he wanted. He knew where she worked, where she lived, and there was no escaping him if he decided to seriously harass her—short of calling the police. She didn't want to resort to that. If Adrian was really innocent, Tony had scarred his life as badly as hers, even more.

She nodded at the ham, pretending she hadn't understood his threat. "Your first home-cooked dinner?"

He raised his eyebrows and didn't smile, but held out the slice he'd chosen for her inspection. "Care to join me?"

"For fried ham? No, thank you. When will your cousin be returning my car? If I have to rent one, it could cost me a fortune."

"He's coming up to see your gallery and bring you the porcelain consignment tomorrow. I wasn't certain if you were open on Mondays. If you need a ride, I'll be happy to help."

"I can survive another day. I don't have the case and lighting ready yet for Juan's figurines, though. I hope he won't be disappointed." She needed to get on with her shopping, go home and fix her lonely meal and do her books as she did every Monday night. She shouldn't be standing here shamelessly lapping up this male attention, for that's what it was. Adrian had an appreciative way of looking at her that made her feel young and flirty and as unburdened by life as she had been at eighteen. She was playing with fire.

"I don't think he's expecting miracles. He's just curious and had to come in for supplies anyway. He'll probably be in around lunch. I'll bring him by."

She would see him again tomorrow. Her head wished he would go away. Her heart pattered a little faster with anticipation. She needed to get a life if playing with fire was her idea of excitement these days.

"I'll see you, then." She could have made a graceful exit right there, but the haunted look in Adrian's eyes held her back for one second too long. Holding her breath for the courage to actually meet his gaze, she offered, "Thank you for bringing me home last night. I hope you didn't have to sleep in the truck."

"It was quieter than the shelter." His self-deprecating grin twisted her heart even harder. "Don't look like that. I didn't want anything happening to the truck, so I didn't bother going to the shelter."

Oh, shoot and filth, a man who had probably once driven a BMW was protecting his cousin's wretched excuse for a truck by sleeping in it. The all-too-familiar guilt crept under her skin. She fought it with a brittle smile and a nod. "I'll see you tomorrow, then."

With the feeling that Adrian's dark gaze pierced her spine, she walked away.

"Mama's sick, Quinn, real sick. Belinda can run over after work and look after her, but Belinda doesn't have time for all the young ones, and they're running wild after school. I'm working after classes, so I can't be there often." Cesar, Adrian's half brother, stalked up and down the tiny furnished room without noticing his surroundings.

"I can take the youngest home with me," Juan suggested, "but the twins are at that age . . ." Adrian's cousin shrugged. "They're just into middle school and don't wish to leave their friends. Isabel is pregnant. I don't know if she can look after them if they come to us."

"I can quit school, get a full-time job," Cesar suggested awkwardly.

"Over my dead body." Grimly, Adrian crushed the soft drink can in his hand and threw it at the trash basket. "What kind of job could you find that would let you be home when the kids come in after school? If you really want to help, get your teaching degree. Why aren't Dolores and Elena looking after the younger ones?"

His half brother exchanged glances with his cousin, and Adrian's temper surged another notch. There was so much they'd kept from him while he was locked helplessly behind bars. And instead of going directly down to his family, he'd come up here, chasing after a spoiled ice queen who'd robbed his family of their future.

"Tell me," he demanded.

"Dolores is sixteen now," Cesar said apologetically. "She thinks she is grown. She's working at Burger King and talking about quitting school and getting married. Elena . . ." He struggled for an explanation. "She turns the boys' heads. We couldn't afford the cheerleading for either of them, so Elena sulks and flirts and is headed for trouble."

So the very ones he'd counted on to help with the younger children were behaving like children themselves, as they were, actually. Just because he'd carried responsibility for the world at that age didn't mean the girls should. Adrian balled his hands into fists and tried not to let the fury and frustration inundate him. "I'll come home," he agreed. So much for his rationally planned choices. Life had never given him many options. "Just don't ask too many questions when I show up."

Cesar's youthful brow pulled down in a frown. "I'll quit school before I'll let you do anything else to get you sent back to that place."

Adrian cuffed his half brother upside the head. "Quitting school won't help, I tell you. I can still find work. I just wanted to correct a mistake first. We'll go admire Juan's exhibit, then the two of you go back where you belong. I'll be home in a day or two. Tell those sisters of ours they'd better straighten up before I arrive."

Cesar looked relieved behind his frown. "My courses are easy this semester. I can take a second job."

"We'll talk about that later. Let's go visit Ms. Hope and her fancy gallery."

Juan took his truck while Adrian and Cesar folded themselves into Faith's turquoise beetle and led the way. Feeling murderous, Adrian strangled the steering wheel, but choking it didn't relieve his escalating tension. Tony's widow knew more than she was revealing, he was positive.

For Cesar's sake he put on a pleasant face as they found parking places behind the gallery. Adrian had been the result of his mother's one mistake in life. She'd had him at seventeen, while unmarried and without a high school diploma. It had taken her several years to get back on her feet, earn a diploma, and fall in love with a decent man. Adrian had been almost six by then, and used to taking care of himself.

His stepfather had been a loving man and a hard worker. He adopted Adrian and added the name Raphael to his father's given name of Quinn, but even his stepfather had found it difficult to make ends meet when the babies started coming. Adrian could damn the church and its teachings for that, but he loved his half siblings and the rest of his family and didn't waste time cursing their beliefs. Instead, grateful for the father he hadn't had until Rick came along, he'd shouldered as much of the responsibility for his younger siblings as he could. When Rick died in a car accident before the birth of the youngest, Adrian had assumed the responsibility for supporting them. He'd been twenty-five and just out of law school at the time.

That didn't excuse his criminal negligence.

Locking the car, waiting for Juan to park his truck, Adrian dismissed the past and concentrated on the present. Cesar didn't need to know the pressures he had felt at that age. He draped his arm over his half brother's shoulders and steered him toward the front of the small plaza of exclusive shops.

The shop door chimed as they strode in, three brown-skinned men in faded jeans and their best dress shirts and still looking like trash collectors. A few tourists turned and stared. A silver-haired matron expertly examining a contemporary Navajo piece glanced at them and frowned.

Faith's blond head tilted up and a smile of pleasure curved her glossy pink lips as she set aside her invoice pad and emerged from behind the counter.

The impact of that genuine smile smote Adrian right where it hurt, and for a change, it wasn't below his belt.

❧ SEVEN ❧

"Mrs. McIntyre, come meet the artist who created that bowl you commented on." After Adrian's surly introductions to his half brother, Faith turned and gestured at the matron currently admiring the Navajo pottery. She didn't know what had set Adrian's hackles up this time, but she wasn't being paid to care. Juan, now, was a different story. She could promote his work with genuine pleasure, and profit.

The tourists drew closer as they realized the man carrying the cardboard box was actually an artist. Faith gestured for them to enter the gathering circle. This was what she enjoyed most about her shop—bringing the art-deprived public together with the artists and encouraging their interest.

"Is this the consignment?" she asked eagerly, letting Juan set his box down on the empty exhibit table she'd been preparing earlier. "May I show everyone?"

A little overwhelmed by the audience, Juan deferentially nodded agreement. Faith sensed Adrian's cynicism as he leaned against her counter and watched the proceedings, but she didn't have to put on a show for his sake. She smiled as she lifted the first piece out of the box. "The tiger! You brought me the tiger! Thank you." She held the delicate figurine up so their audience could appreciate its beauty. "The details are exquisite. Look at the whiskers, and the eyes! This one looks like a protective father watching over his cubs."

"*Sí*," Juan agreed quietly. "I am still working on his mate."

"Then they should be sold as a pair," Faith declared firmly, setting the tiger aside. "I'll display this one until his mate is ready."

The silver-haired matron picked up the tiger and studied it as Faith pulled out the rest of the pieces. The tourists oohed and aahed over a sleek panther and a cardinal ready to burst into song. A set of tumbling kittens brought a chorus of ecstasy. Haltingly, Juan recited a brief story behind each piece, and before she'd emptied the box, Faith knew she had sold almost the entire consignment. She'd studied her catalogs and had the prices she wanted firmly in mind. There was hesitation on the part of the tourists, but Mrs. McIntyre's definitive purchase of the largest piece and a demand to be notified when the tiger pair were ready swayed them to open their wallets.

As the shop gradually cleared of the triumphant new owners of original hand-signed porcelain, Faith slumped onto her stool behind the counter and beamed. "Juan, that was brilliant! You practically hand-sold every piece. You need to make limited editions of all of them, sign and number them, and I could line up other galleries as well as this one. If you don't mind a little travel . . ."

Smiling at last, Juan shook his head. "Isabel is carrying our first child. I'll not travel far from home. But I've never seen such enthusiasm before. That was your doing, not mine. They believed in your expertise."

"She received a nice percentage for that enthusiasm," Adrian interrupted rudely. "Don't give her too much credit."

Adrian's half brother—Cesar, Faith thought he was called— still looked amazed as he checked the few remaining pieces on the table. "But did you see how much she sold them for? Maybe I should take up pottery—"

Adrian cuffed him lightly. "After you own a farm like Juan and can raise your own food so you don't starve. It's taken Juan—what?" He turned to his cousin. "Fifteen years? And this is the most money he's ever made. And you've never shown any talent in that direction before. It's not something one can learn."

"And the bowl didn't sell," Faith gently reminded the youth. "That is the most original piece of work, the one with the highest price. It could be months before I find someone willing to pay the cost. The porcelain figurines are brilliant and take forever, but once the molds are created, they can be reproduced a million times. The hand painting can be turned over to artisans. The vase, on the other hand, is one of a kind. There will never be another like it, but most people don't understand or appreciate uniqueness."

Undaunted, Cesar merely stepped back from the table, shoving his hands in his pockets and shaking his head in admiration. "Adrian, you are missing your opportunity."

Not acknowledging this enigmatic remark, Adrian turned his dark gaze on Faith. Somehow, she always fell for the depth of his eyes, as if he had some mesmerizing power. Refusing to succumb to any man, she stuck her chin up in defiance, waiting for his next cynical pronouncement.

"Juan and Cesar must go back to . . . Encee." A smile tugged at his lips as he used her version of the state's name. "But we could celebrate the occasion this evening. Would you have dinner with me?"

Faith thought she might faint with shock. She dug her fingers into the metal stool seat and stared. He'd stood there and blatantly dismissed her selling abilities, behaved as if she were no more than a used car salesman unloading a clunker, and now he wanted to celebrate? There was something definitely odd about this, especially since he shouldn't have two cents with which to buy dinner.

"You want to renegotiate the consignment contract?" she asked doubtfully. "The one we have is legal. You said so yourself."

Juan stuffed wads of bubble wrap and newspaper into the now-empty box and tidied the table while Cesar's head swiveled back and forth, trying to follow the undercurrents of the conversation. Juan shoved the box into the young man's hands. "It's time we go. I don't want Isabel alone after dark."

"Isabel would take an ax to any intruder's head," Adrian threw after him as they headed out. "You're the one who would invite a thief for supper."

Juan gestured rudely as he opened the door. "Pardon my French, Ms. Hope, but my cousin grew too big for his britches long ago. He needs his mama to cut him back down to size."

Faith bit back a snicker and waved. "Let me know as soon as you have another consignment ready and I'll come get it. I have no wish for you to be parted from Isabel longer than necessary."

Juan grinned. "When she sees what I have earned on this trip, she will have me in the shop night and day. You have just bought our baby's nursery. She will want a college education next."

Feeling good again, Faith waved them off but remained firmly planted on her stool, with the counter between her and Adrian. Another customer wandered in, and she called a greeting, ignoring the dark man looming over her. She didn't trust him, or any man.

"The shop closes at five. I will come by for you then," he stated without question, straightening from his relaxed position against the glass.

"I have to close out the register and deposit my receipts, and I promised to stop in and see Annie," she argued. "We really have nothing else to say to each other."

With a lift of his eyebrows, Adrian produced a familiar ring of car keys from his pocket. "You might want to reconsider that. I'll make it five-thirty, then."

He strode out, taking her car keys with him.

The minute Adrian walked in the door that evening, Faith looked for her keys, but he'd already stuffed them back in his pocket. She considered going after them, but just the thought as her gaze followed the lazy grace of his lean hips caused her mouth to seal shut.

"I've already been to see Annie," he announced without preamble as he approached the counter. "I took her new charges over to the battered women's shelter. The husband showed up today looking for them, and the woman was finally convinced they'd be safer elsewhere."

Faith closed her eyes to block out all thought of Adrian's

dangerously male prowl, but his voice still licked up and down her nerves. "Did Annie have to call the police?"

"Joe was already over there. Feeding them doughnuts on a regular basis was a piece of genius. I gather that was your idea?"

She shrugged and closed her record books before reaching under the counter for her purse and jacket. "It always helps to know your neighbors, but Annie is a little wary of policemen."

"I can understand that reaction." Adrian reached over the counter and helped her with the jacket.

Faith assumed her miniskirted suit and silk blouse were too dressy for any place he had in mind, but that was the least of her concerns. "The innocent have nothing to fear around cops. You're the one breaking parole." She shoved her arms into the jacket and pulled away.

"I mean to correct that shortly. I'm eager to turn over a new leaf and become a model citizen again."

"I'm not renegotiating the contract," she reminded him as he opened the door and gestured for her to precede him. "It's a standard percentage and a fair price for my expertise. Juan would never have managed those prices on his own. Just because they happened to sell quickly today doesn't mean it will happen again. Every inch of my floor space has to turn a profit. The rent here isn't cheap."

"I'm not arguing," he said mildly, taking her key and locking up. "Juan couldn't sell those pieces for any price in Asheville. I suspect he earned in one day what he made all last year."

Mollified, Faith didn't object as he opened the passenger door.

Uncertain of the polite way of approaching the obvious, she waited until Adrian had taken the driver's seat before asking, "Did you find a job?"

"I got my deposit back on the room." Without further explanation, he eased the VW into the heavy rush hour traffic outside her shop.

Understanding it took intense concentration to navigate some of these tricky streets with trucks and sport utility vehicles looming large over the tiny beetle, Faith tried not to distract him with idle conversation. But when his direction appeared to be the interstate out of town, she tensed up. "Where are we going?"

Hitting the accelerator and expertly adjusting the stick shift as they rattled from the ramp into roaring traffic, Adrian didn't bother glancing at her. "Charlotte," he replied curtly.

Faith's eyes widened as she watched her car and her life roar down the highway back to the place she'd left behind. She didn't want to go there again. Not ever.

She eyed the keys dangling from the ignition and the grim man at the wheel and her stomach sank to new lows. She could scarcely believe it—he was kidnapping her.

Cautiously, she reached for her purse.

He shot her a glare. "I liberated your cell phone earlier. You ought to lock up your purse. Prisoners learn interesting things whiling away time in county jails."

Sitting back, she clasped her hands nervously. She refused to let him terrorize her. He seemed a fairly intelligent man. Perhaps he responded to reason. "I have a job here," she reminded him. "I don't have time to go to Charlotte."

"I've wasted four years of my life. You can waste a few days."

He was serious. She clenched her teeth against panic. She just had to think.

With rush hour traffic roaring all around them, she didn't dare do something rash like jerk on the keys or grab the wheel. At this hour, they wouldn't leave the traffic until they neared the mountains. Fighting fear with rationalization, she figured Adrian Raphael was an educated lawyer, not a professional kidnapper. He wouldn't hurt her, would he?

"I could have you arrested for this." Dumb, Faith, dumb. Remind him of what he had to lose. Guaranteed to make a desperate man sane.

"I'm living in purgatory anyway. What difference would it

make?" He jerked the VW to the right side, avoiding a lumbering truck cutting too close on the left.

The heavy traffic and narrowness of the aging interstate made her sick on a good day. With growing darkness and terror, her stomach pitched furiously. She closed her eyes and tried not to watch. With her luck, they'd catch a rock slide on the mountain.

"I can't help you," she insisted. "I gave everything of value to the court. What on earth do you expect me to do when we get there? Wave a magic wand?"

"I've been thinking about that." Adrian jerked his head in the direction of the backseat. "There's a box of fried chicken back there. Help yourself."

She reached in the backseat for the box. Maybe food would relieve the distress clawing at her stomach.

"All right, genius, and what has your male-inflated brain thought of that I haven't?"

"Safe deposit boxes." He reached over and grabbed a biscuit. "Tony had boxes in every bank in town. That's how I knew he was a crook. I just didn't bother investigating, figuring it had nothing to do with me." He snorted in deprecation at his naiveté.

"I didn't have access to any safe deposit boxes." Refusing to fall for his pretense of vulnerability, Faith tore into her chicken. They had to stop sometime. She'd call for help then.

"Somebody did," he insisted. "I told the court about them, but Tony testified he'd shown the contents to the prosecutor, and no one called his bluff. I tried, but the judge ruled it out. Sandra claims she knows nothing about them. Your divorce wasn't final. As his wife, you can go to the banks and ask if he still has active accounts. They may have already turned the contents over to the state, but you can verify that and start the process to recover them. I'll wager six-to-one that at least one of those boxes contains computer disks with his files."

"This is a wild-goose chase." Wiping her hands on a napkin, Faith glared at him through the growing dusk. "My clerk isn't scheduled to come in tomorrow, so I'll lose a day's business and endure this horrible trip all the way to Charlotte because you're obsessed with the impossible. Tony handled everything through a corporation he'd set up, and there were no bank boxes. I should know. I was an officer of the corporation." She settled back in the seat with a sigh of satisfaction. That had been Tony's big mistake. He'd given his mousy little lovestruck wife authority over his corporation, thinking she would never grasp her power.

Boy, had he been wrong.

❧ EIGHT ❧

Four and a half years earlier

"Marianne? You know when Tony said we were thinking of selling this house, you said you had someone interested in property in the area?" Biting her bottom lip, Faith fought for the carefree tones of a Southern-belle housewife. She'd played the part for years. She could do it. "Is he still looking? We've found a place over in Myers Park we'd like to offer on, and it would be easier if we knew we had this place sold."

Her fingernails should have left dents in the receiver as she listened to the real estate agent on the other end. On the desk in front of her were neat stacks of canceled checks made out to one Sandra Shaw. In the back of the safe she'd found a picture of a well-endowed strawberry blonde in short shorts. Tony had always lacked imagination.

"Tony's out of town," she said into the receiver, "but I have authorization through his corporation. You know how lawyers are." She laughed knowingly while grimacing. She'd never appreciated lawyer jokes before. She still didn't.

She'd thought and planned this for weeks. She'd made inquiries. She'd driven out to the trailer park address listed in the city directory and watched three dusty boys playing on a swing set. The younger two looked like identical twins, but they were too far away to search for a resemblance. She might not know for certain whose kids they were, but she recognized the strawberry blonde from the photo as soon as the woman stepped from the trailer. Mobile home. Double-wide. Paid for through the loan company with the checks from the safe. The first check dated before Faith's marriage. The last check was dated two weeks ago. Tony had been keeping her all through their marriage.

The woman piled the kids into a luxury utility vehicle, paid for with the next stack of checks. Faith stared after the cloud of dust for a long time while her heart slowly crumbled. She tried holding it together, tried rationalizing away the evidence before her eyes, but even rationality led her straight into a whirlpool of pain.

While she'd been scrimping and saving, working in Tony's office without pay, giving up her hopes of college and a career, this Sandra person had been living in a new trailer and driving new cars and raising babies. The babies Faith had yearned for with every ounce of her being.

She'd never needed the fancy house. She drove an aging Volvo rather than go into debt. And all that money she'd saved, Tony had lavished on this woman who had given him children.

Shaking, too stunned even to cry, Faith drove away from the mobile home and allowed fury to well up in place of pain. She used fury as the glue to hold all the shattered pieces together, fury as the fuel to keep her moving forward.

As she drove back toward Charlotte, she was still reeling, but she'd found her focus. Tony was "out of town" again. She hadn't seen his car at the trailer, but that didn't mean anything. He could have floozies all over the state for all she knew. He'd just told her he wouldn't be home for a week. A week gave her lots of time.

After arranging for Marianne's client to see the house, Faith checked off one more item from her list and picked up the phone for the next. She had learned to be very organized while working for Tony. She would make someone an excellent secretary. With professional courtesy, she called the office of every credit card in her purse and asked for her name to be removed from the account. Then she snipped the cards in half and followed up the calls with a letter and the mutilated cards. She kept copies of everything.

She'd already been to the bank. She'd withdrawn every cent in checking, savings, money market, and certificates of deposit. She'd worked hard for eight years, given up her career to put Tony through law school, given up her education to provide him with the perfect hostess and housekeeper and bookkeeper and decorator and ... She had calculated his debt to her at far more than the sum total of their personal assets.

She had never been so blindly furious in her entire life. She hung on to that fury as she called the broker and ordered the sale of their stocks. Later, she would weep for what she had lost and what she could never have, but not now. Now, she would get even.

She'd read about women who had lost everything when their men left them, women thrown on the streets—helpless, uneducated, and unemployable—when their husbands found younger women. Well, she by damn wouldn't be one of them.

Sandra wasn't even a younger woman. Tony had been supporting Sandra before she came along. He'd been supporting Sandra when Faith's grandmother had died, leaving her a small but significant inheritance—the one they'd invested in his law office after Tony's graduation.

She wouldn't consider the ramifications of any of this. It was painfully apparent Tony had married her for her little bit of money and her boarding school manners and her eagerness to please. She suited his image of a wealthy professional's country club wife. The Sandra person was too blowzy, too common, too beneath his dignity. She was only suited for being the mother of his children.

She would almost feel sorry for Sandra if it weren't for the agony searing through her. Forcefully ignoring the acid burning holes through her stomach, Faith picked up the cruise tickets that had started it all and shoved them into her purse. The travel agency was next on her agenda. Sandra wouldn't be able to afford a baby-sitter by the time she was done, so she wouldn't need the cruise tickets. She was doing the other woman a favor.

Briefly wondering where Tony had found the money to

support his other life, Faith grabbed the odd copies of accounting records and canceled checks drawn on the law firm's escrow account and added them to the contents of her purse. He'd probably filtered the money through the corporation accounts his bookkeeper kept at the office. She would ask Headley about them. She'd met the old reporter while working on publicity for community groups, and knew he liked puzzles.

As she walked out to her old Volvo, she glanced at Tony's gleaming new Jaguar in the drive. He treasured that car as if it were a child. She was pretty sure it was titled to the corporation—the corporation of which she was treasurer. She'd love to see his face when he realized she'd sold it. But she'd be long gone.

How convenient that Tony had allowed her to handle all their personal finances. She knew to a penny how much he brought home in salary, how much she'd saved by keeping them out of debt, just exactly how much he owed to her. The Jaguar ought to just about cover her grandmother's inheritance money.

The Present

Adrian cast his companion's lingering smile a suspicious look. He'd thought she'd be furious, perhaps terrified, definitely frantic. Instead, she'd clasped her hands into tense fists and sat as straight and taut as a ramrod, but the trace of a smile warned of the evil direction of her thoughts.

The fried chicken hadn't filled the hole in his belly. He doubted if any food would. His gut burned with things he wanted and couldn't have, and inexplicably, this female was one of them.

"By the time we reach Charlotte, it will be too late to drop in on my family." Stick to the mundane, he told himself. Worry about the next meal, the next bed, the safe deposit boxes. He couldn't cure his mother's illness or the kids' neglect or world peace. He couldn't bed an ice queen. One did what one could. "Do you have friends, family, who might be up that late?"

In the growing darkness, he couldn't read the expression she turned on him, but he figured it was haughty, if not downright derisive, judging by her tone.

"I have nothing and no one in Charlotte. I'd hoped never to go back there again."

Well, after the scandal of the decade, he supposed he could understand that. Charlotte was the city that never forgot and never forgave. "Headley sends you his best wishes." She ought to know there were a few people who didn't blame her.

She looked out the windshield and didn't reply.

"Do you have a credit card?" Back to calculating one thing at a time. He didn't have patience for analyzing human equations.

"Why? So you can steal it, too?"

Well, hell. Adrian gripped the steering wheel tighter, as if he could keep the bug from flying off the road from the force of the semis roaring past. "I don't want to steal anything. I just want to get to Charlotte, locate Tony's safe deposit boxes, and pray they contain the evidence I need to clear my name. Then you can go back to whatever little game you're playing in Knoxville, and I can go back to my family. I'll never have my license reinstated as long as the legal fund has to pay off all those widows and orphans Tony cheated, but at least they'll know I don't have it."

"Neither do I," she stated firmly. "I figure it went to support Sandra. Let the lawyers pry it out of her."

"You're a cold-hearted bitch. Don't you ever spend a sleepless night worrying about the people Tony cheated?"

"Up until you showed up, I'd thought you were the one who pocketed the escrow funds. None of it had any relation to me."

"What in hell did you think was paying for that fancy house in Dilworth and the shiny Jag and the country club dues?" She was an enigma. He couldn't fit all the pieces of her together into one whole. How could someone this cold-hearted find time to buy books for homeless kids and appreciate fine porcelain and sing like she meant every word of her songs?

"I paid for it," she answered calmly. "My inheritance bought the law office. Tony's salary paid for the house. My scrimping and saving and working for nothing paid for everything else. I controlled our personal checkbook. I know precisely where our money came from. I have no idea where anything else came or went."

The traffic was too intense for him to turn and look at her, but he actually wanted to believe her. He couldn't, of course, she'd been the one with the falsified copies of the books. She'd been the one who testified against him. She had to be hiding something.

"And that's the reason you packed up and moved away with no forwarding address and hid up here under an alias?"

"I left a mail-drop forwarding address," she said primly, cleaning her fingers on a damp wipe from a package in her purse. "And Faith Hope is my name, not an alias."

"I spent years trying to trace you. You're hiding, all right. And you don't want to go back to Charlotte for a reason. You have an accomplice who's looking for his share of that money?"

Again it was too dark to see her look of scorn, but it scathed him just the same. Pure vitriol laced her reply. "I had a husband looking for his Jaguar, among other things."

"His Jag?" That caught him so off guard, he laughed. "You stole his precious Jag? My congratulations to you, my dear. I didn't know you had it in you."

"I didn't steal it, I sold it. I sold the house, the stocks, the furniture, and anything that wasn't nailed down. What I couldn't sell, I gave to charity. I left him his suits, though. I sent them to Sandra."

Adrian chuckled. She looked so prim and proper sitting there, as if she should be wearing white gloves and one of those little fifties hats and be sitting in a church pew. She'd sold Tony's car! His chuckle escalated. She might as well have sold his penis. "The country club membership?" he asked out of pure spite. Tony had spent hours bragging about the CEOs he dined with at the club.

"That, too," she agreed demurely. "I told them Tony had decided to give up material possessions and donate his wealth to charity."

He roared. He simply couldn't hold it back any longer.

"You'd better pull over to the side or you'll run us off the road," she said calmly, watching him without so much as a smile.

"I'm okay." He wiped the tears of laughter rolling down his face but he couldn't stop grinning. "Do you have any idea how I schemed to strip Tony to his briefs?"

"I spent eight years of my life with Tony, dreaming," she said softly. "I decided it was time to take action."

That shut him up. This demure, dainty little housewife had dared to enrage a murderous bull by stealing his balls. Tony must have gone ballistic. He would have torn the state apart looking for her. He'd probably charged her with grand larceny and every statute he could find in the book.

"How did you get away with it?" he asked in pure awe.

"I had the canceled checks from his private account, the account that supported Sandra. And I had the copies of those account pages I sent to Headley. He didn't know what else I had, so he kept quiet. That's how I knew he was guilty of something. But I still didn't want to take chances. I filed the divorce papers and left the state. Tony knew too many people in Encee, and I didn't have anyone. He bad-mouthed me from the mountains to the coast before he left."

He believed her. He really believed her. He must be losing his mind. Even knowing the agony she must have endured to have her revenge, he grinned all over again. His mother would love Miss Faith Hope Nicholls. They were both brave women who'd done what they had to do to survive.

Which placed him in a hell of a lot of danger. His mother would come after him with a kitchen knife if she knew he'd kidnapped a woman. He didn't want to contemplate what Faith would do to him now that he knew her strength. Faith Hope could be one vicious female.

"You had Headley on your side," he reminded her, "and I bet a lot of other people you didn't give a chance. You could have gone back after Tony died." Reason and persuasion, he told himself. He needed her trust.

"I didn't want to go back. I made a new life, and I like it."

His lawyer's training heard a note of something behind the defiance, some smidgen of doubt, some yearning he couldn't quite label. He probed for more. "You like singing in a dive?" he asked. It seemed so out of character.

"It paid the rent until the shop showed a profit. Now it helps support the homeless. I'm not so blind as to not realize I could easily have been in their place had Tony thrown me out first."

In the dim light of the dashboard, she shrugged. "Besides, I'd always wanted to sing, and I'm not denying myself any of my dreams anymore. I lost years of my life for my stupidity, and I don't intend to be a victim ever again."

He heard the threat even though it was uttered in a perfectly even voice. She gave new meaning to the phrase "steel magnolia." But he was tough, too. He wasn't a mild-mannered Southern gentleman. He didn't wear kid gloves. Between them, they'd have to find ways of working together without killing each other.

He made the first overture. "You used those years to become a stronger, better person. I don't count that a waste. And you walked away with a sizable amount of cash, so you got a gallery out of it." And the clair-de-lune piece, but he held back his knowledge of its pricelessness. He still looked for a trap.

"I only kept the amount that would have been mine if we'd invested my inheritance in stocks instead of Tony's office."

She lied. He knew she lied. He had her now.

"That fancy house in Dilworth was worth more than the office. Who kept all the rest?"

"Not that it's any of your business," she shot him a look that he knew wasn't happy, "but I set it up in a nonprofit trust fund. I didn't lie to the country club. The worth of Tony's material things was donated to charity. I figured that made us even."

She was downright certifiable. She'd had enough wealth to subsidize a modest lifestyle for the rest of her life, and she'd given it all away? Uh-uh, sister. He didn't buy that one.

"And the clair-de-lune piece?" he asked nonchalantly, waiting for her to explode with wrath at his trap.

She folded her hands neatly in her lap. "That was my grandmother's. Tony never knew its value."

Oh hell. She'd beaten him again.

Either she was a liar par none, or she had waters deeper than the deepest ocean.

And he was seriously beginning to believe the latter. He was kidnapping a damned saint—one who could make a blind man drool.

❧ NINE ❧

Mist covered the windshield as they drove out of the mountains into the foothills. If they took I-26 out of Asheville, the traffic would ease, but Faith knew she couldn't summon the energy to take a flying leap out of a car going sixty-five miles an hour. She couldn't summon the energy to do more than watch the aging wipers slap back and forth. She'd never told her story to anyone. Why had she told this man?

And how did a lawyer and an ex-con know the value of a clair-de-lune bowl, or even what one was?

She wasn't as good at asking questions as he was. She'd grown up traveling from state to state with parents who taught her that asking too many questions was impolite. Besides, he was a lawyer, like Tony, and could probably interrogate while never giving a straight answer.

She shouldn't show any interest in him at all, but if she wasn't going to jump out of the car, she was stuck sitting here beside him in the dark for another two hours or more, worrying about what lay ahead, fearing her attraction to another man she should despise. She watched through the darkened windshield as they turned from I-40 to I-26, leaving the lights of Asheville behind. There was little more than empty road from here to outside Charlotte. What would they do when they arrived in the city?

Considering Adrian's grip on the steering wheel, and his silence after his earlier laughter, she debated the wisdom of trusting him. How far around the bend had four years in prison sent this man?

A good question, but somehow his laughter had reassured her. If Adrian was really innocent, he had a right to prove it.

"You must have worked with Juan quite a bit to know so much about pottery," she said abruptly, introducing a safe topic.

His grip didn't loosen, and he continued to focus on the taillights ahead of him. "My mother's family brought the skill with them. They thought to make a living with it in the land of the free."

She'd spent enough time in Mexico to know about Mexican tiles and pottery. It sold for pennies south of the border. It didn't sell for much more here. "We're a technical society. Appreciation for creativity and artistic ability is limited."

He snorted impolitely. "Tell me something I don't know. My grandfather became a tile setter. My mother worked in the mills. They survived. That's what we do best—survive."

"Survival is the first step," she agreed. "But once we have a roof over our heads and food in our bellies, then we can look for what makes us happy."

"Try it with nine kids."

Nine. She tried to imagine it, but her longing for a child of her own mixed with her knowledge of the struggle to afford decent housing, and she couldn't reconcile either one. Maybe she'd been a little hasty in giving everything away. If she really could conceive—how would she afford a child? "Maybe having children made your mother happy?"

"She wept bitter tears when Ines was born after my stepfather died. She can't be overjoyed to see her firstborn jailed for his stupidity. We won't go into all the trials and tribulations between the first and last. Children are a burden and a responsibility. They do not guarantee joy any more than money does."

He'd steered her off the conversational track, just as she'd figured. Not willing to deny her newly awakened dream already, she switched back to the original topic. "Mexican pottery does not lead one to recognize an antique piece like the clair de lune."

He shrugged, wriggled his lanky frame uncomfortably in the small seat, and reached for the radio. "I have an inquiring mind. I took art courses. The clair-de-lune glaze fascinated me. How did your grandmother acquire it?" The radio crackled but produced no music.

Art courses! She couldn't name a single lawyer of her acquaintance who could do more than mention the names of a few famous painters or discuss the investment appreciation on artwork their wives had acquired. Still, she supposed it made sense given the family trade.

He was leading her down the garden path again.

"I never asked her." She defiantly switched the topic back to him. "You have eight brothers and sisters? How old are they?"

"I'm the eldest. Belinda is next at twenty-five. Ines is the youngest at six. My mother named us alphabetically, so you can always know where one of us stands in the family."

Adrian, the eldest, letter A. Faith smiled at the whimsy. "Did she intend to have the whole alphabet?"

He shrugged and seemed to relax a little. "Who knows? She was only eighteen when she had me. She could have thought anything. Teenagers have their heads in the clouds."

"And their hearts on their sleeves," she agreed quietly.

"They grow out of it."

"What about you? What did you dream of at eighteen? Did you have a sweetheart?"

"Rick was still alive and supporting the family then. I guess I just dreamed of getting rich and moving us all into a big house with a swimming pool. I worked every minute of every day to put myself through school and didn't have time for girlfriends."

"But you had them." She knew he would have. A man with his striking looks would attract women like bees to honey. "Did you have someone special waiting for you to get out of jail?"

He hit the gas pedal and skirted around a semi, pushing the little car as hard as it would go. "She liked that attorney's shingle on my door better than she liked me. She was no major loss."

But the bitterness was there. If Adrian were to be believed, Tony had cost him his livelihood, his family, everything he possessed, as well as any hope for the future. Tony had died with a lot of woe on his shoulders. She hoped he went straight to hell.

"Maybe I should have stayed more involved with the business," she said thoughtfully, mentioning a topic that had preyed on her mind for years. "I used to keep the books when he first started out. I would have noticed if something was wrong."

"You kept the books and never noticed Sandra on the side," he pointed out.

Score one for the lawyer. "You actually signed the transfers," she countered.

"Heaping blame won't help us now." He slowed down and shoved his thick ponytail behind him. "I knew he was up to something, but I ignored it. Tony offered me a job when no one else would, and he paid me well to buckle my mouth. I had an ethical responsibility to know what the firm was doing, and I failed miserably, but I've paid my debt. I want to at least try to have my license reinstated, but I can't if Tony spent all the money on Sandra."

"The legal fund paid the people who were cheated. If there's any proof that you weren't involved, why wouldn't they give you your license back?"

His laugh was cold. "Because that fund is paid for by lawyers, and their insurance bill skyrockets every time the payoff is large. If it hurts their pockets, they'll make me pay."

"Then this is an exercise in futility, isn't it?"

"Probably," he admitted. "When I thought you had the money, I had some purpose. If you really don't have it . . ."

"I really don't have it." She said it quietly, but forcefully. She wanted him to turn the car around and go back. She didn't want to rake through cold ashes in a town she'd left behind. She didn't believe in looking back.

"Some of the money or the books could still be in the safe deposit boxes," he insisted.

Did that mean he believed her, or was this some sort of test? What did it matter? He didn't turn around. He'd made up his mind to keep going because he didn't know what else to do. She understood that sort of desperation. She just didn't understand forcing other people to go along.

"Don't you think Tony would have emptied the boxes first chance he had?" she asked. "He left town after the trial. I'd cleaned him out. He had nothing but his law practice, and no one wanted to buy it after the scandal. He would have cleaned out every dime he'd hoarded."

"The D.A. impounded everything in the office. If Tony had safe deposit keys there, the D.A. would have found them. I don't think Tony would have left something so dangerous in Sandra's hands. She's a loose cannon. You're the one he trusted. He would have left those keys in the house, and you sold everything before he could get to them."

She was the one Tony trusted. A few years ago that would have been sweet music to her ears. Now, it hit her as bitter and cold. Tony trusted her to be a safe dimwit who would ask him polite questions he could avert with ease. She closed her eyes and leaned her head against the seat. "Then they're gone. I emptied his safe and his desk and there weren't any keys there. I hauled all my personal stuff to storage and haven't seen it since I left, but there's nothing in there that Tony would have touched."

"Then we'll start by questioning the banks. I'll be your lawyer, you'll be the widow who's just learned your husband left his valuables in a box you didn't know existed. We'll need a death certificate."

"I don't have a death certificate," she said wearily, eyes still closed. She didn't want to remember any of this. She just wanted her secure, quiet life back.

"You don't have a death certificate? Why not? You were still married when he died, weren't you? How did you collect his life insurance?"

The sound that emerged from her throat was too brittle for laughter. "He died in South America. They don't just automatically ship out death certificates. When I thought I could use his life insurance for the trust fund, I knew I'd have to find out how to obtain one. But after I located the policy, it had Sandra's name on it, so I mailed it to her and let her handle the death certificate business."

"Sandra never mentioned that to me," he muttered suspiciously.

"Sandra's the loose cannon, remember? Why don't you kidnap her?"

He snorted, then chuckled. "The first time I called Sandra, I could hear the kids screaming their heads off, and she tried to put a move on me over the phone. Suggested conjugal visits. She thought I had Tony's money."

In the darkness, Faith grinned. "They were made for each other. You should have taken her up on the offer."

"And paid child support for the rest of my life. No, thank you, ma'am. Having kids is definitely not on my agenda. I have to figure out how to feed the family I have without making more. By the time Ines is out of college, I'll be forty-seven. I don't see me starting a family at that age."

That thought inexplicably saddened her. She hadn't known a twinge of hormones since leaving Tony, but this man with the sexy eyes had her reevaluating her sexless life. An ex-con and lawyer, for heaven's sake! Could she stoop any lower?

That didn't mean he wouldn't make a good lover, the Eve in her argued.

And he'd make handsome babies.

"A lot of men start late these days." She did the calculations and concluded he was only a couple of years older than she. While she'd grown up in the relative cocoon of family love and security, he'd been toughing his way through a harsh world she hadn't experienced until late in life. He'd known it from birth. That made him decades older in terms of living. She didn't know where she was going with these crazed thoughts. She needed sleep.

"Maybe I'll marry a rich lawyer," he answered with sarcasm.

She chuckled. "There you go. Serve both of you right."

"We can start tracking down the death certificate in the morning." He returned to his objectives. "No reason we can't call banks while we're at it. And maybe you should open your storage and poke around. If Sandra was desperate enough to proposition me, he must not have left her much. That proves the money is still out there somewhere."

"You keep dreaming." Yawning, Faith curled up in the seat and tried to sleep.

"What else have I got to do?"

She couldn't argue with that, and he didn't say anything more. She dozed until the car halting woke her. She considered not opening her eyes, until Adrian reached over her arm for her purse. She caught his wrist and twisted hard, the way she'd been taught in her self-defense courses.

With his other hand he twisted back, disarming her without hurting her.

"It's after midnight. This place is cheap. I'll pay you back later. We have to get some sleep before we tackle the banks."

Blinking, she looked up into a flashing neon sign advertising vacancy.

"You think I'm paying to shack up with you in a cheap motel?" she asked incredulously.

"You'd prefer an expensive one?" Grabbing her purse, he removed the billfold she kept her credit card in and helped himself.

He took the keys with him when he went in to register.

Faith tried to gauge their location but they were still in the middle of nowhere. It figured he wouldn't take her to one of the big intersections laced with hotels and restaurants.

She could get out and walk and see if anyone would answer their door at midnight, but he'd find her before she walked half a mile. What's more, she risked being run over by a car in the dark, raped by the first person who saw her, or robbed, at best.

She wasn't a brave person. Better the devil she knew than the one she didn't.

Slumping in the seat, she practiced cursing.

❦ TEN ❦

Four and a half years earlier

"Where the hell is my Jag?"

Tony's frown wrinkled every inch of his brow as he glanced again to where the carefully shrouded sports car should be. The historical society hadn't allowed a garage addition to shelter it. "You didn't drive it, did you?" he asked in horror as he walked up the oak-lined drive from the chauffeur-driven car at the curb, accompanied by two men considerably larger than he.

Looking up from the notes she was scribbling for the couple beside her, Faith glanced toward the approaching men and fought back a frisson of alarm. She recognized Al McCowan, Jr. as an old friend from the university and one of Tony's favorite golfing buddies. The other bulky blond man was one of Tony's childhood friends she hadn't seen around in a long time. Tony didn't like admitting to his rural origins.

Had Tony already discovered what she'd done? Fear iced her blood, but anger boiled too strongly for her to act on any sense of self-preservation, "I sold it," she called sweetly, handing her scribbled recommendations for gardeners and repairmen to the extremely well-muscled football player tensing up beside her. She patted his arm. "Would you be so kind as to escort me to my car?" she asked politely. She had thought to be gone before Tony arrived, but she'd counted on the house's new owner being sufficient protection against surprises.

She had been right. Tony turned purple and hurled obscenities, but even with his bulky bodyguards in tow, he didn't dare
attack one of the Panthers' newest linemen. Without a word
of explanation to anyone—too terrified to speak if the truth
be known—Faith marched to her aging Volvo, climbed in,
and drove away.

Once safely out of reach, she let exultation balloon inside
her, crushing all fear. She wished she could have seen Tony's
face when he discovered his house was no longer his home.

The Present

Staring wearily at a bathroom mirror with irregular dark
splotches where the silver backing was missing, Faith grimaced at her reflection. She would turn thirty on her next
birthday. Already she could see the crow's-feet at the corners
of her eyes. What did she have to show for them besides the
music of Tony's curses as she walked away? She had a life
without a single deep relationship, without love, without any
of the things she'd thought to have by now.

And the damned man in the other room was forcing her to
examine everything she'd done these last few years, everything she'd so proudly based her new life on. The result
wasn't pretty.

He'd *kidnapped* her, damn it. She didn't need to take life
lessons from a criminal.

Pulling her hair back in a barrette from her purse, she
stalked back into the shabby motel bedroom. It was clean.
That was all she could give it. At the sight of Adrian propping
the room's one chair against the doorknob, she scowled.

"Keeping thieves out or me in?"

He dropped into the chair, crossed his arms over his chest
and stretched his long legs out in front of him, practically
filling the narrow aisle between the end of the bed and the
dresser. Her tired gaze focused on the scuffed soles of his
worn wingtips—courtroom shoes, she used to call them.

"Both," he responded warily. "The way your mind works,
you'll have figured out how to have me locked up and be

halfway back to Knoxville before I wake up. I need my sleep."

Faith glanced at the double bed. She wasn't about to suggest that they share it. Let him suffer.

He hadn't asked to share the bed.

She dropped wearily on the sprung mattress, wrinkled up her nose at the thought of checking the sheets and, removing her comfortable Easy Spirits and suit jacket, lay down as she was. He'd brought in a duffel bag probably containing all his worldly possessions. She didn't even have a toothbrush.

A forty-watt bulb in the reading lamp still burned between them. Adrian's eyelids were already drooping. The shadows from the lamp highlighted the hollows of his sculpted cheekbones, and she wished she had enough talent to draw him. The glimmer of his silver earring captivated her. If all she wanted was sex, she might as well have taken up with Artie from the band. He'd be a lot less trouble.

She flung the spare pillow at her kidnapper.

Adrian jerked up, caught it, and glancing at her warily, shoved it behind his back.

"Kidnapping is a federal offense." She couldn't go to sleep like this. He might as well suffer with her.

"So sue me." He shut his eyes again.

She wanted to turn the lamp off so she wouldn't see the breadth of his shoulders straining against that damned flannel shirt. She was afraid to be left alone in the dark with him. Panic began to build in her throat. She didn't know where it came from. Could she pry her phone out of his pocket? *Touch* him? Not a chance.

"There are a blue million banks in Charlotte. We can't possibly visit all of them. I have to get back to my shop." Maybe voicing her fears would help. It would certainly drive him as crazy as her, at least.

He opened his eyes again, and she wished he hadn't. The "lean and hungry" look that Shakespeare wrote about couldn't compare to what she saw in this man's eyes. Large and dark, shadowed by indecently long lashes, they narrowed as they focused on her, forcing her into awareness of how she lay sprawled across a bed big enough for two.

She breathed a sigh of relief as he turned off the lamp.

It didn't help. In the darkness she was even more intensely aware of the vibrations. He'd been in prison for four years. She'd been on remote control longer than that. It was just human nature, she told herself.

She could escape. All she had to do was seduce him.

"Don't," he warned.

She didn't even have to be told what he meant. She understood from the tautness of his voice and the dangerous depths from which it emerged.

She didn't know which she wanted more, escape or the seduction.

"I can't trust a man who kidnaps me," she whispered into the darkness, more for her own benefit than his.

"And I'm not about to trust a woman who holds my life in her hands," he retorted with just enough anger to be convincing.

"Then I suppose you'd better find a way to resolve that problem." Snapping the words, Faith rolled over to face the wall and closed her eyes.

In the blinking light of the hotel sign through the thin curtains, Adrian stared at the tempting silhouette of rounded hip and slender waist lying on the sagging bed, and only years of control prevented him from doing something he shouldn't.

A package of dynamite would be safer.

He'd been on the edge of arousal since he'd first seen her on that stage. He ached so fiercely with it now, he'd never go to sleep. And if he didn't go to sleep, he'd sit here all night imagining all the ways he could get her under him.

He didn't think it would be difficult. He'd seen the sexual awareness in her look. He knew women like her were tempted by the dark and forbidden. He'd taken advantage of their kind once or twice in the past. It was pure animal curiosity, nothing more. But this time he had a feeling it could be a hell of a lot more for him and three times as dangerous.

Convincing his mind was one thing. Telling his body was quite another.

He could do this a lot easier when angry. He needed to summon that anger boiling within him, stir the cauldron that seethed in his soul, spice it with the hot pepper of indignation. But she looked more like a bewildered child than a cold-blooded villain, and he couldn't even kindle the coals—not of anger, anyway. Lust would have him bursting into flames any minute now.

She wanted trust. How the hell could he give her that? It wasn't in him. Tony—her husband—had burned what little bit of trust he'd once possessed. For all that mattered, it looked as if she'd never trust him for the same reason.

Finally, her breathing evened, and he relaxed enough to contemplate tomorrow. His eyes had scarcely closed before they jerked open again to the sound of running water and the glaring light of dawn blazing through the curtains. He'd never curse another Carolina dawn as long as he lived. The freedom to walk out into the cool morning air was a blessing he'd never really appreciated until he'd lost it.

His gaze swung from the rumpled, empty bed to the closed door of the bathroom. At least she hadn't stabbed him in his sleep, so maybe violence wasn't on her agenda.

The door swung open and Faith emerged, all shiny and bright-eyed like a brand new toy under his Christmas tree, and he almost swallowed his tongue in longing. She'd let her hair down and it swirled around her shoulders like thick white-gold silk. In this light, her eyes were almost blue, and as crystal clear as a mountain lake. If he started investigating the way the tailored silk of her blouse clung to her breasts or the thin cloth of her skirt emphasized the sexy curve of her hips, he'd be salivating. Her legs were definitely out of bounds.

"I'm hungry," she announced with a challenge in her eyes.

Well, so was he, but he didn't think they had the same hunger in mind. He couldn't keep from wondering what she would do if he stood up and started kissing that pouty pink mouth of hers. His imagination had her blouse unbuttoned and bra unfastened and his hands full of soft warm flesh before he could rein in his fantasies.

He groaned and shut his eyes. He'd made some big mistakes in his life, but this was one of the most agonizing.

"The minute I go in there and wash, you'll run for help, won't you?"

"Thought about it," she agreed.

Shit. They'd send him back to the slammer before he could taste a woman's mouth again. His mother would curl up and die and his family would go straight to hell.

"But I'm not about to fish the car keys out of your pocket, and I'm not in the mood for police before breakfast. I don't suppose this joint has a café?"

Oh, God, thank you. Whatever he'd done to deserve this, he would repeat twice over. He opened his eyes to narrow slits to see if she was laughing.

She tossed her hair and gave him one of those mouth-watering smiles she bestowed on the bar crowd. He didn't trust it for an instant.

"You're waiting for me to feed you and *then* you'll call the cops." He surged from the chair and stalked toward her, feeling every ache and pain from a night in his awkward bed.

She stood her ground. "Touch me and I'll *feed* you to the cops," she warned, "in bite-size pieces."

Warily, Adrian waited. If he touched her, he'd have her on the bed and rolling under him before she had a chance to utter another syllable, aching muscles or not. He'd best wait to see if she'd discovered a more reasonable alternative.

"We can use my cell phone to call the banks on the way to the storage unit. I don't know if they'll even give out safe deposit box information without a death certificate, but we can find out that much. You can sort through my junk until you're satisfied Tony left nothing in there. Then I can leave you with your family and I can go home." She waited a moment, and when he didn't immediately reply, she added, "You'll have to trust me with the phone."

He had a feeling it wouldn't be as simple as that, but if that's what it took to make her happy for the moment, he wouldn't disagree. "That's a plan." Gathering up the reins of his control, he marched past her into the bathroom and slammed the door.

He would have short-circuited on frazzled wires of frustration as soon as the door closed, but his gaze caught the shower, and with determination he jerked on the cold faucet. He'd survive this, somehow.

Faith checked off another phone number from the list she'd copied from the hotel's directory. "Death certificate, identification, and/or the key before they'll even bother looking. Damned banks charge more and more and do less and less. It's a good thing I don't have enough money to worry over which one of the monsters to give it to."

Adrian steered through the morning rush hour traffic on I-85 into Charlotte. He had the windows rolled down, and even the smell of exhaust fumes was perfume to his nose. He was free. He was home again. He could almost hear his mother's joy and the clamor of the kids as he walked through the front door. What was he doing chasing down a ghost?

Looking for his life, he reminded himself. Otherwise, he'd be bagging groceries or flipping hamburgers. "All right. We'll track down how to get that death certificate. And we'll search the storage unit for a key. I'll assume identification isn't a problem for you?"

He turned his attention away from the road just enough to catch her sticking her tongue out at him. Grinning, he turned back to the road in time to prevent the Mercedes in the next lane from ripping off the VW's bumper in its hurry to cut in front of them.

"You wouldn't do that if you had any idea what it does to a starving man's hormones," he warned without a trace of delicacy. She might as well understand where things stood here. They'd fenced around it long enough.

"As if I give a damn about your hormones," she retorted calmly enough. "Obviously, deprivation has given you testosterone poisoning. I'm not hanging around here. I'm going home."

"I'll follow you. If you have any care for my family, you'll avoid that."

Silence. He could almost hear her simmer. He had her number, finally. She might think he was scum of the earth, but she had a heart as mushy as warm cream cheese.

"Annie will pick up my deliveries, but she can't sell anything. My clerk won't work full-time. I can't afford to lose more than a day's worth of sales," she protested.

"We're talking about lives here." He used his best sincere voice. He hadn't become captain of the debating team without knowing all the answers. "Is a few dollars worth the futures of seven kids?"

"I thought there were eight," she answered suspiciously.

"I've already put Belinda through nursing school. She's married and on her own. I should have talked her into becoming a doctor, but she had marriage on the mind at the time."

She sighed dramatically. "Just give me one good reason why I should care."

Telling her she had a heart like cream cheese probably wouldn't do it. Adrian grinned anyway. It was a beautiful Carolina-blue morning. The heat of the sun poured through the windshield. Puffy white clouds flitted above and willow oaks flashed past as he gunned the engine and eased into an opening in the next lane. He was free. He was sitting beside the most beautiful woman he could ever remember meeting. He could do anything.

He debated all the possible answers he could give her. He could lie and promise to love and cherish her forever. Women loved hearing that even if they didn't believe it. And this one wouldn't believe it for an instant, not after what Tony put her through. She probably didn't even want to hear it.

He could tell her about each of his siblings, about the athletic twins, about Cesar's genius, about Hernando's crippled leg and Ines's adorable grin. He could tell her about the loving mother who had literally worked her arthritic fingers to the bone trying to keep them all fed and healthy.

But he'd bared his heart enough. He wouldn't give her

more. Looking straight ahead, he offered the only reason he could afford. "Because you're the kind of woman who wants the right thing done, no matter what it takes."

She didn't reply, and he knew he had her.

❧ ELEVEN ❧

"I told you the storage unit was on South Boulevard. You just turned uptown." Faith figured even if he hadn't given her the car keys yet, she still had the phone. She could always call 911.

She could see tension bunching the muscles beneath Adrian's shirtsleeves. His earlier easy laughter had disappeared behind a grim mask as he negotiated the heavy traffic. She didn't think it was the traffic bothering him. She tried to put herself in his shoes and wondered why he didn't go straight home to his family. She would.

"I have a friend who used to work at Nations. Hit the number for them and ask for David Wilkins."

She hit the requested phone number. "They're called Bank of America now," she reminded him. "A lot of people have moved on."

He nodded curtly in acceptance of that. From this angle, she thought she detected Native American origins in his coloring, but the blade of his nose and the sharp jut of his cheekbone was pure Castilian Spanish. She suspected his height came from some redneck side of his family. She grinned at that and asked the operator for David Wilkins. Never let it be said that she was afraid of a man with a ring in his ear.

She handed the phone to him as his friend's secretary came on the line.

He scowled, eased the car to the side of the road and stopped, letting traffic flash by in the sunlight. Well, that was interesting. A lawyer who couldn't do two things at once.

She heard the wariness in his voice relax as he made an appointment. He handed the phone back without comment and watched for an opening in the traffic.

"Well, you didn't promise him your firstborn child, so I assume he's still speaking to you."

"I saved his butt once. He owes me."

She'd heard that before. Men had a peculiar way of keeping score. If she did someone a favor, she didn't count it as a point on her scorecard to be called in whenever she liked. Admittedly, it might be advantageous at times like this if she could.

Autumn didn't touch Charlotte this early in the season. The magnolias still gleamed emerald, the willow oaks had paled a little from their summer color, but they weren't brown yet. The decorative flower beds decorating every office and shopping center still contained the crimson red of summer geraniums and salvia. After the first frost they'd be replaced by pansies, but the sun beamed warm as they descended the ramp into the shadows of the high-rise office buildings of uptown.

"Concrete jungle," Adrian muttered as he turned toward the financial district. "This town used to have shopping and sidewalks and parking. Now it's all concrete."

"So is every city in the country. Get used to it."

He found a parking place in the Seventh Street Station garage.

"Why not the bank's garage?" she complained. "We'll have to walk blocks."

"Because I'm assuming they still give ninety minutes free here. My pocket money is limited, unless you're offering to pay."

He opened the door and unfolded from the low seat with a groan, giving away the discomfort of last night's sleeping arrangement.

She wouldn't feel guilty. She wouldn't even like the man for coming around the car and opening the door for her. He was just being polite to get what he wanted.

"We don't look exactly impressive in wrinkled clothes." She tugged at her rumpled skirt with distaste.

"Want to go to the airport and have the valet press them?" he joked, pressing a hand to the small of her back and practically pushing her toward the exit.

"No, I want to play the wall." Refusing to be pushed, she halted and examined the mosaic artwork decorating the parking garage wall. The artist responsible for it had built a riddle into the pictures. The correct answer punched into lights outside the garage produced a computerized reward of chimes and flashing lights. She'd always wanted to try her hand at it.

Adrian looked at her as if she were crazy. Then glancing around, it slowly dawned on him. "The riddle. Haven't they solved it yet?"

"Yeah, but there's a new one. I never had a chance to solve the old one." She knew she was wasting time. Tony had never let her come in here because he'd known she'd dally over the painted clues, but she thought it would be wildly satisfying to solve the puzzle and make a building chime.

"It could take hours. We'll stop on each floor and you can look, and then when we come back, you can try it out."

Faith stared at him incredulously as he grabbed her arm and steered her toward the wall. He seemed to be as fascinated with the puzzle as she was. His eyes lit with interest and intelligence as he avidly scanned the mural. He'd probably solve it faster than she would. She was just amazed that he'd bother with something so useless.

"Come on, next floor." He pushed her toward the exit, and they raced for the stairs.

Laughing, she shoved past him and hit the stairs running, emerging into the bright light on the next floor and hurrying to scan the clues in the mosaic before he could.

There was something freeing in just enjoying the moment, in forgetting the world and its problems and behaving like a child. She couldn't remember when she'd last laughed like this.

By the time they'd raced to the bottom floor, punched the chiming lights, and hurried up the block, they were breathless and almost late for the appointment. Adrian grabbed her hand

and together they dodged traffic and ran into the imposing office tower.

It seemed perfectly natural to be holding his hand. It shouldn't. She tugged it away as soon as the stone cold quiet of the imposing foyer hit her. She brushed at her wrinkled skirt again, wished she'd powdered her nose, and tried not to look too intimidated by her surroundings as they rushed past men in Armani and women in business-tailored suits. Tony had always been at home in marble surroundings. She'd always thought wistfully of the small-town banks of her childhood where the clerks offered her lollipops and asked about school.

"You have a smudge on your nose," Adrian whispered wickedly as the elevator door closed behind them.

"I look like last night's leftover mashed potatoes," she grumbled, reaching for a clean-wipe.

He licked his finger and rubbed the smudge off. "More like tousled silk sheets."

She melted clear down to her toes. How did he do this to her? She looked into solemn dark eyes and almost believed every word they promised. She never let anyone this close to her. Then the elevator door clanged open and they stepped back into the real world.

Adrian's friend greeted him with a wariness that relaxed slightly upon sight of Faith. She didn't recognize the banker, but she recognized his readiness to accept her as helpless, witless blonde, ready to flirt. In Tony's time she would have smiled and batted her lashes and oozed honey. She didn't owe Adrian that kind of aid.

She nodded curtly, ignored the banker's hand, and took a seat without asking.

Adrian didn't even notice.

Sitting back in amazement, she watched as Adrian concentrated on spinning his tale, delivering appropriate facts judiciously and leaving out everything in between. Not once did he glance in her direction or appeal for her help. She might as well not be there for all it mattered to him.

Tony had always used her as a social icebreaker and a shield he could throw up when he felt threatened. She'd never fully understood how he'd used her until she watched Adrian step in front of her, protect her from questions, and act for her. She wasn't certain she ought to like being sheltered, but she appreciated a man prepared to assume full responsibility.

She could tell from the way Adrian's knuckles whitened as he leaned forward that he didn't like the answers the banker was giving him, but he didn't explode in a temper or throw out impatient threats of lawsuits as Tony would have done. Adrian's future lay in finding those safe deposit boxes, but he remained as calm and civil as he had from the first greeting. His tough exterior concealed a wealth of willpower. Considering she'd seen the wrong side of Adrian's temper, she thought his control nothing short of remarkable.

The banker's phone rang, interrupting the conversation. "What?" he asked curtly. Then his expression changed. "All right, tell Al just a minute." He hung up and glanced at them apologetically. "I'm sorry. I've got an angry VIP waiting. Call if I can answer any more questions."

The two men stood and shook hands without resolving a single issue, and Faith wanted to sit there in bewilderment and figure out what had just happened. They'd been told they couldn't get any help at all, and they were just walking out?

Stunned, she let Adrian guide her from the office. Out of the corner of her eye she caught sight of one of Tony's golfing buddies waiting impatiently, and shivering, she hurried to hide in Adrian's shadow. It was foolish to hide from the past, but she saw no point in causing trouble if it could be avoided.

Faith studied the grim set of Adrian's jaw and the way his mouth thinned in anger, but he didn't utter one explosive word as they rode the elevator down. If a high-powered bank officer couldn't find those deposit boxes, how the devil did Adrian think they would?

She hated to ask, but she couldn't bear his silence any longer. "What do we do now?" she whispered as they left the air-conditioned foyer for the autumn heat.

"Solve the riddle?" he asked wryly, staring at the traffic

rushing past. "Clanging bells and trumpeting chimes might just hit the spot."

Her mood for childish games had fled with the intrusion of reality. "We could file for the death certificate, I suppose. I probably should have done that long ago."

He shoved his hands in his pockets and shrugged. "Yeah, that's a start."

She didn't like seeing the energy drain out of him. It was as if he'd used up all his resources in controlling his hope and anger back there, and now he'd finally faced the inevitability of defeat. Oddly, instead of using the moment to escape, she didn't want him giving up.

"The death certificate first, since we're down here," she suggested. "Then we call the state and have them start tracing unclaimed assets, as your friend suggested."

Faith started down the street toward the courthouse.

Adrian's long stride easily caught up with her. His long hair and earring were as out of place in the conservative tide of business suits as coconuts on an apple tree, but Faith noticed the sidelong, admiring glances he attracted from the women around them. He seemed oblivious to the attention. He was probably used to it.

"That needs to be done anyway, but then you may as well go home. I need to go back to my family. There's no point pissing into the wind."

She grinned. Tony would never have said anything so ungentlemanly. "We may as well check the storage unit while we're at it. I can't imagine there's anything in there, but it's been years and I don't remember what I packed away."

"Fine," he said curtly, as if he were humoring her and hadn't kidnapped and plagued her for just that purpose.

"I know a groin punch that can bring a man to his knees," she said conversationally.

The grim look around his eyes eased as he cast her an interested glance. "Planning on trying it on any bankers?"

"My lawyer specialty."

Although it didn't reach his eyes, he flashed her that heart-stopping white smile in appreciation. "Maybe I better feed you. I bet you're one of those skinny women who turn nasty when their blood sugar drops."

"No, and I don't have PMS either. I only turn nasty when men play games with me. You kidnapped me and dragged me from my work to look for those blamed books, so don't quit on me now, Sherlock."

This time the laughter reached his eyes. "You're kinda cute when you're riled."

She almost smacked him until she saw the teasing lift of his lips and sunlight caught the sparkle of his earring. He'd been ground up and put through hell. She'd allow him a sulk or two.

"Fine." She headed for a small Chinese restaurant where the food was cheap. "Now you can feed me."

Adrian admired the way Faith continued to look brisk and breezy even after they'd climbed ten thousand steps, rode two dozen elevators, questioned three dozen officials, and ended up only a few feet from where they started. She'd knotted her shiny straight hair into a businesslike bun, and silken strands had started to escape at her nape, giving her a more vulnerable look than she probably appreciated, but she filled out the last form with a crisp flourish and turned it in without batting a lash.

Outside the glass door she slumped noticeably. "Tony's still a bastard after he's dead," she muttered.

"Damned inconvenient of him to choose South America," he agreed amiably, although he hoped the fiend had died painfully and horribly in some thick jungle after the plane's crash. Maybe a tribe of headhunters had found him.

She glanced at her watch. "We have time to call the state offices before they close. Did you want to do it from here, or would you rather go home?"

"Make the call." He wasn't ready to go home. He didn't want to go home as a failure. He'd hoped to appear triumphantly, with news that all would be well, that he'd turned things around. Telling them he was just an ex-con, an ex-lawyer, with no prospects except as a dishwasher wouldn't help anything.

When he heard her reciting her home address into the phone, he grimaced. More forms. This could take weeks. Months. What the hell would he do with himself? And she could change her mind about helping him at any moment.

She sighed as she closed the cell phone and stuffed it back into her purse. He wanted to tuck that straying piece of hair behind her ear, but he knew to keep his hands to himself. One wrong move and she'd leave him high and dry. He was used to women as window dressing. He wasn't entirely certain how to handle one who didn't want to be handled.

"It's late." She held her hand to her back as she straightened. The concrete bench they'd chosen to sit on wasn't precisely comfortable. She glanced up at the storm clouds scuttling across the sky. "We'll have to drag boxes out of the storage unit to examine them. Is that wise at this hour?"

"You have a better idea?" Watching her breasts push against her blouse gave him plenty of ideas, none of them useful.

She didn't even seem to notice the direction of his gaze. She shoved the straying hair into a pin and watched the beginning of rush hour traffic barricade the intersection. "Why don't we look for Headley? Maybe he has some suggestions."

Oh yeah, let's look for Headley, Adrian mocked to himself. Headley hung out in bars. Ten good stiff drinks ought to do the trick. Then he'd be out cold and it wouldn't matter what he did next.

"You spring for dinner." With resignation, he stood and held out his hand. Might as well get used to living on welfare.

❧ TWELVE ❧

With a few calls they located Headley's latest hangout at a country-western club on the north side. After paying a ransom to retrieve the car from the parking garage, Adrian eased into rush hour traffic and turned north.

"Stupid urban assault vehicles," he muttered as a Rover nearly took off their fender while changing lanes. "Their drivers need the monsters to protect them from their own incompetence." He slammed the VW's brakes as another SUV ran the red light in front of him.

"Well, we can all hope that driving like that, they'll eventually turn the top-heavy things over and be obliterated. My personal preference is for a dash-mounted laser gun that will disintegrate them without littering."

Adrian cocked one eyebrow but didn't remove his gaze from the road. "Bloodthirsty sort, are we?" She'd removed her jacket, and the top button of her tailored silk shirt had come undone. With her miniskirt riding more than halfway up her thigh, she looked better than sin, Ben and Jerry's cherry-cream-cheese ice cream, and pure gold all wrapped in one.

"Only when tired," she admitted, tucking her shoeless feet under her. "I don't miss this traffic at all. From now on I'll always live close to where I work."

"Even if you have to live in slums?" he asked in disbelief.

She shrugged. "What's more dangerous, a slum or this traffic?"

He grunted in acknowledgment. "You're not what I thought you were."

"You thought I was a thief and a cheat and an embezzler."

"I thought you were a rich bitch who wouldn't give up her lifestyle at the cost of others. I still can't figure out what the hell you are. Why haven't you called the cops or knocked me over the head and taken the keys and got the hell out of here?"

She'd like the answer to that question herself. Crossing her arms, she glared out the windshield. "I ought to, but Tony's treated you worse than me, so maybe I feel like I owe you." Or maybe she'd developed a fascination with raven-haired men with rings in their ears. Or her hormones had riddled her brains with holes. Anything was possible.

He turned the wrong way down a one-way alley, cut through a parking lot, and emerged a few blocks from their destination. "One of these days this town will learn to build cross streets." He downshifted and parked without acknowledging her response.

So he didn't like accepting help from a woman. Big deal. She didn't have to live with him. Slipping on her shoes, she opened the car door without waiting for him, and took off across the parking lot. Adrian was beside her within a few steps. He loomed over her, every bit the protective male as he took her elbow and steered her toward the corner.

"I intend to pay back every penny," he said abruptly as he held the restaurant door for her. "And you can have free legal advice for the rest of your life."

Faith flashed him a look of disbelief, then almost laughed out loud at the fierce look of determination on his face. He really, *really* didn't like taking help from a woman.

They brought Headley a barbecue sandwich along with sandwiches for themselves and slid into the booth across from him as the DJ spun an old song about taking a job and shoving it. Peanut shells crunched beneath their heels, and Faith observed the empty stage with professional interest. It was wider and more crowd accessible than the one she used. She could walk out in the audience when she sang—

"Joining us anytime this evening?" Adrian asked wryly, shoving a beer into her hand.

She popped back into the moment and smiled sheepishly at the old man across the table. "Hi, Headley. How you doing?"

"Bored with retirement. Bored with city life. Watcha doin' exciting?"

It was apparent the old reporter had already drank his supper, but he held his beer well. Interest was bright in his eyes as he looked from Adrian to Faith. Headley had befriended her after she'd brought him the pages from Tony's ledger, but she hadn't tried to keep in touch with him any more than with anyone else here since she'd left.

"Adrian here thinks he was framed and that I can help him out of it. Heard any rumors that might be relevant?" Faith said, putting down the sandwich and sipping her beer. After the hot barbecue, she could use it.

Headley raised his shaggy gray eyebrows and bit into his sandwich before answering. He took his time thinking about it, then shook his head as he finished chewing. "Can't say that I have. Tony's plane crashing was a nine-day wonder a few years back. There was some speculation at the time, people wondering if he could be as innocent as he claimed, or if he'd taken the money and run, but that's about the last of it. You've probably heard all that before."

She'd left before she heard that, but she could imagine the way tongues wagged.

"The prosecutor would have gone after Faith to get the money back if he'd had any evidence against Tony," Adrian interjected. "So that was gossip and nothing else. If you've not heard more, then they must consider the case closed."

The bar was dark and about half full. The canned music provided just enough background noise to prevent anyone from hearing them, not that anyone was close enough to hear, Faith observed.

She tried to still her tapping toe and realized both men were looking at her again. She sighed in exasperation. "Look, I don't know the law, I don't know the case, and what little I do know—Tony—is dead. What do you want from me?"

She knew the instant the gleam appeared in Adrian's eye that she'd said the wrong thing. His half-lidded gaze dropped to her breasts, and she wanted to kick him under the table. He had no right to look at her like that. She'd done nothing to encourage him—except look at him the same way. Sticking out her bottom lip, she blew an annoying strand of hair from her face and glared at him. "One word out of you, Adrian Raphael, and I'll teach you that trick I told you about."

He grinned in blatant male admiration. She was used to Artie's adolescent looks of longing and the catcalls from a drunken audience. She wasn't used to a predatory gleam in a handsome man's eyes. In business suits, she aspired toward mousy, so men seldom looked at her twice. Her stage persona wasn't her, and she considered the looks she drew there as impersonal. There was nothing impersonal about the heat of Adrian's gaze.

"I'll let you teach that trick to the district attorney when we find the evidence." Smooth and seductive, his voice rumbled close to her ear.

"Not to put a crimp in your style, Quinn," Headley interrupted, "but you might want to talk to the D.A."

Adrian scowled. "You realize Tony insisted I use the 'Quinn' on letterhead instead of 'Raphael' because it sounds less ethnic?"

Headley shrugged. "It's your name, don't knock it. The D.A.'s office will have more facts than I do."

Tearing his gaze from Faith, Adrian sipped his beer with an air of annoyance. "I won't give those bastards the time of day. They looked at the color of my skin, looked at the color of Tony's money, and decided the case there and then. I want my license back just so I can run this case through the court and show them up for the asses they are."

"Your skin is brown," Faith pointed out prosaically, buoyed by the alcohol she didn't usually consume. "If I remember rightly, the D.A. suns himself at the country club and is browner than you are."

Headley chuckled.

Adrian scowled. "Did anyone tell you that you have a smart mouth, Miss Hope?"

"Did anyone tell you that you have a chip bigger than Everest on your shoulder, Mr. Raphael?" she replied sweetly. "Want me to knock it off?"

"Knocking it off is an excellent idea, children," Headley remonstrated. "You can fight it out in bed, but have pity on an old man and put a lid on it in public."

Reddening to her hairline, Faith sank back in the booth and wished she hadn't finished her beer. Adrian's maddening grin told her what he thought of Headley's idea.

"Miss Hope has some energy she needs to work off on the dance floor," Adrian commented, sliding from the booth and hauling Faith after him. "You know where to reach me if you think of anything else that can help us."

Headley nodded and did nothing as Adrian dragged Faith to the nearly empty dance floor.

"I don't want to dance with you," she muttered as the DJ purposefully started a slow song, probably after some unseen male signal from Adrian. Despite her protest, her body lined up with his as if they were made to go together. A shiver shot up her spine from the point where his hand rested.

"Maybe you don't want to dance with me, but you're practically vibrating with the music." He shifted her closer, spun her around in a tricky step, and moved them across the empty floor with expertise. "Either that, or with nervousness, and I can't imagine why you'd be nervous."

She heard the self-mockery in that last. They both knew why she should be nervous about him. He was not only desperate and unpredictable, but they had another night ahead of them, and they were both starved for something they shouldn't have. She'd never dated much, had known only one man, but Adrian left her with no doubts as to her desirability in his eyes.

She had to remember who he was, what he wanted, instead of responding to his physical grace and those soul-dark eyes burrowing into her. Lots of men had wide shoulders, narrow hips, and taut abdomens. What the hell was she doing looking at his belly anyway?

She could feel it pressed against her, along with another

pressure she didn't want to acknowledge. She pushed away a step, and he let her. She missed the contact.

"I'm not nervous, just anxious," she said tartly, hoping that would end any speculation on his part. "I need to get back to my shop."

"Yeah, and I need to get my life back."

Fortunately, the music changed to a faster beat. He danced a two-step just as easily, and now she couldn't avoid looking at his chest and all parts south. Biting her lip, she tried to focus on his face, but the taunting quirk of his mouth and the hungry look in his eyes didn't help matters. Through his gaze, she was aware every time her hair brushed her shoulders, knew how her blouse gaped slightly to reveal the curve of her breasts if she straightened, knew what happened when she moved her hips instinctively to the music.

By the time the music changed to another slow song, she was tingling in places she'd forgotten existed, and she nearly melted into his arms. Grateful for the crowd forming on the dance floor, she said nothing, just clung to the strong arms enfolding her while she pretended none of this was happening. She ought to pull away, but it had been so long. . . .

He smelled of the hotel soap he'd used to shower this morning. He hadn't shaved, and his beard stubble grated her cheek as he leaned down to her, but she hadn't felt a man's beard in ages, so she absorbed the texture without complaint. She had to stop this, knew she had to stop it, but a little voice in her head kept whispering it was just one more song.

The crowd formed into a line dance, and Faith saw how the other women laughed, flirting, trying to catch his attention, but Adrian's gaze never left her. She'd never had that kind of male attention before, and her insides contracted with the power of it. If he'd concentrated on his law practice as he focused on her, he must have been one hell of a lawyer. Tony had never looked at her that way. Ever.

One dance blurred into another, but she no longer noticed the music or the crowd building around them. Her world consisted of the muscled arms holding her, the desire in the gaze of the man watching her, the way their bodies moved as if of one accord. She could dance like this forever.

Until they reached a frenzied beat that imitated the urges driving them, and the rocking, swinging, swaying motion of hips and torsos burst the bubble they'd hidden behind.

Muttering a curse, Adrian caught Faith's elbow and dragged her into the darkness behind towering speakers. Without a word of apology or explanation, he grabbed her waist, hauled her against him, and sucked all the breath from her lungs with just one kiss.

A kiss, a simple, mindless kiss. She'd never been kissed like this before. Her mind exploded, her hands grabbed his shoulders to prevent sliding to the floor, and her mouth fused irrevocably to his. She felt his muscles bunch beneath her hands, tasted the taut narrow line of his lips before they parted and his tongue seared a path to her soul. Not a kiss, then, but a conquering invasion and a claim of ownership against which she had no defenses. None. She drank the sharp tang of his beer-flavored breath and rejoiced as long, skillful fingers slid to cup her breasts.

Her gasp at the contact undid both of them.

Wordlessly, Adrian dragged her back to the booth where they'd left Headley. He was gone. He gestured for the waitress, who hurried over to assure them the bill had been paid.

Without explanation, he steered Faith out the door into the darkened street.

She'd played with fire and now she didn't know if she would go up in flames or internally combust. Adrian gave her no signal but merely opened the car door and all but flung her in. She slid into the seat and watched in silence as he started the car and would have peeled rubber from the tires as they left the lot, had the engine possessed that much power.

She wouldn't ask where they were going. She didn't want to know.

❧ THIRTEEN ❧

Heart thumping so hard she thought it would burst through her chest, Faith sat silently as Adrian took the next ramp off the interstate, maneuvered into a motel parking lot with a blinking vacancy sign, and switched off the engine.

The lights of the motel office beckoned. If she could just shut off her mind and listen to the humming of life Adrian had woken in her . . .

"I can't do this," she murmured, calling herself coward even as she said it. Other women did this. Who did she think she was?

Hands frozen to the steering wheel, Adrian stared straight ahead. "It's a crummy, cheap motel. I'm sorry. It's all I can afford with what's left in my pocket. I should have known better." He reached for the ignition key.

The note of self-disgust turned Faith's head, giving her a view of his angular profile outlined against the motel sign. "It's not the motel."

His hand halted above the key, and she could see the effort it took before he withdrew it and looked at her. "You deserve more than this," he said with a hitch in his voice as he ran his hand over his hair. "I know better. I'm just not thinking clearly right now."

"It's not you either," she said wryly, hearing the pain of rejection behind his calm admission. Tony had *never* understood rejection. He'd been so full of confidence she could have said no with her fists and he wouldn't have understood. Not that she'd ever told him no. She'd always done whatever he asked.

Tonight she had a choice, and she was flubbing it. Badly.

Adrian braced his forearms on the edge of the steering wheel and watched her warily. She didn't want to know what she looked like after a night of sweaty dancing. Her hair had come down and it probably stuck to her face and flew around her shoulders like a rat's nest. Any makeup had long since worn off. And the red and blue neon light probably did wonders for her complexion. But Adrian didn't turn away.

"I'm a desperate man," he said carefully, enunciating each word as if it were his last. "I want you so much, I think the top of my head will blow off. I thought the feeling was mutual. Am I wrong?"

His words and tone stole into those dark, hidden recesses of her soul that had been empty for so long. He wanted her. No one had ever really *wanted* her, not with this primal hunger bubbling up out of nowhere. The intensity of Adrian's raw need terrified her.

"You're not wrong," she admitted. Her body wanted this criminal, this ex-con lawyer who had all but kidnapped her. She'd lost track of her mind, but not her honesty.

"All right," he said in acceptance, not moving his hands from the wheel. "What would I have to do to persuade you to walk into that cheap motel room with me for a night of messy, sweaty sex?"

Faith almost laughed at the wryness of his tone. He was being as honest as she was. This wasn't any long-term commitment. This was two diametrically opposed people coming together in the heat of lust.

She still couldn't do it. She sighed at her conventional morals. It wasn't as if she'd been brought up that way by her free-spirited parents. It was just who she was. "You'd probably have to be a pirate and that motel would have to be your ship," she admitted. "I've never done this before and I can't—"

He stopped her with a disbelieving gesture. "You've never done this before? You ran with Tony's crowd for how long and you've—" He cut himself off by banging his head against the steering wheel. Resting it there, he sat very still for a moment.

"I'm insane. I'm clearly insane. Let me have the shower first, all right?" He climbed out and stalked off to the motel office without looking back.

Faith wrapped her arms around herself and tried to stop shivering. She *wanted* what he had to offer. She wanted mindless, steamy sex. But this was the wrong man and the wrong time. She blocked out all images of what they could do in that cheap hotel room. She'd been used before. She simply couldn't do it again.

Adrian didn't touch her when he returned from the office with a room key in his hand and opened the car door. He barely even looked at her as he jerked his duffel from behind the seat. Once inside the room, he slammed the key on the dresser and aimed for the bathroom. In minutes she heard the shower beating down full force.

She sank into the plastic molded chair and in the dim light from the hotel parking lights through the window stared at the dismal room. She was turning into a dried-up, shriveled-up creature who wouldn't take risks.

She hadn't turned thirty yet, and she felt a hundred years old.

She couldn't even convince herself with that argument. She would just have to accept that she was a grown-up now and couldn't act as stupidly and impulsively as she had as a teenager. Look at what that had gotten her—Tony.

By the time Adrian emerged, still rubbing a towel over his dripping hair, wearing jeans but not his shirt, Faith had the courage to walk right past him and into the bathroom. He'd probably had some hope that she'd weakened while waiting and that the sight of him half undressed would change her mind. If she looked closely, it might have. She simply wouldn't look. She wouldn't look, wouldn't listen. She would set her mind to achieving her goal and going home.

By the time she'd showered and donned a long T-shirt from his duffel, Adrian had pulled the comforter off the bed and lay sprawled on the floor, watching the flicker of the television. Wordlessly, she stepped over him and climbed into the empty bed.

There really wasn't anything they could say to each other. She turned to face the wall, stomach clenched in knots.

Faith sent Adrian a covert glance as he backed the VW from the motel parking space the next morning. He had scarcely said two words since she'd woken to discover him returning to the room with a sack of Krispy Kremes. His silence stirred her easily susceptible guilt.

Setting her mouth and staring straight ahead, she refused to fall into that trap again. She didn't have to please anyone but herself. She didn't owe Adrian a thing. In fact, he owed her. Maybe that's what bothered him.

"Wanta talk about it?" she asked cautiously.

"I'm thinking. I learned to keep my thoughts to myself these last few years." He steered the bug into the morning traffic. "You sure those doughnuts were enough?"

"They settled my stomach, if that's what you mean." She refused to look at him. The doughnuts weren't enough for what really bothered them. Even with the beer and the music and the night behind them, the quivering itchiness remained. She would not think of how Adrian Raphael looked with his shirt off, or the way the sun sparkled against his earring, or that moment of vulnerability when he'd thought she was rejecting him.

"I used to take my fiancée to that pancake place in South-Park. You ever had one of those monster apple things they fix?"

Faith relaxed and let the sun and the memory replace the night. "Way too big for me. I had a bite of Tony's once. I like the strawberry crepes best. We always went there in May, when the strawberries were so fresh you could practically see the dew on them."

"Yeah, Misty liked them, too, but she'd order only half a portion and then eat just a few bites. Wasted more money on that girl and food." He shook his head in disbelief.

"Do you know what she's doing now?" Faith asked quietly. He didn't talk much about his prior life.

Adrian shrugged. "She married a doctor. I heard they're already separated. I'm better off without her, so I'll thank Tony for that one."

She didn't have anything to say to that. Maybe happy relationships existed only in romance books. Her parents were happy. Of course, her parents were weird.

Adrian steered around a semi trying to make a left turn over a double yellow line across two lanes of rush hour traffic. Faith closed her eyes and prayed as the VW toddled around the blockage and straight into the path of a towering SUV hurtling out of one of the many shopping center driveways. South Boulevard needed six lanes—all out of town.

"I've got to get back to work." She needed to return the focus of this little jaunt to the impersonal. "I figure it shouldn't take more than an hour to search the unit, and I can be on the road in time to reach the store before closing."

"You really don't think we'll find those keys, do you?" Adrian asked as the traffic flowed again.

"I packed that stuff. I would have remembered keys. You may be right about the bank boxes—Tony liked his secret caches. But I cleaned out his safe before I moved. All I uncovered was Sandra."

He grimaced and his shoulders slumped. "I've waited four years. I guess I can wait a few months more for bureaucracy to crawl along and produce that death certificate."

"What will you do with yourself?" Faith asked, understanding his unhappiness. He wanted his reputation cleared right now, so he could go back to work and help his family. She'd hate to have this blot on her name, too.

He shrugged. "Fry hamburgers. I don't know. There aren't too many law firms willing to take on ex-cons as legal aides. I sent out a few letters before I left prison and didn't get any response."

"Can you write wills and give legal advice to people too poor to pay the big firms?"

He gunned the VW into an illegal left turn across oncoming traffic and into the storage company's drive. "I'd make more flipping burgers. Give me the code." As they pulled up to the computerized entrance gate, he rolled open the window and punched in the buttons she recited. The gate creaked open. "Nine, twenty-two, seventy?" he asked with a grin. "Your birthday?"

"Wanta make something of it?" She crossed her arms and glared straight ahead. "Turn left. It's the third row, the one past the exit gate."

Adrian glanced in the rearview mirror. "That pickup followed us in before the gate closed."

"Probably forgot his number. Good luck on getting out, though. Unless he follows us again, he's stuck. He needs the code to exit."

Forgetting the pickup, Adrian focused on finding the right cement box in rows of cement boxes. Intense concentration had always been one of his better traits, but he was having some difficulty ignoring the sexy female wrapped in his flannel shirt. The collar was so big on her that the first button fell at the top of her breasts, and she hadn't fastened the damned thing. She wasn't wearing a bra either. He'd watched her stash it with her crumpled blouse. The tail of his shirt came to the hem of her skirt, so she looked as if the shirt was all she wore. She should look like a slob. Instead, with that silken tawny hair caressing her shoulders, she looked like every man's *Playboy* fantasy.

"That's the one." She reached for her purse on the floorboard, and the overlarge shirt gaped enough to reveal the curve of her breast. "I should have the key in here somewhere."

The pickup rattled past, then backed up and returned to the exit row. Adrian clutched the VW's steering wheel with both hands and tried not to stare at Faith's nearly bare breast as she rummaged through the satchel she called a purse. He needed his focus back. She'd be gone in another hour, and he had to get a life.

"Here it is." She singled out a small key in a ring of keys and opened the passenger door without waiting for him.

Taking a deep breath, Adrian swung out of the wretched small car without knocking himself out or emasculating himself. Faith already had the padlock unfastened.

He helped her lift the door, then gazed dispassionately at the neatly stacked and labeled cartons in the dim interior. Organized and efficient. She must have been one hell of a secretary.

She hadn't finished more than a year of college. She'd been a secretary and a country club housewife, but went on to develop two successful careers, while he'd poured years of his life down the drain for a law degree he might never use again. Someday, he'd ask himself if a college education was worth it.

"Most of this stack is books." She gestured at the front row of small boxes. "I can't bear to give away books, but I have no shelf space."

"All right, let's not mess with them just yet." Rolling up his shirtsleeves, Adrian started hauling the heavy boxes into the lane between the buildings. Maybe physical exercise would soothe his straining libido.

Faith clambered past him to tear at the tape of the top box on the next stack. "This should be mementos, yearbooks, report cards and the like."

He pulled out his pocketknife and systematically ripped open every box so she wouldn't have to break her nails. She wore them unfashionably short, but perfectly manicured. He'd wanted them dug into his back last night.

Focus.

They rooted through old papers and files, ornate and useless wedding gifts, sentimental keepsakes, and all the other foolishness a woman like Faith couldn't throw out. They would have all had a place in the pricey house she'd called home, but not in her Spartan closet of an apartment.

"Look!"

They'd reached the back corner of the unit, and he had swatted enough spiders for one day. Sweat poured from his brow in the unventilated heat, and he straightened his aching back to glare at whatever silly treasure she'd uncovered this time. She had already filled the car with old photos and books she'd decided to take back with her. He'd been out of his mind to kidnap her for this.

Reverently, she pushed aside wads of cotton batting to lift out the contents of the box. In the dusky light, Adrian couldn't immediately discern what she held, but the shape and a flash of color tugged at a broken chord somewhere inside him.

"I'll give Tony credit for one thing," she murmured as she lovingly fondled the object in her hands, "he always had perfect taste in gifts. I've never found anything as beautiful as this."

She eased through the box stacks toward the sunlight. Adrian backed out of her way so she could hold the object to the light, and his stomach nearly dropped to his feet when he saw what she held.

It sparkled with a particularly luminous pale silver-green, the porcelain luster so bright it nearly blinded. Sunshine gleamed through the translucent fineness of the vase's scalloped lip. The line and curve of the base flowed smoothly into a perfect fit for Faith's small hands.

His vase. The one he'd sweated blood over. A year's worth of nights he'd spent developing the perfect glaze. He'd experimented with clay compounds for years to find the perfect mixture of alabaster and kaolin. Billed out at the rates he'd charged for legal work, the damned thing would be priceless. He'd sold it to Tony for a pittance when he needed ready cash for Belinda's last semester of school. He remembered Tony saying his wife liked pretty glass.

"Better wrap it up good if you're taking it back with you," he said curtly, returning to the dim interior to rip open another box. He'd known even as a kid that he couldn't earn a living with talent or creativity. He had to use his brains. His brains now told him he was an idiot to keep searching.

But he couldn't bear facing his family as a failure. He needed a little more time.

"I'd always hoped to find the artist so I could put together a display." Apparently abandoning their fruitless search, Faith perched sideways on the driver's seat, her tanned legs stretching out from beneath the shirt hem. She wasn't wearing panty hose. Not noticing his interest, she turned the porcelain in her hands, then poked her fingers inside to remove the packing that prevented full appreciation of the china's fineness. "Most artisans prefer the simplicity of stoneware. I've only seen fine china like this in Europe."

She wadded up the packing and threw it at him. Adrian caught it and shoved it in a box. He could tell her it wasn't profitable to make pieces like that, that Americans wouldn't pay the price of the labor and materials, much less for the creativity. But she knew that. She just wasn't listening to herself. Since he had no intention of ever wasting more time like that, he didn't feel behooved to reveal his artistry—or his stupidity.

She frowned as another piece of packing stuck in the wide bottom beneath the narrow neck. Turning the vase upside down, she shook it until the packing caught in the throat, where she could almost reach it with her fingers. "Why in heavens name did I pack so small a wad in this thing?"

"Too angry to care?" he suggested, taking the vase from her so he could stick his longer fingers inside. "I'm amazed you didn't break it over Tony's head."

"He wasn't worth it. Besides, the only time I ever saw him after I left was in court at your trial. It wouldn't have been too cool to attempt assault and battery in front of a courtroom full of judges and attorneys, most of them golf buddies of his."

Adrian grunted acknowledgment of that as he caught the packing and eased it through the vase neck. "Sure you didn't pack your diamond necklace in here while you were at it? This thing is hard."

Faith's eyes widened as she stared at the crushed yellow legal paper he produced from the vase. "I didn't do that. I used packing paper from the movers."

A mockingbird sang into the silence as they stared at the wad of crumpled paper. Adrian couldn't bear the tension. He handed the package to her to do the honors. Still holding the smooth surface of the porcelain vase, he tried not to hope. He'd lived on hope and determination for four years. He couldn't believe anything would come of it now.

"Keys," she whispered as she folded back the paper. "Tony's keys." The yellow wad dropped to the ground as she produced a silver trophy key ring from a golf tournament. On it dangled half a dozen small keys—bank box size.

"Why the hell would he put them in a vase?" Adrian growled, refusing to believe that his prayers had been answered this easily. "It's a wonder you hadn't filled it with flowers and water and rusted them."

"I don't think keys rust." She turned them thoughtfully, measuring one against the other. They were all different.

"Let's pack and get out of here. You taking the vase with you?"

She emerged from the fog she'd lost herself in. "If the deposit boxes are in the corporation name . . ."

"We'll clean up and start looking as soon as we leave here," he said, his heartbeat finally returning to normal. He didn't know what he'd done to deserve this break in fate, but he wasn't one to be ungrateful. He'd make the most of it.

She looked at him as if she'd just discovered his existence. "If you're right and Tony really did abscond with those funds—"

"What do you mean, 'if'?" he asked angrily. "He damned well took every penny. Or what he could without those keys," he amended, his mind taking another giant leap forward. "Do you think they'd be the only set?"

She looked from him to the keys. He ought to be annoyed that she still didn't believe him. But he was still having a hard time shaking his own entrenched convictions that she'd profited from Tony's embezzlement. So, neither of them had a reason to trust. They'd figure it out somehow.

As if reading his mind, she held out the key ring. "I don't know if safe deposit boxes have two keys, but if they don't, it's a miracle Tony didn't kill me when he discovered I'd packed these up and moved."

That was a thought to ponder. He was grateful Tony was dead. Adrian traded her the vase for the keys and shoved the ring in his pocket. Tony would probably have strangled her with his bare hands if he could have found her back then, but he probably had too many other problems to juggle after the trial, and before he could search properly, he'd died.

"Maybe we'd better think this thing through a little more," Adrian said thoughtfully, heaving the last of the boxes back into the building. He took her silence for agreement.

Lost in their separate thoughts, they passed the pickup on the way out of the exit lane, and neither noticed as the truck followed them through the gate.

❦ FOURTEEN ❦

"I can't go into a bank and act like a corporate officer in these clothes." Faith tugged at the soft flannel of Adrian's shirt as they drove down the highway.

"You're about the same height as Belinda. We can borrow something of hers. I just don't know her work schedule and don't have her phone number. She lives in one of these anthill apartments out here. I'll try finding it." He eased into the slow lane to look for the next ramp.

"I don't know if these corporate papers are enough. What if they don't believe me?" She'd wrapped the precious vase in cotton batting and packed it in a sturdy box, but she held it securely in her lap for extra protection. The vase was a treasure she understood. The keys worried her. And the old corporate papers she'd retrieved from one of the boxes should have been things left in the past.

"You've got the seal and the corporate resolution. That should be enough. You're an authorized officer—"

Adrian shouted a curse and slammed an arm across Faith's chest as a truck swerved from the left lane onto the ramp in front of them. Fenders collided with a grinding crunch, and the VW tires skidded off the pavement.

Faith screamed and clutched her box as the lightweight car careened off the banked ramp, into the air. Before she even realized they were tumbling, the roof crunched. Glass shattered. Pain shot through her head and neck. Somewhere, she heard Adrian screaming her name, just before she blacked out.

* * *

Crawling out of the wreckage, Adrian heard cars screeching to a halt on the road above him, but he had no problem focusing on the situation at hand. Faith was still strapped in her seat, and she wasn't answering him.

The car lay on the passenger side. He couldn't pull her out without righting it, or possibly hurting her worse.

Debris lay scattered across the field. The photos she'd so carefully chosen, books, everything that had been under the hood, now blew in the breeze. The vase box rested on the shattered and bent window beside her.

Blood poured from a gash on her forehead. The impact must have thrown her against the window. He tried to think, take one step at a time as panic shrieked through his veins. He needed to stop the bleeding.

He took off his shirt and ripped a sleeve from the seam. Folding it into a pad, he leaned into the car to hold it over the gash. What should he do next?

"I've called 911," a good Samaritan called, sliding down the embankment toward them. "They should be here soon."

"Help me right the car. I have to get her out of there."

The minutes blurred into a haze of hot sun and sweat and blinding panic. People appeared out of nowhere. He couldn't have said if they were white, black, or yellow. The turquoise VW blazed across his eyeballs, its trunk hood crushed, its roof flattened, with Faith lying quiet against the blood-soaked seat.

Ambulance sirens wailed as he and the others righted the vehicle and eased Faith from the interior. Someone shouted not to move her, but Adrian saw her eyelids flutter, and nothing could have prevented him from lifting her into his arms.

She was frail and light. Choking on a lump in his throat, he eased her out of her bent position and sat with her across his lap. He'd tied his other shirtsleeve around her forehead to hold the bandage in place, but blood still seeped beneath it, matting in her hair.

His fault. He should never have brought her here, never involved her. He should have understood that she'd made a new life, risen above the ashes, and he should have followed her example. Why had he insisted on dragging her down into the cesspool with him?

She was everything he couldn't have, and he'd destroyed her in childish revenge.

Faith's eyelids flickered again. As the paramedics scrambled down the hill carrying a stretcher, she blinked and stared straight into Adrian's soul.

"The vase?"

He wanted to laugh and scream and throttle her. He was holding her life in his hands, and she worried about that shitty vase? The woman was crazier than he was.

"It's fine. I've got it. But I smashed the bug."

She closed her eyes and smiled. "Now I can get a Miata."

Oh, hell. Oh, triple hell. A vast emptiness yawned within him as he hugged her close while the paramedics set up the stretcher. He thought maybe he'd wrecked more than the car. He didn't want to let her go. Her heart beat steadily next to his, pouring life from her into him. He had been dead inside longer than he'd realized, and she was so very much alive. He had to see that she stayed that way.

A police car arrived, giving him something new to worry about. He still hadn't renewed his license. He couldn't let Faith out of his sight, and they'd want a report. They'd probably haul him away in chains.

Ignoring the cop still sitting in his car, talking into his radio, Adrian clutched the box with the vase under his arm and held Faith's hand as they carried her up on a stretcher. Let them track him down at the hospital. They could lock him up after he saw that Faith was safe.

Adrian called Cesar from the emergency room. His brother arrived as the police completed their report and admonished him to renew his license. Adrian half listened while he paced the waiting room floor. He nodded at his brother but didn't involve him as the cop handed him a ticket.

Some jackass had sideswiped the car he was driving, rammed them off the road, injured Faith, and *he* was the one who got the ticket. Fate had a funny way of laughing at him.

"You okay?" Cesar asked as the policeman departed.

"I'll ache all over in the morning, but yeah, I'm fine. Faith's not. She's down in X ray."

Cesar whistled and shoved his hands in his pockets. "How bad does it look?"

"She was awake when we brought her in, that's all I know."

She'd treated him like a human being, a desirable male, and soothed all the wounds these last years had knifed into him. And what had he given her in return?

Mistrust and a broken head.

He wasn't in any humor for talking. One thing about Cesar, he knew when to keep his mouth shut. Pity he couldn't say the same about the women in his family. They'd be all over his case when they found out. And they'd find out. He had nowhere else to take Faith but to his mother's house.

Eons later a nurse emerged from the forbidding depths of the interior to assure them Faith was lucky. She had a badly bruised knee, pulled ligaments, and maybe a minor concussion. She was groggy from painkillers and needed bed rest, but she'd be all right.

They rolled her out in a wheelchair with a crutch across her lap. She looked pale and almost ethereal beneath the white dressing on her forehead. A huge elastic bandage encompassed her bare knee. She wouldn't be dancing anytime soon. From beneath the hideous white gauze she offered a shaky smile.

Adrian's heart plunged to his stomach, but it had already shattered into a million pieces anyway and wasn't worth much. Wordlessly, he helped her from the chair, tried to help her balance on the crutch, and then, cursing, simply swung her into his arms.

"This is ridiculous," she whispered against his throat as he carried her out. "I have to walk."

"Yeah, well, I have to hold you, and I'm bigger, so I win." He sounded gruff, even to himself.

"Sexist pig," she murmured into his collar. "I'm feeling *really* good right now. You ought to let me go while it lasts."

"Like hell I will. I'm taking you home to my bed where you can feel even better."

She couldn't reply to that without embarrassing Cesar as he opened the door to his rusty van. Faith let Adrian slide her across the bench seat. She was too groggy to think of a good reply anyway. Happily, she embraced the vase Cesar handed her and said nothing.

"How much of those drugs did they give you anyway?" Adrian grumbled as she leaned against him while the truck took off.

"Lots and lots of tiny little pills." She didn't have any idea.

"Bet you're one of those high-metabolism twits who sky-rocket on a cup of caffeine. Fool doctors, haven't figured that out yet." He circled her shoulders with his arm and she snuggled happily against his ribs. She was injured and drugged and beyond worrying about how this looked.

She was nearly asleep by the time they reached their destination. These Raphael men were hardly the talkative type, she mused drowsily as she tried to ease out of the truck after Adrian. They hadn't exchanged two words the entire trip. Maybe they were making evil plots that involved her.

"I'll run in and ask Mama which bed to use," Cesar offered, as if she wasn't there.

She ought to say something in protest, but Adrian picked her up again, and her breath departed from her lungs and her brain took leave from her head. Gad, he was strong. She felt like a helpless Scarlett O'Hara as he carried her into the house. She wasn't the Scarlett type, but she didn't have the presence of mind to protest.

She should be telling him she had to go home. She rested her head on his shoulder instead. Adrian's arms tightened around her, and she wished she had two heads so she could lay the other one against him, too.

She wasn't quite right in the head she had.

"It's just my luck I have a sexy woman helpless in my arms, and the only place I have to take her is my mother's," Adrian griped from somewhere above her.

"The credit card is probably good for another night." She yawned.

"I'll take you up on that when you're awake. Want to play nurse and doctor?"

She heard the grin in his voice, but her eyes were closed and she couldn't see it. He had such a lovely grin, when he used it. "Doctors have cold hands," she grumbled. "Might as well do space aliens."

He chuckled as he laid her on a bed to which someone had directed him. He had a lovely chuckle, too, she decided. And a lovely chest. A nice, broad chest she could snuggle against. She didn't like it when he lay her down and backed away.

"Sleep it off while you can. The cops were easier than the interrogation I'm about to endure about you."

The door closed and she was alone. She wondered about a thirty-something lawyer who was afraid of his mother, but she kind of liked the idea that she'd discovered his weak spot.

Much longer in his company, and she might even like the man.

That had to be the drugs talking, she thought as she slipped into sleep.

"Wake up, wake up, we have to make certain you're not a vegetable," a cheery voice sang as someone shook Faith's shoulder.

She blinked and looked up into long-lashed dark eyes identical to Adrian's.

"Good. You're awake. I've brought you some gazpacho, much tastier than the dishwater the hospital would have given you."

Faith obediently struggled to sit up against the pillows being plumped behind her. Belinda, she decided. Adrian had a sister named Belinda who was a nurse. The B child, second in birth. So, she wasn't brain dead. She remembered that much.

The dark eyes and equally dark hair were the only similarities between brother and sister. Belinda was shorter than Faith, and rounder. She wore her hair chopped in a breezy cut and exuded good cheer instead of Adrian's taciturn grimness. And there didn't seem to be a mistrustful bone in her body.

"Cesar told us how you sold Juan's little animals. Isabel is furnishing the nursery with the money. We have to get you all better so you can go back and sell his next consignment. The baby will need linens and car seats and all manner of things."

Through her pounding headache, Faith smiled at the slight accent. Apparently, Adrian's parents retained enough of their Spanish accents that their children still possessed some of the flavor. Adrian hid his well, but lawyers learned clear enunciation and practiced their speech.

"I will raise Juan's prices so the baby can have its own car." Faith tasted the delicious soup before testing the movement of her knee. She definitely preferred the soup. Hiding her grimace, she resolved not to move that leg again soon.

"How is your head? Are you seeing two of everything?" Belinda asked with concern.

Obviously, she hadn't hid the grimace well. "My head hurts, but there's only one spoon in my hand, and the soup is heavenly. Thank you." She wanted to ask about Adrian but was afraid that would open a can of worms her aching head couldn't handle yet.

"I brought you clean clothes, and took yours to the cleaners. Adrian thought we were the same size, but he hasn't seen me in a while." Belinda wrinkled her nose. "Don't tell him, but I'm pregnant, not just fat."

"Why haven't you told him?" Faith asked in amazement at this revelation. "That's wonderful news. And you're not fat. We're just different shapes. I have none and you do." She didn't know why she was feeling so cheerful. It had to be the drugs. This was definitely better than the hospital, and her personal nurse seemed to be a fountain of information.

"Oooh, I like your attitude, but I won't have a shape much longer. Adrian told me I shouldn't have kids until Jim and I can afford a house, but the price of houses . . ." She rolled her eyes expressively. "Adrian thinks kids are a money drain. He doesn't understand what it's like to want one. I can understand that he's spent his whole life raising us and doesn't see the benefits, but we're not him," she ended rebelliously.

"Well, I'd say you're old enough to run your own life, and he's not a sterling example to follow. Feel free to tell him I said so." Faith finished her soup and sighed in pleasure. She needed to worry about going home. How could she work if she could barely stand?

Belinda ran her hand anxiously through her thick, short hair. "I'll need all the ammunition I can find when he starts yelling. He's much better at arguing than I am." She brightened. "But he is good for some things. He's gone to find your car and look for all the things he said you had in it. He says I should find out if you have disability insurance. He'll help you file a claim."

Faith's smile broadened. "A lawyer, through and through. Sometimes, they're handy to have around."

Belinda shrugged. "A man, anyway. Sometimes, they're handy. Other times, you want to smack them." She removed the tray to the side table and readjusted the pillows so Faith could lie down. "Mama is dying to meet you, but I told her you couldn't get out of bed for at least a day, so she'll have to wait."

"I can't vegetate here that long. I need a toilet and a shower, in that order. Then, if I'm still standing, I can meet your mother."

"I'd use any excuse I could to avoid that fate," a whiskey-smooth voice rumbled from the doorway.

"Adrian!" Belinda nearly dropped the tray she'd just picked up. "You still walk like a cat."

All lean grace concealed behind too-loose black shirt and jeans, Adrian sauntered into the room. Faith wanted to pull the sheet over her head. She must look like hell, and he looked as if he'd just walked off the cover of a Western novel. His eyes lit with some hidden amusement as he towered over her.

"I've got a Stetson that will hide that bandage," he assured her. "But you can't wear it in the shower."

Holding the sheet up to her chin, wondering who had put

this nightgown on her, Faith tried to ease her leg toward the edge of the bed. "Go away, Quinn. Go far, far away. You're a walking, talking jinx if ever I saw one."

"Yeah. Go figure." Without warning, he leaned over and scooped her off the bed, still trailing the sheet in her clenched fists. "But sometimes," he whispered in her ear, "you need a man."

She'd have to drop the sheet to rip his hair out.

❧ FIFTEEN ❧

You could tell a lot about the character of a family by their bathrooms, Faith mused as she removed several pairs of panty hose from the shower bar and folded them over the counter. This bathroom was obviously used by Adrian's teenage sisters. Judging by the cosmetics, towels, hair apparel, and scented lotions strewn across the counter, they were as self-conscious as all girls that age.

Still, everything was well-scrubbed, and stacks of neatly folded towels filled the narrow closet, so someone in the family was cleanliness oriented. A colorful dried flower arrangement decorated the white rattan shelves over the commode, and crisp yellow eyelet curtains picked up the bright designs of the stunning cobalt and yellow tiles surrounding the mirror. Their creativity added originality and interest to what would have been a dull, ordinary ranch-style house arrangement. Of course, an ordinary family wouldn't produce a man like Adrian.

Belinda had liberated a white T-shirt with lace inserts and a pair of denim shorts from one of her sister's dressers. After washing—not an easy task while keeping her bandages dry—Faith carefully maneuvered into the new clothes. She was less groggy now, but the various aches and pains still made her feel less than herself.

Grateful the clothes came close to fitting and weren't so outlandish as to make her feel like a clown, she leaned on the crutch for the two steps to the door. Opening it, she discovered Adrian lounging against the wall, arms folded, waiting for her.

He looked her up and down with an interest that shivered her insides, then shook his head in disbelief. "You're wearing my baby sister's clothes. She was playing with Barbie dolls last time I was here. I don't know whether to give you a doll or hide Elena away so men like me can't see her looking like you do now."

She didn't want to feel that frisson of sexual interest. Not now. Not here. Not ever. Maybe she should have gone to bed with him at the motel last night and worked this out of her system. Half the interest lay in anticipation, she was certain. "I can assure you, she doesn't wear clothes like these so she can hide from men. Or boys. A girl that age likes to test her powers on the opposite sex. I've grown past that stage," she warned as she swung from the bathroom.

Adrian unfolded his length from the wall. "I used to change Elena's diapers," he complained. "I definitely don't want to hear that. Makes me feel ancient. How are you feeling—besides grouchy?"

"Alive. Almost. Better steer me to your mother before the real pain sets in."

He looked as if he were about to carry her again, but he backed off at her scowl and offered his arm instead.

"Mama's been undergoing chemo. The doctors say the cancer is under control, but the treatment has caused complications. She's been on other medicines for osteoarthritis and high blood pressure and who-the-hell-knows-what, and now she's really weak. They're saying she'll gain her strength now that she's off the chemo, but . . ." He shrugged expressively. "Just keeping her in bed is a full-time job."

"Is there anything you could have done to change anything that's happened?" she asked quietly as they limped down the narrow hall.

"I should have been here."

She heard the bitterness, recognized it because she'd suffered the same. Not as painfully, perhaps. She'd hurt only herself and not others. But it was unproductive either way.

"It was your fault you were framed?" she asked bluntly. "You want to take responsibility for your mother's cancer, too? Why don't we just move on to the wars in Africa and world hunger?"

"And you're the sweet little woman Tony bragged about?" he asked incredulously, stopping outside a closed bedroom door.

"Not anymore, I'm not. Now, are you going to introduce me to the poor woman who's had to endure your arrogance all these years, or shall I just go in and offer her my sympathy without you?"

Faith faced the door, refusing to look at him. Physically, Adrian was far too attractive, and she was feeling far too weak. She had to remember she detested arrogant lawyers and kidnappers who thought they could push women around. If she could keep thinking of him in those terms, perhaps she could ignore his indefatigable loyalty and love for his family.

"You might as well make my day complete." He knocked, then pushed open the door at a call from within.

"Pobrecita!" the woman in the bed exclaimed as Faith awkwardly dragged the crutch through the door. *"Mi hijo es un idiota mayor."*

Faith grinned. *"Solamente un idiota menudo, señora."*

A wide white grin like Adrian's broke across the woman's tired face. Even though her thinning black hair was streaked with gray, and worry wrinkles lined her brow, she still laughed like a young woman. "My son has finally learned some sense in his choice of women. That's better than any pill the doctor can prescribe."

"I figured you'd approve of any woman named Faith Hope," Adrian said dryly from the doorway. "Shall I leave the two of you alone to shred me into little pieces?"

"No, you take that poor girl back to bed where she belongs. Dolores and Elena will be bringing the little ones from after-school classes. Let's not scare her off too soon. I can rest easy now, knowing you're in good hands." Smiling, she leaned back against her pillows. "Faith Hope, we will visit more tomorrow, *comprende?*"

"Sí, señora, con su permiso."

"She doesn't speak Spanish, Mama," Adrian threw over his

shoulder as he steered Faith toward the door. "She's faking it to make a good impression."

Faith didn't understand the rapid spate of scathing Spanish that followed, but Adrian was grinning as he closed the door behind him.

"I take it she's feeling better?" Faith asked as she stumbled down the hall. Exhaustion was setting in.

"She called me three kinds of fool if I let you go, among other things," he admitted cheerfully as he pushed open the door to her assigned room. "So I guess I'll just have to hold you hostage, and we can make beautiful babies together. We'll all flip hamburgers for a living."

Damn, he was good. He'd just warned her off with an irony that would have done Shakespeare proud. Not that she needed warning. She wouldn't mind a beautiful baby, but she'd had enough of men with serious problems. She'd enjoy her own life from here on out, thank you very much.

Besides, she knew making babies was the last thing Adrian wanted. Or needed.

"I think your mama will understand perfectly when I escape. I need to call my insurance company and arrange transportation."

He snorted and removed the crutch from her hand as she sat on the bed's edge. "Not today you won't. First thing tomorrow, maybe. If I know my sisters, that telephone will be occupied for the rest of the evening, and you look as if you're dead on your feet. Besides, your insurance company will be closed for the day. You slept the afternoon away."

Muttering a curse under her breath, Faith accepted the inevitable. She felt like death warmed over. She didn't even want to think about how long it would take to drive back to Knoxville.

She scowled at Adrian. "One of these days, I'll make you pay."

"You don't think I already am?"

Quietly, he closed the door, leaving her alone.

* * *

"Call around. Find someone presentable with sales experience who knows pottery, even if they don't know fine porcelain," Adrian told Juan as he paced the floor with the cordless phone at his ear. He frowned threateningly at his sisters who were waiting impatiently to reclaim the phone line. "She has a clerk but she can't work eighty-hour weeks. We have to keep her store open. It's in your best interest, if nothing else."

The twins ambled in, bouncing a basketball between them, as self-consciously insouciant as only thirteen-year-olds can be. They eyed Adrian with a mixture of hope and skepticism, and his guilt climbed even higher. Boys that age needed a man around the house, a man they could trust and use as a role model. Like he fit the bill. Right.

Not acknowledging that painful thought, he concentrated on Juan's end of the conversation. After rejecting several of his cousin's suggestions, he pounced on one with the kind of class Faith's store needed. "Yeah, team her with Bill. Bill will know the merchandise. Pearl can sell it. Grab a pen and I'll give you directions to the friend who has a key."

Hanging up after giving him Annie's address, Adrian turned to face the growing collection of family in the tiny living room. Little Ines was hiding in the kitchen, pretending to help Belinda with supper. Cesar had gone back to campus. But ten-year-old Hernando had limped in after the twins. Along with Dolores and Elena, the teenagers, that made a houseful.

"Do you *all* need the phone?" he asked wryly.

Dolores chewed her gum and twirled an ugly hank of shorn hair between her fingers. "You've got *her* installed in my bedroom. Where are *you* going to sleep?"

Leave it to too-old Dolores. Adrian was certain that wasn't the question bothering the boys, who slept together all in one room. He'd installed Faith in his old room. Dolores was actually asking if he was moving back in, and how Faith fit into the picture.

He didn't have much choice. Aside from the fact that he was broke and had no job, it was obvious his mother was in no shape to keep an eye on six kids.

He'd hoped to be so far beyond this by now—

It could be worse. He could still be in prison.

"Faith will only be here until she's a little better. I'll sleep on the couch until then. But you may as well resign yourself to sleeping with Elena and Ines again. I'm home, and you're not a princess."

Dolores gave an exaggerated sigh, grabbed the phone from his hand and flounced out, followed by a muttering Elena. The twins broke into excited chatter about ball games, and Hernando took it all in silently, apparently reserving judgment.

For better or worse, Adrian was home.

After the kids were all fed and ushered out to the school bus the next morning, Adrian returned to the kitchen to find Faith balancing on her crutch while filling a coffee cup.

"I could have brought you that," he grouched, conveying the cup to the table. "You just had to wait a minute."

Her look was eloquent as she lowered herself to a kitchen chair, glanced from his harried expression to the assortment of dirty cups and cereal bowls scattered across every conceivable surface, then leaned over to mop up Ines's spilled milk with a paper napkin. "I don't suppose you ever pulled kitchen duty in prison?"

"White collar criminals are treated better than that. You don't think they put lawyers in with cop killers, do you?" He grabbed the napkin, sponged up what he could, and heaved it at the trash can. "What do you want to eat?"

Belinda had apparently helped her to wash her hair and arranged a smaller bandage over the stitches. Faith still looked fragile. He wanted her back on stage, dancing in red boots, hair flying around her shoulders again. No, he didn't. Not unless he was the only audience.

Cursing his perverse nature, Adrian turned his back on her and poured a cup of coffee for himself.

"Toast, if you have it," she said. "Then I need a phone. I really have to arrange some transportation and get back to the shop." She glowered at her damaged knee. "I suppose I better call the guys and talk about a replacement for this weekend. I won't exactly be a ball of fire on stage."

He popped bread in the toaster and handed her the cordless. "Transportation is fine, but you're not driving anywhere with that knee. Forget the shop, too. Juan knows a couple of people who can handle it for a week or two."

"I can't let strangers run my shop!"

He could hear her irritation but ignored it. He hadn't given up his own mission yet. Returning to this house where he'd spent his adolescence had forcibly reminded him of all the reasons he had to prove his innocence.

"They're not strangers. They're good friends of ours. Bill's a potter and knows what's what. Pearl used to work at a fancy store in Atlanta until she married some jerk who skipped town ahead of his creditors a few months ago. They can both use jobs. Will minimum wage and commission hurt you for a few weeks?"

She sighed, and he knew he had her. Bleeding heart liberals were suckers for a down-on-their-luck story. He popped the toast, stuck it on a plate, and carried it to the table. Butter and jam were already there, probably mixed together, courtesy of Ines.

Faith looked decidedly grim as she poked numbers for information into the phone. "Why do I have the feeling you're usurping my life?"

He couldn't answer that one. He had worse to tell her, but he thought he'd break it a little at a time.

She made the report to her insurance agent, jotted notes on a pad Adrian shoved in front of her, and sipped her coffee. He wondered what it would be like to have a wife sharing his breakfast every morning. He twitched at the idea. He'd spent over half his life burdened with the responsibility of family. He'd be damned if he'd take on any more. He'd like the luxury of freedom for a little while.

He wouldn't have that or any other luxury unless he proved his innocence.

Faith hung up and pried nervously at the bandage on her head as she straightened out her notes with quick, decisive pen strokes. "I hate this. We pay half our income to insurance companies. They ought to work for us instead of the other way around."

"I can't believe you had collision insurance on that rolling wreck."

"I carry expensive pottery." She shrugged, as if that was explanation enough. "The insurance company refused to cover it unless I had collision."

He thought she ought to find a new insurance agent, but he didn't argue. "Cesar has a friend who's a good mechanic. He recommended a couple of good body shops for estimates. They'll handle it."

She looked up sharply. "I thought the car was totaled."

"It is." He sipped his coffee and wondered if he could balance his limitless supply of family against all the damage he'd done to her. "But they won't believe it without estimates. Cesar will stop by and pick up the police report for you, too. Let me assure you, Cesar and his friends have *lots* of experience with accident routines."

"Why does that not reassure me?"

She was wearing Elena's shorts again, and she stretched her leg to examine the knee bandage. Adrian could swear her legs belonged on a woman twice her height. They went on forever, and he struggled with the urgent need to wrap his hands around them, to hold and explore and—

"The agent gave me the name of a rental car company I can use until something's decided," Faith said, jerking him back to reality. "They deliver to the door."

She was exercising her leg, planning her escape. "You have one little problem with that," he said carefully, handing her a jam-slathered slice of toast.

Faith looked at his offering with suspicion. "I don't want to hear this, do I?"

"You need to report your credit card stolen."

Her eyes widened into blue pools of accusation.

Adrian held up his hands. "I said I was sorry. You kept calling for that stupid vase, and I made sure you had that. I didn't think about your purse."

"My purse?" she asked weakly.

"Credit card, keys, license, everything," he admitted. "All gone. Some jackal stole it from the wreckage."

Saintly, angelic Faith Hope uttered a string of expletives that would have made a sailor proud.

❦ SIXTEEN ❦

"I'm fine, Annie, really. I just want to clear up some old business while I'm here, and let this knee rest a bit." As she spoke into the phone, Faith chewed on a piece of her hair and stared at the small living room where Adrian had led her. Her parents had never lived in one place long enough to build a wall of photos like the one proudly displayed in here. "I've called the band. They've had a pest hanging around, wanting to try out. They'll put her on stage in my place this weekend. I'll be back before next weekend."

Adrian paced like an angry panther, picking up a framed photo on the end table, kicking a soccer ball, glancing out to the street of identical houses beyond the front window. He looked far too exotic to be in this commonplace cage. Faith contemplated opening the front door and letting him escape.

"Thanks for the offer. I'd appreciate that. My plants probably need watering by now, and the mail will pile up. Help yourself to anything in the fridge before it perishes. The boys promised to change the lock, just in case, but it may be a day or two before they get over there. I told them to stop by your place first."

"The boys," Adrian snorted as she hung up. "If you're referring to your band members, they're almost as old as you are. They're not boys."

"They're like younger brothers, with the maturity of teenagers. Quit picking at me. I didn't ask you to turn my life upside down. Tell me what we're going to do about the bank boxes." She hung up the phone and retreated into the couch cushions.

He pulled back the curtains at the sound of a car arriving

outside. "There's your rental. After we take care of the car, you can rummage through Elena's closet. There ought to be something in there that isn't ten inches above your knees. Then we go bank shopping."

What did he care if she wore a miniskirt to the bank?

She let Adrian take care of the rental car proceedings. She signed the sheet where told, then manipulated her crutch into Elena's bedroom. There wasn't much point in worrying about her stolen purse. Her credit card was already almost maxed. She hoped the thief got caught trying to use it. Anybody low enough to steal from an accident victim ought to fry in hell.

She could replace the stuff in her purse. She couldn't replace the vase, and Adrian had saved that. He'd rescued most of her books and photos and the corporate papers. She'd survive. She'd been through far worse than this before. Far worse.

She sighed at fifteen-year-old Elena's choice in clothing. Crop tops and miniskirts. Maybe she could wear something belonging to Dolores. The sixteen-year-old was bigger through the bosom than Faith, but considering the tightness of teenage shirts, she thought that could be a boon.

Adrian appeared carrying a nearly see-through blouse and a camisole. "Wear these, and you could wear jeans and no one would notice."

Faith raised her eyebrows, but he was right. The gauzy shirt would look elegant and distracting at the same time. "They'll wonder what kind of corporation I run," she murmured, taking the garments. She didn't want to know what he was thinking about when he chose the shirt. She had a suspicion she knew.

"With me at your side, how could they doubt?" He leaned against the doorjamb as if he intended to watch her change.

"You could ditch the earring and ponytail and look like a lawyer," she reminded him, catching the door and easing it closed in his face.

"I'd rather look like a pimp," he called as she pushed him out. "That's at least more honest."

She grinned at that. She might want to lop his head off

more often than not, but sometimes she couldn't help but like the man.

"No, I'm sorry, Mrs. Nicholls, we have no safe deposit box registered in that name," the bank clerk said without inflection.

Adrian wanted to punch the man's eyes out. They'd spent hours creeping through traffic from one uptown bank to the other, without success. Until now, all the clerks helping them had been women. They'd looked at him speculatively, raised their eyebrows at Faith's story, but he'd give Faith credit, she'd stayed as cool as any sophisticated SouthPark matron, and every one of them had fallen for her tale. This jerk, though, was seeing only Faith's breasts. Maybe if he gripped him by his fancy silk tie—

"Thank you for your time, Mr. Weaver." Faith offered the clerk her hand, shook it, then with the sexy little shimmy that had Adrian drooling every time he saw it, she turned and walked, shoulders straight, hips swinging in tandem with the crutch, out the door.

"Now I remember why I've always worn tailored suits," she said thoughtfully as he caught up with her at the tiny egg-shaped rental car. He'd rather have the VW back. At least it had character.

He unlocked the door and helped her in, whether she needed it or not. She'd learned to manage the crutch with grace and expertise, but he liked pretending to be useful. Her choice of subject left him gasping to keep up. "You like looking like everyone else?" he suggested as he climbed in on the driver's side.

She sent him a sideways glance as he pulled into traffic. "Never mind."

"If you look like everyone else, then men won't look at you like that one did," he concluded, despite all his best intentions.

He felt her surprise more than saw it as he maneuvered the car through traffic toward the next bank.

"I think it's because I'm blond," she answered obliquely. "Maybe I should dye my hair."

"Maybe you ought to examine why you don't want men looking at you."

She tilted her head, and all that glossy hair caught in the sunlight. "Maybe you ought to examine why you want everyone looking at you," she said sweetly.

He steered the car into a parking space and shot the shift into park. They were practically shoulder-to-shoulder, and Adrian couldn't stop himself from grabbing her chin and taking the taunt out of her eyes. "I damned well *want* people to know I'm here. They'll look right through me and pretend I don't exist otherwise. So tell me why you go up on a stage wearing red boots and miniskirts if you don't want to be noticed?"

Her nostrils flared and her lips set in a grim line as she jerked her chin away. "I like to sing, and that's what I have to wear for the job. That's not *me* up there."

"Tony really screwed with your head, didn't he?" he demanded, suddenly furious. "That's you up there, all right. That's the you he didn't want you to be. That's the you who would have gone to bed with me the other night. That you is as sexy as any movie star who walked across the screen. And you *like* that feeling."

He slammed out of the car, leaving her to follow as she willed. He hadn't meant to get messed up inside her head. He didn't want to know Tony had screwed her around as badly as he'd screwed with him. He just wanted his damned life back.

She didn't have a life to go back to.

He could see it now. She'd built that little stage persona to act out all those things she wouldn't let herself feel, kept all that anger and sex in a little box that didn't touch her so-called real life, and then played the part of little Miss Politeness and Humanity the rest of the time.

By the time he reached the bank, she was standing beside him, stiff and unyielding, waiting for him to hold the door for her. Good. Let her stay angry with him. That would take the pressure off.

He waited in the background as she smiled politely at the clerk. He'd be her chauffeur and nothing more. She didn't need him. She could turn on her plastic Charlotte career woman efficiency and the clerk would buy right into it without a qualm. *He* was the holdback here.

It took Adrian a minute before he realized Faith was walking away, not out the door, but toward the bank safe. Jerking back to the moment, he hurried after her.

The clerk glanced at him with surprise, but Faith introduced him as an employee and no further questions were asked. Adrian felt his stomach rise into his throat. They'd actually found one of Tony's boxes. If one of the keys fit . . . He might just have a heart attack here and now.

After using the bank's key to unlock the vault, the clerk left them to remove the box to an examining table. Adrian carried it for her, his palms turning sweaty and his heart rate increasing. The box was too small to contain much. No actual printouts, but maybe some computer disks, a few rolls of bank notes. What would he do with them?

He'd given Faith the keys when they'd started out that morning. Now, she handed them back, her hand brushing his lightly, as if she sensed his fear. Adrian couldn't look at her, couldn't look at anything as he tried first one key, then another, in the lock.

It turned on the third key.

He realized Faith was praying as he pulled out the drawer. He offered up a prayer of his own. He'd been raised in the Catholic church. He'd not attended since adolescence, but he'd like to light a candle right now as he pulled the box completely open.

He stared at the empty drawer in disbelief.

"Shit," she murmured beside him, with the lovely Southern inflection that made it more a two-syllabled "sheet" than excrement.

Adrian's tongue stuck to the roof of his mouth. He couldn't say anything. Slowly, he shut the drawer and locked it, handing the keys back to Faith.

"Maybe if I cancel the box, I can get a refund on the rent," she mused. "We have to pay for gas somehow."

He couldn't think of any good reason why. Tony had probably emptied all these boxes before he moved Sandra to

Florida and took off for parts unknown. Why bother hunting down more disappointment? Four years he'd waited for this moment, counted on it. He'd kidnapped an innocent woman, wrecked her car, ignored his family, for what? Because he'd thought Tony stupid enough to leave evidence behind?

He didn't bother listening as Faith removed the key from the ring and made the arrangements with the bank clerk. He needed to find a job. He had a college degree. Businesses were begging for help. Maybe he could find one that would ignore his criminal record. One that didn't care if he was an embezzler. A car wash ought to do it.

He opened the glass door so Faith could swing out. Nearly the middle of September and heat still hit like a blow to the face as they emerged into the concrete and sunlight of the parking lot. If it weren't for his family, he'd move back to the mountains and help Juan turn out cutesy animals for Faith's collector trade. His ego balked at the thought.

"I wonder why Tony paid the rent so far in advance if the box was empty?" Faith asked as he assisted her into the car.

What did it matter? He steered the car into traffic and headed for home. Might as well let Faith return to her real life. She could probably drive fine with her other foot.

"Where are you going? I thought we agreed on the Bank of America in SouthPark next."

He shot her an incredulous look. "You want to keep burning gas to collect rent deposits? You can write and ask for them with the same effect."

"Not if I don't know where they are." She shrugged her slender shoulders beneath the gauzy shirt. Through the sheer material he could see the mole at the edge of her camisole strap. He wished he'd had the opportunity to see a lot more.

"Just heave the keys out the window and forget it," he said wearily. "Tony cleaned house before he left. He wasn't completely stupid."

"The last time Tony opened that box was in December, before I found out about Sandra. Want to make any wagers that he bought her something snazzy with whatever he'd stored in there? He just hadn't had time to steal enough to refill it before I packed everything up and moved out with the keys."

"Or he had another set of keys and cleaned house before he left." He was tired of this argument. He needed to remove Faith from his life so he could think.

"Nope," she said confidently. "I asked. The bank has one set; I have the other. They don't make duplicates. Can't."

His brain was so dead he'd steered onto I-77 before what she said completely registered. "Those are the only set for all the boxes?"

"The only. If Tony was using those boxes to store his ill-gotten cash so I wouldn't find out about it, then there's more out there somewhere. We just have to find it."

If the damned dangerous road had any shoulder, he'd pull off and kiss her.

As it was, he swerved off at the next exit, whipped around a parking lot, narrowly missed a trailer hauling a race car, hit the shift into park, and reached for Faith. Before she could react, he gripped her shoulders and kissed her. Hard. Not even the high of reviving hope could match the ecstasy of Faith's lips opening beneath his. He breathed in the sheer joy of it.

When she finally regained her senses and shoved him away, he hit the gears and careened out of the parking lot in the direction of SouthPark, shouting, "Faith Hope, I think I love you!" over the radio blaring some moldy oldie with the same verse.

❧ SEVENTEEN ❦

"How many damned banks are there in this town?" Adrian griped as they left another empty hope behind, the glass doors behind them slamming shut for the day. This time, Adrian pocketed the box keys. Apparently they were now too valuable for him to trust her with them.

"Too many." Faith dragged her aching leg across the parking lot. "And Tony used to travel to Raleigh and Durham and who-knows-where-else. Maybe we ought to consult the D.A."

Beside her, Adrian groaned. After their earlier jubilation, she understood his disappointment. She really would prefer ecstatic kisses to the grim reality facing his family.

"I'll write a letter and circulate it to every bank in the country before I talk with that prick," he said fiercely. "I want it all lined up nice and neat so he can't ignore me as he did at the trial. Word processors make official-looking stationery."

"Works for me." He was the lawyer. Who was she to argue? She sank gratefully into the hard car seat. "I need food."

"A dozen hungry-man tacos coming up."

How a poky little cow town like Charlotte had turned into a traffic planner's worst nightmare would make a good *Dummies' Guide to Gridlock*. As Adrian breezed across the worst intersections, Faith closed her eyes and tried to relax. She trusted his driving, but the accident had left her tense and fearful of other cars. She kept waiting for the bone-chilling sound of grinding metal. "Maybe we're going about this the wrong way. Maybe we should try thinking like Tony."

"If I could think like Tony, he'd be alive and in jail right now, and I'd be filthy rich and living in Florida."

She let the sarcasm slide by. He had a right to it. "Tony was always in a hurry. He had so many balls in the air, he couldn't always keep up with them. He practically lived in his car."

Adrian steered the car into the driveway of his mother's house but didn't climb out as he considered her earlier suggestion. "So maybe Tony chose banks along his favorite routes?"

"Or near places he visited frequently."

"We searched uptown, Dilworth, and SouthPark," he pointed out.

"Maybe they were too obvious? Maybe he only kept that uptown box for fast emergency cash. He might prefer the others to be somewhere he wasn't recognized. Sandra lived out past Lake Norman. He could stop in that area on his way to Raleigh."

"Okay, tomorrow we head north instead of south. And I'll ask Cesar for his laptop with the word processing program. I can't ask you to scour the state if we don't turn up anything soon. Letters will have to do."

He offered his arm, and Faith accepted it wearily. Her head throbbed and her leg ached. Or maybe it was the other way around. Whichever, the instant she relaxed into the strength of Adrian's support, the aches and pains faded like magic. It felt good not to have to endure this alone.

She was such a damned wimp. She had *liked* being married. She had liked having a husband to share things with. At first, anyway. She had to remember how it had deteriorated into a cage with ever-narrower boundaries. The price of sharing her life was much too high.

"I can create the letterhead," she offered. It would be a relief to go home. She was grateful he had seen reason. "We'll need some good quality paper. Invent a really officious firm name and use my mail-drop address."

"Who do you have picking up your mail?" he asked, holding open the kitchen door for her. "I had friends watching that damned box in hopes of catching you or at least tracing you."

"I figured Tony would kill me if he found me, so I didn't give them a forwarding address. I bribed one of the mail-drop clerks to open the box from the back once a month. One of the guys in the band has family down here, and they'd stop by and pick it up. I don't receive much mail through it anymore, but it's habit to keep doing things that way."

Faith took the kitchen stool Adrian offered. She didn't have the strength to stand.

"Simple and devious at the same time. You have a wicked mind, woman." He reached in the refrigerator for a pitcher of sweet tea. "Can't keep alcohol in a house with teenagers, so this will have to suffice. Let me check on Mama and the kids, and I'll be back in a minute."

"Give me an onion to chop or something so I'll feel useful."

"And trust you with a knife?" He grinned and produced a knife and an assortment of vegetables from various hiding places. "I can hear the TV, so the twins are here. We'll need *lots* of everything."

As he disappeared to check on family, Faith settled in to peel and chop. She'd always wondered what it would be like to be part of a large family. She had hoped by now to have at least a couple of kids of her own. Perhaps she'd been naive to think a close-knit family would be fun and more fulfilling than her empty life. The burden Adrian carried seemed almost crushing, too overwhelming for him to enjoy the company of his family or any of the benefits.

A car door slammed in the drive, and tires squealed as the vehicle backed out again. Faith looked up from her paring as the back door opened and Dolores slouched in.

The sixteen-year-old would be attractive if she hadn't gone overboard on every fashion trend out there. She'd butchered her lovely black hair into a weedy crop that revealed a shaved billboard space at her nape. Her left ear sported more earrings than Faith owned. And she'd encased her full figure in spandex topped by a man's shirt three sizes too large. The six-inch-high soles of her mules clunked noisily across the worn linoleum.

"You fixing supper?" she asked warily as she watched Faith peel and chop. "I was gonna throw some noodles in a pot."

"Adrian said he'd fix tacos. I'm just the kitchen help." She'd not worked much with teenagers, and she eyed Dolores equally warily. Awkwardness welled between them.

"Yeah? Then I guess I'm off the hook. Let me know when it's ready." She removed the cordless receiver from the wall, sauntered across the kitchen toward the door, and cursed as she hit the Talk button. "He's on the damned phone," she griped, punching it off again. "Gets out of goddamned prison and acts like he owns the place."

"Doesn't he?" Faith asked innocently, concentrating on the onion and not the unhappy snarl on the girl's face. She'd pieced together enough knowledge of Adrian and his family to suspect he'd been the one to purchase this fairly spacious ranch house. Even in this blue collar part of town, real estate was exorbitantly expensive. Housing couldn't keep up with Charlotte's booming population.

Dolores shrugged. "Mama's had to make the payments while he was locked up. The rest of us work to pay the bills and buy groceries. That ought to count for something."

Considering the cost of the jewelry in the girl's ear, Faith suspected her meager earnings were spent on clothes and gold more than bread and milk, but working as well as attending school was a big responsibility for a teenager. She wouldn't argue with her.

"You know Adrian didn't steal that money, don't you?" Faith asked quietly, still concentrating on her chopping.

"He's got you believing that?" Dolores snorted. "The two of you sleeping together or something?"

Faith's stomach clenched but she pretended nonchalance. "No, we're not sleeping together. I know the man who framed Adrian."

Dolores punched the telephone again, and apparently still finding it occupied, punched it off. "Do tell," she said snidely.

Suspecting the girl would have slammed out of the room by now if she wasn't interested in hearing proof of her brother's innocence, Faith searched for a path of reason. "His partner in the law firm was living a double life and needed the money," she said quietly. "Don't you think if Adrian had stolen the money, he would have used it to pay your bills?"

"He was driving a cherry red 'Vette and living in a fancy apartment in SouthPark," Dolores exploded. "He was shoveling money into that girlfriend of his while we lived in this hovel and wore hand-me-downs."

"Misty paid for the apartment, and the 'Vette was ten years old."

Faith nearly bit her tongue as that bitter voice intruded. She looked up to see Adrian in the doorway behind his sister, leaning his forearm against the doorjamb as if he'd been there for a while. The cynical, taut lines of his jaw pulled tighter as he saw Faith watching.

"You're a liar and I hate you," Dolores shouted, swinging around to aim a fist at his stomach. "I wish you'd never come home!"

Adrian didn't dodge as she slammed her punch home. He didn't even gasp for breath at the impact. "You only hurt yourself when you strike out at others," he said mildly as she drew back and cradled her hand.

"Bastard," she spat, before squeezing past him and into the front of the house.

Still slumped against the doorway, Adrian lifted his gaze to Faith. "I am, you know." At her questioning look, he explained. "A bastard. My father never married my mother. Of course, that makes *him* a bastard in my book." He lifted himself from the wall and entered the kitchen to examine the contents of the refrigerator.

"Labels don't solve anything."

"Nope. And 'bastard' isn't precise enough to be descriptive except in the one definition. If she'd called me 'thief,' you'd have a better picture of my character."

"But you're not a thief." Faith figured he was many things, but thief wasn't one of them. She ought to know. She'd lived with the biggest thief of them all, one who stole lives and hope as well as money.

"Fool, maybe, not thief," he agreed producing an assortment of jars and half a chicken carcass.

He was taking his sister's explosion much too calmly. If she'd learned anything at all about this man, it was that he harbored passions so flammable, it was a wonder he didn't incinerate. Something was wrong.

"Dolores said you were on the phone."

Adrian reached for a butcher knife and began whacking the chicken into slivers. "We had messages."

Faith shivered as she waited for further explanation. He sliced viciously at a hunk of meat as if he were disemboweling someone. In a moment, fury would steam out his ears. She worried more about seeing him implode than about whatever bad news had visited them now.

"I'd suggest you spit it out," she offered conversationally, "or you'll be punching me like Dolores did you. I don't think I have the stomach for it." She eyed Adrian's flat abdomen speculatively. Dolores hadn't held anything back. He truly must have abs of steel.

His jaw tightened into a flat plane beneath sharp cheekbones as he finally looked up. "Tony didn't hit you, did he?"

"I would have been out of there a lot sooner if he had. I'm not that messed up. Who called?"

"Juan. Annie." He dumped the slivers of meat and vegetables and the contents of several jars into a large skillet with the ease of experience. "Juan called to say someone broke into your shop before Bill and Pearl arrived."

The images of her grandmother's precious bowl and her meticulously selected inventory trashed beyond repair flashed through her mind so vividly, she almost moaned.

Fingernails biting into her palms, she tried to sound calm. "The clair de lune?"

"Safe." He shook the skillet instead of stirring. "They've called the cops and made the report for insurance purposes, but you may have problems collecting."

Head spinning, Faith clung to the counter and tried to organize her thoughts. "What else? What was stolen if they didn't take the clair de lune? I keep only fifty dollars in the register at night."

"I don't know if Annie has been making deposits. Pearl couldn't tell. But whoever it was didn't just steal the cash. They ransacked the place. They found the clair de lune lying on the carpet and its pedestal broken open. Anything else that may have held anything was either trashed or on the floor. Apparently the intruder flung around a few curios for good measure."

The clair de lune was safe. Faith tried to take a deep breath and nearly choked. Her windpipe closed in panic. Breathe easy, she told herself. She was insured. She couldn't possibly have insured her grandmother's bowl for what it was worth to her, but the other things were replaceable. Mostly.

She'd had an alarm installed on the bowl display. Her head shot up. "Why won't the insurance company pay?"

Adrian turned down the stove, leaned back against the counter and crossed his arms. "Because the store wasn't broken into. It was unlocked and disarmed with keys."

When she merely stared at him, open-mouthed, he continued relentlessly. "First, you report your car totaled. Then, you report your store robbed and vandalized. And Juan's already told me what Annie has to report. They've hit your apartment, too."

She couldn't think of a thing to say. Four years she had lived safely and uneventfully. This couldn't be coincidence.

"They were *all* unlocked with keys," he said gently. "Whoever stole your purse used your ID to locate your apartment. How many criminals would bother traveling all the way to Knoxville on the off chance the owner of an ancient VW might have something worth stealing?"

"Tony?" she squeaked. Dizziness and lack of air collapsed her head to her arms and she nearly slipped from the stool before Adrian caught her.

not real in any case, not for her, not for this sham of a marriage...

MARRIED TO A STRANGER

148

❧ EIGHTEEN ❧

Adrian watched Faith all through supper as she pulled together her calm mask, spoke pleasantly with Dolores and Elena, asked questions of the twins, and helped the younger ones with their tacos. Only he knew she was splintering into little pieces inside.

So he watched her carefully as she managed to lay claim to the phone before the teenagers could finish eating. Belinda finally appeared, and Adrian left her to handle the kids while he followed Faith into the other room. She was talking to Annie, and her face was as pale as it had been after the accident.

He'd done that to her.

Beneath that tightly controlled facade she was approaching hysteria and not thinking clearly. He'd have to do the thinking for her until she grasped the full implications of this disaster.

When she hung up the phone, she didn't even look in his direction. She brushed past him, into the kitchen, where she picked up the car keys he'd thrown on the counter. Damn, but the woman didn't miss a thing. At least he still had the bank keys.

He expected her to waltz right out the back door, but he'd forgotten her proper upbringing. One didn't leave without saying farewell to one's hostess. Ignoring her crutch, she limped down the hall to his mother's bedroom.

Adrian didn't feel inclined to listen to what they had to say to each other. He caught Hernando as he raced out of the kitchen, directed him toward the bathroom to wash the sauce off his face, and waited.

Faith emerged from the back hall carrying her box with her few precious possessions a few minutes later. This time she at least acknowledged his presence. "I'm going home," she announced, before unfastening the front door latch and walking out.

She was making him crazy. He really ought to let the fool woman get herself kidnapped by a professional this time. Maybe Tony really was alive and he'd murder her. Even Faith the Invincible wouldn't have the kind of violent mind necessary to escape from a real criminal. She was tough, but she wasn't that tough.

He didn't want her to be that tough.

With a sigh, Adrian stalked out the front door after her. She was already in the driver's seat of the rental, testing the strength of her injured knee on the brake pedal.

"It won't hold up that mountain," he warned her. "You'd have to use your left foot. You want to try driving that road at night, with all those semis, working the gas and brake with your left foot?"

"Yes." Determinedly, she caught the door handle and tried to yank the door shut.

Adrian caught the door top and held it firmly open. "You're not thinking," he chided her. "You're reacting. Just stop one damned minute and think."

"I don't want to think. I want to go home. They've already done their damage. What more can they do? Annie said they're installing new bolts in the morning. I'll stay with her until then."

He wanted to grab her and shake some sense into her pretty head. He figured shaking was the last thing he'd do if he got his hands on her, though. "You want to think that through again? If they didn't find what they wanted in your apartment or your store, where do you think they'll look next time?"

"Who says there'll be a next time?" she asked fiercely, glaring out the windshield, her fingers glued to the steering wheel.

"Do you think this was all coincidence?" He didn't want to terrify her. He wanted her to be defiant and courageous and all those insane things, because she would need it. "Do you really think that we were accidentally run off the road and some thief accidentally came along and stole your purse and that same thief accidentally turned up in Knoxville to search your stuff right after I accidentally got out of prison and found you?"

Her arms stiffened. Her mouth tightened into a pale line. He figured she would twist the wheel into a pretzel any minute.

"Tony is dead," she said stonily. "No one survived the plane crash. No one could. It was in the mountains. In winter. It took rescue teams days to reach the site."

"Maybe Tony *is* dead," he agreed softly, "but he had friends. Maybe someone else knew about the money."

She collapsed then. She buried her face against her arms, and her shoulders shook, and she seemed to melt into boneless jelly.

He squatted beside the car and caressed her leg through the jeans she'd borrowed from Elena. "Someone has to be after that money."

She shook her head, whipping her fine hair back and forth. "Only Tony."

Ah, he was beginning to see the hang-up here. He had his guilts; she had hers. He pressed her leg tighter to catch her attention. "Not your money. The other. The tons I'm supposed to have stolen."

That caught her, all right. She lifted her head, and he could see the tears glistening in the blue of her eyes.

"They think *I* have *your* money?"

"The stolen money," he said gently. "It's all tied together, don't you see? We're not the only ones who suspect Tony may have stolen from those accounts. And I'm not the only one who thinks you may have the clue to where the money is hidden. They just couldn't find you until I led them directly to you."

"Remind me to thank you sometime." She dropped her head back to the steering wheel, but this time she wasn't shaking. "We've not exactly been hiding our presence. Anyone could have followed us the other day. That pickup . . ."

"It was a truck that hit us," he agreed. "They could have seen us with Headley the night before, followed us to the motel."

"Oh, charming. So now they think I'm in collusion with a criminal."

"You could have found a better way of wording it." He stood. "Let me get my stuff. I've already called Cesar. He should be here shortly. I don't think we'd better stay here any longer."

She stared up at him. "You think they'd hurt your family?"

Well, at least she was thinking again. "They could have killed us both with that accident. What do you think?"

He wanted to smile at her two-syllable pronunciation of a four-letter word but he couldn't. He should have known this could happen, but he'd been focused on only one thing—himself.

Cesar's van rattled into the drive, saving him from any further introspection. Primeval instincts for survival came first.

"This is ridiculous." As the car lurched into the gravel drive, Faith glared at Cesar's ramshackle boardinghouse near the community college. "We have no money, no jobs, and this is the next best thing to being homeless. Did anyone ever tell you that you're a bad influence?"

Adrian parked under the low-hanging branch of a willow oak and turned off the key. He supposed anger was better than her earlier hysteria, but not by much. He already felt cad enough without her rubbing it in. "We're just calling a time-out until we develop a better plan," he reminded her.

"Cesar's roommate returns Monday," she goaded him. "You'd better think quick."

Swinging his duffel over his shoulder, he helped her out of the car, removed her box from the back, and led her toward the rickety outside stairs. He winced every time she limped.

"I could carry you up," he suggested as she clung to the rail as if it were her crutch.

"Screw you, too." Favoring her injured leg, she took another step.

That would suit him fine. One good long screw would go a long way toward taking some of the edge off. He could scarcely tear his gaze from the way her rounded posterior swung as she limped up the stairs in front of him.

One look at the interior of the apartment and he knew tonight wouldn't be the night he got lucky. "It's worse than a cheap motel," he muttered as he threw the duffel and carton on the littered carpet. "Prison was better than this."

Faith glanced around at the empty beer cans, the tottering stacks of books and paper, dirty dishes and glasses, and shrugged. "We can always check out the homeless shelters."

"You're gonna rub this in, aren't you?" He peered into the filthy galley kitchen, then checked the tiny hall. "Two bedrooms. I recommend you take the one in back. It looks like it may actually have sheets."

She sank onto the overstuffed couch instead. "I want a definite plan of action or I'm going to the police. I can't live like this."

Heaving two dictionaries, a stuffed monkey, and a whiskey bottle off a battered armchair, Adrian collapsed into the seat and nearly sank to the floor. He leaned his head against the chair back and stared up at the ceiling. He thought he saw tomato spatters on the cracked and filthy plaster. "Do you really think the police will listen? Do you think they're even bothering to trace the bastard who broke into your places? The guy had keys. They're figuring it's a domestic dispute or that the crook is long gone."

"The D.A. here will understand the significance if we explain it."

"First, he'll throw my ass in jail for parole violation if he finds out I've been in Tennessee. Second, the break-ins are out of his jurisdiction. Third, we have no proof the accident wasn't an accident. And lastly, we'll just give him the idea to have someone tail us so he can lay his hands on the money first. And don't think he'll be much help if the bad guys get to us before he does. He'll count on going in and cleaning up after. He doesn't have enough investigative force to do anything else."

"Cynic," she grumbled. "Paranoid cynic," she amended.

"I prefer to think of it as realism. Give me credit for having a little more experience with the criminal justice system than you have." If he'd had any character at all, he'd have been one of the good guys in white hats who represented the little people against the cold cruel world of that system, but no, he had to make his millions first. Somehow, he just didn't think his punishment fit the crime.

"All right, Mr. Realism, what do we do next, then?"

He wished he knew. Lifting his head, he tried a seductive leer. "Go to bed?"

She flung an empty beer can at him.

He caught and squashed it. "All right. Let's take the basics first. It's probably not safe to return home, agreed?"

"No," she said mutinously. "They know there's nothing there now. Why should they go back?"

"Because you're there?" he suggested. That shut her up. "As I said, we can't go home. If this person is as dangerous as he seems, he could threaten our families, our friends, anyone within our vicinity. What would it take to break you?"

"Not much, but I'd have to make up a story to break since I don't know anything. Why didn't they continue following us around town if they think we know where the money is?"

"Good question." Tossing the can up and down, Adrian thought about it. "Maybe they already know where the money is and they just want the keys? Maybe they thought you had the keys in your purse, and when they weren't there, they checked your places?"

"They couldn't open the boxes unless they were officers of the corporation. And Tony was the only other officer besides me." She grimaced as logic returned them full circle to that unpalatable prospect.

She was sharp. If he'd had her around a few years ago, he'd never have gotten into this mess. She would have pulled him up short before his ego and ambition tumbled him over the edge. "Okay, but forging papers similar to the ones you have wouldn't be difficult. The bank wouldn't know the difference. And now they have your ID."

"Sandra!"

He thought about that and shook his head slowly. "Sandra has the wattage of a Christmas tree bulb. She has a houseful of kids. Admittedly, she might know about the keys and the boxes and everything, but she couldn't personally carry this off. She'd have to hire someone."

"Or someone could have found her in Florida after Tony's plane crash and made her think she had a lot more money coming to her. She probably went through Tony's life insurance pretty fast."

"If she had the life insurance," Adrian reminded her. "If you don't have a death certificate, what are the chances that Sandra managed to get one? She wasn't even his wife."

Faith made an unladylike snort. "Maybe she had a husband like Tony had a wife. Or a lover. The whole world, or at least most of Charlotte, would know that money is still out there."

"Well, that's helpful. Now all we have to do is suspect the entire city. I suggest we find the money and run."

"I suggest you go to hell. I wouldn't touch that money if you buried me with it."

"Rise right up out of the grave, huh?" He smiled at the tomato-splattered ceiling. She had pluck, Miss Faith Hope did. And integrity. Damned dangerous combination. That thought triggered another. "How much money is left in that nonprofit trust fund you set up from Tony's assets?"

"It's invested in stocks, and they've appreciated," she said grudgingly. "The income goes to charity, but there's still a few hundred thousand or more."

He heard her reluctance and figured she might be deliberately underestimating the amount, but she was trusting him a little more each day. Maybe if they could build up a few layers of trust . . . Experience had taught him not to hope.

"All right. Now, did you leave papers in your apartment or shop that would have let the thief know about the account?"

He heard her intake of breath and sat up straight again. She'd gone back to pale.

"It's all in my desk," she whispered in horror. "I'm the trustee. I write the checks."

He'd figured that. He'd seen what she'd done to help Annie and the shelter. That money hadn't come from singing in bars.

"Let's call Annie and have her gather up some of your things, including that checkbook and any ID you might have that the thief didn't take. You'll need to notify the bank if the checks are gone, and if they're not, maybe you could make a temporary donation to the homeless that we can repay later."

She raised her eyebrows in question.

Adrian sighed. "To us. We're destitute and homeless, remember?"

❧ NINETEEN ❧

She couldn't sleep. She might never sleep again. Her knee throbbed. Her skin felt too tight. Thoughts whirled and crashed in her pounding head. Her breasts ached.

That last brought her up out of the narrow bed. Tony had used sex as a sleeping pill. She'd be better off taking a Tylenol rather than consider the same thing.

It would help if she could label Adrian Quinn Raphael as a fast-talking con artist, an arrogant egotistical lawyer who was ruining her life or any of those other things he deserved to be called. But no matter what else he was, she didn't doubt that he was also a worried man concerned about his family. That side of him appealed to her entirely too much for peace of mind.

How well did Tylenol mix with beer? She figured that's all she'd find in the refrigerator.

Anything was better than lying here tossing and turning, images dancing through her head of Tony rising from the dead and Sandra with ax in hand. The faceless, nameless driver of the pickup couldn't be as vivid as the monsters already inhabiting her mind. Any of them could easily drive her to the arms of the man sleeping on the other side of the wall.

She opened the bedroom door and heard voices. Her heart instantly hit a tattoo and she glanced over her shoulder at the garret window. She could climb onto the roof. . . .

A familiar velvet baritone stopped that thought in its tracks. Adrian was conspiring behind her back. She should have known.

She pulled on Elena's jeans under Adrian's long T-shirt,

then slipped silently down the hall to the shadows outside the littered living room. Adrian's cousin Juan now occupied the armchair. Cesar sprawled across the dilapidated couch. Beer in hand, Adrian paced the narrow space between, avoiding the stacks of books as if he'd memorized their placement.

"We can't know how desperate this person is," Adrian said with an urgency that made Faith's skin crawl.

"We can't even know if he's more than a stupid crook," Juan pointed out. "Kids have cars. They could have looked the shop up for a lark, took the cash, and gone on a drinking spree."

She and Adrian had already covered this ground thrice over. They'd argued half the night. She turned away, deciding she didn't want a beer bad enough to be trapped into repeating the argument.

"Stupid crooks and kids don't systematically turn a place upside down, then terrorize a homeless shelter and some harmless musicians. They're looking for Faith."

Faith froze.

Juan whistled and Cesar sat upright.

Unaware of her presence, Adrian crumpled his can and hefted it toward a wastebasket. The can cleared the hoop easily but he'd already turned his back on it. "I don't want to tell her about Annie and the band, okay?"

"When did all this happen?" Cesar demanded.

"A little while ago. Annie left a message at the house, and Dolores called me with it while you were out. Annie was pitching a wholesale fit. She wanted to come after me with a shotgun."

"I don't blame her." Caught between fury and fear, Faith stalked into the room and stopped in front of Adrian. He stood nearly a head taller than she, and the eye-level contact with his wide shoulders ought to terrify her. It didn't. "I'd punch you, but I'm not up to repeating Dolores's performance. Who the damn hell do you think you are?"

Both Juan and Cesar eased to their feet and glanced nervously toward the escape hatch of the door. Adrian propped his fists on his hips and glared back at her.

"Want me to help you get to sleep?" he taunted.   £

She hauled her hand back and would have smacked the smirk off his face if Juan hadn't caught her wrist.

"His jaw is as hard as the rest of his head. Ask him sometime how he worked his way through law school."

Faith dropped her hand and fought the overwhelming urge to break into tears. She would not fall back on that age-old weakness. "How's Annie?" she demanded. "And the boys?"

Since neither Cesar nor Juan could answer that, they turned to Adrian, who shrugged. "Annie's furious. The guy pulled a knife on her from behind. The police figure it was a wino gone berserk and told her she needed a bodyguard or a safer job. Winos don't demand to know where Miss Rich Bitch lives."

"Rich Bitch?" That sounded like a bad B movie, not like Tony or any of the sophisticated lawyers he'd hung out with.

"The band said he used the same term when he locked them in the bathroom at the bar. He might be thorough in tracking down all your identities, but I guess he can't remember your name."

"The guys know I'm as perpetually broke as they are. They must have wondered who the heck he was talking about." She was calming down now. None of this seemed quite real.

Adrian stalked to the window without speaking. Cesar offered her a beer. Juan offered his chair.

"Adrian doesn't like sharing," Cesar confided as Faith took both the beer and chair.

"Swell. Then he should have left me out of this from the start. It's a little late to start the lone gunman act now." She sipped the beer and ignored Adrian's back. All riled with anger, eyes flashing as he donned his protective male armor, Adrian looked sexier than all Satan's angels put together.

"But Annie and the guys are okay?" she demanded.

"Once your musical friends climbed down off their cloud and figured who their jailer was talking about, they lied through their pretty white teeth. Told him you'd run off to Hollywood with a hot agent who promised to put you in movies. Even gave him an L.A. address. From what I gather, they were having so much fun making up stories, they didn't even know when the guy gave up and went away until someone unlocked the door and let them out."

Faith grinned. Whoever was after her hadn't spent much time investigating her friends.

But Annie . . . She closed her eyes as she came off that brief high. "Annie told him about you, didn't she?"

Adrian shook his head as Cesar offered him another beer. "She thinks I'm a homeless vagrant who's fast-talked you into trouble. It doesn't matter. He had to know about me already."

"And thought Faith was an easier target?" Juan suggested from his perch on the couch arm.

"Probably. He's hoping to get his hands on the money without going through me."

Faith didn't like the way he said that. She didn't like the way Adrian's eyes lit with the holy fires of hell or the way his fingers balled into fists. And she definitely did not like his defiant stance as he stared at her.

"I think it's time I visit my parents in Mexico," she said brightly, lifting her beer can to her lips.

"Over my dead body, *señorita.*"

She'd been afraid he would say something like that.

"Maybe everyone else should visit family in Mexico," Juan suggested dryly.

"If you can figure out how to afford that, be my guest." Adrian returned to pacing. Faith looked defiant enough to do something stupid, like running away. He couldn't let her do that. He needed her here, where he could keep her safe. The crook might know where her parents lived—especially if the crook was Tony. He simply couldn't overlook that possibility, no matter how much Faith rejected the idea.

Tony wouldn't be personally capable of terrorism, but he might have considered hiring stupid thugs for the occasion.

"He's after me and Faith," Adrian continued curtly. "The coward is evidently trying to work around me, but he sounds desperate enough to consider women and children. Belinda's husband still works nights, doesn't he?" At Cesar's tentative nod, Adrian plowed on. "Jim's police cruiser parked in front of the house all day should deter the stupidest of crooks. Can you and your roommate move into the house with Mama at night?"

"Caveman thinks he can protect everyone?" Faith asked sarcastically. "What about you and me? Did you think we're invisible?"

She grated on his nerves. He didn't like his authority challenged. He was in charge here and whatever he—

"She's right," Juan said quietly. "This person has no need to go through your family if they know where to find you and Faith."

Adrian fought the idea that he couldn't keep everyone safe by himself. He'd worked and scraped and . . . Botched everything. Admit it, he was a complete failure. Obviously, he didn't have the sense God gave a taco.

"The cruiser and Cesar and his roommate staying overnight are probably a good precaution," Faith said thoughtfully.

Adrian refused to look at her. She sat there all silver and gold and angelic, as if her whole world hadn't burned to the ground not once, but twice. If he looked hard enough, he could probably find ways to blame himself for both times. He ought to buzz out of her life now, while she was still almost in one piece.

Except it was too late for him to back out. Whoever was after Faith could find her now, thanks to him. And that person had waited four years to get what he was looking for. He wouldn't give up easily.

"You and Adrian would stay here?" Cesar asked dubiously.

Adrian almost snorted aloud at that thought. Faith would rather stay in a homeless shelter than this pigsty. She'd rather live with derelicts than with him. Faith was not a stupid woman. She probably had lots of rich friends she could move in with if she decided to stay in Charlotte, and who was he to stop her?

"If I can throw out your beer cans," she answered dryly.

Adrian dropped his head against the cool glass. He didn't want her living here. His pride screamed to give a woman like

Faith a fancy house and fancy car, and if he couldn't do that, he didn't want her at all.

Like hell he didn't want her.

He didn't think he could honestly survive living under the same roof with Faith Hope. He wanted her so badly it set his teeth on edge.

"Whoever is looking for us will probably be on his way back from Knoxville now," she said calmly, as if she didn't speak the voice of doom. "Cesar had better go back to the kids. If Adrian and I are visible enough, they should be safe, but let's not take chances."

"You'd better install stronger bolts for the doors and windows," Juan advised.

"We'll have to tell Jim what this is all about if we ask him to park his police car at the house," Cesar warned. "He's bound to report it. Word will get back to the D.A."

Adrian could hear his half brother and cousin heading cautiously for the door, waiting for him to argue, but he couldn't move. He'd been rendered powerless. Faith didn't seem to be leaving with them.

"Someone will have to pick up the stuff Annie gathers for me," Faith said. "We'll need that checkbook before we can install locks."

We. She'd said *we.* They would be living here together. Alone. Under the same roof. She was volunteering to stay with *him*, the monster who had ruined her life. Maybe she was as crazy as he was.

The door closed, and Adrian knew they were alone. Still, he didn't turn around. He didn't want to see that luscious raspberry mouth, those grave gray eyes as they accused him of bringing her down to his level.

"I guess I'll look for a job in the morning," she said into the ensuing silence. "I don't suppose any of the bars want a singer with a bum knee."

He listened as she limped away.

The crazy woman had just offered him heaven and hell on a platter. She was trusting him to protect her, when his only rational thought at the moment was getting her naked and jumping her bones. Did the damned woman have no sense at all?

He was more desperate than the damned thug who'd driven them off the road. She'd be safer anywhere else but here.

❧ TWENTY ❧

Closing the bedroom door against the sight of the weary man in the other room, Faith leaned against it, caught her elbows in a nervous grip and took a shaky breath.

She was out of her mind. She should be running for the door right now, driving as fast and far as she could go. She was an intelligent woman perfectly capable of taking care of herself. She'd proved that once.

She'd run away last time. This time she'd built a life she didn't want to lose. She'd have to stand and fight.

Okay, a little harmless insanity. Take another breath.

The image of Adrian staring out the window, all the burdens of the world crashing down on his shoulders, haunted her. He'd stood straight, hands in pockets, head thrown back, as one blow after another hit him. He hadn't cringed or whined or blamed anyone else. He'd just accepted the responsibility and looked for some means of handling it.

That he'd chosen the macho route of assuming he had to do it all himself didn't surprise her at all, but she couldn't let him bear the entire burden. He wasn't responsible for her.

But he was right. She couldn't fight criminals on her own, and the police here couldn't do anything until a crime was committed. Besides, she felt safer with Adrian. She didn't want to go home with monsters at the door. She was a selfish coward.

She heard him coming down the hall, halting in front of the other door. She trembled, desperately wanting the company of strong arms and the reassuring murmurs she knew he would provide if she opened her door. She couldn't afford to be that weak again.

She listened to him enter the other room and shut the door. Slumping against the wood panel, she buried her face in her hands. What in hell had she done?

She was standing here wanting to fling herself into the arms of the man who had kidnapped her. She'd just offered to help him find the evidence to clear his name at the risk of her own health and security.

And she knew damned well she'd done it because she wanted to go to bed with him—with still another man who didn't want children and didn't really want her.

As soon as she got herself out of this, she would have her head examined.

The apartment was empty when Faith finally dragged herself from the uncomfortable cot the next morning. Without much expectation, she blearily opened the ancient rounded refrigerator and discovered a pristine bottle of milk, a carton of orange juice, and a box of cereal. Considering what might be lurking in the dark recesses of the cabinets, the refrigerator seemed like an excellent place to store cereal.

Adrian must have used the last of his money to buy groceries, and then he hadn't eaten.

Glancing around at the stacks of dirty dishes, she could understand why.

Well, she had absolutely no clue what else to do.

The familiar twang of country music pouring through the apartment door greeted Adrian when he returned at noon. He could hear water running and Faith's voice accompanying the chorus as he stepped inside. He wondered if she'd just gotten out of bed and was in the shower.

The image of Faith naked and glistening nearly crippled him.

He couldn't have her, he told himself ruthlessly. He couldn't take advantage of her vulnerability when he had absolutely nothing to offer except sex.

So he'd better solve their problems before testosterone poisoning set in and his balls rotted off.

His lascivious images of Faith naked in the tub disintegrated the instant he entered the kitchen to see her blue-jeaned rear end stuck in the air and her head hidden in a cabinet beneath the sink. Faint echoes of song emerged as her tight posterior swung in time with the music from Cesar's boom box. Adrian thought it was almost worth being hunted by a stupid crook to have this vision to carry with him for the rest of his life.

Deciding he'd scare the wits out of her if he spoke, he leaned against the wall and enjoyed the show.

As she ducked her head out from under the counter and painfully straightened her injured leg to sit back on the floor, she caught sight of him. She flung the sopping sponge at his head but bent to massage her knee rather than stand up. "Next time, knock," she grumbled.

"And forfeit that show? Not on your life. Want me to massage that for you?" He threw the sponge at the sparkling sink. Now that he was capable of looking elsewhere, he could tell how she'd spent the morning. He could actually see enough of the counter to know it had cracked white tile and that the sink needed new porcelain.

"Keep your fantasies to yourself." Remaining on the floor, she leaned against the newly scrubbed pine cabinet. "I thought maybe you'd run away."

She had her hair tied back in a borrowed bandanna, and a smudge of dirt streaked the side of her delicate nose. She should look like something dragged in from the street. Instead he caught the worried frown between crystal-gray eyes, the heated pink of her cheeks, and dropped his gaze to admire the full mounds of her unfettered breasts beneath the thin cotton. The hard points pressing against the shirt reassured him that he wasn't trapped in this fantasy alone.

Reluctantly dragging his gaze away, and grateful he had to hobble only a few steps to the refrigerator, he removed the bottle of milk. Maybe if he didn't look at her, he'd be able to

walk again in the near future without emasculating himself.
"I found a job."

"Clean glasses in the cabinet to your right. Throw me a
towel, will you? My knee isn't ready for action yet."

He dropped the towel in her direction and poured the milk.
They were tiptoeing around each other like nervous cats.

"So, where are you working?" she asked casually as she
dried her hands.

"I have a friend with a kiln who needs someone who can do
decorative design." He chugged the milk as if it were beer.
He'd spent the better part of his life acquiring an education so
he wouldn't be reduced to his family's trade of catering to
tourists who wanted pots to match their decor. But they had to
eat somehow.

"You can do design?"

He heard her effort to remain casual. He'd never had much
patience with designer plates. Any kid with crayons could
color a paper plate with the same effect. But it was better than
flipping hamburgers.

"It's a job, and he'll pay me cash daily, so we'll have food
and gas money. I can work at night so we can still hit the
banks come Monday." The domesticity of that "we" and the
assumption that she'd stay worried him, but he was at a loss as
to what else to do. He couldn't send her home with a knife-
wielding nutcase looking for her. He prayed no one would
know to look for the immaculate Mrs. Tony Nicholls in this
flophouse.

"I found a map of Charlotte and a telephone book while I
was cleaning, and I've plotted a list of banks along Tony's
major routes."

He could hear her scrambling to rise, and he turned to offer
a hand. She weighed next to nothing, but the imprint of her
hand in his burned like hot coals.

Play it cool, Quinn. He realized he was using his father's
name in the same derogatory tone as Faith did. Striving for
nonchalance, he untangled their fingers, and flustered, she
reached for a glass. He couldn't help the heady triumph
at knowing she was as aroused as he was. They didn't have

the time to waste on those feelings. Should they ever be insane enough to give in to impulses, they'd probably bang themselves into oblivion. A week in bed wouldn't be enough for him.

Tearing his mind from that thought, he acknowledged her efficiency. "We'll start first thing Monday. In the meantime, we need cash, so I told Rex I'd be in this afternoon."

"Rex?" She poured orange juice and rested against the counter. "Does anyone honestly name their kids Rex these days?"

"His real name's Ralph but that wasn't kingly enough." Adrian grinned at the disbelieving flare of her nostrils.

She drained her glass and set it in the sink. "Eat something," she ordered. "Cereal may be boring, but it's good for you."

He hadn't had someone tell him when to eat since he'd been living at home, a million years ago in a different incarnation. In these last years he'd perfected an air of aloofness, grown his hair long, wore an earring, accentuated his differences so people would think twice before crossing his path. He'd been known to intimidate grown men by the way he stood. And this bubble-headed female ordered him about as if he were a child.

He reached for a cereal bowl. "Keep the doors locked and don't let anyone in until I come back," he ordered.

"I'll do that."

She said it so sweetly that Adrian jerked his head up. He didn't trust her innocent smile. "You're working on the bank letter, right?"

"That will take all of fifteen minutes." Her innocent smile disappeared as she leaned against the counter, folded her arms, and did her best imitation of him. "Do you really think I mean to stay in here and be your housekeeper?"

"There's a jerk out there with a knife looking for you!" He tried to keep his voice to a low roar. His only other alternative was to throttle the stupid woman. Did she have any idea what folding her arms like that did for her breasts?

"I'm perfectly capable of defending myself. I keep telling

you that, but you don't listen well." She leaned forward and all but stuck her face in his. "I'm not yours to take care of, Quinn. I won't be your prisoner, your burden, your responsibility, your anything. Got it?"

Oh, he had it all right. He could grab her neck right now and kiss her until her head spun and they were both writhing on the floor. But he didn't need the hassle. Not daring to lay a hand on any other part of her, he covered her pretty nose with the flat of his palm and carefully pushed her back. "I get it. I'm only 'Quinn' when you're irritated, right?"

She stepped away. "Shove it where the sun don't shine, mister."

He even lusted after her when she was being stupid. He grimaced. Who was he calling stupid? "I'm not Tony. I don't have patience with stupid females. What if this jerk has a gun? You have a defense against that?"

"That's my concern and not yours."

The milk and cereal curdled in his stomach, and he threw the rest in the sink. "You'll just let me carry that guilt on my conscience for the rest of my life? Thanks a lot. I really need one more albatross around my neck."

"Get this through your head, Quinn." She boxed his temples with the flat of her hands. "I . . . am . . . not . . . *yours*. Period. We may temporarily live under the same roof, but that's it. We may temporarily share this little problem, but that does not mean we share anything else. I have a life in Knoxville and I lead my life the way I want. You can't lead it for me. These are hard lessons, but I've learned them well." She tapped his temples again. "Practice."

Some other time. Right now, it only took her touch to ignite the fuse. Grabbing her wrists, Adrian jerked her tight against him and lowered his head.

Faith gasped as her breasts crushed into an immovable wall of muscle, and the hot kiss she'd desperately tried to forget seared across her mouth. He held her wrists behind her back so she couldn't move, couldn't do more than accept the slide of his lips across hers, the milky taste of his breath as he plied her with reckless kisses that she couldn't fight, that she needed as much as she needed air. She opened her mouth to him, surrendered to his invasion, didn't even notice when he released her arms until his hands firmly cupped her buttocks and lifted her closer. She had tried to pretend that other time hadn't happened, that it had been a mistake of beer and music and fear, but she couldn't pretend this away.

She slid her hands to his shirt to shove him away. Instead her fingers curled in his collar, and the heat of his chest through the thin cotton nearly scorched her.

Adrian was the one with sense and strength enough to pry her fingers loose and set her back, although he continued holding her wrists. If she looked half as stunned as he did, she didn't have a chance against him.

"Come with me to the pottery," he demanded. Or asked. She couldn't tell which.

She shook her head instinctively. "No," she whispered, unable to quite catch her breath. He was still too close, and she couldn't seem to step back. "You have to let me do this on my own."

"Do you want to kill me?" he asked with clenched jaw.

"Sometimes, yes." Defiantly, she threw back her head and met his glare. "In ways, you're much, much worse than Tony, and I don't want you anywhere near me. I don't want your macho culture or your take-charge attitude or any of those other things that make you who you are. I want to be left *alone*."

He dropped her hands. "Fine. Will you be here when I come back?"

"Don't lock the doors if I'm not here. I'll be back," she said calmly.

"Dammit, there are dangerous men out there looking for you!" he shouted, totally enraged all over again. "Have you no sense at all?"

Here it was, the moment she could stand up and fight back, or retreat to the complacent little woman Tony had thought her.

Adrian looked as if he would grind her bones to mincemeat. He had enough on his mind as it was. Maybe now wasn't the time for defiance in the face of anger. "I'll need groceries," she said sweetly, trying not to grind her teeth.

"I'll get them." He slammed out, and Faith winced as the door rocked in its frame.

She was a wimp. Okay, maybe she just didn't want to worry Adrian more than necessary.

But it was damned well time for him to realize she wasn't one of those things he needed to worry about. This time, she wasn't staying home to please any man.

❧ TWENTY-ONE ❧

"Dolores, I know it's Saturday night!" Exasperated, Belinda set down her mother's tray and refrained from heaving the soup remains at her younger sister. "Forgive me for having a life of my own, but I have to go home to fix Jim some food, and we can't leave the little ones here alone. You have to be in by eleven. That's final."

Dolores stuck out her lower lip in the same manner as six-year-old Ines. "I'll marry Mike and move out and then I can leave this place anytime I like. What will you do then?"

"I'll take the little ones to your love nest." Belinda heard her sister's defiance but wanted to laugh at the naive belief that she could leave anytime she liked. Family didn't work that way. Life didn't work that way. "Don't be ridiculous, *chiquita*. Marriage is far, far worse than being home by eleven. You would spend all your time trying to earn enough money to pay the rent and buy groceries and make car payments, and then you'd never have time to go out on Saturday night. Consider yourself lucky."

"Yeah, well, why doesn't Adrian do all that?" Dolores shouted, before flouncing off to primp some more for her date.

Adrian had been out of prison for a month and had yet to contribute to the family's finances. Belinda sighed and began scraping scraps into the disposal. Well, at least he'd moved Cesar back in to help with the little ones. Except now he'd sent him to Knoxville and that wasn't much help. Still, she couldn't blame Adrian. As the next eldest, she knew how hard and how long he'd worked to keep them all together with a roof over their heads, as well as fed and educated. She was having a hard time telling him that she couldn't step into his shoes.

The doorbell rang, and she let Dolores answer it. A man should be here to interview the sullen teenagers the girls were dating. Adrian used to straighten her dates out quick enough. She couldn't do the same. They looked at her as if she were a bug on a rug.

Dolores popped back into the kitchen doorway with an odd look on her face. "Maybe you'd better talk to this lady."

Immediately alarmed, Belinda dried her hands, ran them through her hair to set it straight, and brushed down her khakis. Strangers never meant good news.

Dolores had left the woman standing on the other side of the front screen door. Instead of castigating her sister for rudeness, Belinda checked to make certain the lock was fastened. Call her a bigot, but in her experience blond, white women wearing more makeup than Tammy Faye did not call on them for sociable purposes.

The scent of cheap musk perfume and cigarette smoke engulfed Belinda as she approached. The leopard-print silk tank top screamed Wal-Mart, and her black leggings stretched far too tight over wide hips. Belinda didn't like discovering that she was not only a bigot, but a snob for thinking this creature spelled trouble with a capital T.

"May I help you?" she inquired politely, striving to hide her accelerating heartbeat. Ever since Adrian's arrest, she'd been suspicious of the motives of strangers.

"This where Adrian Raphael lives?"

"No, I'm sorry." That wasn't a lie. Adrian didn't live here. He was temporarily sleeping at Cesar's, but he didn't live anywhere.

"You know where he is?"

That was a little tougher to skirt around, but Belinda definitely did not like the sounds of this. "May I ask who's inquiring?" she asked stiffly.

"Just an old friend. I heard he was out, and wanted to come by and wish him well."

Belinda thought that highly unlikely. Adrian had a taste for sophisticated women, and considering the one he'd brought home the other day, that taste hadn't changed. Faith might not be Hispanic like his other ladies, but she was definitely sophisticated. Belinda found it hard to believe that the woman on the other side of the door could be the menace who had driven Adrian off the road, though. She barely looked bright enough to drive.

She glanced to the street and noticed a red Ford Explorer, one that looked a little worse for wear. Adrian had said it was a pickup that hit them, not an SUV.

"Perhaps when he calls I can tell him you were asking after him. Would you like to leave your name and number?" Manners had been pummeled into her at an early age, and in this case they were convenient. Adrian would want to know who the visitor was.

"No, I'll find him. I want it to be a surprise." Giving Belinda a dismissive look, she tottered back down the cracked walk on her high heels.

Some men preferred voluptuous, Belinda thought as she watched their unexpected visitor climb into the SUV. Jim certainly didn't mind her own less than svelte figure. But the leopard-woman carried "voluptuous" to the point of ridicule. No one could look like that naturally. Leopard-woman had spent a lot of time and money on that huge hair and those huge . . .

Okay, she was being catty. Carefully closing the door and locking it, she wondered who she could call to warn Adrian. Faith. She would start by calling Faith at Cesar's.

Dolores watched her with avid curiosity. "Who do you think that was?"

"Not anybody Adrian met in prison," Belinda said decisively, reaching for the phone.

Faith wasn't in the apartment when Adrian arrived a little after nine.

Terror skyrocketed his blood pressure as he lowered the grocery sack to the kitchen counter. Where the hell could she be?

Had anything happened to her?

Fury met terror and both ripped through him at once. He'd damned well told her . . .

Racing to her bedroom, discovering no sign of disturbance other than clothes strewn across the bed, he tried to check his temper and think. Nothing could have happened to her here. She'd been perfectly safe behind locked doors. The damned woman had just taken it into her head to defy him.

He wanted to wring her neck for terrorizing him like this. He'd told her . . . He'd warned her . . .

Ah, hell. Rubbing his hand over his eyes, Adrian tried to accept his insanity for what it was. She'd said she could take care of herself. He didn't believe her, but there was only so much he could do. She'd made up her mind that she didn't need him or any man, and he sure as hell couldn't blame her.

He'd just have to get used to living in paralyzing terror.

Returning to the kitchenette, he tried to ignore the silence. No country music, no swinging posteriors, no sassy-mouthed blonde. He should be grateful for a chance to be alone.

He'd had four years of near solitude, enough to know he despised it.

Shoving a six-pack into the refrigerator, he leaned against the sink and tore ravenously into the sandwich he'd bought at the deli. He'd brought one for Faith, too, a fancy gourmet thing with bean sprouts and who-knew-what on it. He was hungry enough to eat both.

Was Faith hungry? She didn't have any cash.

Shit. She was a grown woman, as she'd told him repeatedly. He didn't have to worry about her as if she were Ines.

If he hadn't kidnapped her from her well-ordered life, she wouldn't be out on the street now, hungry and half dressed. This was his fault. He'd deal with it.

Throwing off his paint-stained shirt, rummaging through the duffel and vowing to find a Laundromat, Adrian ticked off a mental list of places Faith could have gone.

A neatly penciled page of telephone numbers beside the phone caught his eye as his head popped through his sport shirt. He could use Cesar's laptop to check the directory. . . . One of the numbers had a check mark beside it.

Tucking the shirt in, Adrian picked up the phone and dialed. The open page of the newspaper's entertainment section confirmed his suspicions when the number connected with a local country dance bar.

The address to the bar wasn't far from there. She'd probably walked. He wouldn't have her walking back at night. Stupid female. Even suburbia wasn't safe late on a Saturday night, and this wasn't suburbia.

So much for his rational decision to let her spread her wings and fly. He slammed out in search of his runaway canary.

"Uh-oh."

Faith slid off Belinda's high heels and rubbed her foot, glancing at Belinda as she did so. "Uh-oh?"

"Big brother cometh." Belinda slid farther down in her seat behind the huge amplifier and tried to make herself small.

Faith ignored the tightening knot in her stomach. She'd agreed to help Adrian. She hadn't agreed to be his prisoner.

"The band's ready to cut to the last set. You on?" George, the lead singer, stepped to the side of the platform.

"I'm ready. And forget funny. Let's do this sexy." Slipping on her shoes, Faith took George's hand and climbed back onto the stage.

George raised his eyebrows but didn't question her decision. Behind her, Belinda squeaked and covered her eyes. Adrian's sister had forgotten her fears about her strange visitor when Faith told her about this gig. Belinda had eagerly called in a neighbor to baby-sit and volunteered to bring clothes Faith could sing in. But, obviously, she hadn't expected her half brother to show up. Did the whole family fear the big bully?

As the band struck up the first chord of the duet, Faith searched the crowded room for Adrian, finding him without much effort. He'd propped an elbow on the bar not ten feet from the stage and was watching intently. She'd fry his damned eyebrows off. That should teach him not to follow her around town.

She couldn't look real sexy with jeans covering her knees and a borrowed cowboy hat hiding the bandage on her forehead, but she figured given Adrian's current state of abstinence, it wouldn't take real sexy. She ought to be ashamed of herself. Instead, she felt confident and just a little bit wicked.

Adrian sipped his beer as he watched Faith's slender figure limp out on stage in jeans and a sparkly red vest. He glared at the polished and grinning male vocalist who accompanied her. He didn't like the way his palms got clammy and his heart skipped a beat, but he'd calm down in a minute or two. Just because his sexual frustration had fixated on a blond demon in heels didn't mean he had to act on it.

She opened on a sultry note that almost instantly quieted the loud chatter at the bar. Even though she completely ignored him, Adrian could feel every damned note strike and slide under his skin like daggers.

He gulped his beer as Faith turned big gray eyes up to her partner and crooned low notes that crawled right up Adrian's spine and mined a hole through his middle. He tried to remember she was just a stupid housewife who had believed Tony's lies for eight years. A woman like that would settle for anything in pants, and a smooth-talking snake like the singer would suffice. Maybe she wanted a little excitement in her life this time around, instead of Tony's security. Adrian knew he couldn't offer her either.

Sullenly, he turned his back to the stage. Let her have her fun. It wouldn't be at his expense.

The duet ended and she started on one of her lighthearted songs. A drunk at one of the tables offered a ribald commentary in accompaniment. Adrian wanted to smash his fist in the man's face and tell him to shut the hell up, but he didn't need any trouble with the law. He was simply here to see the stupid woman home.

Glancing around the darkened room, Adrian spotted a lawyer he'd gone to school with who studiously ignored him. If he stayed in Charlotte, he'd have to grow used to the slights.

Lawyers didn't like losers, and despite all its claims otherwise, Charlotte was still a small town. Everyone knew about him.

Even if he proved his innocence, there would be those who would sniff and claim where there was smoke, there was fire. It had been difficult enough for him to find a job after graduating from school. He had no family connections, no contacts, no money, and the color of his skin against him. He should have been suspicious when Tony offered him a position. He had been, but was too hungry to refuse.

He wouldn't have that opportunity again. He lifted his beer and tried not to dwell on it. As the guy in the movie said, a man had to do what a man had to do.

The drunk at the front table got louder. Adrian tried to ignore him, but he caught a hitch in Faith's voice as she sang, and he swung around.

The blamed moron was trying to climb up on stage. Where the hell was security? Better yet, where in hell was the pretty boy she'd been singing with?

Faith continued smiling and making love to the microphone. The drunk's friends tried to pull him back. Adrian still didn't see a sign of security.

Elbowing into the mob forming in front of the stage, Adrian cursed their passivity. Stupid sightseers. Didn't they have the sense to realize the drunk wasn't part of the show—although Faith damned well did her best to make it seem like it. She sent a taunting chorus in the drunk's direction, but the guy was too far gone to be insulted. He seemed to be fascinated with her red shoes.

Adrian saw the male vocalist easing into view, but it was too late. He was too mad to stop now.

Another step or two and he could reach the seat of the bastard's pants. He elbowed aside a giggling redhead holding a martini. Yuppie moron.

Before Adrian could extend his arm over the shoulder of the jerk in front of him, Faith surrendered her high heels, leaving them in reach of the pervert.

As the man lunged for his prize, Faith raised a small,

nylon-shod foot, and deliberately slammed him backward with the force of her heel.

Women screamed and men lurched aside as the drunk flailed, unbalanced, into his table, collapsing backward until his weight drove the table across the floor and straight into Adrian.

Faith continued singing, leaving her red shoes where she'd removed them as a dare to any other man drunk or stupid enough to reach for them.

Catching the table's edge, Adrian shoved it aside, leaving the drunk floundering like a beached whale. The damned woman had taken the breath out of his lungs but not the heat out of his temper.

Adrian's temper finally fizzled as he forced his way to stage right and discovered Belinda huddling behind the tower of amplifiers. She squealed and peeked up at him, then glanced at the stage as if seeking Faith's help. When his own sister was terrified of him, he'd gone too far.

"What the hell are you doing here?" he asked wearily, collapsing into a chair beside Belinda's. The amps vibrated so loudly, he didn't expect her to hear him. Faith had slipped into a song he recognized as her signature number, and he figured the set would be ending soon. He needed time to adjust to the image of porcelain-fragile Faith shoving a two-hundred-pound gorilla off the stage.

Belinda gestured helplessly and sipped her soft drink rather than reply. His sister had dark circles under her eyes and didn't look well. He didn't think Faith should be keeping her out at this hour.

The crowd roared its approval as Faith sang her last note, and the male vocalist thanked her and the rest of the group. The noise from the amps died, the spotlights switched to the dance floor and a DJ, but Belinda still didn't say a word. She rubbed the moisture off her cold glass and refused to look at him.

Slapping each other and laughing, ribbing Faith as they leaped and stumbled down the stairs, the band broke up as they hit the main floor and drifted in different directions. Limping toward Belinda, Faith shook off any offers of assistance.

"I have to change and clean this goop off my face. I'll be back in a few minutes." Barely acknowledging Adrian, she followed the band behind the stage.

The pretty boy vocalist didn't follow. Watching Adrian with amusement, he stuck out his hand. "George Olson. Friend of Faith's?"

"My brother, Adrian Raphael," Belinda belatedly introduced them.

Without invitation, George straddled a chair. "Saw you riding to Faith's rescue. As you can see, she doesn't need help."

"She shouldn't need help," Adrian growled. "Where was security? She could have been hurt up there."

"Security leaves us alone unless we signal for them." George shrugged and regarded Adrian with unconcealed interest. "You don't know much about Faith, do you?"

"That's scarcely any of your business." Feeling irritable, he just wanted out of there.

"Faith and I are old friends." George pushed the subject mercilessly. "I lost my lead singer a few years ago, and Faith auditioned for the spot. She was terrible."

Adrian scowled. A man would have to wear a bag over his head and beans in his ears to think Faith could come even close to terrible.

George leaned back in his chair and patted the rump of a beaming waitress. "Just lemon water, sugar. Have to save the voice." The waitress scampered off, and he returned to nettling Adrian. "She was white as a sheet, combed her hair in a tight schoolmarm knot, wore this hideous long skirt, and lost notes every time anyone looked at her cross-eyed. But she wore those damned red boots . . ." He sighed reminiscently.

Adrian thought he might throttle the jerk. Belinda dug her fingers into his arm, and he realized how tense he was. This was stupid. He tried to relax and enjoy the story. He could see the uptight SouthPark matron Faith had been standing in front of a rowdy crowd looking like that. They'd howl her off the stage. She must have been desperate. That had to have been right after she left Tony.

"Something about those red boots made me give her another chance. That, and I really needed a singer to keep that gig." George shrugged deprecatingly. "Business wasn't all that hot back then. I thought she'd give us a little class if she could loosen up."

"She looked plenty loose tonight," Adrian said dryly.

George laughed. "She learns fast. First time a drunk came after her, she ran like a rabbit and fell off the stage. Made her mad. God, don't ever get that woman mad."

Considering what Faith had done to Tony when she'd discovered his perfidy, Adrian could appreciate the warning. She was definitely not the type to take a beating lying down.

"I introduced her to a friend of mine after that," George continued. "He teaches martial arts, not specializing in any particular kind but mostly teaching teenage nerds not to get beat up. He had a class in self-defense for housewives, too. Faith took to it like a swan to swimming. I think she took the balls off the last guy who groped her."

Adrian didn't want to hear this. He didn't want to imagine Faith desperate enough to sing in front of drunken crowds. He didn't want to think about men groping her. He wanted to see her all prim and proper, behind the wheel of a Mercedes, where she belonged.

But she had definitely left a heel print on the forehead of a two-hundred-pound gorilla. And politely removed her stilettos before she did so.

Belinda patted his arm. "Doesn't she sing beautifully?"

"No." Undeterred, Adrian clung to his anger. "She doesn't hit half the notes right."

George grinned and pushed back his chair. "But she's got passion and drive, and that's what sells. If I could have persuaded her to Nashville with me, she'd be at the top of the charts by now. There's a damned lot of talented singers out there, but only a few of them have that kind of focus and determination. And smarts."

He stood and nodded at someone behind Adrian, who

didn't have to look over his shoulder to know who it was. She wore baby powder—*baby* powder, for chrissakes—and he could still recognize Faith's scent.

"I have no ambition, George," she chided him. "I just needed some easy money to pay the rent."

"I dread the day when you find ambition then." George leaned over and kissed her cheek as she circled the table and took the chair he offered. "See you at practice Monday? We can work out some new routines."

"Monday it is," she agreed, watching Adrian challengingly as she did so. Someone had apparently retrieved the red shoes for her, and she plopped them in a canvas tote she set on the table.

He didn't know this woman. He couldn't presume to tell her what to do. But he sure as hell disliked her advertising her presence to the entire city. "Like living dangerously, do we?" he mocked as George departed.

"What do you think will happen to me in front of a crowd?"

"Planning on having the crowd follow you home?" Anger simmered without an outlet, but he didn't know how to frighten the fool woman into understanding her danger.

"I could do that. Or I could ask George," she goaded.

"Or Jim," Belinda intruded weakly, gesturing toward the door. "He's on dinner break this time of night."

With a sigh of resignation, Adrian turned to see his cop brother-in-law strolling through the crowd, his blue uniform sending several bar patrons scurrying for their cell phones to call taxis.

"Jim, good to see you. Since when do you let your wife hang out in bars?" Adrian stood and shook the younger man's hand. He could have wished Belinda had chosen a wealthier husband, but she couldn't have found a better man.

"I'm not stupid enough to tell Belinda what she can do," Jim said mildly, wrapping his arm around his wife's shoulders as she joined him.

"Only Adrian does that. Faith, meet my husband. I wish he'd arrived in time to see your show."

"Maybe another time." Faith reached over the table to shake the policeman's hand. "I put Belinda's things back in the bag." She nodded at the canvas tote. "I'm glad you can escort her home. I hated having her drive down here like this."

"Wild horses couldn't have kept her home." Jim dropped the bag over his shoulder and affectionately rubbed Belinda's abdomen. "She'll slow down soon enough."

"What?" Adrian shouted in outrage at the gesture, his anger finding a new focus. "Are you out of your mind?"

Faith dug her fingernails deep into his hand and interrupted his tirade. "You can congratulate Belinda later. Did you recognize the description she gave you of the visitor?"

Growling irascibly, Adrian diverted his attention to the new subject. "Visitor?" he demanded.

He radiated anger and tension, but at least he'd found a new focus for his intensity. Faith watched his expression change from anger to suspicion to incredulity as Belinda described the blowzy blonde in the red SUV. Faith had seen the woman only once, but she couldn't think of another person on earth who would fit the description better.

"Sandra," Adrian swore before Belinda even finished. "Why the hell is Sandra looking for me?"

❧ TWENTY-TWO ❧

"Sandra's too damned dumb to plot anything." Wearily, Adrian glanced over the set of professional letters Faith had produced from Cesar's laptop. She'd created letterheads for an imaginary attorney's office with his name on it, and another letterhead with the name of Tony's corporation and her official title as president. He figured she'd promoted herself. Tony would never have given her that designation.

"Sandra wouldn't have downtown connections." Faith curled up in the ratty recliner and massaged her knee. "But she was smart enough to hold onto Tony and have his children. Don't underestimate her."

Reading the succinct letters requesting notification of any safe deposit boxes in the corporate name, Adrian tried not to watch Faith. He was tired, he was angry, and he was too worried about his family to get mixed up with this contrary female. He couldn't believe Belinda had gone and got herself pregnant. The burden of his family threatened to overwhelm him.

Setting the letters aside, he sipped his beer and contemplated the path Faith's conclusion had opened. Faith made instinctive if not altogether logical deductions. "All right, if we assume no member of my family told anyone I'd found you, then we have to start with our day in town. Who down there would know you or have reason to call a loose cannon like Sandra?"

She grimaced and gave up the massage. "It wouldn't be a matter of knowing *me*. I was just the corporate wife, the ornament on Tony's arm. No one at the courthouse had reason to

183

know me. Some of the bankers and lawyers from the country club might recognize me—I saw at least one of Tony's golfing buddies that day. But they would think nothing of seeing me around. It was seeing me with you that set someone off."

"Aside from the D.A.," Adrian mused aloud, trying to distract himself from wanting to massage her leg for her, "the only other person I can think would be interested in us is the guilty party." And the guilty party was Tony—who was dead. This wasn't getting them anywhere.

"I don't want to believe he's alive," Faith whispered, so faintly he almost didn't catch it.

She looked defeated. The proud, confident woman from the stage had crumpled into a scared woman whose safe world had been shattered. He could comfort her, but his self-control wasn't great at the best of times, and right now didn't qualify as anywhere close to a good time.

"Why the devil did you marry a creep like Tony anyway?" Hell, that was a fine way to comfort a distraught woman. Cursing, Adrian headed for the refrigerator, hoping for a beer.

"I don't know. For the same reason you went to work for him?" she suggested with a large dose of sarcasm.

"Desperation?" He grabbed a bottle, popped the lid, and took a long swig.

Demure Miss Perfect gave a piggy snort. "Probably, although I'm certain that's not what I thought at the time. I was *eighteen*. What did I know? I'd traveled the entire western hemisphere but didn't know a single soul. My older sister died of meningitis on one of our jaunts, and I felt as if I'd lost my only friend. After that, my parents wouldn't take me with them, and then my grandmother died, and I was the loneliest person in the world."

"That's when Tony stepped in," Adrian finished for her, offering her the bottle instead of the physical consolation she needed. Even he wasn't desperate enough to play on her vulnerability like that.

"He'd just graduated." She shook her head at the beer. "He was headed to law school. He turned my world upside down—an older, handsome, reliable man, what more could a girl ask? He said he wanted what I wanted—a pretty house and a stable home and someone to love. I thought he'd offered me heaven. I *adored* him."

Knowing he was out of his mind, Adrian tugged her from the chair, took her place, and pulled her down on his lap. Talk about *heaven*—she felt good there. He wrapped his arm around her waist and wouldn't let her go when she struggled. He'd be in hell real soon if she kept up the wiggling, but he figured they both needed a human touch right now. "Tony knew all the right buttons to push," he agreed. He could scarcely condemn her for her innocence.

She gave up the fight easily. Pulling her feet into the chair beside him, she curled up in a ball and rested her head against his shoulder. "Yours, too?"

He grunted and took another swig of the beer, but it didn't distract him from the round curve of her bottom snuggled into his lap. "He graduated law school just as I was starting. He got pissed, once, when his debating partner lost to me, a lowly undergrad, and a spic at that, but we didn't have much contact until after I started sending out résumés my final year. Nobody was particularly impressed with my credentials, or lack of them."

All that seemed so trivial now. Adrian tested the slender curve of her waist beneath his hand, waiting for a protest. Damn, but she felt good. If only—

"Tony said it was all about who you know, and he made certain he knew all the right people," she agreed sleepily.

Hell, she was exhausted. He had no business taking advantage of her now. He withdrew his hand to a less tempting spot. "I had to work to support a family. I didn't have time to make connections. So when Tony offered me a position, I snapped it up, no questions asked. We cordially despised each other, but I'm good at detail and he wasn't. So he found the clients, and I did the work. It seemed fair at the time."

"*That* was Tony's talent," she said dryly, groaning as she unbent her knee. "He knew precisely how to play a weakness to his advantage."

She struggled to rise, and however reluctantly, Adrian

helped her. He didn't think he was in any state to follow her, unless it was into her bed. And after that last comment on Tony, he didn't dare say a word and risk falling into the same category.

He threw his can at the newly emptied trash basket. "I told Rex I'd work all day tomorrow. Come with me?" She hesitated, and he figured he'd been too hasty. "If you have other plans, that's all right."

"No, I don't have plans," she said softly. "I just wish you could be with your family, is all."

"You and me both, but they've managed without me for four years. They'll hang on a little longer."

From the corner of his eye he could see her nod agreement. He tried not to take too deep a breath. He didn't know what he was doing here. He only knew he would lose some piece of himself if anything happened to her, and he didn't have much left to lose before he vanished entirely. More had ridden on her answer than he cared to examine.

"All right." She limped off without giving him any argument or excuse.

She had class, and he liked her a hell of a lot more than was good for him.

"How can you be sure this is the color you want?" Faith wrinkled her nose at the leaden gray oxide glaze in the pot Adrian handed her. "It doesn't look anything like the cobalt in the example you gave me." She knew glazes didn't match their color, but she needed conversation to break the awkward silence.

"Heat gives it color." Adrian wiped sweat from his forehead with the hem of his T-shirt as he glanced over her shoulder at what she was doing. "You have to work quickly with that brush. It's not like oil. The clay sucks it dry the instant you brush it on."

"It's a simple design," she said doubtfully, studying the sample plate he had given her. "I used to draw flowers like that on my schoolwork in high school."

His laugh was curt. "Whoever ordered these might as well

have gone to the factory outlet and bought manufactured stoneware. Crude and boring. But Rex caters to customers with more money than taste."

"Well, the plates you did yesterday were colorful," she said doubtfully. "I don't think those hues would be available commercially."

He shrugged, leaned over her shoulder to show her how to hold the brush for the best effect, then stepped back. He was soaked in sweat from working with the kiln, but it was a healthy male musk that Faith enjoyed. His sheltering, non-demanding arms around her last night remained imprinted on every cell of her body.

"It isn't art," he said bluntly. "It's dinnerware. But we both know one pays for the other."

She glanced around at the crowded shelves. "From what I can see, Rex should stick with dinnerware."

Adrian chuckled. "I tried to teach him how to use slip coloring once, but it was messy and took more imagination than he possesses. He's good with a brush, has an eye for color, and he knows how to turn a cup. We all have our skills."

Faith bit her lip and concentrated on filling in the flower design Adrian had sketched for her. She would rather have watched him, found out more about his knowledge of stoneware, but they were back to treading carefully around each other. She didn't think she could look at him without drooling over that sopping shirt plastered to his chest. He'd obviously spent the last four years working out a lot of frustration in a gym.

"Juan seems to think you have talent. Could you make a living at this?"

He snorted and tested the tackiness of the glaze on a freshly painted saucer. "Not and support my family. My mother's family would have starved if they hadn't taken outside jobs. Playing in clay is just a hobby."

She wanted to disagree, but she'd seen how many potters lived. Supplies were hideously expensive. One badly glazed batch, a poorly heated kiln, a sudden drop in temperature, anything could ruin a week's hard labor and a fortune in supplies. It had to be a labor of love. Art didn't pay in an industrial world.

Adrian carried out a tray of already glazed dishes ready for firing. Faith knew there were many ways of achieving color and design on stoneware. Rex had chosen one that was more labor and risk intensive. The pieces she was working on had already been fired once to produce a hard, dry bisque. She would hand paint the design, and later a transparent glaze would coat the entire piece. Then he'd fire it again. Two loads of fuel and twice the danger of the dishes cracking.

She grimaced at the dull color her brush produced, but the bright blues, reds, and yellows of the finished dishes on the table gave her hope. It might not be art, but it was useful and unique. She thought it relaxing—far better than contemplating how they would dodge Sandra and a knife-wielding thief while trying to locate a needle in a haystack.

Adrian worked more quickly than she did. While she painstakingly filled in the designs he sketched with a quick sure stroke, he glazed the painted stoneware and kept the kiln at an even temperature. In his spare moments he wielded a deft brush to finish painting the plates she hadn't completed.

She could tell he knew the business, with an inborn talent and appreciation for the clay. He was also far too intelligent and ambitious to waste his life baking dinnerware.

Finishing the last plate, she rose and stretched her back. She was limping less, but she tried to keep her weight off that knee as much as possible. She needed it to heal.

Wandering in to see what Adrian was doing in the kiln room, she nearly swallowed her tongue at the sight of him stripped half naked as he stoked the fire. Like some mighty Vulcan outlined against a fiery inferno, his bronzed back and shoulders glistened with sweat and rippled with power. The impact of all that raw male strength knocked the breath from her lungs.

Adrian swung around while her eyes were still wide and her breath hadn't returned. Using his shirt to mop the perspiration from his chest, he eyed her speculatively. His thick black hair looked as if he'd just washed it, and the clip he used to hold it back had slipped on the slick wet strands, leaving a short piece to fall forward around his ear, accenting the high plane of his cheekbone. In the flickering light from the kiln the silver ring on his ear gleamed against his dark skin.

"See something you like?" he asked when she said nothing.

"What I like has nothing to do with anything." Recovering some of her equilibrium, she turned to leave. *For heaven's sake, Faith,* she scolded inwardly, *you're almost thirty. You've seen naked men. Deal with it.*

"Why doesn't it?" he demanded, following her, grabbing a dry pullover golf shirt from the back of a chair. "Why can't you let yourself go, admit when you want something and go after it?"

He was too close, too raw, too physical, and too damned male. She rubbed her arms and stopped retreating at the worktable. She still didn't look at him. "That's what a child does," she snapped. "Adults measure the cost."

"Sex doesn't cost a damned thing."

She could hear him pacing. She hoped he'd put his shirt on, but she wasn't certain she was even ready for that. It had never occurred to her to compare male buttocks as other women did. She'd never looked at a man and wondered what he would be like in bed. Tony had taught her sex, and she'd found it a passable duty, a wonderful example of how he needed her. So, obviously, sex was a lie.

She'd never, ever, looked at a man as she'd looked at Adrian, and imagined him naked, shoving her against a wall and pumping inside her. Her body was still weak from reaction.

"Maybe sex doesn't cost you anything," she replied bitterly, "but it costs me far more than I can afford."

He stalked around the table and slammed his hands down in front of her, staring into her face at eye level. "Why? It's a physical act of release, far more pleasant than tormenting ourselves like this."

Guilty pleasure shivered under her skin at knowing he wanted her—mousy little Faith. But then, he'd been without sex for four years and would probably make love to a chair leg at this point.

"Sex without an emotional commitment is an animal act," she stated firmly, trying not to look too closely at the flash of his dark eyes. He had a thin, jutting patrician nose she admired entirely too well, and if she gazed at his mouth . . .

He jerked away from her to stalk the room again. His hair swung back and forth, and his lean hips moved with the lithe grace of a caged panther. She was shut up in a small room with a dangerous animal.

"Emotional commitment," he spat out in disgust. "What the hell is an emotional commitment? Fury is an emotion. Frustration. Bitterness. Hell, I can give you emotion in spades. I could melt a little Nordic ice princess like you in a matter of minutes."

That's what she was afraid of. "Adrian, we're both on edge and not thinking sensibly." She tried to calm him, but she figured she had as much likelihood of accomplishing that as she would of dousing the kiln with words.

"We wouldn't be on edge if you'd let go and be yourself and forget all that prim and proper garbage Tony wanted from you."

As soon as the words escaped him, Adrian threw up his hands in disgust with himself as much as her. There it was, in all its ignoble glory, the barrier that stood between them. Shoving his hands in his pockets, he swung to face her.

Her cheeks were pale and her eyes had hardened to shards of ice. While he burned like a cauldron of hot coals, she froze up tighter than any iceberg. He must be out of his mind, he thought, to think of making love to a female as frigid as this one.

Except he'd seen her on stage. She wasn't frigid.

"Sex is just a physical release," he repeated. "Going for it on stage is a poor substitute."

"I don't wish to continue this discussion," she said coldly, gathering up her purse. "If you're done here, I'd like to leave."

Oh, hell, he didn't know why he'd tried. Or he did know. That wide-eyed look of admiration in her spectacular eyes had shot straight to his groin, and he'd turned rock hard in an instant like any adolescent. But he knew better than to listen to hormones.

He checked his watch. "Rex should be back shortly. Let me see if the temperature is holding steady, then we can leave."

He damned well wanted her more than anything he'd wanted in his life. Right now he'd give up his law degree and his search for the evidence of his innocence if he could have this woman in his bed for a week.

He left her standing there, pale and shaken, while he checked on the fire. He *knew* better than to come at her that way. She didn't deserve his rage. But he was rapidly reaching the limit of rationality.

Returning to the workroom to find her examining Rex's god-awful tea sets, he put a hand to her spine and steered her toward the door. Even that contact shot steam through his ears.

"Come on. Cesar should have your things back from Knoxville now. You can dress like yourself again."

❦ TWENTY-THREE ❦

In the familiar comfort of her navy blazer and cream silk slacks, Faith tucked her chignon into combs and wrapped confidence around herself once again. Cesar's tiny bathroom mirror told her she looked like Faith Hope, businesswoman, and not the shattered, ridiculous female Adrian had made her feel yesterday.

She didn't need sex or any man to make her whole. She was quite happy as herself. She'd be even happier once they found the money and the books and she could go home.

Returning her makeup kit to the tiny bedroom, she glanced in admiration at the vase she'd removed from the cardboard box in which Adrian had packed her storage items. She should never have hidden a thing of such beauty just because Tony had given it to her. She couldn't blame the vase for what Tony had done. When she returned home, she would put it in her window and redecorate.

Picking up her nearly empty purse, she joined Adrian in the kitchen. He was leaning against the kitchen sink, eating cereal. He looked up as she entered, but his gaze stayed shuttered, hiding the inferno he'd revealed yesterday.

"You talked to Annie?" he asked curtly.

"She called the Charlotte shelter," she said. "They'll cash a trust fund check in exchange for a donation. Once this is all settled, I'll personally make good the difference."

"*I* will," he corrected, setting down the empty bowl.

She eyed him skeptically, but he stared at her with the pride of an arrogant aristocrat, and she didn't argue.

"We'll need good quality paper to print the letters," she reminded him. "It could take us all week to scout the banks between here and Raleigh. I can't stay away that long."

Politely, he didn't bother reminding her of the burglar. She didn't want to think of the violation of her home and shop right now. She was placing her bets on finding Tony's books in Charlotte, turning them over to the D.A., and returning to the business of living.

Sending letters to every bank in the state and waiting for their return would take far longer than she was prepared to wait. "You have the box keys?" she asked.

Adrian silently produced them from his pocket—his ticket to paradise.

They rode in silence to the shelter to cash the trust fund check, stopped at an office supply for the letterhead, then steered into traffic bound for the first bank on Faith's list.

"How can we tell if anyone is following us?" Nervously, she clasped her hands and watched the sideview mirror.

"We can't, not in this traffic." Adrian expertly steered into a gap in the fast lane. "But unless someone knows where we're staying, they couldn't find us to follow us."

That made sense. If someone knew where they were staying, they wouldn't *need* to follow them. They could have broken in during the night or anytime. Somehow, she didn't feel reassured.

"Could someone have followed Cesar from my apartment?"

"Going ninety miles per hour down those mountains at night when all anyone can see is headlights? They'd have to be crazy."

He glanced over at her, and she tried to look composed. He was right. Knoxville was hours of heavy traffic away.

"We'll think of something," he said soothingly. "For all we know, one of your bar admirers decided to stalk you. The burglaries might have nothing to do with any of this."

That wasn't any more reassuring, and she knew better than to believe in coincidence. "I have new locks now. They can't get in. I'll be fine. I'd just like to find those books and get this over with."

Maybe sometime in the next million years she'd rid herself of the vision of Adrian, nearly naked. Only right now, the vision grew clearer and more graphic every time she looked at him.

She didn't know if she was more afraid of him or the bad guy.

"Here's our first exit. Are you ready?" He asked it calmly, as if he had nothing riding on their success.

"I'm ready." Far more ready than she had been last time. It was a miracle how her own clothes made a difference. She was Tony's wife in these clothes, the SouthPark matron who hobnobbed with the CEOs who commanded thousands of these tiny little branch banks. She fondled the strand of pearls at her throat, the symbol of the power and wealth she'd once possessed. She hadn't realized what a crutch money had been.

They had no luck at the first bank, or the second. Every exit was littered with branches from a dozen different financial institutions. If Tony had stuck with just one bank, the task would have been immensely easier.

By the time they reached the eighth or ninth brick box with columns, they had their routine perfected, right down to their polite smiles of regret at disturbing the manager with their request for a box that didn't exist.

"We knew it wouldn't be easy," Adrian reminded her as they returned to the car after still another defeat. "Let's get some lunch."

Well, at least they had some cash for food, thanks to the trust fund. Faith figured she should be grateful for what she had.

Instead, she simply wanted to kill Tony all over again.

"There are probably more banks in the Lake Norman area than there are in the whole world," she grumbled as he headed for a nearby fast food outlet. She hadn't sampled so many different kinds of fast food since she was a kid in school. She'd already concluded half of America must subsist on grease and mayonnaise.

"I figure there's more in the south end. You still have a lot of farmland out here."

Faith raised an eyebrow at a mile of brick and concrete shopping centers and offices. "Money is a crop these days?"

He grinned and accepted the greasy bag from the drive-through window. "I can see I'd better take you out of all this for a while. You get mean when frustrated."

That had several connotations but neither commented on them as he drove toward a small grassy space near the lake and away from the shopping center. Other people had had the same idea, and several office workers strolled the path, dipping into their lunch bags as they walked, or finding seats in the grass. The September sun still shone brightly, but a cool front had chased away the heavy humidity.

"What will you do if we don't find the books?" Faith knew she shouldn't ask, but his problems took away from her own.

He sprawled in the grass, unconcerned about his jeans or white dress shirt. "I can't even go into law enforcement unless I clear my record. The only things I know are law and pottery. And wrestling."

"Wrestling?" Faith licked mayonnaise off her fingers and studied him dubiously. Professional wrestling was a popular entertainment here, but she had difficulty imagining Adrian in spangled tights.

He shrugged and finished chewing. "Good money to put on a show. Figured law was half acting anyway, and so's wrestling. Put myself through school that way."

"Good heavens." Stunned, Faith tried to see it, but she wasn't a wrestling fan. Her mind's eye conjured hunky bodies, flowing blond tresses, and outrageous costumes. She couldn't see lean, sleek, unadorned Adrian in a ring.

"Called me the Black Panther. I wore all black, and had to lose most of the time. Nothing I couldn't learn in a gym. It kept me in shape after hours in the law library."

Faith shook her head in disbelief. "You're a natural in pinstriped suits and wingtips. You're making this up."

"Ask my family sometime." Finishing his sandwich, he

crumpled the lunch bag and tossed it toward a barrel container. It hit.

"You should have taken up basketball." Brushing grass off her slacks, Faith dropped her empty cup in the trash.

"Don't get paid for college ball. I worked off a lot of energy with wrestling, but I think I'm a little too old for that now. We'll find the books."

Grabbing her hand, Adrian pulled her toward the car, showing no sign of age diminishing his restless energy. After last night, Faith didn't object to the contact. She trusted him not to pounce on her until she was ready.

Ready? She shivered at the tangent her subconscious had taken. She'd never be ready.

"The next exit is the turnoff toward Sandra's trailer park," she commented, examining the map and avoiding any more personal revelations. "Do you think she's moved back?"

"We could take a look." Adrian wrinkled his brow in thought. "How dangerous could she be?"

"Never underestimate a woman," Faith warned.

He snorted in agreement. "All right, let's just drive by, see how things look. It's always best to know where your enemies are."

They traveled down a long country road in the opposite direction from the lake and its million dollar mansions, past farms, jungles of trees and kudzu, and an occasional shabby cottage. Twenty years ago the whole area around Charlotte had looked like this.

"Sandra's was the third house on the right. She had a play set for the kids in the backyard." She couldn't hide the hitch in her voice as they approached a lane of shiny mobile homes.

They slowed down in time to watch a young boy emerge through the front door and run next door to a neighbor's.

"Could that be Tony's oldest?" Faith asked, trying to hide her wistfulness. She'd calculated the oldest would be about twelve now. If she and Tony had had children as soon as they were married, her child would be eleven. She didn't think she would ever make sense of what Tony had done. He'd had *chil-*

dren when they married. He'd had a mistress, whom he never stopped seeing. She'd never comprehend it.

"I never saw them, so I don't know. The kid's hair is the same crummy brown as Tony's, that's all I can tell you." Adrian hit the gas and turned around in a driveway down the road. "But Sandra's SUV isn't there."

"She could have sold or rented the place, I suppose." Faith sank into her seat and wondered what self-destructive devil had urged her to make this detour. She should be grateful she'd never had Tony's child. She never could have escaped if children had been involved.

"I have some friends who live out in this direction. I'll ask them to drive by occasionally, see if they ever see the Explorer there." Dismissing Sandra, Adrian snapped on the radio.

They didn't say anything else as they drove back to the interstate and the next round of banks.

By mid-afternoon they were ready to admit defeat. They'd reached the last exit before the interstate stretched through miles of farmland, and they hadn't found a single bank with any knowledge of Tony's corporation.

"I told George I'd be there by six to rehearse," Faith said tiredly, stretching her aching knee as far as the tiny car would allow.

"I don't suppose it would do any good to tell you it's dangerous for you to make public appearances." Adrian glared at the heavy traffic blocking his access to the last bank on the list.

She figured it was only sheer bullheadedness that prevented him from simply turning around and going home. "I don't think your potter friend would be interested in paying me for my inept attempts to paint. And I refuse to rely on a man for my support. I'll earn my way, and singing is the easiest way I can make a quick buck."

She could see the muscle jerk over his cheekbone and his fist grip the wheel tighter, but he didn't argue. "I'll take you there and pick you up."

"That will cut into your time at the pottery. One of the band can see me home."

"Just tell me what time you'll be done, or I can give you a phone number, and you can call me when you're ready to leave. I don't want anyone else knowing where we live." He cut between two cars, hit the gas, and entered the parking lot, swinging into a parking space, shifting, and shutting off the engine in one swift motion.

He was trying to be reasonable. She'd try to do the same. She could vehemently deny any need for any man's help, insult his machismo, and protest—for the thousandth time— that she could take care of herself, or she could compromise. Deciding she wasn't half so independent as he liked to believe, she settled for compromise. She liked his concern for her welfare, even if it derived from his guilt in involving her.

"There's only this bank at this exit," he said grimly as he climbed out. "What are the chances they even have safe deposit boxes?"

Faith shrugged, figuring the question was rhetorical. They'd have to go in and ask, no matter what they thought.

The bank's temperature sign flashed eighty as they dragged across the blacktopped parking lot and entered the air-conditioned coolness of the interior. At this hour on a Monday, the clerks were busy counting cash and tallying receipts. Customers were a nuisance.

A woman in gray gabardine eventually offered her services, took them back to the vault records, and scanned the index. Well, as the only bank in town, they apparently had deposit boxes, Faith decided. Lucky them.

"Yes, the Nicholls Corporation," the woman acknowledged to Faith's total surprise. "The rent is paid through the end of this month. Do you have your keys?"

Heart in mouth, Faith couldn't say anything. Adrian produced the key ring. The woman nodded, and marched back to the vault.

Not even looking at Adrian, Faith followed on her heels, heart pounding a rapid ticktock in time with the huge bank clock over the vault door. The last box had been empty. The last box had been conveniently located near home. This one was in the middle of nowhere. Could they really have found Tony's secret cache?

She waited patiently as the clerk opened a lock with her key, checked her ring for a similar key, and inserted it. It fit.

Adrian reached past her to lift the heavy box from its space, and the clerk guided them back to the viewing room, where she left them alone in a private cubicle. By this time Faith was holding her breath and suspected Adrian was holding his.

Setting the box down on the table, he cautiously turned the key until it clicked. Not glancing at her, he slid the drawer open.

"My God!" Faith exclaimed in a whisper as she stood at Adrian's side, staring at the same vision that held him captive.

"It's impossible to keep a few million dollars in a single box," he said pragmatically, lifting out a crisp bundle of green. "If they're all fifties, stacked side by side like this, I doubt if there's fifty thousand."

"No ledgers," she whispered, still in awe of that much cash in one place.

"Computer disks," he corrected. "Tony put the books on computer after you left."

He sounded so cool and collected, as if they handled fifty thousand dollars every day of the week. "You can pay back some of the money," she suggested. "Would that help?"

Removing his handkerchief from his back pocket, he wiped the bundle he'd touched, replaced it in the drawer, then using the handkerchief again, closed it and wiped the handle and the rest of the surface, before returning the keys to his pocket. "All this will do is convince the D.A. that you were in cahoots with me." He carried the box back to the vault and slammed it into place. "You'd better pay the rent on this thing for another year so we have time to gather more evidence. If the bank opens it and sees all that cash, they'll have to report it."

She couldn't believe this. They'd spent days hunting down Tony's cache, and they were walking off and leaving it behind. Instead of screaming in celebration, he treated it as if it were a contaminated nuclear device.

❧ TWENTY-FOUR ❧

Adrian sat at the back of the barroom watching Faith rehearse and sipping the beer he'd brought in with him. The bar was closed on Mondays, but he figured he ought to take the edge off before he faced Faith with the latest development. Discovering the cash had been a mixed blessing in the face of recurring disaster.

Up on stage, Faith listened to the band leader, nodded her head, and waited for her opening cue as the guitarist started a new riff. She'd changed into a bright red T-shirt reading WARNING: I HAVE AN ATTITUDE AND I KNOW HOW TO USE IT, and a pair of cutoff blue jeans that must have been molded to her shape. Adrian gave thanks to the powers that be that she'd had the sense to wear the shirt on the outside of the jeans so he didn't have to watch every little jiggle and bounce from here. He was almost certain he'd internally combust if he had to look much longer without touching.

As she sank into a slow, seductive song in a husky voice that hit him in the gut, he nearly crushed his beer can before he drank the contents. God, he wanted her so badly everything else became a murky haze in the back of his mind. Maybe he should send her to her parents in Mexico. He could assume she'd be safe from him there, at least.

She wouldn't go. If he'd learned nothing else about Faith Hope Nicholls these last days, he'd learned she didn't give up and she didn't give in.

He couldn't predict how she would react to more bad news. Instead of trying, he sat back, sipped his beer, and tried not to let the hot poker in his pants dictate what they would do next. He had to be logical about this.

She knew he was out here, but she was studiously ignoring him this time instead of playing the part of siren. Still, the song shivered along his skin, digging in and not letting go.

He shouldn't torture himself like this, but he'd prepared a little surprise for her, and he waited to see if the band carried it out. She deserved a little compensation, some recognition that she was special, that today was special. He couldn't do much for her, but he had done what little he could.

As she lowered her voice to sob out the last notes of the song, the band broke into a crazed guitar rendition of "Happy Birthday." She stopped in mid-note, stared blankly into the darkness outside the stage lights, then swerved around to look at the band. Adrian got up from the table and sauntered forward as one of the stagehands entered carrying a huge chocolate cake covered with flaming candles. They'd probably broken every safety rule in the book and would set off fire alarms in a minute, but it was worth it just to see Faith's face.

She looked startled, as if uncertain the band's impromptu outburst into song was for her. Her jaw literally dropped at sight of the cake. Adrian grinned as her eyes widened and a smile of disbelief finally lit up her entire face. She was so beautiful, he could eat her instead of the cake. Something internal yearned to claim her as his, to pamper her like this forever, to give her a life of surprises just so he could see that look on her face over and over again.

He'd have to be satisfied with the accusing look she finally swung in his direction.

"You!" she shouted. "You told!"

He vaulted onto the stage in front of her. "Of course I did. How else could I claim the birthday kiss?" Without waiting for her to take that in, he caught her by the waist, hauled her against him, and covered her mouth with his as he'd been dying to do since the last time.

The band whooped and hollered, the music screamed into something suggestive, but Adrian knew nothing beyond the moist press of her mouth against his and the subtle powdery scent mixing with the heat of Faith's skin as she wrapped her arms around his neck and surrendered without a protest.

She was slim and rounded and soft in all the right places as he crushed her against him. She nestled right where he needed her as hunger consumed them both. Fire should have shot from their heads instead of the candles. Skyrockets couldn't have been more heady. If he didn't stop soon, they'd have to break out the fire extinguishers.

Gasping, Adrian set her back on her feet, although his hands couldn't quite let go. She looked as dazed as he felt, but he had word skills she didn't possess, and he used them to ease the tension. "If that's my reward for remembering, what do I get if the cake is good?"

"Fat." Shoving her hands against his shoulders, she pushed away, but not so far that he couldn't reach out and grab her again if he wanted. She wasn't retreating. She was embarrassed.

He grinned at her response. So, her word skills were almost on a par with his. *"Feliz cumpleaños, querida."*

"I didn't even realize the date until I signed into the register at that last bank," she murmured, wrapping her arms around herself as the band's noise died down and the others surrounded them.

"Do we all get birthday kisses?" George asked with interest.

"Not unless you want to die young." Adrian possessively hauled Faith into his arms again. He noticed she didn't protest, although he could attribute it to her desire not to be mauled by anyone else. "Who's hoarding the champagne?"

On cue, another stagehand meandered out with a massive silver bucket of ice and a magnum bottle. The band cheered ecstatically, one clever member scaled the bar to release the champagne glasses, and the party began.

"You shouldn't have," Faith whispered, still not fighting his embrace.

Her bottom fit snugly beneath his hips, his arm encompassed her waist with ease, and he would easily sacrifice cake and champagne to stay this way. "Rex pays me well. And a friend of Belinda's gave me a discount on the cake. I'd rather give you something more memorable, but I was afraid you'd throw anything else at me."

She chuckled. "You're probably right. The last time anyone remembered my birthday, Tony gave me a string of pearls and told me he had to go to D.C. for the week. That's the only time I ever returned one of his gifts. I was so mad at him for going away and not taking me on the cruise I wanted that I bought plane tickets to Mexico to visit my parents. He never even noticed I wore fakes."

Adrian looked down at her as she smiled at the boy bringing her a glass of bubbling liquid. "You mean those pearls you wore today aren't real?"

"Nope. They were designer fakes, but they're fakes. Can you imagine living where I do and trying to hide expensive jewelry from thieves?" She took the champagne glass and held it in her hand as George made a flowery birthday speech.

"Thank God for small favors," he breathed, accepting his glass and chugging a gulp before George finished. At the inquiring look she threw over her shoulder, he shook his head. "It will wait. Let's enjoy your party first. Belinda and Cesar wanted to be here, but I told them Mama and the kids came first and that you'd understand."

"I don't need a party. Just being remembered is so nice."

Tears glinted in her eyes, and Adrian heard the break in her voice. He hugged her closer. She deserved someone who could make the world beautiful for her. All he could do was make it worse.

"Blow out the candles, Faith!" the guitarist, with one arm around a girlfriend, shouted.

"You have no idea what you've started," Faith murmured as she stepped away from Adrian's hold.

"But I know exactly how to end it," he murmured back, following her across the stage. She shot him a look of suspicion, but he could play innocent a while longer. They were safe here for a while, and she deserved a little party.

With the cake served and another round of champagne begun, someone stuck a CD into the sound system and music poured forth. Deciding he'd watched Faith accept enough kisses on the cheeks and hugs and inane patter from the band, Adrian drew her into his arms again and began the dancing. He knew it was a mistake, knew he should keep the entire barroom's distance between them, but he might as well cut off his tongue as to try.

"Thank you," she murmured into his shirt front, swaying easily into his rhythm. "I know you're making the best of a bad deal, but I've . . ." Faith didn't know how to continue. She hadn't realized how alone she had been these last years, how hungry for a human touch, a simple acknowledgment of her presence, anything to show she was alive and not a super-human robot. A tear trickled from the corner of her eye, and embarrassed at the stupid sentimentality, she surreptitiously tried to wipe it.

Adrian raked his hand through her hair and tilted her head back so he could press a kiss against the place she'd wiped. "I'm not making the best of a bad deal. I'm thanking you for understanding, for being better than any person I've met for a long time, for reinstating some of my faith in the human race." He grimaced at the pun of her name.

She grinned. "For reinstating Faith *into* the human race?" she countered.

"Have you ever considered changing your name?" he grumbled, moving into a quick two-step required by the change of songs from the speaker.

"I did once, it didn't work out." She slipped from his grasp and, ignoring the complaint from her knee, executed a tricky dip and swirl with her hands on her hips, and defied him to match her.

He did. Adrian might be out of practice, but he kept up with an innate agility that had her heart racing with admira-tion and glee. Tony had never danced with her like this. He'd manage a slow waltz if required, but then he'd always wander off to talk with people far more important than she, leaving her to idle her time on the sidelines. She'd never known what it was like to have a man's full attention focused on her, espe-cially a man with a focus as intent as Adrian's. Like paper in

the hot sun under the magnifying glass of his gaze, she sizzled. She forgot her knee.

When one of the band members discovered an open keg of
beer, Adrian caught Faith's hand and drew her out of the stage
lights and toward the darkness near the door. "Time to go. I
don't need breaking and entering on my parole record."

She didn't object. She was exhilarated by the man and the
music, not the champagne and the party. She floated after
him, as high on bubbles of happiness as on champagne. She
might come down with a thud in a little while, but she wasn't
in a hurry. She was thirty years old today and had little of
what she'd hoped to have by now, but she was all right. She
would make it. The next ten years were going to be good
ones. She could feel it in her bones.

She tucked her T-shirt into her jeans and grabbed the
blouse she'd worn over it earlier.

"Where's the egg?" she asked, buttoning up as they emerged
onto the night street and no familiar vehicle waited. The evening was cool, and she hugged the blouse around her.

"Cesar has it. Maybe we should take you car shopping in
the morning. You'll have to call Annie and see if the insurance
check is in the mail." He steered her down the street, avoiding
the streetlights.

She liked the solid feel of his hand at her back. Adrian had
amazingly strong hands.

"I don't suppose the bug was worth enough to buy a
Miata," she mourned, still not feeling any pain.

"Not unless it was classified as an antique vehicle," he said
dryly, pushing her into a dark alley after the next building. "If
we don't find Tony's books, we could always take his ill-
gotten gains and buy you one."

"And let his fellow lawyers pay for his crime. That's only
fair," she agreed, trying not to stumble in the darkness. She'd
worn comfortable shoes, but Adrian was proceeding entirely
too fast. "Where are we going? Are we walking home?"

"I have Cesar's van. That should confuse them a little while
longer until I can come up with a better idea." He peered
around the corner of the next building, and apparently finding

it all clear, pulled her into a darkened parking lot where the looming shadow of the van waited.

He threw open the door and all but pushed her in. Confused, Faith bumped her sore knee, cursed, and clambered into the high seat as the door slammed behind her. The champagne high was rapidly fizzling into something less pleasant.

"What's going on?" she demanded as Adrian yanked open the driver's door and slid in.

"Nothing we can't handle," he assured her. "Let's just pretend it's all part of your birthday celebration."

She'd like to pretend that, but she had a sneaking suspicion that Adrian didn't play games lightly. She sat silently as he maneuvered the van out of the alley, into the street, and turned toward the interstate instead of Cesar's apartment. "I never liked Blind Man's Bluff, and this is beginning to feel like Pin the Tail on the Donkey. I think maybe you'd better explain the rules."

In the faint light from the dash she could see his jaw tighten. She knew she wasn't going to like this. A streetlight glinted against the ring in his earlobe, and she took a deep breath. He looked more like a pirate than ever.

"Someone's been through the apartment. They tossed your suitcase and my duffel. They took Cesar's laptop. That means they'll have those letters you wrote and know what we're doing." His hands clenched on the wheel as he glanced over at her. "They took that little bag of jewelry you had, with the pearls in it."

Faith forced herself to face the facts calmly. "It's all costume jewelry. Admittedly, the pearls cost a couple hundred, but they're not worth crying over. What about my vase and photos?" she asked anxiously.

He jerked his head toward the back. "I picked them up and put them back there with our clothes."

"Then it could be just a regular thief, a crack addict looking for quick cash?"

"It's possible. I don't think it's likely. They tore through everything as if they were looking for something. I'll admit, you relieved me tremendously when you said the pearls were fake. I didn't know how I would replace a fortune in pearls."

He was doing the same thing as she, trying to sound normal. He was probably doing a better job of it, but then, he'd had more time to accept this new violation. She tried to assemble all the pieces of the puzzle flitting around, but champagne bubbles and weariness and panic kept careening off each other and colliding with the walls of her mind.

"We could always live out of the van, I suppose." Adrian interrupted her tired struggle to think. "I'd rather trap the bastard and wring his neck." He took an exit ramp and seemed to be aiming for a well-lighted hotel.

When he steered into the turn lane and bumped into the parking lot, Faith clutched the purse in her lap. "Why are we going here?"

"Because it's your birthday, and I'm not taking you to a cheap motel this time."

That made about as much sense as anything. She said nothing as he parked in front of the office and climbed out, leaving her behind. They didn't have credit cards. He'd have to use cash. Did hotels still take cash?

Her mind was wandering, avoiding the memory of that star-spangled kiss of earlier, of the teasing laughter, the warm looks, the hot dancing. Adrian could not be thinking what she was thinking. She had made herself perfectly clear on the matter. Surely he could find a room with two double beds in a place like this. They would take the night to think about what to do next.

But the deep dark recesses of her brain didn't buy any of this. In the fermenting murk of her fertile mind, other ideas coalesced, frothed, and emerged like little amoebas from the river of life. This was her birthday. Adrian would give her anything she wanted. She wanted a child.

That was the one thing he would refuse to give her, for very good reasons.

As Adrian emerged from the office carrying a key card, Faith fought the war between need and honor, but paranoia won. She didn't want sex unless she could have a child.

Adrian would never let her walk out carrying a child of his, and just the thought of Adrian permanently in her life had her staring over the brink into insanity.

CAPTIVE OF HER BEAUTY???

that gleam in his eyes with one eyebrow raised a mild clue that plan the next part of his plan. He conventoned in his man'd by staying until don't know what they thought.

❧ TWENTY-FIVE ❧

Faith gaped at the king-size bed dominating the center of their assigned room.

"They didn't have anything else?" she asked, incredulous.

"That's what I asked for." Adrian locked and bolted the door, then yanked the draperies closed. "I'm relieving you of any need to make a decision by kidnapping you. This is my pirate's cabin, the ship's set sail, and you're mine to do with as I will. I distinctly remember you telling me that's what it would take."

Faith tried to absorb his words while staring at the bed. Her insides were tumbling in nervous flips and she didn't dare look at him. "Pirate's cabin?" Her voice quavered in disbelief, but she had a vague recollection of telling him that it would take a pirate and a ship to persuade her into bed with him. She didn't know which one of them was crazier—she for saying it, or he for remembering.

"Yup." He turned on a lamp and glanced at her. "You either share my bunk or I'll throw you to my men."

Faith glanced at the "bunk"—a huge bed that would easily contain Adrian and six other people. She gulped and turned to meet dark eyes smoldering with desire. Instead of the pragmatic lawyer she was starting to know, he looked every bit the dangerous pirate captain with silver earring, beard-stubbled jaw, and ponytail. Her subconscious had worked overtime when she'd handed him that suggestion. As she watched, Adrian yanked open his shirt buttons.

"Take your clothes off," he ordered, staring at her breasts instead of meeting her eyes, as any good pirate would do.

She knew he was playacting, but he was very, very good, and goose bumps shivered down her arms. In the semi-darkness of the strange hotel room, she could almost believe they were dangerously alone on the deep blue sea. Something primitive stirred within her as Adrian dropped his shirt and stalked closer. The powerful build of sleek brown shoulders and chest held her fascinated gaze. He was all lean grace and animal muscle—and so sexy, her teeth chattered.

"Me, or my men," he challenged, his gaze searing through her bulky work clothes as if they were invisible. "Your choice."

Except he was taking away her choice, accepting all responsibility for what they both wanted. He'd understood what she hadn't understood herself. She wasn't Tony's protected little wife anymore, but she hadn't been able to step out of that role. She was a horrible hypocrite expecting him to act as enabler. But he'd told her once that he was a desperate man.

And she was a desperate woman. Afraid she would shatter if she moved too fast, Faith nervously unfastened the first button of the shirt she'd pulled on for warmth. Adrian's avid gaze egged her on.

"Remember, it's me or my men," he warned. "A cozy warm bunk or the cold dank recesses of the hold."

She could almost believe he would give up on her and throw her to whichever criminals were tracking her every movement. She shivered, and unfastened the next button. She still had a T-shirt on. This was no big deal.

She could do this. Adrian wouldn't reject her. He wouldn't roll over and go to sleep before she finished undressing. Tony had liked it fast and furious. She'd always been slow. But Adrian seemed ready to watch all night, as if every move she made was a thing of wonder.

Perspiration broke into little droplets on his brow as she finished unbuttoning her blouse, revealing the outline of her breasts beneath the T-shirt. Nervous, she didn't know what to reach for next.

"Take it all off," he commanded in a sandpaper rumble that

revealed how close he was to losing it. "I want you on my bed and under me for the rest of the night."

Moisture pooled between Faith's legs at the mental image she'd carried with her of Adrian naked. Now her mind's eye could see him naked and on top of her. She gulped, dropped her blouse on the floor and reached for the hem of her T-shirt. He helped her tug it over her head, then threw it across the room.

Without warning he reached over and unsnapped the front closure of her bra.

Her breasts spilled from the lightly padded cups. She'd always been embarrassed by her petite size, and it took every ounce of her courage to keep from covering herself as Adrian's hand brushed hers away. Reverently, his long fingers cupped and nearly swallowed her breasts.

"Oh, God, you're more beautiful than I imagined."

She didn't have time to doubt his praise before he closed his mouth over hers. With his palm heating her flesh, and his mouth to persuade her there was no turning back, any notion of choice disappeared. She melted into his hands, as surely his prisoner as if he held a cutlass to her throat.

He'd eaten a candy before they'd left the bar, and she inhaled the sugar and spearmint as his tongue plied her mouth with desperate longing. She couldn't catch her breath. It was as if she were oxygen and he was the flame, and a ball of fire engulfed them.

His hand swept down her back, pulling her closer until his zipper pressed against her belly, and she instinctively arched into him, her body demanding more even if her head hadn't quite caught up. He popped the snap of her jeans and pushed them over her hips, stripping her to her panties. The rough brush of denim against her skin warned of where they were rapidly headed.

As terrified of her arousal as she was of him, Faith tried to ease from his grasp, but the bed hit behind her knees. Thrown off balance, it didn't take more than Adrian's gentle shove to send her sprawling backward, across the comforter, leaving her exposed and naked except for a thin layer of silk. He stared hungrily as he reached for his jeans.

"We're in the middle of the Atlantic and you have nowhere to run," he reminded her as he released the snap. "By morning, you'll be my woman and virgin no more."

She ought to laugh; he said it with such a straight face, but she knew him too well to be afraid of force. It was a silly game and she had only to say no to halt it.

She was afraid to say no, afraid he would stop—equally afraid he wouldn't.

She was naked and trembling in his bed, as much the virgin as he'd proclaimed her. And there was very definitely something piratical about the way he dropped his loose jeans and stepped out of them. His black briefs weren't standard pirate fare, but they disappeared quickly, and what remained was every inch marauding pirate, holding her captive with wonder.

Had she ever looked at Tony like that? Probably not. Tony had never *looked* like that.

Adrian jerked the covers to the bottom of the bed as Faith scooted for the top at his approach. His gaze had become a physical force that scorched her everywhere it touched. Her breasts burned with the heat and rose to hard, aching crests. She was so wet she almost cried out in relief as he stripped off her last vestige of clothing. She did cry out in surprise as his hot hand immediately cupped her there.

"Virgin territory." He smirked as he joined her on the bed, trapping her with his length as he leaned over her. "You make this too easy. Want to scream in useless protest? No one will rescue you."

Screams lurked on her lips, but not of protest. Or maybe in protest, but not of the sort he meant. She needed his hands and his mouth all over her, and she needed something entirely different where he played now.

"I'll throw myself overboard," she whispered in self-defense.

"You are already in over your pretty head and sinking fast." He grinned and claimed her breast with his mouth, and she nearly shot off the bed at the sudden heat of him all over.

She was in *way* over her head.

He tugged her down until she was completely under him, pinned beneath his greater weight as he thoroughly explored her breasts with hands and mouth. She grabbed his arms and tried to pull away, to somehow touch him as he did her, and reduce him to the same smoldering ashes and aching need, but it was like tugging on tree trunks. He couldn't be moved. His knees held her captive, and she struggled to reach him, to take him, to force him to hurry.

"I apologize in advance for this first time," he murmured, raising his head to trail kisses across her jaw. "I can't hold out much longer."

Body screaming for release, she didn't argue as he shifted his knees to part her legs. Opened wide and vulnerable, she surged against him, no longer wanting to play. She wanted the real thing, craving the solidity of him inside her.

Only when Adrian reached for the condom he'd apparently taken from his pocket did Faith remember how much of the real thing she wanted. She wanted a child almost as much as she wanted sex. Adrian was willing to offer her one. She couldn't blame him for not offering the other.

"I think it will take a very long time for this ship to reach shore," he murmured in her ear, just before bending to suckle her breast.

With a small cry of joy, she arched upward, offering herself to mindless pleasure rather than hopeless dreams. Pleasure was all she needed, she told herself—a few hours of intense, mind-bending pleasure to make up for all those cold, lonely nights.

Just as she thought she would come apart without him, Adrian surged into her, and thought became a thing of the past.

He filled her until she tightened around him, and release would have come instantly if Adrian hadn't struggled to prevent it. He wanted her all night, and for the rest of his days. He didn't want to disappoint her this first time. Sinking to the hilt, he tried to stop, to rest a moment and gain control again, but Faith's inner muscles did a little dance that blew his mind, feminine murmurs brushed his skin, and soft malleable breasts beckoned. Giving up with a sigh, he pulled back and plunged deeper, making her scream as he exploded over and over, pushing her into the bed until he had everything of her he'd thought he wanted, and knew it would never be enough.

Not stopping to take a breath, he caught her mouth with his, ruined her skin with his sandpaper jaw, and filled his palms with her breasts. Her nipples were still hard, taut points, and within moments she was writhing beneath him as he teased them into aching sensitivity. As he worked his mouth downward, absorbing the splendor of her with his tongue, conquering her with his fingers, he knew he wasn't giving her time to think, time to panic, time to reject what he was and what he never would be.

They just needed time to work the out-of-control hormones from their systems, he reassured himself as she fell apart beneath his marauding fingers.

When he had taken her to the sky and back, and he was ready for her again, Adrian dug his hands into her thighs, spread them wider, and drove deep within her a second time, relishing the narrowness of the passage as he grew even harder and she whimpered in pleased surprise.

Maybe by the time he was done here, she would understand that sex could be just that—sex. A physical release, and a lot more fun than the self-torture of abstinence.

Within minutes he had her rocking to his rhythm, and her cries were ones of impatience. All that pent-up passion he'd known she possessed spilled into this act that he'd taught her.

Tony obviously had never wasted time on lessons.

As dawn lightened the draperies, Adrian blissfully inhaled Faith's delicate perfume and tugged her back against him. It had been so long since he'd had a woman, he'd forgotten how good they smelled. Even her perspiration was sweetly musky. Now, she smelled of him as well as her perfume. He wanted to rub himself all over her, mark his territory like a dog.

Except she wasn't his to claim. He glanced down at Faith's sleeping figure where she curled against him. She was built on delicate lines, but gentle muscle molded her arms and thighs. She took care of herself. Dancing across a stage several nights a week must do that.

He'd made her scream every time last night. He'd like to hear her scream a few times more. She had a lovely, musical scream, a lilting scale of tones from chirp to full throttle. He definitely wanted to hear full throttle again before dawn broke and the fantasy ended.

He hadn't needed the pirate role to be turned on, but the fantasy of having her for as long as he wanted had been good. He'd like to fantasize that she would roll over and regard him through sleepy, come-hither eyes without need of role-playing, that she would come to him readily every night. He'd like to fantasize a lot of things, but he was an intelligent man. He knew what he couldn't have.

He reached over her arm and caressed the tip of her breast. It responded instantly to his touch. She moaned sleepily as he tweaked her hardening nipple and nuzzled her nape. When she pressed her buttocks back against him, he slipped his arousal between her thighs, branding her with his heat. He could play pirate captain ravishing his victim one more time.

"I can't," she whispered in protest as he adjusted her more firmly against him.

He slid his fingers down her belly and between her legs, caressing her where she needed touching. She was definitely ready. "You can't?" he taunted, sliding one finger inside.

"Adrian!" She gasped and wriggled as he stroked deeper. "You can't—" But she lifted her leg higher at his insistence.

She was all silk and scent and too tempting to resist. He knew famine too well. He would feast while he could.

He caressed her breast again, kissed her warm shoulder, nipped her nape as she attempted to roll from his grasp. She shuddered as he held her still and rubbed against her moisture. He lifted her lovely, slender leg over his and stroked her spine, positioning her gently as he reached her buttocks and explored.

"Adrian!" she protested again, but it was a weak, breathy protest, asking what he intended more than complaining.

He wanted her in too many ways to care which way he took her. But he needed to know she wanted him.

He stroked the tight nub hidden in folds of soft flesh, readied her with his fingers, and slipped partially inside her.

"The ship has landed and you're free," he whispered in her ear.

"This time's for real, then," she murmured sleepily. To prove it, she adjusted her position and rammed down on him, impaling him to the hilt.

His thoughts went no further as Adrian accepted her offer with a lusty groan of relief, slamming into her over and over again, until they were both screaming for release.

She convulsed as he shattered inside her, pouring a flood so hot he thought he'd pass out as her muscles contracted and pumped him dry.

Only then did he remember he'd meant to pull on the last condom before he entered her fully.

Shit.

❧ TWENTY-SIX ❧

Still quivering from a night unlike anything she had ever known, Faith stepped from the shower and wrapped a thick towel around her. Adrian was already there, drying his hair, watching her intently with those dark eyes that could hold her spellbound. *Had* held her spellbound. She couldn't think of any other excuse for her behavior. Pirate, indeed!

She didn't think so much of the soreness of all those places he'd used and bruised so much as the liquid heat of her womb as he'd done so. Right this minute she had only to look at him to know she would fall into his bed if he so much as nodded his head in that direction. She turned her back to him as she reached for her suitcase.

"I want you to take the van and get out of the city."

Faith ignored that stupidity as she pulled on clean underwear. She wished he'd leave the bathroom so she could have some privacy, but it was stupid to wish for privacy after what they'd done last night. She even knew the place on his thigh where he sported a vaccine scar. "I have nowhere to go but home, and that's not any safer."

"Surely you have friends or family somewhere," he insisted.

"Other than my parents, not since Charity died." She'd been searching for security ever since. Last night had been a major aberration. Major. She didn't dare repeat it. She wanted to so much, it scared her right down to her toes. She was terrified time wouldn't change that feeling.

"Fine. I have more family than Attila had Huns. I'll send you to one of them."

She supposed caveman protectiveness acted as a substitute for anything resembling emotional commitment, or even tenderness. She was used to that and didn't expect more. She might *wish* for it, but she knew the meaning of impossible.

She fastened her bra and shimmied into an electric-blue tank top before turning to glare at her fantasy lover. He'd donned his jeans but hadn't fastened them. His unbuttoned shirt hung loosely from his shoulders, revealing way too much of the dark hairs between pronounced pectorals.

"I am a coward, Adrian Quinn Raphael. I do not like adventures. I would much rather write letters and wait for answers. But I will not let some semiliterate moron terrify me out of house and home, threaten the innocent, or otherwise terrorize my friends in my place. I will stand out in the middle of I-77 and scream until he finds me, if that's what it takes. *Comprende?*"

He threw her a black look and started buttoning his shirt. "You're certifiable. He's only after you because he figures you're weakest. Keep you out of the way, and he'll come after me. Let's give him something to think about."

"Such as?" she asked sarcastically as she pulled on gray slacks. She had assumed they would plot a new route of banks for today. She could be assuming too much.

"Only Tony or I would be interested in accounting records." He unselfconsciously tucked his shirt into his unfastened jeans. "So we have to figure whoever is tailing us is after the money."

"Fine, we'll spread a trail of money leading straight to the police station." She elbowed him aside so she could see the mirror and use the hair dryer and brush. This was entirely too intimate a scenario for her narrow world, but it felt completely natural. He'd obviously pushed her over the edge of desperation into insanity.

Maybe not total insanity. He'd been inside her in more ways than one, and knew the way her head worked as well as she knew his. She knew he was eyeing her breasts in the knit top, knew the shiver of desire lighting both their fires, and knew neither of them would act on it right now. They both knew how to set priorities. The intimacy of understanding was almost as scary as physical intimacy.

"That's actually a possibility." Without looking in the mirror, Adrian raked a comb through his still damp hair, pulled it over his shoulder to tie it with a strip of rawhide, and then leaned over to burn a hole in her nape with a kiss.

She nearly dropped the hair dryer.

"I'll stop by the apartment, pick up a briefcase, and drive slowly back to the bank where we found the money. If he's watching the apartment, he ought to be salivating by the time he follows me there."

"They won't let you into the vault without me," she reminded him.

"I don't need to get into the vault. That money stays right where it is until the cops can collect it. I just want our stalker to *think* I have it."

Alarmed, Faith turned off the hair dryer and glared at his image in the mirror. "He'll drive you off the road and kill you for that briefcase!"

"That's one scenario, I suppose, if he's stupid enough to think Tony left everything in one box. But the van is a little more substantial than the bug. It won't be easy."

"And if he doesn't drive you off the road?" she asked in suspicion.

Adrian shrugged. "He'll follow me to see what I do with it. I can have Cesar and Jim tail him as we enter the city, then I can park, and we can surround the devil. I want to know who we're dealing with here."

She reflexively swung around to turn his shirt collar down, caught herself, and stuck her hands under her armpits as she glared at him. "He could run over you in the parking lot at the bank, sideswipe you on the highway, gun you down when you stop. He could drive right by and not do anything but note where you take the briefcase. I vote we track Sandra down first."

"Sandra did not ransack the apartment." Checking the mirror, Adrian turned his collar down and shoved his hair back before stalking into the bedroom.

The king bed was a rumpled wasteland and the room smelled of sex. The sooner they got out of here, the better off they both would be. Faith grabbed a gray silk shirt to wear over the tank top and retreated to the door with her suitcase. "IHOP," she demanded. She was starving, and she didn't want him acting on any harebrained notions before they'd had time to formulate a safer plan.

She didn't know why she was worrying about the macho ape, but she was.

Adrian shoved his toiletry kit into his duffel and zipped the bag shut. She really didn't want to get involved with another man. Men expected entirely too much, and a man like this would walk all over her. She wanted to go home to her safe, sane—lonely—life.

Damn, she'd known better than to do this. One night of terrific sex and she was turning into a doormat all over again. At least she'd had terrific sex out of it this time.

When Adrian threw his bag over his shoulder and pushed her out the door, she dodged his hand and held out her palm.

"Give me the keys."

He looked at her in incredulity. "Why? We're just going to IHOP."

"You still don't have your driver's license renewed. I'll drive."

His brow drew down in a frown, but he dug the van keys out of his pocket and handed them over. He still possessed the bank keys. "You're not planning something silly like driving back to Knoxville, are you?"

"I'm not entirely certain that's silly, but no, I want breakfast." Feeling giddily triumphant over such a small battle, Faith unlocked the van door and climbed into the driver's seat. She'd never driven anything this huge. While Adrian waited patiently on the passenger side, she leaned over and unlocked his door.

"I suppose you ought to learn to drive this while I'm in it." He threw his bag in the back, slammed the door, stretched out his legs in the roomy front, and watched her with interest.

All right, she was an idiot who preferred someone else do

the driving, but she could do this. Fastening her seat belt, she plugged the key in the ignition, located the shift, and clenching her teeth, had the van running and rolling toward the exit. She'd just asserted herself—now she needed to prove she knew what she was doing.

"If your insurance check has arrived, we need to look for a new car for you. This van doesn't quite match your style." Sitting sideways against the door, arms folded, Adrian watched her maneuver the van into traffic.

"Put your seat belt on," she ordered.

"Yes, ma'am." With a grin, he sat up straight and snapped on the buckle. "You want to be the pirate tonight?"

Delight and terror shot straight up her spine. She hadn't even thought so far as tonight. "No, sir, I want to be Cleopatra, and you're Antony. I want you worshiping at my feet." She didn't think she could survive another night like last night, but she could contemplate it. She'd always been better at dreaming than doing.

She had done a whole lot more last night than she'd ever dreamed in all her born days.

Out of the corner of her eye she could see Adrian eyeing her feet with interest.

"I've been admiring those pearly toes," he said suggestively. "I think I could get into foot fetishism real easy. Yes, ma'am, worshiping at your feet could be real interesting."

Double damn. That voice of his had liquid desire pouring through her like hot syrup. She'd never been a slave to sex before, but she could see its appeal right now.

He was trying to distract her, and doing a fine job of it. "Back to business," she ordered curtly, braking for a vehicle changing lanes without warning.

"I like this chauffeuring thing. I haven't had time to admire the scenery. Wonder how many more stores they can jam onto this road before traffic explodes at the seams?" He gazed out at the wilderness of malls and shopping centers.

"I doubt if 'exploding' is the right word. Exploding implies movement. One accident, and it's instant gridlock." Easing into the right lane, she bumped across the curb into the restaurant parking lot. She'd done it. She'd driven an unfamiliar, overlarge vehicle without a single incident.

And Adrian hadn't once flinched. He was definitely a higher life form than Tony. With Adrian, she could push back, and he let her. She had only herself to blame if she didn't push.

She parked in the back where she had two spaces to maneuver into, then pocketed the keys before Adrian could reach for them. She wouldn't let him waste his life on stupid crooks. They'd think of a better means of finding their tormentor than using him as bait.

"Something tells me I've unleashed a monster," he said contemplatively as they walked toward the restaurant. "You're not going to get bitchy on me, are you?"

"I might." She opened the door before he could reach for it, and marched into the lobby, ordering two seats in non-smoking before he could catch up with her.

"Maybe *you* should have gone to law school instead of me." He slid into the booth across from her, ordered coffee, and picked up the menu, but his gaze was still on her.

She wrinkled her nose. "Never had any interest. I wanted to be a singer and an artist, in no particular order. Mostly, I wanted to be a wife and mother, with a little cottage on a quiet street with a white picket fence and neighbors I knew."

"You almost had it all with Tony." Sitting back, Adrian tried to relax, but he was sitting across from the most beautiful, intelligent, likable woman he'd known in his lifetime, after a night of incredible sex, and relaxation wasn't precisely on his mind. He didn't know what *was* on his mind because he was too antsy to think about it. He didn't want to think she'd been happy as Tony's ornament sitting in her expensive "cottage." He didn't want to think of her walking away from this table as she'd already proved she could do. He needed more time to figure out exactly what it was he wanted from her—not that he had any right to expect a damned thing.

"Yeah, well, that proves I didn't know anything." She doctored her coffee with a pink packet of stuff and an ocean of cream. "I'm wondering if Tony might not have laundered his money through some other source. If that box could only hold fifty thousand and he stole millions, he couldn't hide it all over the countryside."

Adrian sipped his black coffee, relieved at this change of subject. He couldn't handle personal relationships right now. "I never kept the books, just signed the transfers when he left memos on my desk. As best as I can piece together, he invested the escrow monies in different mutual funds and brokerages under a name other than the trust's. Then he withdrew from these separate accounts at will. I assume the D.A. confiscated all funds and recovered everything from the fraudulent accounts."

"Then the millions you supposedly stole were partially recovered?" she asked. "I didn't follow any of this since I'd assumed you were the culprit, and I had other concerns besides Tony or his office at that point."

"We had a very large estate department. Tony cultivated widows and old people with grandchildren. At the time, I thought he might be skimming a huge commission from each estate, but I assumed he did it legally. I knew about Sandra, but I didn't know how much he was pouring into keeping her. I thought the money was going into your lifestyle, and commissions would have covered that."

"He only brought home his salary." Faith played with her cup handle, not looking at him. "If he was skimming huge commissions plus stealing money, I wonder . . ."

Adrian shook his head firmly at the path of her thoughts. "He didn't gamble, and he didn't drink. I would have left if he had. The commission alone would have been enough to support Sandra if he didn't spend it on you. With the size of the missing amounts, he had to be stockpiling it somewhere. I never heard of any other woman. I don't know how he had time to balance the two of you as it is."

Faith shrugged, and Adrian caught a forlorn look in her eyes before she hid it. Tony had put her through the wringer. He'd had a real treasure in his possession, and he'd ignored it for the luster of fool's gold. Stupid, stupid man.

If Tony was that stupid . . . Bits and pieces of the kaleido-scope of memories fell into a pattern. "Tony wanted power and influence."

Faith glanced up, eyes widening. "He talked a lot about politics, but I knew we'd never have the wealth he'd need to run for the kind of office he was interested in."

"He was dabbling." Adrian slapped down his cup. "He contributed to men who encouraged his interest. He spent a lot of time in Raleigh cultivating contacts."

"He was stockpiling a campaign fund?" she asked dubiously.

"Manipulating investments so he could skim profits as well as commissions. He may even have intended to return the principle to the trusts once he'd made a killing at whatever he was investing in. He'd need a separate account and books to keep it straight, and I can assure you, the D.A. never found any. All leads led to cash withdrawals with my signature on them, my *forged* signature, I might add."

She blinked in what might have been relief. "Then . . . the person he was investing through . . ."

"Could be sitting on a chunk of cash and trying to cover his rear end."

❧ TWENTY-SEVEN ❧

"I'm sorry about your laptop, Cesar." Faith rubbed her hand up and down the icy tea glass as Adrian's younger brother dug into a sandwich. "If I had my credit card, I'd buy you a new one. And the bank switched my checking account numbers, so I don't have new checks yet. I can call Tommy and have him pick up my office laptop and bring it down here next time he comes. He has family here."

Cesar waved away the suggestion and finished chewing before answering. "It's the beginning of the school year. I don't have anything major due. I can always use my roommate's if I need it." He glanced with concern at Adrian, who was pacing up and down his mother's kitchen. "You decided it's safe to come here?"

"This asshole likes empty houses, and this place is never empty. Must be frustrating the hell out of him."

"We really need to talk with the D.A.'s office," Faith interjected quietly. "They'd have a better list of Tony's associates than we would. Maybe if we told them what we suspect, they would cooperate."

Cesar snorted, glanced at his brother, and returned to his sandwich. Adrian continued pacing.

She wanted to slap some sense into him, but she could see it wouldn't help. Adrian was convinced the D.A. harbored a grudge and a prejudice. Maybe he was right. What did she know? She was just a dim-witted housewife. "All right, don't go to the law. They're all a bunch of redneck stuffed shirts anyway."

Adrian grunted something that could have been agreement or muffled laughter.

Cesar was the one who replied. "Jim passed the info on to the D.A.'s office. They told him the case is closed. There's nothing they can do."

Well, so much for that idea. She supposed there wasn't a case unless they spelled it out for them. "All right, can you remember all the places Tony transferred funds to?" she demanded of Adrian.

He jerked a chair around, straddled it, and reached for the legal pad he'd thrown on the kitchen table. "Yep. What about you?" He started scribbling.

"I handled all our personal transactions. I'm the one who dealt with the broker. I can call and play the poor widow and ask if Tony was involved elsewhere, but I doubt if Tony even knew who I was dealing with."

"And I doubt if the guilty party would admit it." He glanced at his notes, jotted down another, and crossed his arms over the chair back. "We need account numbers. If we had those, we could go on-line with most of these places and pull them up."

"I imagine Tony kept all that information in another box. If he had time, he would have taken it with him. But if I took the keys before he could claim them . . ." Faith bounced a pencil on the table. "He still probably had numbers or something in his billfold. He had to have banked the bulk of the cash."

"We're right back where we started. We need to trap the guy who's following us and find out what the devil he wants."

Cesar finished his sandwich and wiped his mouth with a paper napkin. "Friend of mine lives out past that trailer park you told me about. He drove by last night and said there was a red Explorer in the drive."

Adrian immediately shoved away from the table and started to rise. Faith smacked his arm and pointed at his chair. "Sit right back down there. Sandra knows who you are. She won't tell you anything she doesn't want you to know."

"You're turning out to be damned bossy," he protested, but

he took his seat again. "What do *you* suggest?" he asked snidely.

"A little more respect, Mr. Macho." Faith sipped her tea and thought about it. "Chances are, if it's our mysterious broker who's tracking us, he doesn't know about Sandra. She wasn't someone Tony would flaunt in financial circles."

"Sounds like Sandra would have spent every dime Tony stole if she knew about it," Cesar commented, reaching for the refrigerator door behind his back and producing a carton of milk without getting out of his seat.

Faith grabbed the half-gallon carton as he lifted it to his mouth. "Don't do that. It's rude. I bet your mother wouldn't let you drink from it."

Cesar grimaced and glanced at Adrian. "You could have picked someone less like the women we already have in this family." He stood up to fetch a glass.

Adrian grinned briefly and looked her up and down. "I thought I'd found someone as far different as I could."

"I'm the same sex as your mother and sisters. That's all it takes. You want to live like animals, go find a cave." Unperturbed by the complaint, Faith swung around the legal pad Adrian had been writing on. She recognized most of the names and firms he'd written down. Tony liked dealing with the biggest names, whether or not they were the best at what they did. "I can't believe any of these men would have anything to do with illegal funds. If we want to believe it's anyone except Tony or Sandra ransacking our houses, then we have to figure it's someone who knows they've been doing something wrong."

The phone rang. After a silent exchange between the brothers, Cesar reached for it. Adrian scribbled abstract designs across the bottom of the legal pad.

"Yeah, she's out sick. I was supposed to call and forgot. If she's feeling better, she'll be in this afternoon." Cesar hung up, ran his hand through his badly cut hair, and glanced uncertainly at Adrian.

Adrian shot him a glare. "You shouldn't lie for them. Dolores?"

"Yeah. She was at the bus stop this morning. Someone must have picked her up."

Wearily, Adrian shoved the chair out from under him. "I suppose the boyfriend has an apartment?"

"Probably, but I don't know where it is."

Faith warred with herself about becoming involved, but she was already involved. She knew what it was like to be a confused and hurt teenager. They did stupid things, like marrying stupid men. She didn't want Adrian's little sister to go through that. "She'll have an address book. It's probably in her purse. If she took her purse, she'll still have notes jotted in her notebooks, on her desk, under her bed. She wouldn't want to lose something that important."

Adrian raised his eyebrows but didn't question. He took off for the far reaches of the house. Cesar grimaced and finished his milk. "I should be on my way to class. She's the one who's supposed to take over for me. Girls have no sense of responsibility."

"Belinda doesn't?" Faith challenged him.

He shrugged. "Okay, maybe Belinda. Sometimes. But getting pregnant right now isn't all that responsible."

"But maybe it's better if she has a life than following Adrian's route. It's hard being yourself and being there for everyone else at the same time."

Cesar shook his head. "A family like ours can't afford the luxury of being ourselves. We have to work twice as hard for everything. Dolores has to learn that."

Faith pitied the teenager faced with that attitude. Not everyone could have the brains, energy, and ability of Adrian. He'd set a difficult example to follow. Her own sister had always been the smart one in the family, the one most destined to follow in their parents' footsteps. Maybe the eldest children were blessed with more responsibility than the ones who followed. That didn't make them any better. Or worse.

As Adrian stalked into the room carrying a piece of school notebook paper, Faith stood up and snatched it away from him. "I'm going with you."

"This is none of your damned business." He tried to snatch it back, but she stuffed it into her purse.

She didn't like arguing, had never nagged in her life, had always given in to Tony and her parents and everyone else simply to keep the peace. She couldn't go back to being that cream puff anymore. She patted his chest, recognized the tensing of his muscles beneath her hand, and met his gaze firmly. "You want to keep your sister, you'll let me come with you. Cesar has to go to class, and Dolores hates you right now."

She shouldn't have been so harsh. He looked defeated and accepted her offer without further argument. Maybe it was time Adrian Quinn Raphael learned to accept the help of others.

Faith contemplated locking Adrian in the van when they located the apartment in a run-down boardinghouse on one of the city's more dangerous streets. Steam almost visibly poured from his ears as he grabbed for the door handle before she'd even parked the van.

She hastily turned off the ignition and pocketed the keys before running after him. Damn good thing he didn't carry a gun, but a man like Adrian could be deadly without any weapon other than his fists.

She grabbed his arm before he could rip open the door. "She may not be here," she reminded him. "You could be scaring the poor boy to death for no reason."

He pounded on the door instead of ripping it off the hinges.

A lanky teenager in torn T-shirt with tousled blond hair answered. He looked blankly at them and said nothing.

"Who is it, Mike?" a familiar feminine voice called from the interior.

Faith groaned as Adrian bunched the kid's shirt in his fist, shoved him backward, and stalked inside without invitation.

"Get yourself out that door this instant, Dolores!" he shouted at the terrified girl sitting on the sway-backed plaid couch. "So help me, I'll handcuff and tie you—"

"I'm not going home," Dolores replied sullenly. "I refuse

to be a slave any longer. You're back. You do it. You take care of the kids and Mama and clean the house and work yourself to death in a crummy fast-food place. I won't."

"Shut up, Adrian," Faith intruded before he could open his mouth. The boy looked terrified now that he knew who they were, or maybe because of Dolores's declaration. Chances were good that he'd never considered marriage or responsibility or anything except Dolores's rather bountiful breasts. Boys that age were like that. "Dolores, if you love Mike, you won't saddle him with the same burden you're complaining about. He needs to finish school, find a good job, and provide a decent place to live before he can even think about taking you in."

"I can live anywhere," she said sulkily, refusing to look at them. "I can work full-time. I don't need school. They don't teach anything that will help me work anyway."

"Dolores, so help me—" Adrian started across the floor, but Faith grabbed his arm and hung on.

"Adrian, listen for a change, will you?" She shook his arm to capture his attention.

He glared down at her, and when she didn't flinch or release him, he glared at the boy. The boy tucked both hands under his armpits and managed to look defiant. Both had the sense to shut up and let the women do the talking. Faith gave thanks for small favors.

"Dolores, look, you've had to grow up much too fast while Adrian was away."

Dolores snorted at the term "away" but didn't interrupt.

"You have to help him back into the swing of things. Adrian doesn't understand that you're not a little girl anymore, and that the others aren't babies you can tuck into bed at night. You're a lot more grown-up than he gives you credit for, but you really don't need to grow up this fast. You need to be cheerleading again, going to football games and parties, not working at a crummy fast-food chain. If you don't like it now, wait until you've done it to support kids and a family for a few years."

"Mike's a good mechanic. He'll make a lot of money." She

tucked a loose strand of hair behind her ear. She still wasn't looking at them, but she was listening.

"Mike could get run over by a bus tomorrow," Faith answered harshly. "Life happens. You have to be ready for it. Unless you enjoy being a burden on someone else, you need to finish school, get some kind of technical training at least. Adrian can help, once we knock some sense into his head. But right now he has a lot on his mind and hasn't been paying attention."

Dolores threw an uncertain look at the silent Mike. He shrugged and looked a lot less defiant than earlier. Not finding what she wanted there, she dared a look at Faith. "Is he coming home, then?"

Faith figured this was the time for Adrian to step in, but he remained tight-lipped, fists at his side, waiting for her to answer. She didn't have any answers.

"Actually, we could use your help a little. . . ." she said tentatively.

Adrian's eyebrows flew up, but he was obviously biting his tongue. Hard.

Dolores scowled, but she wasn't protesting.

All right, so she'd have to wing it. Trying to remember what she would have liked to hear when she'd been that age, Faith mentally rolled her eyes and tried again. Separate magnet and nails first, she reminded herself, turning to the boyfriend. "Mike, this is kind of a family thing. Would you mind if Dolores called and told you about it later?"

Treated as if he were an adult, the boy looked relieved and a little anxious as he glanced at Dolores. "You know I'll be here. You do what you need to do."

She shot him a black look and stood up. "Fine. But I'm coming right back here. I'm not baby-sitting those brats again."

Hearing Adrian's growl, Faith smiled, dropped an arm around the girl's shoulder, and practically shoved her out the door. "Thank you for listening."

Out at the van, Adrian held out his hand, and deciding she'd already tested his patience beyond endurance, Faith slapped the keys into it.

"I'm entering a monastery as soon as I figure out how to escape this nuthouse," he grumbled, flinging open the passenger door and gesturing for them to climb in.

"We'll visit." Refusing the front bench seat, Faith opened the rear door, leaving Dolores to sit with her brother. She did so, reluctantly.

"What's this all about?" Dolores demanded once the car was under way.

"Ask Faith. I'm just the dumb male here. What do I know?"

"Are your grades good enough at school that you can afford to skip today, or should we come back for you after school?" Not to be forced into anything, Faith sounded out the situation. Years of pacifying Tony had given her a few talents, anyway.

"I have a test today, but I don't see any reason to take it. I don't need school."

"She's testing your temper, Adrian, so keep it canned," Faith warned. "When I was sixteen, I decided I'd never be the beloved daughter my sister had been, and I ran away, too. Dolores probably had a better excuse than I ever did."

Dolores glanced over her shoulder with her first display of interest. "Where did you go?"

"I didn't have any money and couldn't go anywhere. I tried hitchhiking, hoping to reach my grandmother's. The police picked me up and I spent a night in jail."

Adrian hooted. "Miss Dilworth spent a night in jail? Did Tony know that? That might have shot down his political aspirations."

"Shut up, Adrian."

Dolores giggled.

"Let's get this back on track. Take Dolores back to school so she can take her test." She was winging this, interfering where she had no right, but if she couldn't have kids of her own, she might as well mess up someone else's. Somebody had to do something, and Adrian's mother didn't need this burden. Before Dolores could poker up and refuse, Faith offered the carrot. "Adrian is trying to find the guy who helped frame him and who took the money. That woman who came to your house the other night might know some things we need to know, but she won't tell us. If we fix you up so she doesn't recognize you, do you think you could help?"

Dolores blinked in disbelief. "You want me to talk to that slut?"

"Good Catholic girls don't use words like 'slut,' " Adrian said dryly.

"Shut up, Adrian," they both replied in unison, and the tension unexpectedly broken, laughter filled the van.

❧ TWENTY-EIGHT ❧

"One night of sex and you turn into a manipulating, demanding bitch," Adrian griped as they left Dolores at the high school. "And don't you dare tell me to shut up again."

"Yes, sir, Mr. Raphael, sir," Faith answered meekly from the seat beside him.

He could hear her muffled laughter and bit back a grin. He wanted to throttle her but couldn't. Her way of doing things was far more effective than his would have been.

"What the devil do you think Dolores can do with Sandra? She's a kid. She doesn't understand anything."

"She's sixteen, going on sixty, and she understands a lot more than you give her credit for. She may not react appropriately to what she understands, but she isn't dumb."

She reached over to pat his thigh, and his libido shot skyward. He'd hoped to work some of this out of his system so he could think clearly, but it was obvious thinking clearly in Faith's presence wouldn't happen in his lifetime. "I don't want the kids involved," he warned. "This is my problem. She has enough of her own."

"I hate to tell you this, but it doesn't work that way. You want Dolores to step into your mother's place, accept an adult's responsibility, then you have to treat her as an adult and let her decide if she wants to be involved in what is, after all, a family problem. It's affecting the whole family, Adrian. Can't you see that?"

He didn't want to see that. He was the eldest. He took care of things. His stepfather would have wanted it that way.

He'd felt worthwhile and useful when he was doing the providing. He felt like a piece of garbage now.

"Hell, I can't see anything clearly," he admitted. "I just want this over so I can pick up what pieces are left and go on." He wanted a hell of a lot more than that, but he'd always been a greedy, arrogant piece of shit. He knew he'd really hit bottom when he was agreeing with his worst enemies. Hell, maybe *he* was his own worst enemy.

"You're not Superman. You can't do everything. We need to find out if Tony really was diverting funds through a firm you didn't know about. We need to find out who knows about the fund. Sandra is our only starting place, unless you want to go back to canvassing banks. I need to put together those bank letters again while we're at it."

"All right, we'll go to the library. You can compose them again, print them out, and we'll take it to the copy store."

Faith seemed to relax as he gave up his plan of trapping the stalker. Maybe she cared just a little. It didn't mean anything, couldn't mean anything, but right now he needed one person in this world who didn't think he was a piece of shit. He couldn't believe he'd fooled a woman as smart as Faith, but it gave him reason to stay grounded.

Faith reformatted and repeated the letters she had drawn up earlier. While they were printing, she hovered over Adrian's shoulder, watching his on-line manipulations.

"If Tony had any accounts at these places, they're not letting me find them," he complained. "Hard to come up with a password if we don't even know there's an account."

"Ummm." She sounded hesitant. "It occurred to me that if the bad guy is Tony's broker, he could do anything he wanted with the money if he thought Tony dead and no one else aware of it."

"Now she tells me." Adrian threw up his hands in disgust and shut down the computer. "So what exactly is our agenda here? He doesn't need us if he already has access to the account."

"Maybe it's not the broker?" she suggested. "Maybe someone else knows of the account but has no authority over it?"

"And they think you do?" He wanted to sound skeptical, but that's what he'd thought when he went after her.

"They're obviously after me. They think I have *something*."

"You have the bank keys, but you're the only one who can use them."

"Unless . . ." She leaned her lovely silk-covered rear end on the computer desk and stuck a fingertip between her luscious lips, and he had to fight to keep from pulling her on his lap.

She brought him back to the real world with a sharp look. "Unless the 'he' was a 'she' and she's as good at forging my name as yours."

"Oh, shit." He slumped back in the tiny chair the library provided. "You're not suggesting that barmy little bookkeeper Tony kept—"

"I'm not suggesting anything," she said curtly. "Let's have these letters copied and devise some way of questioning Sandra. She has to know something."

"With her hair back, wearing a business suit and heels, she'll look old enough," Faith protested, pinning up what there was of Dolores's hair to show the effect.

"She's a kid!" Adrian shouted, pacing his mother's front room while various of his siblings sprawled across chairs, watching as if this were pay TV. "She looks like a kid. She doesn't know anything about investments and insurance. She'll sound like a kid."

"Act-u-al-ly," Dolores drawled haughtily, "our class invested in the stock market last year and did quite well. I bet I know more than you do about stocks."

"Considering I never owned any, you're damned right." Adrian glared at Hernando, who'd commandeered his chair. The ten-year-old giggled and scrambled up on the arm. So much for scaring some sense into anyone.

"If Sandra thinks she'll get money out of it, she'll answer

anything. I would if I had three kids to raise and their bastard of a father left me no way to take care of them."

"One should not say such words in front of the little ones," a soft voice protested from the doorway.

"Mama!" several voices yelled at once. Little Ines leaped from behind a table and raced to capture her mother's legs, nearly toppling her. The others were a little more respectful, standing to offer the best chairs in the room.

"Mama, you shouldn't be out of bed." Adrian gently took her arm and led her to the big upholstered recliner, helping her into it and covering her legs with an old afghan.

"I am not helpless," she said with dignity, sitting up straight. "I can sit here and watch my little ones, and they will look after me." She nodded in Faith's direction. "Dolores tells me you make my headstrong son behave. You will keep him out of any more trouble?"

She reduced him to the age of three with words like that. Adrian growled, but Faith dipped her head politely, acknowledging the responsibility his mother laid on her. She had no business accepting any responsibility for him, but he liked that she didn't argue with the irritating old woman.

He brushed a kiss across his mother's thin hair, and she slapped his arm. "Dolores needs a man to teach her to respect herself. You take care of her."

"Yes, Mama." With resignation, he nodded toward the hallway. "Dolores, let Faith go with you to help you choose what to wear. We'll rehearse the questions on the way out there."

Faith hesitated. "Perhaps I ought to stay here to help. . . ."

His mother waved away the suggestion. "Belinda will be here later, and Elena can start supper. There are plenty enough to help." She pointed at the twins. "You two, you should be cleaning the kitchen before your sisters arrive. Off with you now."

The boys looked tentatively to Adrian for help, but he merely raised his eyebrows expectantly. Maybe Faith had the right idea. Shouting and glaring didn't have much effect.

Maybe the silent treatment would keep them guessing. They slid off the couch and dragged into the other room.

"See, we are fine," his mother said softly. "Go with your lady. Clear up your trouble, and do not worry so much about us."

He would always worry about them. It wasn't in his nature to do otherwise. But watching Faith lead Dolores off to the bedroom, he wondered how he would train himself not to worry about Faith once this was over. She'd become a part of him he didn't want to let go, but she had another life that didn't include him, couldn't include him. She'd fare much better on her own—if he could just convince his towering ego of that.

Faith watched with jaded wisdom as Dolores bounced up and down in the front seat. Adrian had ignored her since she'd brought his sister out in her best Sunday suit, with Dolores's irregular hair slicked back and hidden in a silk scarf of their mother's. The multiple earrings had been scaled down to a sophisticated gold pair from Faith's collection, and the tattoo was hidden behind long sleeves. The platform heels were a little incongruous, but neither of them could come up with anything better. Adrian had growled something like approval, claimed the car keys, and stalked out to the van.

Faith didn't know why she should care if he ignored her. He'd gotten what he wanted last night, and obviously his concentration had returned to clearing his name. She shouldn't expect more than that. He needed to apply his attention to his family again. She wholeheartedly approved, but couldn't help it if she felt left out.

"Can Elena and I really go back to cheerleading?" Dolores pestered.

Well, they couldn't expect a teenager to behave like anything else but a teenager. Their concerns teetered between child and adult with reckless abandon. Dolores had some catching up to do on the child part.

"If they still want you on the squad, I'll see what I can do," Adrian agreed, not taking his gaze off the busy highway.

With the cost of uniforms, and travel, cheerleading was a hideously expensive sport, and that didn't count the loss of Dolores's fast-food job to keep up with it. Adrian would have to live at the pottery, painting dishes to earn just a portion of what he needed to help his family. Faith wondered about the legality of giving Tony's money to this family her husband had robbed of four years of Adrian's life. Maybe she shouldn't have so hastily locked it up in a trust.

Dolores glanced down at the official-looking printed form of questions in her lap. "What if she doesn't believe I'm an insurance agent and won't answer any of these?"

"Then you thank her politely, tell her you'll get back with her, and leave. Don't try anything smart. I don't think Sandra is dangerous, but we have no way of knowing who she's hanging out with these days."

Faith could tell Adrian hated letting his sister do this. He probably hated knowing Dolores was almost grown up as well. He'd simply learned from birth that men ought to protect their women. She'd fallen for that nonsense with Tony, and look where it got her. She'd have to straighten out Adrian's thinking.

But she had no right to straighten out his thinking, and men weren't likely to change because a woman told them to. She sat back and glared at the traffic flashing past. The sooner she removed herself from Adrian's life, the better off she would be.

Caught in rush hour traffic, it was after six before they reached the exit to Sandra's house. But they'd already discussed that. If Sandra was working, she was more likely to be home now, feeding her kids. They drove past the mobile home, noted the lights on and the Explorer in the drive, and pulled into a gas station parking lot down the road.

"I don't like this," Adrian complained.

"You want to go in and ask Sandra if Tony left her any stock accounts or safe deposit numbers?" Faith unbuckled her seat belt and opened the rear door.

"She'd probably tell me if I offered to share the results with her." With a sigh, Adrian flung open his door and glared at his little sister. "You're sure you know how to drive this thing?"

"Cesar taught me in this 'thing,' " Dolores reminded him. "And it's not even a quarter mile down the road. I may not get any answers out of that weirdo, but I can drive the van."

Climbing out, Adrian draped his arm over Faith's shoulders and watched as Dolores took his place in the driver's seat and drove off. Faith couldn't decide if she liked his high-handed presumption, but she didn't push him away. The bigger they were, the harder they fell, and she had a feeling Adrian was in for a harsh landing.

"If I buy clean sheets for Cesar's bed, will you sleep with me tonight?"

Well, so much for feeling sorry for the man. Faith headed for the gas station minimart, dodging his encroaching arm. "I thought you had to work."

"Not all night." He kept up with her easily. "And you're going with me. I'll not leave you in that apartment alone."

"I thought the apartment was safe." Actually, she was barely thinking at all. The idea of sleeping with him filtered every single thought straight through her hormones.

"No place is safe until we figure out who we're dealing with. But I had a locksmith install bolts, and we can't afford a motel every night." He halted her outside the plate-glass door, pulling her next to a towering stack of Pepsi six-packs. His face held no expression whatsoever as he stared down at her. "I don't expect anything of you, Faith. It's your choice. But the thought has been driving me crazy all day, and I wanted matters clarified so I wouldn't expect too much."

Oh, heaven help her! He was afraid she'd say no. He would actually respect her decision. He thought far more of her than she did herself.

With that realization, she rested her head against his chest and let him wrap his arms around her. As much as she valued her independence, she couldn't deny him what they both wanted, for now.

Any day now they'd clear Adrian's name and return to their normal selves. Maybe they could remain friends, distant ones, probably. But for one more night, they could be lovers.

❧ TWENTY-NINE ❦

The cement curb still held the heat of the sun's rays as they sat and sipped Cokes and watched the old van rattle into the gas station lot again. Adrian stiffened anxiously, and Faith rubbed his thigh as he squeezed her shoulders. She liked his need to touch her, and she was learning to return the favor.

He caught her hand and held it tightly against his leg as the van stopped in front of them. "I'll try not to yell," he said. "But I can't promise what will happen later tonight if I bottle it up now." He slanted her a knowing look.

She pressed his leg and stood up, brushing herself off as he rose beside her. "I'm sure Cleopatra allowed Antony his moments of passion," she answered obliquely.

She thought he chuckled, but he brushed past her to help Dolores down from the van. It was a courtly gesture that obviously pleased and embarrassed the teenager. The man had his moments.

"Coke? Hot dog?" he offered, resisting grilling her before seeing to her welfare.

"Diet Coke." Dolores nervously twisted her skirt into place, checked the scarf covering her mangled hair, and watched Adrian stride off to buy the drink.

"He's been worrying himself sick over you," Faith told her quietly. "He really hates dragging us into this."

Dolores nodded. "My father was like that. He wanted to do everything himself. He worked two jobs while Adrian was in college. They think he probably fell asleep at the wheel and that caused the accident that killed him."

Faith drew in a deep breath. The girl understood more than

243

they gave her credit for. "And Adrian still feels guilty about that, as well as everything else. We all have problems we have to learn to deal with."

"Yeah, I guess." She shuffled the toe of her platform heel and looked up gratefully as Adrian returned with the can of soft drink. "Thanks."

"All right, tell us what you've learned. I can't stand the suspense anymore." Adrian pushed Faith into the front seat first, then helped Dolores in beside her.

Faith didn't dare object. If he needed her support, she could lend it. She just had to remember that's all it was—the support of a friend.

Dolores took a big swig of her drink, then swiped her mouth inelegantly. "The woman's crazy," she declared. "Do they really let people that ignorant loose?"

Faith laid her head back against the seat and let the laughter simply roll out of her. Adrian and Dolores looked at her as if she were crazed, but she couldn't help it. Dolores had sounded exactly like her big brother. The girl would definitely be all right, given a few years to grow up.

"You could let us in on the joke," Adrian grumbled, starting the van and pulling back to the road.

"You wouldn't get it, and Dolores wouldn't appreciate it." Still smiling, she sipped from what remained of her drink. "Some men need women like Sandra to make them feel important," she told the girl. "I think they have to work at being that stupid."

Dolores nodded agreement. "Yeah, I know some girls at school like that. Mama says if a boy doesn't like you for who you are, then he's not worth your time."

"Enough girl talk," Adrian said. "Let's get on with this. What did Sandra say?"

"She filled out the form as Mrs. Nicholls. She claims the government is deliberately withholding her husband's death certificate so she can't collect benefits, but her brother has hired someone to help her get what rightfully belongs to her. He's promised to sue for the papers Mr. Nicholls's ex-girlfriend stole." She glanced questioningly at Faith. "I think that means you."

Faith made a rude noise. "She can tell it to the court."

"Anyway, she doesn't know anything about bank accounts or bank boxes or investments. She just knows Tony told her he had money and they would be rich. But then the plane crashed, leaving her to raise three kids while . . ." She gave an embarrassed shrug. "She used some impolite terms. She thinks Faith has his money and won't share."

"But she didn't say who was helping her locate the money?" Adrian demanded.

"She said her brother had hired an attorney friend of his. She came up here because they're about to 'crack the case open.' She was thinking of buying a Land Rover in place of her Explorer." Dolores said the last dryly. "But she refused to give me any names, said her brother had forgotten to tell her and she was bad about names anyway."

"Yeah, right, like she doesn't remember her own." Adrian gunned the engine onto the highway and turned toward Charlotte. Once in the line of traffic, he glanced at Faith. "Know anything about Sandra's brother?"

"Not a blamed thing, but Tony had a friend from home called Sammy Shaw. That's Sandra's last name."

"Shit, yes! That almost makes sense." Adrian gripped the wheel and glared out the windshield. "I want that clown, and I want him now."

Wearing Adrian's T-shirt, Faith sat cross-legged on the new sheets adorning Cesar's bed, trying not to look nervous as she jotted notes on a legal pad. She still felt like a fallen woman, sitting here waiting for her lover to come out of the shower. The Faith Hope she knew didn't do things like this.

She knew perfectly well that was an antique attitude, but she couldn't change who she was overnight. She had never entirely given up the idea of finding a nice man, maybe one who already had children, marrying again, and having the life she'd always thought she wanted. But it had never occurred to her, not even once, to simply take a lover in the meantime.

She glanced up as Adrian entered the room with a huge bath towel wrapped around him, toga style. Her brain slipped into neutral and all parts south revved into gear. She obviously had never met a man like Adrian before.

He kneeled on the bed and crawled over her, scattering notes across the mattress and to the floor as he steamrolled her into a prone position. "I want to worship at your toes," he told her solemnly, before backing up the way he'd come, aiming for her feet.

"If I were Antony, I'd watch out for Cleopatra's asp," she said tartly, trying to release her trapped legs in punishment for his not giving her the kiss she'd wanted.

He nibbled at her thigh, licked behind her knee, then looked up with a gleam in his eye. "I will gladly watch your ass, Your Majesty." He bent and nudged her shirt up with his nose, planting a kiss on her abdomen. "And then your breasts . . ." He nibbled higher, tumbling the shirt past her breasts so they stood erect and expectant in the cool air. "And anywhere else you so command."

By the time his mouth fastened on her nipple, she was beyond even the simplest of commands. With a cry of complete surrender, Faith didn't argue the point but succumbed to waves of pleasure shimmering through every nerve ending. If she had to settle for a lover, then choosing one who'd had four years to imagine what he'd do once he had a woman in bed had been the smartest thing she'd ever done.

By the time they'd exhausted themselves in the wee hours of the morning, Faith was too satiated to do more than roll into Adrian's arms and fall asleep. In another time and place she might have questioned her ability to do this, but not now, not tonight, not after he'd taught her more about her needs than she'd ever known. With her mind asleep, her body trusted his with the security she craved.

She woke to Adrian's lips nuzzling her nape as sunshine poured through the slits in the blinds. "They'll have to send you back to prison to rest if you keep this up," she murmured sleepily into her pillow.

"I can rest after I'm dead. I have a lot of lost time to make up." He caressed her belly, teasingly avoiding the more erogenous zones north and south. "Besides, I'm terrified that once you realize how much I want you, you'll run screaming back to the hills. I intend to take advantage of every minute I can steal."

It was nice being wanted for something besides her checkbook or secretarial skills. It was even better being wanted by a man who was so gorgeous he wouldn't even have looked at her under other circumstances. She was the one who should take advantage.

"I bet you say that to all the girls." She yawned and snuggled her posterior more securely into the curve of his hips, then yelped as he rolled over, taking her with him. She ended up sitting on top of him, facing the wrong direction. "Idiot." She tried to scramble away, but Adrian caught her waist and stroked a hand down her spine. There was only one thing she could do in retaliation, and she clasped him firmly, stroking until he bucked her off and caught her beneath him.

"Idiota," he murmured against her mouth, followed by a jumble of other phrases she couldn't interpret between mind-stealing kisses as his body joined hers and they rocked together.

She didn't know if it was deliberate or subconscious on either of their parts, but they were taking a lot of chances without protection. She couldn't stop to think in the white heat of the moment. She needed this, they both deserved this, and whatever happened, happened. For one small moment out of time, she wouldn't think, plan, organize, or worry.

Later, as they showered together and Adrian lathered her hair, smothering her with kisses before abruptly cursing and retreating, Faith knew he'd remembered what they hadn't earlier and regretted it, but she didn't. As he returned with a condom, Faith didn't complain, but held him close as he released himself into her.

Whether he wanted to or not, Adrian Raphael had gifted her with the one sweet hope she'd lost long ago.

"We have to pry more info out of Sandra." Faith lay her pen down on top of the legal pad and sipped her coffee while

Adrian took Cesar's faucet apart to stop the constant dripping. "She came to you. She must have wanted something."

"Yeah, an ex-con who hadn't had sex in four years." He grunted as the rotten washer loosened and fell down the sink.

"Don't overrate yourself. She has three kids she can't support. I don't think she's looking to make another one. She had money on the mind."

He shrugged as he scraped decades of goop off the faucet base. "Then she should have known better than to come to me."

"Look, if she thinks I owe her, she might figure you feel the same. She might think you've found a way to get the money out of me. Maybe you can even talk with her brother. They're the ones with the answers, or at least part of them. We're not accomplishing anything on our own."

He scattered Ajax over the caked grease and left it to soak as he reached for his coffee mug and finally turned his attention fully on her. "Fine, I'll visit Delilah in her lair, but if I come back with my head shaved, you've no one to blame but yourself."

"Maybe she'll shrink your ego while she's at it." Since she had no clue what he was angry about, she couldn't even begin to follow this conversation. She just knew she couldn't live like this much longer. He was messing with her mind, derailing all her goals, and making mush of her emotions. She'd be a quivering idiot all over again if they didn't find a solution soon.

"If I had any ego left after prison, you've tromped on the remains of it. It's all right, I'm getting used to it." He waved away her protests as he straddled the kitchen chair and took another swig of coffee.

"We're wearing on each other's nerves already," she said calmly. She refused to be insulted, refused to act the part of lovesick moron. "We need our lives back. That's not going to happen while we wait for banks to answer those letters. You said you'd call the D.A. personally. What did he say?"

"Just that I'd better be certain to report to my parole officer on time or he'd come after me. Face it, they won't take this seriously. I'm not part of the Establishment, and I don't count for anything more than gum on the soles of their shoes."

Faith shoved the legal pad in his direction. "Fine. Then when we crack this case, I'll bring a whole pack of chewing gum with me to the courthouse."

"You're as certifiable as Sandra, you know that?" Looking at her in disbelief, Adrian shook his head and picked up the paper. "What's this?"

"The questions you need to ask Sandra, or her brother." Faith spun her pen in circles on the table. "Considering Sandra's chronic lack of cash, what are the chances that her brother is behind the break-ins?"

Adrian glowered at her. "That's how I have it figured. I just need to break a few heads first so I can get at him." He shoved his chair back from the table and stood.

"You won't find him without Sandra's help."

"You want to put a little wager on that?" Without stopping to hear her reply, he reached for the phone and began pounding numbers.

She would have to remember that Adrian wasn't Tony in more ways than one. Tony had been even-tempered and imperturbable, seldom indulging in tantrums. When he did indulge, they exploded uselessly, damaging only her.

Compared to Tony's passivity, Adrian was a fountain of moods and emotions, but not only had he never damaged her, he'd showered her with more pleasure than she'd known in her life.

In return for that pleasure, she could tolerate quite a few temperamental fits.

❧ THIRTY ❧

Adrian sat in the darkened bar booth, nursing a mug of coffee. He'd come a long way from the night when he sat waiting for Faith to appear on stage, slowly cracking with brittle tension as his life fell apart. He was still angry, and he was still tense, but his sense of purpose had strengthened and focused. He was calm and certain and on top of things for a change, and he had Faith to thank for that.

He sipped the coffee and tried not to dwell on how Faith had turned him around. He owed the lady a lot.

The "lady" in question would tear *him* apart when she discovered what he was doing. She thought he was at the pottery. He'd left her merrily preparing a tortilla fiesta with Belinda and the kids. Jim had the night off, and his cruiser sat outside the house as a warning to Shaw or any other pervert who might think Faith an easy target. Once he reached the bottom of this little matter, she would never have to worry again. She could go back to her real life.

That was a little time bomb he wouldn't dwell on. Faith had her own life. He couldn't keep her from it any longer than necessary.

If he could actually find the evidence of Tony's crime, he had a shot at having a life of his own. He wouldn't raise his hopes to the level of what he could have if he found the money, too.

His stomach churned as he watched the woman working her way across the dance floor toward him. For whatever reason, Sandra had chosen the "country" look for this meeting—

skintight jeans, fake alligator boots, and a fringed leather shirt hanging over a spandex tank top that revealed everything beneath. Time was not kind to a figure like Sandra's.

"How ya hangin', honey?" She slid into the seat across from him and dropped her feathered ten-gallon hat on the table.

Adrian signaled the waitress and ordered a beer while fighting for a straight face. He had a feeling Sandra watched entirely too many movies and needed a real life. Tony had probably done that to her. He ought to feel sorry for another of Tony's victims, but she'd had four years to pick up and move on—as Faith had done.

"How did you recognize me?" Adrian sipped his coffee while waiting for Sandra's beer to arrive.

"Saw you at the trial, honey. I was there, in the front row. Don't you remember? I kept hoping they'd fry that little bitch of Tony's. I hated to see a man like you go to waste. I was real glad to hear from you."

He hadn't watched the audience at the trial. It had been too humiliating, and he'd needed all his concentration on the proceedings. He took her word for it now. "Well, I was sorry to hear about Tony, even if he was an elephant's ass." They'd got the preliminaries out of the way through phone calls during his prison days, when he'd convinced her Faith had the money and they could get it if they worked together. He'd been interested in evidence at the time, but Sandra's fixation had been money. He was probably solely responsible for Shaw trashing Faith's store and apartment. At the time he'd planted the seeds of suspicion in their infantile minds, it had never occurred to him that Faith might be completely innocent.

"If I had a penny for every promise Tony made me—"

"He might have kept them had he lived." He didn't want sob stories. He wanted facts. "We just need to figure where he left it. Have you come up with any new clues?"

She looked coy as she sipped her beer from the bottle and batted her lashes. Setting the bottle down, she left red stains on her paper napkin as she politely dabbed her lips. "Now, honey, we've been over this. I told you I don't know anything about anything."

"Don't play games, Sandra," he warned, sitting up straight and staring her in the eyes. She shrank back slightly, and he didn't feel guilty in the least. "All I'm after is the books. You can have the rest. Can anyone else honestly tell you that?" Of course, he was lying through his teeth, too. If he could turn that money back to the bar association and prove his innocence at the same time, he could have his license back.

But his words had their effect. She looked momentarily uncertain. Adrian gave her credit for a certain wily cleverness when it came to men and money.

She sat up straighter and wiped the sweat off her bottle with her finger. "Sam wouldn't cheat me or the kids. He's looking out for us."

"Sam? Your brother?" At her vague nod, he pushed further. "Wasn't he best buddies with Tony? And maybe with Tony's buddies?"

She looked a little startled but didn't deny it. "Sam didn't have no fancy education like Tony, but he's done good. He knows all Tony's lawyer and banker friends."

"Did he tell you he's found Tony's wife?" He was shooting in the dark, but he was a darned good lawyer. He knew his target.

He watched as Sandra's expression clouded with suspicion and fury, just as he'd calculated.

"Where is the bitch? I'll pull all that straw hair out of her head for what she's done to my boys. They've practically been starving on the streets while she lives a hog's life."

He'd have to remember to tell Faith that one. A hog's life. She'd love the irony. "I think you'd better ask your brother that. Sounds like he's been keeping a few secrets."

"What do ya mean?" She took a big gulp of the beer, nearly draining it.

Adrian signaled for another. "Did he tell you Faith is here in town?" If Sammy-boy hadn't told her Faith was in town, he hadn't mentioned she was with him either.

"Here? In Charlotte? Since when?"

He could almost see the smoke rising. He wouldn't jeopardize Faith this way if he thought Sandra dangerous. He could handle her. It was Sammy-boy he wanted to smoke out of the woodwork.

He shrugged. "Saw her at a nightclub. She doesn't look too rich. I'm wondering if Tony didn't have someone else he gave the money to, one of his banker friends maybe. She didn't look like she's benefited from it."

"Sam was Tony's only real friend," Sandra said adamantly, quaffing the new beer as soon as it arrived. "Sam introduced me and Tony back in high school. Even when Tony went off to that fancy college, he and Sam worked together. We were all just kids when I got knocked up, and none of us had any money. So Tony and Sammy put in a crop out in the back field, and when they sold it, Tony put a down payment on a double-wide for me and the baby. He always tried to do right by us."

Adrian didn't bother asking what kind of crop two men with no equipment could put in that would earn enough for a down payment on a mobile home. He knew. Marijuana was probably North Carolina's biggest agricultural cash producer, if anyone kept records. He wondered how many of those crops Tony raised and if he was still raising them when he married Faith. Tony had to have some way of hiding the payments on Sandra's dream home. The banker friend, perchance?

"Well, if Tony always tried to do right by you," he said carefully, leading her down the garden path, "then he wouldn't have stopped after he was dead. He meant for you and the kids to have something. We just have to find it. If Sammy didn't tell you about Faith, what else isn't he telling you?" Looked to him like Sammy-boy was playing a double game of some sort. Or protecting his sister from his criminal activities?

Talking obviously made her thirsty. Sandra gulped another half a bottle before answering, then slammed the bottle against the table. "That's what I'd like to know. Men are all shit-sucking turds. I've got a thing or two to ask that bastard when he gets home."

"Now, Sandra, let's be sensible." He didn't mind prying Sammy out of the woodwork, but he'd prefer it not be with knife in hand—not until he had what he wanted, anyway. "He may be trying to protect you. He doesn't know you're seeing me, does he?"

She shook her head and batted her eyelashes flirtatiously. *Wrong choice of words, Quinn,* he admonished mentally.

"Well, let's keep it that way for a while," he said nonchalantly. "I'll work at the things I know, maybe try to find out something from Faith. If you can tell me anything your brother has found out, maybe I can use it to pry information out of her."

Sandra muttered something foul and signaled for the waitress on her own. "She's the cause of all this, the whore."

Adrian didn't want to know the convoluted reasoning behind that statement. He didn't want to be stuck with Tony's drunken mistress for the night either. He pulled out his cash to indicate he was ready for the tab to stop rolling. "Well, then, she's paying her dues now," he said offhandedly, counting his remaining dollars. He had time to earn a few dollars more. He still hadn't learned the name of Sam's attorney friend, though.

"She doesn't have three kids to feed." Sandra finished off her second beer as the waitress brought the third. "She snared Tony while I was carrying the twins. He was supposed to get a fancy job after graduation, and we were gonna get married, and she came along, and wham! Claimed he'd knocked her up, and her big-shot daddy would ruin him if he didn't marry her. There's no justice in the world for people like me."

Not when they believed lying sons of bitches like Tony anyway. From what Adrian had gathered from Faith's comments, her father probably would have patted Tony on the back and politely told him to go to hell. "No justice for either of us," he reminded her. "That's why we have to look out for ourselves. If you could just remember who Sam is working with, maybe I could find out something." He shoved his wallet into his back pocket.

Sandra glared at him blearily. "Why should I trust you?"

"Because I don't want anything from you, and I have six kids at home who need feeding as much as yours do," he offered. "I need to prove my innocence so I can work again."

At this point she could either say screw him or tell him what he wanted. He didn't have the patience for more. Time was running out.

She rubbed her hand up and down the bottle and shrugged. "Come home with me and I'll give you the guy's business card."

No way, José. Adrian stood up. "I have to get to work. Give me a call if you remember, and I'll look the guy up, see if he's legit."

Seeing opportunity slip away, Sandra hastily backpedaled. "Wait a minute, honey. Don't be in such a hurry. I might have something right here." She pulled out a wallet splitting at every seam and stuffed with ten years' worth of receipts. Emptying the contents on the table, she shuffled through them until she found what she sought. "Here it is. I can't read it in this light."

The light wasn't that bad. Sandra needed glasses. Adrian scanned the name, whistled, and handed it back to her. "You're a class act, lady. I'll get back to you." He walked off before she could stuff all the bits of paper back in place and follow him.

Outside the bar, he gestured to Jim's waiting off-duty partner. He would owe a hell of a lot of favors if he ever cracked this case, but if he could salvage his license, he could repay them easily. For the first time in weeks, he thought he actually might have a chance, and excitement screamed through his veins.

"She shouldn't be driving, Hank," Adrian told the younger man. "Keep her company, drive her home, and I'll have Cesar pick you up. Be careful. Her brother apparently has a knack for growing and selling pot and may still be in the business. If there's any way you can, keep an eye on him. But if he's doing business with McCowan now, you and Jim may have a case too hot to handle."

The cop raised his eyebrows. "Mac Junior or Senior?"

"I'd say Junior is the right age and temperament, wouldn't you?"

Hank offered a profane description that suited Adrian's opinion completely. The name on Sandra's card had been Al McCowan, Jr., heir presumptive of one of the city's wealthiest bankers, groomed for success in the best schools and best society. As a teenager he'd been in more trouble with the law than any coke addict off the streets. He'd apparently learned discretion with age.

"The D.A. ain't gonna like this one at all." Hank shook his head in sympathy.

"You don't think the D.A. knew about it all along?" With a cynical shrug, Adrian walked away.

He had had no way of knowing about McCowan, hadn't seen it coming, but he should have. Birds of a feather and all that. If Tony had crooked cash, McCowan would have crooked accounts to stash it in. Last he remembered, McCowan, Jr. had a fancy office in the same bank building he and Faith had visited when they hit town. The man must have eyes in the back of his head or spies on every floor, Adrian thought, but he would wager everything he'd ever earn that Junior had known the instant he'd walked through that door with Faith in tow.

Damn, but he was a stupid shit. Why had he dragged Faith into this?

There was no way on God's green earth that McCowan was helping a nobody like Sam Shaw for altruistic purposes. They had joint goals, and chances were good, once they were accomplished, Sam Shaw wouldn't be the beneficiary. Neither would Sandra. Men like McCowan didn't survive by dispensing charity.

Men like McCowan didn't dirty their hands by trashing apartments and terrorizing people either. That had to be Shaw's work. Tony certainly had kept lovely company.

He needed to talk this out with Faith. She knew Tony better than anyone.

He couldn't mix Faith up in dangerous company.

Shit and hellfire, he wished he could call out the National Guard. Instead, all he had for backup was a half-dozen siblings and half the potters in the state.

Would David have tackled Goliath with a pot shard and a taco?

❧ THIRTY-ONE ❧

Faith listened as the back door to the Raphael home quietly opened and shut. She'd recognized the knocking motor of Cesar's van as it pulled into the drive, and she sat up in bed to wait for Adrian's appearance. Something was wrong. She'd known it the moment Adrian hadn't taken her to the pottery with him but left her here instead. She assumed it had something to do with finding Sam Shaw, and Adrian's determination to solve this problem on his own.

She should let him. It wasn't any of her concern. She flatly refused to be responsible for anyone else ever again.

But she couldn't help worrying.

When he didn't immediately come to her, she debated lying down and going to sleep. To hell with temperamental men anyway. Who needed them?

But she'd never sleep unless she knew what was wrong. What if it affected Dolores or Cesar or one of the other kids? Adrian didn't have the right to risk them. She couldn't live with herself if anything happened to them, not after understanding what Tony had done by cheating Adrian of his livelihood. If she'd known at the time, she would have turned Tony's money over to the Raphaels. Of course, back then she'd thought Adrian guilty as hell and hadn't known his family existed.

Creeping down the hallway so as not to wake anyone, she found Adrian sprawled on the living room couch, shielding his eyes against the pale glow of a table lamp as he scribbled on a notepad. She wondered if he'd taken up her habit of jotting down mental notes or if he'd always done that.

"Where's Cesar?" she asked, deriving some satisfaction from startling him into dropping the pen. She'd thought Cesar would sleep on that couch, and that she and Adrian would be returning to the apartment. They couldn't share a bed here.

"Studying, I hope." He picked up the pen again and avoided looking at her.

"Don't think so." She shoved his long legs aside and sat down. She'd never particularly thought of herself as capable of doing anything so shamelessly familiar with a man she'd only known a few weeks, but Adrian had stripped her of any veneer of shyness or reserve she might once have possessed. "Jim called and Cesar took off like cannon shot. Something's up."

He shrugged. "They have lives. It was Jim's night off. They're probably playing pool."

"Jim picked Belinda up at nine. Cesar didn't come back. You're here and not at the apartment. Something's going down and you're not telling me." She didn't even bother disguising it as a question. She wasn't a fool, and she wasn't playing one again.

He dropped the notepad on his stomach and glared at her impatiently. "Look, I'm taking care of things, all right? I've fucked up your life and now I'm going to fix it. We'll go car shopping in the morning, and then maybe in a day or two you can have your life back. That's what you want, isn't it?"

His voice should have sounded challenging or belligerent or even offhand, but she heard only weariness. She didn't need to see his features to know the pain etched across his forehead. His hair had come half undone, and it spilled in a black shadow over the pillow he leaned against. They were sitting on a shabby couch in an aging house, surrounded by the signs of poverty, and he was throwing their differences in her face. Something was definitely wrong.

Afraid it might be personal rather than caused by Tony's screw-ups, she shied away from discussing his problems openly. If she stuck to what she knew best, he couldn't hurt her. "I despise lawyers," she said calmly. "They're all conceited asses. I probably only went to bed with you because you're not a lawyer any longer. But you're still a conceited ass. So, sue me. I don't need this or you or anyone anymore."

She stood up and walked toward the doorway into the hall.

"Faith," he said wearily.

She halted but didn't turn around. She didn't even know if she'd meant what she said. She was too confused to care.

"I'll do whatever it takes to get my license back," he warned her. "You've known that from the first."

She nodded. "Yeah, but for a while there I thought maybe you'd turn into a human being. My mistake." This time she walked out without stopping.

"She's a sloppy drunk. Told my partner all about how she'd been wronged and she couldn't trust anyone and all men are evil," Jim reported through the phone wire.

Adrian leaned wearily against the kitchen counter and nodded at the receiver. "Yeah, been down that road, heard that song. What else?" He wished he was a smoker, but growing up, he could never afford cigarettes. And it was too early for a drink. Besides, alcohol wouldn't cure what was ailing him.

"He says Sammy came home around midnight. He and she had a shouting match that should have woke the neighborhood. Since no one called in a domestic report, I assume the neighbors have heard that before, too."

"Guilty parties don't report guilty parties. So she must have told him she saw me and knew about Faith. Wish I'd been a bug on the wall." Adrian checked the kitchen door to be certain it was closed. He'd seen the kids off to school. The last he'd seen of Faith, she'd been with his mother. That was always a dangerous sign.

"Yeah, well, she didn't throw Sammy out on his ass. The truck's still there." On the other end of the line, Jim hesitated. "You know, Adrian, if this goes down the way you say, heads will roll. I could make detective, or I could get kicked out on my ass."

"I know." Adrian rubbed his forehead. "And with Belinda expecting, you can't take chances. I understand. We have to steer clear of the D.A. with this one, if there's any chance he's involved or even suspects who's involved. You and your buddies lay low, okay? Feed me what you can, and I'll take it from there."

The door opened and Faith propped her shoulder on the doorjamb, crossing her arms and watching him impassively. He didn't want her looking at him as if he were nothing or nobody. He'd almost rather she came at him with a knife than behave as if they'd never crawled naked all over each other.

He hung up the phone and reached for his coffee. "Did you and *mi madre* have a good chat?"

"Somebody from church is coming over to take her to the doctor later. She has a pretty healthy support system here."

"With nobody to rely on for four years, she had to do something," he said cynically, sipping his coffee.

"Go to hell, Quinn." She stalked into the kitchen and poured coffee for herself. "If I'm not of any more use to you, I want to go home."

"Not with Sammy on the loose. I have somebody following him, but Knoxville's too damned far away to keep an eye on you."

"You found him?" she asked casually, stirring sugar into the cup.

He knew better than to take the casual tone at face value. "He's staying with Sandra. Not a hard one." For emphasis he added, "He drives a pickup."

"So, you're figuring Sammy is the one who drove us off the road and trashed my shop and apartment?"

"I figure it's about his speed, yup." He didn't offer more.

"And you think he's trying to find out where I'm hiding Tony's money so he can give it to his sister?"

"Yup," he said noncommittally.

"Which means Sammy doesn't know where Tony hid anything either, so he's a dead end."

She said that entirely too brightly for his own good. Adrian put his cup down. "Yup. So, are you ready to go car shopping?"

"Are you planning on buying Sammy off with the fifty thousand so I can go home?" she asked with wide-eyed innocence.

Except there was nothing innocent about a tortured mind

like hers. Adrian knotted his hands into fists. "Don't push me, Faith. You've done everything there is to be done. Now, we just have to sit back and wait. If there are more deposit boxes out there, we'll find out once we get answers to our letters. In the meantime, I'll handle Sammy."

She slammed her cup down, leaned her hands on the table and glared at him. "If you won't go to Sandra and find out the name of her attorney, I will."

He'd wanted her to break out of her polite little box and unleash the passion she hid, but he hadn't counted on that box concealing an iceberg that could freeze him in his tracks.

Maybe he should be grateful for her reserved upbringing.

He had no such reserves to call on. If he touched her, he would find better ways of shutting her up than arguing.

"I can deal with Sandra. The two of you are better off not meeting." He knew he picked at a raw wound, but he couldn't think of any better way of distracting her.

"And I'm beginning to think it's time we did just that. Ignorance is not bliss. It breeds anger, distrust, and hatred. You either introduce me to Sandra or I'll introduce myself." She didn't walk out, but waited for his decision.

"Don't do this, Faith," he said softly, grasping for some way of defusing the situation. "I got you into this, much to my regret. Give me a chance to get you out."

"No." She straightened and started for the door.

"What do you mean, *no*?" he shouted after her. "You don't have a choice."

She swung around and her hair bounced with her. She brushed at it unconsciously as she glared at him. "I spent too many years letting a man *take care of things*. To hell with that. From now on I take care of things on my own. I don't need you."

She looked like confectioner's spun sugar icing, too pretty and delicate to touch. He wanted to lick her all over and gobble her up like a child deprived of Easter candy. He'd never possessed anything quite so lovely and desirable. Always, he had been content turning his valuables into cold hard cash. Had it been his, he would have sold her priceless clair de lune long ago, right along with a piece of his soul. She was right to tell him to go to hell. She just didn't realize he'd gone there on his own a long time ago.

"I've already talked with Sandra," he answered reluctantly. He couldn't stop her. He had nothing left to lose.

Her fingers dug into the woodwork but she didn't leave.

He freshened his coffee and sat down. He'd be damned if he let her push him into anything he hadn't thought about first.

She brushed by him to pick up her cup and refill it. Instead of sitting down, she popped toast into the toaster. "When? Last night?" she asked with a measured tone that seemed entirely too accusing for his state of mind.

"Yeah." She had no right to make him feel guilty about meeting Sandra without her. Faith wasn't his wife. She wasn't even his girlfriend. They had no claim on each other but a couple of nights' worth of fantastic sex.

Apparently reaching the same conclusion, she didn't comment on his behavior. "What did you find out?"

"That we're in way over our heads, and I want all of you out of it now. I'm the one who stands to gain or lose on this deal, so I'm the one to handle it."

She leaned the lovely curve of her hip against the counter as she worked his words through her formidable brain. Adrian didn't bother trying to read her mind. He'd rather look at the way her shirt clung to her unfettered breasts. Faith liked silk, apparently. And she must like teasing him into a constant state of arousal by not wearing anything under it.

The toast popped, and she threw it on a plate and carried it to the table. "You're saying someone could get hurt or go to jail, aren't you?" She sat down and reached for the jam. "That means someone out there is either dangerous, powerful, or both. I don't understand why Tony wanted that kind of power."

"Because Tony was a jerk. It's probably too soon, but you ought to call Annie and see if you've received any reply for your request for a death certificate."

She carefully spread the jam to the edges of the toast. "You aren't certain Tony is dead, are you?"

That worry lingered in the back of his mind all the time. "He was playing in some pretty deep waters. He could be very dead. Or he could be hiding." There, he'd said it. She would have thought it anyway.

She nodded. "Wonder if my attorney would consider continuing the divorce proceeding when the other party is presumed dead?"

He grunted. With anyone else, he might have laughed. The idea of Faith still being married to Tony was not a laughing matter, however. "He could serve papers to the grave site if there was one."

"Let's not borrow trouble. Unless you have some evidence he's still alive, I'll just keep trying for the death certificate. You don't have any such evidence, do you?"

That, he could honestly answer. "Nope. I'm pretty much figuring Sammy is behind the break-ins. If his brains are as fogged as his sister's, threatening people locked in a bathroom is right about his speed."

"And driving people off the road is something he's seen on TV. He thinks we'll just pop back to life after being flattened, like Wiley Coyote. Got it. Stupid is dangerous, but not powerful. Where does the power come in if Tony's dead and Sammy is stupid?" She waved her half-eaten toast in the air. "No, don't tell me. Heaven forbid that you should tell me anything. Let me guess—Tony's power broker, his investment banker, his partner in crime. Tony latched onto someone as crooked as he was. Charming."

Adrian clenched his jaw and said nothing. If she kept it up, she'd have the whole thing worked out, right down to McCowan. Maybe while she was at it she could tell him what to do about the bastard once she did. Without evidence, his hands were tied.

She chewed thoughtfully, sucked a stray piece of jam from her finger, and drove Adrian's blood pressure straight through his eardrums. How the *hell* did she think he could concentrate when she did things like that?

"This crook must be big enough to be untouchable." She narrowed her eyes over the rim of her cup. "It doesn't make any difference. Once we find all the boxes and have Tony's books, they'll prove your innocence. If we're lucky, they'll also prove who the guilty parties are. We only have to wait. So, what's your problem?"

He had more problems than he wanted to count. This one, though, was hers as well as his. "My problem is that Sammy and friends don't know if we have access to those boxes or any other evidence that might implicate them. My problem is that they may choose to off us rather than speculate."

"*Off* us." She leaned back in the chair and rolled her eyes. "*Off* us? Is that something you learned in criminal school?"

"Yeah, right up there with how to strangle annoying females." He shoved away from the table and stood up. "Now, we're going car shopping. Unless you have any better ideas?"

"Off the bad guy first," she whispered softly.

❧ THIRTY-TWO ❧

Off the bad guy first. It had sounded brave when she said it. At the same time, Faith knew how stupid it was.

She waved her hand to indicate erasing what she'd just said. "I mean, we have to go on the offensive. We have to nail the sucker."

Adrian paced the narrow floor as if he'd rather be anywhere else, but somehow his problems had become hers, and neither of them would sleep at night until this was over.

When he started smacking his fist into his palm, she thought she ought to be concerned, but the more he boiled, the more she cooled down. His fury provided impetus. Her calm added focus. Crazy, but it worked.

He dragged out a chair and straddled it. She slathered jam on a piece of toast and handed it to him. Savagely, he tore into it.

He hadn't shaved this morning, and beard stubble darkened his jaw. His hair still hung half loose, and in the morning sun his earring sparkled against his brown skin. He should look like a dangerous criminal, but Faith's heart did a little jig of joy just watching him.

Finishing her toast, she let Adrian have his anger. He had a right to it. Just as she had a right to do what she thought best for herself. What an *adult* attitude. She might never manage a relationship again, but she finally had her head on straight.

He growled, drank his coffee, and polished off his toast. "You really can't do anything," he reminded her. "I grew up in this town. You didn't. You don't know the political ropes."

"If we were actually talking politics, I imagine I could out-think the entire city council in my sleep, but I assume we're talking a different kind of political rope?"

He shrugged. "Semantics. Ropes are ropes. They'll hang you no matter what you call them. This isn't your fight, and I don't want you hurt."

So, maybe he hadn't come quite as far as she had in interpersonal and personal development. She felt qualified to teach a college level course. "Let's get this straight one more time, Quinn." Teacher to student, that was the tactic. "Someone 'offed' my car, my apartment, my shop, and terrorized my friends. They damned near killed us. I'm involved. I'm staying involved. And you have no power to change that."

"Even if I tell you who else is involved, you won't understand the implications," he insisted. "You still believe the cowboys in the white hats always win."

"I will wear whatever color hat it takes to win," she said coldly. "I will not take this lying down. Besides, whoever you're afraid of is thinking I'm a big zero and isn't even worrying about me."

"Then he sure the hell doesn't know you." Giving up, he drained his cup. "My money is on a guy called Al McCowan, Jr. Know him?"

Faith grimaced. "Porky. Sweats a lot. You'd think, with his money, he could afford a good daily workout in a gym."

He sighed in exasperation, then jerked up straight and glared at her. "You're putting me on, aren't you?"

She grinned. "You're listening at last! Score one for the hottie in the earring."

He choked on his last piece of toast, swiped his mouth with a napkin, and visibly restrained himself by clenching the chair back. Faith smiled sweetly and waited for him to calm down. Given the slow heat lighting his eyes, she didn't think it was anger skyrocketing his blood pressure this time. She really, really liked turning him on.

"I'm not going to live through this, am I?" he asked rhetorically. "All right, so what *intelligent* things do you know?"

"He's a lazy pig. His daddy isn't a bad man, just kind of busy and distant. But Junior cheats at golf, likes cheap blondes and changes them as often as he does cars, and has poor personal care habits," she finished primly.

"You heard this from Tony?"

"No, from the women at the country club. What do you think they do while sitting around the pool and bar all day?"

"Gossip," he said with disgust. "And not even relevant gossip. Knowing Junior is a pig gets us nowhere. And he isn't fat, just well-padded."

"For your information, since you haven't bothered telling me, I'm trying to figure out why Junior would care if Tony or you fried in hell. It doesn't make clear sense. Junior's father practically owns Charlotte. If Piggy needs cash, he sells something. If he wants power, he has it."

"McCowan is the lawyer Sammy 'hired' to help Sandra." Adrian sat back and waited for her to take that in.

She widened her eyes thoughtfully. "That's definitely not the act of a sane man. Junior must be running scared over something."

"And that something would have to be us. You were perfectly safe until we showed up at the bank."

McCowan, Jr. Faith shook her head in disbelief. "He was the VIP waiting outside your friend's office that day. He saw us together." She thought about it a moment longer. "He was a golfing buddy of Tony's. They both went to UNC. Junior could have afforded Duke, but my impression was that he didn't like exercising his brain, and it was easier being the rich frog in a poor pond."

"Tony was growing pot with Sammy while in college." Adrian dropped that little bombshell into the waters as if testing her.

Faith stood up and poured the coffee dregs from the pot. "He said he went hunting. I knew that was a lie. Tony didn't like dirtying his hands. I figured he was studying but didn't want to admit he needed to spend so much time with his books. I think I must have been insane back then."

"Just very, very young." Adrian leaned back in his chair and caressed her hip.

Faith almost dropped the coffeepot. She wasn't used to

these casual touches. She could get used to them real easily. Taking a deep breath, she tried to ice her hormones while repressed desire licked hot flames under her skin. "Anyway, I can't see him growing pot any more than hunting. I'd wager he went out and chose the fields, brought Sammy the equipment and seeds, and let Sam do the real work."

Adrian waited until she had the pot on the burner and the coffee dripping before he hauled her down on his lap.

As if she'd done this every day of her life, Faith wrapped her arms around his neck and snuggled against his shoulder, soaking up the closeness. This was much better than snapping at each other. She liked a man who understood that. "You can do what you will with my body, but you can't have my soul," she quoted mockingly in his ear.

"What the hell would I do with your soul?" He kissed the skin above her scooped neckline and cupped her breast.

Faith smacked him and fought free of his grip. "You're not talking me out of this. If Junior is our guilty party, I'm nailing him to the walls of City Hall." She retreated to her side of the table and sat down.

"Without whatever evidence Tony hid, we can't do anything but stay low. I have friends keeping an eye on Sammy and Sandra. I'll make a few phone calls and see if I can find out what Junior's up to these days, but my sources at that level have pretty well dried up since my recent incarceration." He said that dryly, but anger rippled behind it.

"Junior must know there's evidence out there and that we have access to it," Faith insisted. "Without Tony to connect them, he wouldn't come within a two-state distance of the Shaws. Why the Shaws?"

Adrian tapped the table with the sugar spoon. "Because they know there's money out there somewhere, and they're blackmailing him for a piece of it?"

"Junior could give them his pocket change, and they'd be happy."

He reached back to the counter, grabbed the coffeepot, and freshened her cup before filling his. "Not if Sammy had some inkling of how much was involved. We're talking millions,

Faith. Tony might have emptied the trust accounts to a tune of one million, more or less, but the profits he could have reaped on that money in a bull market are tremendous. With his father's position at the bank, Junior would have had access to tons of confidential SEC information he could use illegally to bump that even higher."

Faith whistled. "I hadn't thought of that. Junior couldn't allow his name on an account like that or federal regulators would have his scalp. Even if the account was in Tony's name, I bet Junior couldn't be listed as broker with those kinds of transactions going on." Faith choked on her coffee as another thought occurred to her. "Sammy? Would they have put the account in Sammy's name?"

Adrian straightened his long legs under the table and rubbed her ankles with his toe. He was barefoot. "Pin the tail on the donkey. I'm amazed they didn't pin it on me."

"What makes you think they didn't? If they forged your name on some of those transactions, they could have forged it on anything. Tony would have had your social security number from payroll records. You could be sitting on a few million."

Adrian thought about it, but shook his head. "Too risky. If I ever discovered the account, I could walk out with it. If I were in Tony's shoes, I'd set up a simple trust account with myself as executor, Sammy as beneficiary, and McCowan's bank as the financial institution. Keep it simple."

"Then Junior and Sammy would be scot-free. Why would they need me?"

"Unless they figure Tony kept memos or written records of other transactions up until the point he disappeared. I imagine he did, but Junior wouldn't worry about them while Tony was alive, because they'd implicate Tony as well. It's after Tony fell out of the sky that things got sticky."

"Maybe some of the money was still there when Tony died," Faith said softly, thinking fast. "Would Junior keep paying Sammy?"

"Probably not. Junior and Tony probably played it cool

during the trial, maybe even moving all the cash out of the fund to somewhere safe. That would have cut Sammy off."

"The money we found could have been part of that?"

Adrian nodded. "Could be. Neither of them would trust the other. They may have paid Sammy off, told him the game was over, but he wouldn't have had any idea how large the pot was. Even with Tony buying Jags and Junior burning it on coke, they'd still have a substantial investment, mostly in stocks."

"My God!" Faith dropped her cup to the table. "That's it! No one keeps their stocks in safes anymore. They're always kept through a brokerage house. But if they wanted the brokerage account closed without losing their gains . . ."

"They asked for the stock certificates," Adrian finished for her, excitement lacing his voice as he thought out loud. "The certificates would have been in the name of the trust fund, of which Tony was executor. Only he could sign them."

"They might even have split them, Junior tucking half away somewhere safe, Tony tucking the other half—"

"In his deposit boxes!" Adrian leaped up and paced rapidly. "We could still recover some of that money! If the stocks have gone up in value over the last four years, I could get my license back. Those boxes could have the evidence on Junior, the books we need to prove Tony's involvement. . . ."

"And you're right, Junior would kill us before he let us have them," Faith said flatly.

❧ THIRTY-THREE ❧

"I can't let the band down. I have to be there tomorrow. It's a perfect setup!" Faith protested.

Grimly, Adrian strangled the steering wheel. "I will not let you set yourself up as a target for desperate men. That's *insane*. I'll simply corner Junior in his office, tell him I have Tony's share of the stock, that I'm turning it over to the bar association, and that I'll happily turn his over as well, no questions asked." He knew perfectly well there were enough holes in that solution to drive a semi through, but he hadn't come up with anything more solid yet. He was working on it.

"That doesn't give you any *evidence*. I'm not letting that bastard go free. Pigs belong in sties, and that's where he's going. He could be sitting on millions in stock!"

"Or he could have forged Tony's signature and sold them all." Adrian swung the van into a used car lot. Despite Faith's death wish, she had to have a car to go back to Knoxville once he solved this mess.

"He would have a lovely time taking a check made out to Tony and cashing it," she said dryly. "I can see the scenario now—a check for a few million, made out to a dead man, and Piggy Junior walking up to a teller and asking for cash with a forged signature on back. Or depositing it in his own account with a forged signature. Even Senior would have a problem with that many millions suddenly bloating his son's pockets."

"He wouldn't be that dumb. As soon as Tony went south, Piggy probably dumped the certificates into a new brokerage account, putting their joint names on it. Once Tony popped off, he probably had a coke-snorting celebration."

Adrian parked the car in front of the sales office, but Faith slammed out of it before he could come around and get her. She was striding in the direction of a cherry-red Mazda before he caught up with her. It wasn't precisely the Miata she craved, but it was a sporty piece of junk.

"A joint account with Tony would implicate Piggy," Faith insisted. "Once Tony conveniently turned up dead, McCowan might have regretted not taking the risk, but it would have been too late. Tony's death was splattered all over the papers. He was stuck with stock certificates in the name of a trust that didn't exist, and which could only be signed by a dead man. Poor baby." She peered in the driver's window at the odometer, wrinkled her nose, then checked the price tag. With a shrug, she scanned the rest of the lot.

Adrian read the specifications on a dull green older model Tercel. Faith walked right past him, heading for a sporty black Celica. Rolling his eyes, he followed her. She was smart. She'd figure out the price differential sooner or later. "This is all pie in the sky," he told her. "We know McCowan's involved, we don't know how, and we can't act until we have concrete evidence. Going out on stage and inviting trouble is not an option."

"I'm not spending the rest of my life waiting for something to happen." She ran a loving hand over the shiny hood and sighed at the price sticker.

Adrian could see a salesman loping in their direction. He debated donning his most ferocious stare and driving the dork, quivering, back to the office, or letting Faith lead the man around the lot by his nose. He could see this was one of those relationship things couples had to work out. Except he and Faith weren't a couple. If he didn't get his license back, he didn't have a chance of even considering anything remotely permanent like coupledom. He didn't like the way his hopes—along with other body parts—shriveled at that thought.

"I'm just looking," Faith said vaguely as the salesman introduced himself. "I don't know what I want yet."

The salesman turned his full-speed monologue on Adrian.

"I can see the lady likes the sporty models. Give me a price range. We've got—"

Adrian crossed his arms and leaned against a hulking SUV. "The lady's the one with the money. I'm just her driver."

The salesman faltered, and Adrian thought he heard Faith snicker, but she stayed at her appointed task without regard to either of them.

Given Faith's determinedly dismissive attitude and Adrian's passive one, the salesman gamely tried a different approach. "Perhaps you prefer high performance? We have a—"

"The lady prefers small, red, and cheap. Far be it from me to advise her otherwise."

Faith swung around and said with a perfect deadpan expression, "I like them pretty, but reliable."

The heat of her gaze rolled over Adrian like a tide of lust. Pretty! He ought to slap the woman silly. He aimed for dangerous, and she thought him pretty. And reliable. She wasn't talking about a damned car. She wasn't even looking at cars right now. The challenge in her eyes was unmistakable.

"You like them cheap and used," he countered, "not to mention useless. Heaven forbid that you should fall for something fast and powerful."

Her eyes lit dangerously as she sauntered toward them. The nervous salesman backed away. Maybe the man wasn't a total dork.

"Um, we have a small BMW. . . ."

Okay, he was a total dork. Lifting himself from the SUV, Adrian caught Faith's elbow and stalked toward a Volvo wagon. "Practical," he asserted.

The salesman hurried to catch up. "Might I suggest—"

Spotting a flash of color, Faith crossed the parallel line of cars to the next row. Adrian didn't let her loose. They left the salesman behind, stuttering and shrugging.

She admired a candy-red Mustang convertible. "I like the color."

"Yeah, it looks good on blondes. Cut it out, Faith. You can buy a cheap piece of junk to spite me if it makes you happy, but I won't let you go out on stage tomorrow with Sandra and

Sammy and company in the audience. Not without half the police force present."

"I'm tired of being practical!" she shouted, pulling her arm free. "I've spent my whole entire life being practical and where has it got me? Trapped in a hopeless situation with another damned egotistical lawyer! I'll ask Headley if he needs some company and go stay with him so you won't feel *responsible*."

She headed back toward the van, apparently having exhausted all the pretty colors in the sprawling car lot.

He ought to get angry, but he couldn't. If she felt half as torn as he did, she had a right to her own share of anger and grief. He should never have pushed her into a relationship on top of everything else.

But he couldn't have done any less.

Sighing over the contradiction, Adrian caught up with her, grabbed her by the waist, and kissed her until both their heads should have spun off their shoulders and into outer space like incandescent balloons.

She gasped and leaned into him when he finally set her down. "You're a bastard, you know that?"

"Yeah, but Rick adopted me, so I'm legit now." He stroked her silken hair and thanked God for sending this miraculous woman to prove he hadn't been forgotten. Maybe he ought to go to mass this Sunday. "Maybe we should be looking at Humvees," he admitted wryly.

"Only if they have cannon barrels and laser guns and come in yellow." She straightened, brushed nervously at her hair, and looked at the ground rather than see if anyone had noticed their public display.

Adrian chucked her chin as he recognized her ostrich tactic. "There isn't a customer on the lot but us. All the salesmen are watching through the plate-glass window, probably with cell phones in hand, hoping to be the first one to call 911 when I strangle you."

She chuckled and wiped discreetly at the mascara beneath her eye. "At least then you'd be safely in jail and out of my way."

He shuddered as he held her lightly. "I never want to be

that helpless again. Don't wish it on me in the name of safety."

He realized what he'd said even before she lifted her chin and glared at him.

"Bingo," she taunted.

"Shit." He released her, jammed his hands in his pockets and scanned the car lot. So, they had an equal dislike of being helpless. That didn't mean she should be the one to risk her neck. "No safe, practical SUV either? It's gonna be full speed ahead, fire engine red alert?"

"What can anyone do to me in a bar?" she demanded. "And I'll have one of Jim's police buddies drive me home, if that makes you happy. I'm not totally foolhardy."

"If you insist on doing this, I insist on being there. And I'll fill the place with Jim and Cesar's buddies and anyone else I can find."

"It's just Sandra and Sammy," she protested. "Sandra might get drunk and come after me with a knife, but you don't think she'll get far, do you? And Sam isn't likely to risk his neck in front of witnesses. I don't know what you're so worried about. I just want to shake things up and see what falls out."

"You want Piggy to fall out." Spotting a gleaming black Amigo, Adrian sauntered in that direction. He fisted his hands in his pockets and fought to hide his fear. He didn't want her hurt. He wanted his license back, and he didn't want to go to jail again, but more than either, he didn't want her hurt.

"It's an SUV!" Faith objected as she discovered the target of his interest.

"It's a four-wheel-drive truck," he corrected. "It could get you over the mountains even in winter."

"I don't drive—" She shut up and slanted him a curious look.

He couldn't say it, wouldn't even hope it. He left it hanging there. He very much wanted her to come over the mountains this winter, even if he was flipping damned hamburgers. He'd never ask it of her, though.

"It's cute," she said reluctantly, peering into the cab. "It's not a great big *monster* SUV."

He figured she was pacifying him now, but that was better than arguing. Maybe he'd get the hang of this relationship business one day.

"Maybe we should look at pickups?" he suggested. "They're cheap."

"I like the idea of a backseat, even if it is a wee little one." She tested the driver door, and finding it unlocked, climbed in.

The salesman hurried toward them again.

Adrian checked the sticker price, grimaced, and wondered if Rex would advance him a few thousand on his salary. Or maybe he could talk Juan into a percentage share of his profits. He knew damned well Faith couldn't afford this thing, and that he would do whatever it took to buy it for her.

"I don't know how you talked him down." Faith fretted at a loose thread on her shirt cuff. "It's not a new car with hidden kickbacks and bonuses on it."

Adrian steered her shiny black Isuzu Amigo through the evening streets toward downtown. They'd spent another night at his mother's house while Cesar and friends watched the Shaws. He'd almost reached a point where he could imagine pulling the damned car into a dark alley to discover what sex was like in bucket seats. He thought he'd left these sex fantasies behind in prison.

"I just gave him a price comparison of available alternatives at other dealers. It's near the end of the month and they're wanting to clear out inventory. When you're poor, you learn how to bargain."

"I've been poor," she said dryly, wiping a speck of dust from her new dashboard. "I never talked a car dealer down that much."

"Yeah. That's why you drove a VW." He added a note of scorn to sound convincing. Good thing she seemed to have forgotten that lawyers were often actors.

"Well, thank you—I think." She glanced at him in the driver's seat. "But I really think you should have let me drive."

"I want to be certain it handles right. After all, it has forty thousand miles on it." Besides, if anyone followed them, he wanted to know about it. He had occasional visions of he and Sammy and Cesar following each other around in perpetual circles like some Three Stooges comedy.

"It's not any taller than the van," she said dubiously, still trying to convince herself she'd done the right thing.

"But it's much safer than the VW," he reminded her.

"And it will hold more." Lovingly, she patted the tall bucket seat while checking out the rear one.

Had his acquisition of the SUV been the only cause for debate, he would have breathed a sigh of relief at Faith's acceptance, but it wasn't. She wanted to make herself a target for desperate men. He was buying her a vehicle that would keep her safe in traffic, and she was planting herself smack in the middle of life's dangerous highway.

"You may as well have run an ad in the *Observer* as having Hank invite Sandra to the bar to see you tonight," he grumbled. "There isn't any way she could resist, and chances are, she'll tell big brother, too. You're begging for trouble."

"Yup," Faith said with satisfaction, swinging back to inspect the glove compartment and fiddle with radio dials. "This showdown was inevitable. I can stomp Sandra's face if I have to, so you needn't worry about her. Have some faith in me." She groaned as she realized what she'd said.

"I'd rather have some Faith *under* me when the night's over," he countered. "And not in a dozen pieces. You might be able to handle Sandra, but not Sammy."

She shrugged. "I've handled worse. You have Cesar and Jim and his partner and heaven knows who all coming in to help out. I'll be fine."

"They won't be there until after nine. You have to promise you'll stay in the back until you come out with the band. Resist peeking. I'll be there as soon as I can, but I owe Rex and can't let him down tonight. I have to pull that batch of bisque out of the kiln."

"I'm sorry I'm turning your hair gray." She leaned over and patted his arm, and her light perfume surrounded him. "I had no way of knowing Rex would be called out of town tonight and that you'd be stuck at the pottery."

"I'll be there," he said grimly, easing her new car into the alley leading to the bar parking lot. "I'll be damned if I let you out on stage without me. So stay out of sight until I arrive."

"We're only going over the material. The guys can set up the instruments. I don't have to do anything out front until showtime." She sat back and unbuckled her seat belt as he parked the car. "I need to talk with Sandra and Sammy, and this is probably the safest way to do it. If we can persuade them to our side, we might be able to trap Piggy Junior."

"Believe me, having Sandra and Sammy on our side is not necessarily a good thing." Trying not to let his panic show, Adrian helped her down from the car and leveled a wary eye on their surroundings as they walked toward the back of the bar. The one security light didn't reveal anything suspicious.

She stood on tiptoe and kissed his cheek as they reached the door. "At least we'll know where they are," she reassured him. "And you have the bank keys. So what can they do?"

If only that were enough. Pulling her more soundly into his arms, Adrian kissed her the way he wanted to be kissed. Reassured more by her eager response than her promises of safety, he let her go and watched her disappear inside.

If this was the first day of the rest of his life, he might as well shoot himself now.

❧ THIRTY-FOUR ❧

"A high speed car chase down I-77 from a bank parking lot in the Lake Norman area ended in a serious injury accident just outside Charlotte today, blocking traffic on the interstate for hours. Police state the unidentified victim of the crash was taken to a local hospital with serious injuries. The driver of the other car escaped—"

Adrian snapped off the radio. He had no patience with drug dealers and their problems. One could only hope they'd eventually kill each other off. Using vehicles rather than guns was an interesting new tactic.

He eased across the speed bump in the parking lot leading back to the pottery, taking great care not to scratch Faith's new vehicle on the spreading azaleas spilling onto the crumbling drive. He'd have to work for Rex for the rest of his life to pay back what he'd borrowed to slip under the table for this damned car, but he couldn't have done less. If he'd left Faith alone in the first place, she would still be safely chugging around Knoxville in her VW.

If he'd left Faith alone, he wouldn't be churning with more confusion than he'd experienced since adolescence. She'd knocked him off the track and left him with wheels spinning and no direction. Somehow, he had to resist the temptation to throw away everything he'd worked for in exchange for some piece of Faith's future. That was a fool's dream. Once he had things straightened out and she'd gone home, his head would fall back in place. He hoped.

Adrian opened the back door of the pottery, not surprised

to find it unlocked. Rex had said he'd leave the key inside so he could lock up when he left.

He didn't have much respect for a potter who would leave all his hard work baking in a kiln and walk off because his boyfriend had called him unexpectedly. Even if he wasn't a creative genius, Rex should have more respect for his craft than that. And for his time and materials.

Even as Adrian realized that Rex wasn't usually that scatty, he turned on the light switch and discovered the reason for his employer's hasty departure.

Silhouetted in the double-wide doorway of the show room, Al McCowan, Jr., otherwise known as Piggy, stood calmly examining one of Rex's creations. He looked up as the back room light came on and smiled at Adrian's appearance. "We have friends in common, it seems."

Adrian's hand froze on the light switch and his thoughts instantly surged to Faith. If Piggy was here, he couldn't hurt Faith. Reluctantly, he released the switch but didn't step away from the door. The back room was narrow and hot and filled with shelves of unglazed bisque—not a place Piggy in his Italian suit would enter willingly.

" 'Friends' might be a questionable description," Adrian replied harshly. Rex had sold him out. He'd extract a satisfactory revenge for that later.

"Rex has expensive habits and owes me," McCowan said casually, halting in the doorway of the showroom. The dangling light bulb in the kiln room threw more shadow than light, and the small table lamp in the showroom illuminated only the ceramic piece beneath it.

"What do you want, McCowan?" Adrian didn't figure this was a friendly visit, but even if Piggy outweighed him by a ton or two, Adrian could throw him. It wasn't physical fear messing with his mind right now.

"The safe deposit keys," McCowan replied, apparently assuming no further explanation was required.

"I don't have them." Adrian didn't see any reason to play coy about his knowledge of the keys' existence. He just didn't want this ox going after Faith next. "We locked the keys in a

friend's box." That should suit Piggy's way of thinking sufficiently to be believable. In actuality, the keys burned a hole in
his pocket. He saw the stupidity of that too late.

"That's a lie." McCowan lost his smile, but not his composure. "I know where you've been and what you've been
doing."

Now that Adrian's eyes had adjusted, he could see the other
man had gained a few pounds since he'd seen him last.
McCowan's jowls were heavier, his face puffier, and his blond
hair thinning enough to make him appear bald. Greed and
laziness didn't agree with him.

Adrian didn't like McCowan knowing of his relationship
with Faith, but it had never occurred to him to keep it secret.
How the hell could he steer Piggy away from her? He stalled.
"I can't imagine why it's any business of yours."

McCowan stepped into the oppressive heat of the kiln
room. "I'm making it my business. Every lawyer in the state
is paying through the nose for your excesses. I don't see any
reason why you or Tony's bitch of a wife should profit from
us. We want our money back."

Did the man think he was an idiot? They both knew it was
Tony's excesses that had cost them. Of course, that didn't
change Piggy's goal. It amazed Adrian how criminals could
sound so convincingly self-righteous. Did they really believe
their own BS? "When and if I find the money *Tony* stole," he
replied, "I'll happily repay the fund, with interest. If that's
your only concern, you've wasted your time. All I want is my
record cleared and my license reinstated."

"You misunderstand me," McCowan said softly in his best
Southern drawl. "You wouldn't see me standing here if I
didn't have the means to tie you up and dump you down the
sewer if I choose. You have no options, Raphael. You give me
the keys and anything you found in those boxes, or I send you
back to jail for a hundred years, and Tony's bitch of a wife
with you. Although, unfortunately, you won't be sharing the
same cell," he said with mock regret in his voice.

Adrian figured McCowan could do it. He'd already used
him as a pawn and thrown him away once. He'd have no re-

morse over doing so again. But this time he knew he had little
to lose. Being at the bottom of the barrel gave him solid
ground to stand on.

"Faith has friends who would tear out your liver if you
came near her. She's not an option," Adrian said adamantly.
"If you knew her at all, you'd know she would have given any
money she found back to the owner as soon as she found it. I
don't know what you're after, but Faith doesn't have it."

"You know perfectly well what I'm after, and if you won't
give it to me, I'll go through the bitch to get it. Women aren't
quite so impervious to danger as trash like you."

Sweat trickled down Adrian's spine. If he'd had anything to
give the fatuous fool, he might consider it just to keep Faith
safe. But the keys wouldn't give McCowan what he wanted—
the money, and the evidence.

"She can't give you what she doesn't have. I've locked the
keys in a friend's box until we locate Tony's hiding places.
Threatening her might give you personal satisfaction, but
you're wasting your time otherwise." Adrian reached for the
doorknob. He wanted to see if Faith was safe. To hell with
traitorous Rex's ugly plates.

"I *know* Tony's hiding places," Piggy stated coolly. "I've
arranged for a few people to keep you both company until I
have the keys as well. Shall we visit your friend with the
box?" McCowan stepped around the worktable as Adrian
flung open the door.

Two men in black T-shirts blocked his escape route.

Without hesitation, Adrian swung around, grabbed the heav-
iest earthenware pitcher on the shelf and flung it directly at
Piggy's head. If he was going down, he was taking McCowan
with him.

Piggy ducked, and the pitcher shattered against the doorjamb. The two thugs in black jumped Adrian at once.

Oh, hell, it had been ten years since his wrestling days, and
those acts had been carefully choreographed. He hadn't practiced his footwork in a long time. He staggered into the wall
of unglazed earthenware, toppling dishes and plates as he fell
under the weight of the other two men.

Needing to reach Faith before these men did, Adrian roared in rage, planted his free elbow in the face of one assailant, rolled to the right, grabbed a broken platter and smashed it against his second captor's ear.

Piggy's cries of fury rang higher than his henchmen's wails of pain. Breaking free, Adrian shoved up and raced for the door. A solid blow to the back of his head sent him sprawling across the threshold, into the gravel of the drive.

"The keys, Raphael," Piggy said politely from somewhere overhead. "Or the bitch."

His freedom, or Faith. It wasn't any choice at all. "My pocket," he muttered, then groaned as one of the thugs flipped him over to search his jeans.

"Faith, there's a gent out here wants to see you," one of the band shouted from the backstage door.

Faith finished unwrapping her knee bandage and massaged the muscle underneath. It felt strong enough. She wanted to wear this skirt tonight. Call it vanity, but she wanted Sandra to see she had an opponent to reckon with.

"I can hope there's more than one who wants to see me," she called back, pushing her boots on over her socks. She didn't want to bend that knee enough to pull on panty hose. "Tell them to wait their turn."

It didn't bother her to follow Adrian's orders about staying backstage. She had no reason to put in an appearance in the bar until he arrived. Cesar and Belinda's Jim and their friends might already be in place, but she wanted Adrian out there, too, if only to see how well she handled the situation.

"I figure he had talking in mind, not singing." The young musician sauntered back. "He gave me a fiver to make certain you got his card." He handed over the battered piece of cardboard, printed side down.

Tony's alive was scrawled across the blank space.

Heart sinking to her stomach, Faith flipped the card over and read the inscription: ALAN MCCOWAN, JR.

She crumpled the cardboard with shaking fingers. "What does the man who gave you this look like?"

The kid looked at her quizzically. "You look kinda sick. Should I get George?"

She tried to pull herself together and act normally, but even the remote possibility that Tony was still alive and walking this earth unleashed explosive fireworks in her brain. The idea of a pig like McCowan knowing of Tony's whereabouts escalated the chaos to volcanic eruptions through every nerve in her system.

"First, tell me what the guy looks like," she demanded.

"Big, beefy, straw-colored hair, maybe your age or older."

Ancient, in the kid's eyes. Faith took a deep breath and tried to think. Not until the kid described him had she recognized the resemblance between Sam Shaw and Al McCowan. Tony apparently liked big bullies on his team. She'd only seen the surface differences between the men—denim compared to silk, bad grammar compared to good, bad teeth . . .

She looked up. "What did his teeth look like?"

The kid stared at her. "Are you whacked? D'ya think he's a horse? I didn't notice his *teeth*."

"All right, did he look yuppie or hick?" She didn't know why it mattered which of Tony's bullies was out there, but she'd developed a strong aversion to surprises. The battered state of the business card evoked suspicion.

"Hick," he said firmly. "Cowboy hat and big-haired blonde with him."

Sam Shaw. She tried to feel relief, but her lungs wouldn't work. The message on that card scared her to death. She wouldn't have to worry about all the implications of still being married. Tony would kill her before the divorce papers could hit his desk.

He would want his money back. *All* his money.

She wanted Adrian here. She could face Sam and Sandra together. She might even be willing to tackle a bastard like Piggy McCowan. But she couldn't face the idea of Tony alive and well and returning to torment her life again. She just couldn't do it, couldn't face him and his charm and all the old neuroses that had held her shackled for years.

Tony could prove Adrian's innocence.

Faith's head shot up and her fist crushed the card into spitball size. "Call George and the other guys for backup. I have to write a note I want you to deliver to somebody in the audience. We have a major creep going down if we do this right."

The kid's eyes widened, but he hurried to do as instructed. Faith had warned the bandleader that there might be trouble, but she'd told him Adrian had it in hand. Adrian wasn't here, and she wouldn't wait for him. If Tony was alive, she needed to know *now*.

She scribbled a note to Jim, checked the audience, and found him sitting with one of his officer friends at the bar. She pointed him out to her messenger and watched to be certain the note was delivered before she made her next move. She might not wait for Adrian's arrival, but she wasn't taking any other chances. She wanted all the force behind her that she could gather.

She searched the dimly lit barroom but couldn't spot the Shaws. "Where's the man who gave you the card?" she whispered as the kid returned to report his task complete.

"Booth on the far side of the bar. You can't see him from here. His old lady was bitching because she couldn't see the stage good."

"Well, she'll see this part of the act real well."

"Faith, you sure you want to do this?" George arrived and put a hand on her shoulder, restraining her from marching out. "We're going on in a few minutes. Wouldn't it be better to wait for Raphael and talk to them after the show?"

It was almost nine, and Adrian wasn't here. Faith fought a new panic. Maybe he was caught in traffic. Maybe the kiln hadn't cooled properly. Any number of things could have delayed him. She wouldn't think about their conversation of yesterday. Men like Piggy didn't "off" people like in the movies.

Retreating from beneath George's arm, she squeezed his hand instead. "I may have stirred up a little more trouble than I anticipated. I don't *think* anyone would shoot at me on stage, but I don't want to risk it. Do you think we could delay the show?"

Alarm rippled across the expressions of the men around her. She'd much rather go out there and sing and pretend nothing was happening, but Adrian's theory scared her to death. She didn't want to endanger innocent people.

"I think we better call the police," George said slowly.

"Adrian's brother-in-law is a cop, and he and a buddy are out there, but they can't stop bullets. Jim's wife is expecting their first baby. I can't involve him in this. It's not as if anyone has done anything that he can arrest them for."

She didn't want to panic and rush into anything without thinking, but she couldn't intellectualize this to death either. If it were just the Shaws out there, she didn't foresee any problem. She could go out on stage and wait for Adrian. But if there was any chance Tony or McCowan were in the audience, it was a whole new ball game.

"Go on without me," she ordered. "They'll be watching the stage and not me." She held out her hand to one of the band members. "Give me that beer bottle. I can cut a man's throat with a bottle, if necessary."

"Not if he has a gun," George said quietly.

"He'd have to be stoned out of his mind to shoot in a room full of witnesses. I can handle this." Faith took the nearly empty bottle and smiled bravely. She'd seen men stoned out of their minds. If they were inclined toward murder, they'd lay out anyone who crossed their path, including witnesses. No one could second-guess madmen. She had to take her chances. No man would paralyze her into helplessness ever again. Not even Tony.

Terrified, she waited for the band to hit the first notes of the opening number. As the crowd clapped and cheered, she clutched her beer bottle weapon, and still smiling, stalked into the smoke-clouded barroom.

❧ THIRTY-FIVE ❧

"You!" Sandra screeched, slapping her hands on the table and struggling to rise from the booth as Faith walked up.

"Sit down, Sandra." Faith poured the dregs of her beer into an empty mug and swung the bottle idly. Sandra got the message. She sat back down.

Faith didn't like it that Sammy had chosen this moment to disappear. Like a gunfighter, she'd prefer having her back against the wall so she could watch for him. Unless she wanted to climb into the booth and stand on the bench with her back pressed into cow horns, she decided that wasn't an option. "We have bigger problems than old grievances. Where's Tony hiding out these days?"

Sandra looked genuinely startled, then fury returned. "You bitch! Don't give me that innocent miss stuff. I know you got that death certificate and claimed what was rightfully mine."

"C'mon, Sandra. If I had half a mil in life insurance, would I be working in this dump? Where's Sammy? Did you think he would actually help with the death benefits? When are you going to quit relying on men?" Faith contemplated sitting down, but the booth made her nervous. She leaned against a post and tried to keep half an eye on the audience. The band had cranked into a loud number, and she had to shout to be heard above the bass notes.

"Sammy has his lawyer friend working on it," Sandra said defensively. "He says you got to it first. I have *kids* to raise. How could you steal food from the mouths of children?"

"Dammit, Sandra, I *sent* you the insurance policy. It had

288

your name on it. It wasn't any good to me. What the hell did you do with it?"

"I damned well never got no policy from *you!*" Sandra shouted back. "Tony said he'd take care of me, but you stole everything!"

Faith sighed. Adrian had been right. Talking to Sandra was like talking to a broken record. She couldn't see past her grievances to find the solutions. "Where's Sammy?" she repeated. "I know he was out here. Maybe he could explain a few things."

"He's gone to take a leak. This is between you and me." Sandra picked up the mug Faith had filled and gulped the warm beer before continuing. "I don't need nothing explained to me. Tony was a horse's ass, but he was *my* horse's ass. Me and him go way back. He was gonna see our kids had better than we did growing up. You were just his ticket into the big-time. He was gonna dump you and put me in one of them big new mansions at the lake. It was gonna be *wonderful*. And then you had to pull the plug."

"Live in your fantasy world if it makes you happy," Faith replied wearily, half watching the action on stage now. She'd built up a bucket load of adrenaline and fear for a drunken moron. "I have to get back to work. But if you think Al McCowan will help you with Tony's money, you're a bigger horse's ass than Tony. He's a crook, pure and simple, and he's out for anything he can steal."

"Now that ain't a nice thing for a lady to say."

Faith recognized Sammy Shaw's drawl behind her. The ominous point of metal pressed against her spine froze her first response.

"Mr. McCowan has a few things he'd like to ask you," Sammy continued. "Why don't we mosey on out of here and give him a visit?"

"Sammy, she says she sent me Tony's insurance policy, and she ain't got it. She's not dressed like she's rich."

Stay calm, Faith. She took a deep breath as Sandra's whine unfroze her thought processes. "Yeah, Sammy, what happened to that policy?" she taunted. "And what was that note about Tony being alive? Maybe you know something Sandra doesn't?"

"What?" Sandra screeched, so furious she managed to shove the heavy table toward the opposite seat so she could stand up. "So help me God if that bastard is—"

"Shut up, Sandra," Sammy hissed. "You're making a scene. I gave McCowan the policy. He was gonna make it right. Now we're gonna make him clear up a few things. She's the key we need."

"I don't think so." Without giving it a second thought, Faith stepped away from the knife at her back, smashed her beer bottle against the table more as signal than weapon, and swung around to face her antagonist.

From the corner of her eye Faith watched a half-dozen six-foot-tall men push back their chairs and start across the room in their direction. Faith smiled. Adrian had really stacked the deck this time.

"Sandy, grab her arms and let's get outta here," Sammy ordered nervously, not noticing the approaching posse. "She can't do nothing with that damned bottle."

"I can, but I won't." Faith shrugged and tried to look nonchalant while Jim and his friends pushed through the crowd. "Unless you have a gun, you won't get more than three steps from here. I'd suggest you start preparing your story for the police."

Sammy glanced around, recognized the determined look on several square-jawed faces, and panicked. Grabbing Faith, he swung her in front of him, holding the knife to her throat.

Oh, hell. She should have figured stupidity into the equation.

With a hard downward thrust, she spiked her boot heel into the arch of Sammy's Nike-shod foot. Sammy howled.

In the next motion, she slashed upward with her broken bottle, aiming for the beefy arm at her throat. Sammy screeched in agony and dropped her like a hot rock as he grabbed his gushing arm.

Counting on stupidity this time, Faith brandished her beer bottle and swung on Sandra, but Jim already had her clapped in cuffs. Screaming protests and obscenities, Sandra staggered backward into the arms of another officer.

The room around them erupted in panic as bar patrons retreated to escape the fracas. The band squealed to a halt as all four members disentangled themselves from instruments and leaped from the stage. Seeing the fight ending before they could reach it, they strolled uncertainly toward Faith.

"Where's Adrian?" Faith demanded of Jim as one of his buddies prepared a hasty bandage to stop Sammy's bleeding.

"I don't know," he admitted worriedly. "But we have to take these clowns down to the station. We'll need you to press charges. Adrian can catch up later."

"Not until we check the pottery," she insisted, fear pushing past her adrenaline rush. "Sammy didn't come in here just to harass me. McCowan's up to something."

Jim nodded, watching the proceedings carefully as his fellow officers led the Shaws away. "We'll go around that way, check things out, but Adrian takes care of himself."

George stepped up, his expression one of concern as he hugged Faith's shoulders. "You all right, babe? Can we help?"

Not realizing until now how shaken she was, Faith stepped away, trying not to wipe hot tears of terror from her eyes. She didn't have time for comfort and tears, not from this man. She wanted Adrian. Oh, God, please don't let anything happen to Adrian. His family needed him. *She* needed him, if only to ease her panic, or so she told herself.

Frantically praying, she edged toward the door. "I'm all right." Her teeth chattered, and she tried to hide her terror with boldness. "I have to go down to the station, so tell Adrian if he shows up. And stay away from any bulky blond guys in suits if they come nosing around."

"Want us to tie them up and haul them down to the station if they show?" George asked teasingly.

"Yeah, just tie up every big blond that walks through the door," Jim answered impatiently. "Works for me."

"I'll check back with you later," George called after her. "We could make a good act."

Faith tried to smile at his insistence, but singing was the last thing she wanted to do right now. She didn't need that outlet anymore. She needed Adrian. She was insane to ever want any man again, but she needed Adrian to be alive and safe and in the same world she inhabited. She looked to Jim, who nodded toward the door.

"C'mon. I've got an unmarked out there. We'll find him."

They caught the Isuzu as it was leaving the parking lot. Faith shouted a warning, Jim hit the brakes and the blue lights and swung the Crown Vic to block the exit.

The Isuzu screeched to a halt and a familiar lanky form stepped into the flash of blue.

"Adrian!" Relief pouring through her like tears, Faith leaped from the police car. Jim followed slowly, but she didn't care if he saw her public display. Flinging herself into Adrian's welcoming arms, she collapsed, babbling, into the unquestioning warmth and security he offered. In a minute she would be herself again. Right now she needed someone who understood and didn't mind if she fell apart.

"It's okay, *querida*. Hush, slow down, let me talk to Jim." As she rattled on about Sammy holding her at knifepoint, Adrian held her close, stroking her hair, but he fixed his brother-in-law with a look over her shoulder. She finally quieted enough for him to sneak a word in edgewise. "There's a barney in back of the shop," he warned Jim. "If he's awake, he's probably not too happy, but he can't go far." Hanging around teenagers had expanded his vocabulary more than prison had. He didn't know if the slang referred to purple dinosaurs or the Fifes of this world, but either worked.

"A barney," Jim said stoically. "I'm not even going to ask. Just make certain you show up at the station to file the complaint."

His car radio spluttered to life and he turned around and pulled out the mike. "Ten-four."

Adrian rubbed Faith's slender spine as Jim conversed with the radio. He ached in half a dozen places, but Faith's collapse in tears shook him even more. He didn't know how to tell her about the keys. Piggy had been long gone by the time he'd overcome his captors. "I'm sorry I wasn't there, *querida*. McCowan decided to go after me instead of you. It took me a while to separate his thugs and straighten things out. I can't believe he sent Sammy after you." Anger rippled through him. He'd lived in terror these past minutes or hours, wondering what was happening to her.

"It's okay," she whispered. "I cut him pretty badly, I think, but he shouldn't die of an arm wound. I think he has his own agenda with Piggy. I was more terrified because you didn't show."

He squeezed her tighter. The wings of justice had fled, along with all his hope. He'd have to let her go soon. Something inside him screamed at the raw injustice of losing the most precious gift in his life right now, but he'd always known she'd never been his to keep. "McCowan's running scared," he told her calmly. "Maybe we can still catch him."

"Run that by me again?" Jim said quizzically into the radio. "She's identified a patient as a dead man? Does she have a doctor with her?"

Faith stiffened at the same time Adrian did. In unison they stepped closer to the car and the conversation.

"My wife's never gone crazy before. All right, all right, I'll be there. Tell her I have Adrian with me, and she'll calm down. I have a probable 10–62 out here; better send a car." Jim hung up the mike, shaking his head.

"Belinda?" Realizing he was crushing Faith's shoulders, Adrian relaxed his grip, but his stomach hadn't unclenched.

Jim shrugged. "They brought in a John Doe earlier. He's in critical condition after a car chase this afternoon. The department is working on tracking his car, but Belinda got nosy and took a look after she clocked out. Sarge says she's hysterical, claims the guy is already dead."

"Tony," Adrian said flatly. "She recognized Tony."

"Either that or his twin. I had to practically hog-tie her and carry her out of the courthouse at your trial, so she knows what he looks like. But it's been four years." He looked uncertainly at Faith. "You up for this?"

"Sammy's note said Tony was alive. I think I've always expected this."

She said it with such weariness that Adrian wanted to gather her in his arms and fly away with her to somewhere safe. But if Belinda was right—Faith was still married. He didn't think the bottom of this hole could get any blacker.

"We'll follow you in the car," he told Jim. The drive to the hospital would be tense in either vehicle, but he'd rather be alone with Faith while he could.

She didn't argue. She followed obediently, didn't even demand to take the driver's seat. Adrian swallowed a lump in his throat as he strapped himself in. The light at the end of the tunnel had appeared, and he had a strong feeling it was an express train.

"He's in critical condition," he reminded her as he bumped the Isuzu into the street in the path of Jim's car. "He can't hurt you."

"I know. It's just so strange . . ." She didn't complete the thought but stared out the passenger side window.

"We'll drag your attorney out of bed in the morning, have him dig out the divorce papers as soon as he hits his office."

"It might not be him. Four years changes people. Belinda could be mistaken."

"Hiding for four years doesn't even make sense," he agreed. "Pregnancy has loosened her screws. She shouldn't be working now."

That riled her enough to shoot him a glare. "She's perfectly healthy and capable of working for as long as she's able. Pregnancy does not rob us of our minds."

Anger was better than terror, he supposed. "All right, Belinda has always had a screw loose. Is that better?"

She crossed her arms and glared out the window. He knew that posture. He might as well give it up now. He wasn't getting anywhere with her in that mood. No point in passing on the rest of the bad news. She had enough on her mind.

If Tony was alive, Tony knew where the boxes were. Could they stop McCowan with Tony's help, or would McCowan be counting on Tony helping him?

Determinedly, Adrian hit the gas. He would do anything to prevent his family from slowly sliding back into the sinkhole of poverty. Maybe he could take a tip from Sammy and hold Tony at knifepoint.

❧ THIRTY-SIX ❦

Jim waited for them at the hospital entrance. "Belinda has gone home. I'd better escort Faith to the John Doe's room."

He looked at Adrian pointedly, and Faith understood. Jim didn't want murder and mayhem on his shift, and he didn't trust Adrian not to throttle the patient if it turned out to be Tony. Jim didn't understand that she was the one most likely to kill her lying, conniving thief of a husband.

Adrian fixed her with an enigmatic glare. "I gave McCowan the keys."

Faith opened her mouth, but no words emerged. Her stomach did an acrobatic tumble and dived to her feet as she heard what he didn't say. He'd traded his future to keep her from harm. The egotistical ass wasn't all ego after all. Just an ass. And her heart wept tears of joy and anguish. She'd finally fallen for a man who thought of her first, and he would walk right out the door to protect her.

She wanted to cry at the extent of his sacrifice, but she'd shed enough tears for one night, and she figured there were more to come. She knew what he was asking now. If he couldn't go back there and throttle the information out of Tony, she must.

This time she had to stand up to Tony in person.

She nodded to show she understood. "Tony can't hurt me anymore. I'll identify him, and Jim can take it from there," she said for the sake of appearances.

Bleakness hid beneath Adrian's fierce gaze, but she couldn't cope with his emotions as well as her own right now. When she'd walked out on Tony, she'd protected herself by thinking of

herself as a divorcée. Even after she'd received news of his
death, she hadn't thought of it as a husband dying so much as
the loss of someone she'd known once long ago. She'd never
really confronted the man who had cheated on her. She'd
walked out on him instead.

If that was Tony up there in the bed, she would be his wife
again.

She tried to be calm as Jim led her down antiseptic-scented
corridors and up in the elevator, with Adrian trailing behind.

While Jim checked with the nurses' station, Adrian picked
up a magazine in the waiting room. Faith didn't look back as a
nurse in white shoes led her to a room down still another corridor. Jim politely waited outside, but the nurse hustled in,
straightening the John Doe's covers, checking the reading on
the machines ticking at his side. Faith stood in the doorway
and stared.

Clear plastic tubes ran up his nose. A bandage hid much of
his mousy brown hair. He needed a shave. Tony would despise looking like that. Faith's glance fell on the blunt fingers
resting on top of the covers. They'd been recently manicured.
She tried to determine his height from the prostrate form
under the white sheets, but she didn't need to know his
height.

She knew it was Tony.

A knot the size of an orange choked her throat. She
clenched her fingers into balls to keep from crying out.

He hadn't even been in that plane crash—he'd run away.
She understood Tony as clearly as she understood herself. He
hadn't been able to deal with his guilt or the collapse of his
practice, the divorce, or Sandra and her three kids, so he'd run
out on all of them to look for an easier solution than facing his
problems.

All the rage and pain she'd bottled inside for so many years
threatened to explode. Throttling him would relieve the pressure, but she'd have to fight the tubing and the wires to reach
him. And probably Jim and the nurse as well. She knew when
the odds were against her.

Besides, Tony had the information she needed for Adrian.

She closed her eyes and let the anger shatter against solid walls. She was whole now. Tony couldn't hurt her anymore. Her freedom was a simple matter of paperwork. What was done was done. The tension rolled out of her, and she breathed easier.

She opened her eyes and discovered Tony staring back at her, but she was ready for him now. "I think your sons might like to know where you've been."

He blinked, breathed a word sounding like "Faith," and the beeping machine beside him escalated to a high whine. The nurse leaped in, adjusted a dial, and made shooing motions. Faith didn't budge.

"He needs quiet," the nurse insisted.

"He needs to be shot and put out of everyone's misery," Faith responded. "But he has three boys who deserve to know why their father disappeared for three years. I'm not leaving until I know." She had no idea why she had taken this tack. Maternal instinct leaping to the fore, perhaps. She realized she didn't have to kill Tony. Sandra would no doubt do it for her. But Tony's children deserved an explanation first.

"Sorry." The word emerged as a sibilant hiss through the ventilator. "Thought better off without me."

"Probably, if you'd left them something to live on. Mighty hard to obtain a death certificate on a man who isn't dead." She should be feeling sorry for the coward, restraining her temper until he had time to recover, but she'd spent a lifetime restraining her temper. No more. He was lucky she didn't cut his throat.

He pounded a fist into the sheet and struggled to sit up. The nurse clucked and protested and pushed him back down.

"Dammit!" The curse came through loud and clear. "She should have had a fortune in insurance! It wouldn't take an asshole to prove me dead. What the f—"

"Hush, now!" the nurse ordered. "You really must rest, mister . . . ?" She turned to Faith for answers.

"Nicholls, Tony Nicholls, father of three lovely boys he deserted."

The nurse tutted and looked less sympathetic as she tucked

the sheets in place. "I'll mark the charts and tell the policeman waiting outside." She bustled off, leaving Faith to administer justice as she saw fit.

"Why did you come back?" she asked, almost idly. After all the panic and fear, she almost felt distant from this man who'd ruined her life in so many ways. He wasn't part of her anymore, just a story left naggingly incomplete.

He shrugged halfheartedly. "Checking on my money?"

"You were driving a BMW, so you obviously weren't hurting for that." He'd taken the stock certificates with him. That thought clicked into place. He'd taken as much of the stock as he could lay his hands on and sold it. Adrian wouldn't be able to refund the debt. But if Adrian could still prove his innocence and Tony's guilt . . . ?

"Election year coming up." He tugged impatiently at the tubing blocking his ability to use his snake charmer's voice. "Sandra's a hindrance, but money will buy her. I still have time to file. Thought I could straighten things out, but when I got in last night and called Sammy, he still hadn't found you."

Faith stared at him in disbelief. "You thought you'd waltz back into Charlotte and everything would be just as you left it?"

"My name's good," he said as belligerently as possible through the tubing.

"Not when I get done with it," she answered sweetly.

Adrian paced the waiting room, occasionally stopping to stare out the window at the lighted parking lot below. What was she doing in there? It had to be Tony for it to take this long.

Agony ripped through him. Tony—alive—was not a score he'd gambled on. Even in his angriest dreams while locked behind prison bars, he would never have considered cuckolding Tony as a means of revenge. All he'd wanted was his life back.

He could never have his life back.

His shoulders slumped as he leaned against the wall and stared into the darkness. He'd known that all along, but fighting was all he knew. He couldn't fight emptiness, so he'd chosen to fight the past. It was over now. Tony was in there, spouting his lies. McCowan would be hiding the evidence. The money was gone. He could fight some more, stir up muddy waters, and get thrown back in jail again. Or he could walk off, flip hamburgers for a living, and at least be there when his family needed him. He couldn't burden Faith with either scenario.

Jim arrived and stood uncertainly to one side. "The nurse says she's identified him."

Adrian didn't move. "Yeah, I figured that."

"I'm gonna call in a report, check to see if the Sammy character is talking."

Adrian managed a curt laugh. "McCowan is his lawyer. What do you think?"

Jim muttered an obscenity and walked off.

He couldn't focus on the reality of Faith walking out of his life, never to be seen again. He didn't know why that wouldn't stick in his mind. She had no reason to stay any longer. All the pieces of the puzzle were here. Maybe they weren't all quite in place yet, but they would be shortly. Tony wouldn't need the keys to open his own boxes. All he had to do was produce identification and say he'd lost them. He probably hadn't left anything of value in them after all—only the evidence that might implicate McCowan, which could be disappearing as he stood there. Of course, if McCowan had blown the funds Tony had counted on, Tony might decide to turn state's evidence to get even. Adrian didn't want to be around while the crooks battled that one out.

His head slowly lifted as a new path emerged through the crowded forest of his mind. He and Faith had put the fear into McCowan, not Tony. Piggy hadn't once mentioned Tony. *Sammy* was the one who had known that Tony was alive.

Someone had chased Tony's car and driven him off the road. Sammy already had a suspicious history of that sort of activity. Sammy's sister was in a position to inherit half a million dollars if Tony could be proved dead.

McCowan might have power, but Sammy was the wild card, playing both ends against the middle.

If McCowan had thought Tony dead, he would almost certainly have found some means of cashing in their ill-gotten gains. Returned from the dead, Tony would scream bloody murder at the betrayal.

If Sammy was in jail, he could be desperate enough to play his wild card by telling McCowan that Tony was alive. From all points of view, Tony needed to be dead.

And Faith was alone in that room with him.

Adrian was already halfway down the hall as all these thoughts snapped into place. He had to get Faith out of there before Sammy called McCowan. Or McCowan found some means of—

Faith's scream shattered the last remaining shard of his peace. Not looking to see who else heard, Adrian dodged IV stands and linen carts, shoved past startled visitors and crashed through the doorway he'd seen Faith enter earlier.

Faith lay still and crumpled on the floor.

Anger seared him. The futility of the loss of all that was good and right washed over him, followed by blind rage at the man who had deprived the world of a treasure.

Swinging toward the bed, Adrian caught the bulky intruder in the process of straightening up, grabbed him by the seat of his pants and shirt collar and hurled him at the wall.

McCowan's shoulder crashed into the plaster, and as he staggered to right himself, Adrian grabbed his shirtfront, rammed the top of his head upward into the larger man's jaw, kneed him in the groin, and flung him along the small stretch of floor not occupied by Faith. Bedpans and IVs crashed and clattered as Piggy slid into them.

Rage flooded Adrian each time he saw Faith's inert form, and without waiting for McCowan to rise again, he leaped on his back and began smashing his face into the tile.

Strong hands grabbed Adrian's arms and jerked him backward.

"Enough, Adrian. I've got cuffs. I'll use them on you if I have to."

Adrenaline still boiled through his veins, but Adrian recognized Jim's voice and forcibly throttled the fury that required he beat the man on the floor into a bloody pulp.

Shoving up without looking at Jim, he fell to his knees beside Faith.

A nurse was already with her, testing her pulse, lifting her head, and providing a pillow as Faith stirred. He'd thought her dead.

Adrian took a deep breath to quell his remaining panic, and with tears stinging his eyes, poured his gratitude into prayer. It took another moment to control his shudders.

He didn't want to be caught wiping his eyes, but he couldn't stay away. He lifted Faith into his arms, so the first thing she saw when her lashes lifted was him.

She smiled, and his heart swelled with joy. And love. He touched his forehead to hers, absorbing that insanity.

"Tony?" she asked.

His swollen heart crumbled back to the dust from whence it came.

Grudgingly, he glanced up. Jim had McCowan in cuffs. A hospital security guard had joined him. An intern bent over the bed, examining the patient, who was fighting to sit up, issuing obscenities through plastic tubing. That was Tony all right. Adrian couldn't believe he'd just saved the bastard's life.

"He's alive," Adrian said, answering Faith's unspoken question. "Sandra doesn't get her half million. McCowan goes to jail. Pity we can't arrange to send Tony there as well."

"Oh, we can." Her smile was stronger as she positioned herself more comfortably in Adrian's arms and poked at the sore spot on her head. Taking that as a good sign, the nurse stood up and returned to her other patient.

"Tony might give evidence against McCowan, charge him with attempted murder even, but he isn't about to produce evidence on himself," Adrian said with suspicion. She might have torn his heart out and made muddy clay out of it, but she hadn't turned his brain to mush. Yet.

"I lied and told Tony I would give the keys to McCowan if he didn't cooperate with the D.A., but first I would tell Sandra where to find him," Faith said with satisfaction. "He hadn't known she was in town."

Adrian stared at her in disbelief. "He didn't come up out of the bed and strangle you, right then and there?"

She snuggled against his chest until her words were muffled. "Nah, I told him I'd just cut Sammy with a beer bottle, and I had no compunction against doing the same to him. I think he believed me—I know where the bank boxes are now."

Adrian laughed. He couldn't help himself. Every head in the room turned, but all he could manage was not rolling on the floor while the laughter billowed out of him. He loved her. Oh God, how he loved this insanely wonderful woman.

And he couldn't have her. That shut him up fast enough.

"So, who does Tony fear most, you or Sandra?" He tried to hide the turmoil boiling through him. She'd given him hope for a future, and dashed it at the same time.

Faith chuckled. "Me, I hope. He thought Sandra had collected the life insurance, was living in wealth in Florida, and had probably married. He'd calculated he had time to provide adequate compensation before she discovered she'd have to pay it all back. Knowing she'd been living hand-to-mouth for three years and that she was here in town scared the devil out of him. That's what comes of keeping dangerous company."

They couldn't sit here like this forever, as much as he hated the idea of letting her go. Adrian set her back from him, stood, and pulled her up.

"He hasn't figured out that Sammy was probably the one who chased him off the road?" he asked as Faith looked at him with a question in her eyes.

"I think he's still a little fuzzy about the accident. Tony had just gone to the bank to pick up some spending money, but he made the mistake of letting Sammy know he was in town. Sammy must have been waiting for him."

Faith clung to his hand and stood close enough that their arms brushed as they watched the intern shooting Tony with a sedative. Adrian didn't want her watching Tony. He looked helpless, and all women liked mothering the helpless. Faith especially. Disgruntled, Adrian dragged her from the room.

"Must have startled Sammy to have the dead rise again," he

said cynically, drawing her down the corridor. They still needed to press charges against McCowan and company. He'd bet his future wages that McCowan had figured it would be easy to shoot a hospital patient full of something painful, and discovering Faith in the room had simply provided him with the perfect suspect. If he hadn't arrived when he did . . . He wouldn't think about it.

"I imagine Tony's appearance more than startled Sammy," Faith agreed, "especially if Piggy had convinced him he could collect the life insurance. Sammy must have totally lost it. McCowan's apparently had that policy for years, and never acted on it."

"I should think the only reason Piggy bothered talking to the Shaws this time was because he wanted Sammy to stop us. If I'd known we'd stir up such a hornet's nest, I never would have brought you here."

"Yeah, you would. You thought I was one of the hornets, and you wanted to stomp me," Faith said complacently as the elevator door opened.

Yeah, just one of the many errors in judgment he'd made over the years. How many more would he have to make before he got it right?

He vowed that this time, whatever errors he made wouldn't hurt Faith, no matter what the cost to him.

❧ THIRTY-SEVEN ❦

November

Adrian hadn't called her—not once in the nearly two months since he'd helped her load her box of photos and her vase into the Isuzu and kissed her good-bye. The kiss had told her everything he hadn't said in words. It had been as cautious as their stilted farewells. After the impact of Tony's return, perhaps they'd needed that civilized leave-taking to collect themselves.

But time had run out, and she wanted—needed—to see where things stood.

Faith sat quietly on a back bench of the courtroom as the judge set bond on Tony to the tune of half a million dollars. Tony might have that kind of money stashed in offshore accounts, but she doubted he could access it easily. Her lawyer told her Tony had spent the last three years in South America with a lovely Brazilian señorita who was undoubtedly far less demanding than Faith or Sandra. The day they'd run off together, he'd decided to take her on a cruise rather than fly down to Rio.

The plane's crash without him must have seemed an act of fate, and Tony had never been one to discard an opportunity.

Faith wondered if his pretty señorita was enjoying his ill-gotten gains now, or if Tony had managed to secure them somewhere where the courts and no one else could touch them. Either way, he could be behind bars for a long time. Not as long as McCowan, however. Tony may have committed perjury and fraud and deserted his kids, and been stupid enough to believe he could live happily in Rio with his new mistress, but he hadn't tried to kill anyone, as McCowan and Sammy had. With all the evidence Jim and his police buddies had jubilantly gathered, none of them would go free for a good long while. With due diligence, the court might even squeeze them of every penny they had stolen as well. Tony would finally suffer as Adrian had.

Her gaze slid to a corner of the courtroom. She wouldn't have come here today at all if it wasn't for the man sitting on the front bench. He didn't need her here. Hadn't asked her to come. But this was excuse enough to see him one more time, and she had come with hope—and heart—in hand.

She still couldn't believe she'd fallen for another lawyer, but she thought—she prayed—Adrian was different. Unlike Tony, Adrian's greed had been for his family. He'd even put her before himself. He had so many good things going for him, she couldn't blame him for his arrogance—if only that arrogance hadn't convinced him he was responsible for the whole damned world.

He looked different already, more like the lawyer she remembered from the trial. The defiant ponytail was gone. Raven black hair still brushed his suit collar, but it had been carefully styled to look civilized, even as it emphasized the savage sharpness of his facial structure. He wasn't wearing the earring, but she wondered if he would pin it on when he walked out of the courthouse. Adrian knew the rules when he chose to apply them.

Faith blocked out the yearning sweeping her. She couldn't change Adrian if he didn't want to change. If he still thought he had to carry the world on his shoulders, that he had to be rich and powerful to deserve a life of his own, then they had nothing to say to each other. She'd had enough of that kind of misery to last a lifetime.

She'd stayed in touch with his family. Juan had told her Adrian was working with him at the pottery while the wheels of justice ground slowly. Belinda had said working with Juan put a crimp in Adrian's visits home, but he was available when his family needed him. He was managing to send them money. The girls were cheerleading again. He was teaching the boys wrestling. Their mother was back on her feet. Belinda was convinced that happiness at Adrian's return had healed her. Faith loved him too much to take him from all that, or to add to his burden.

A twinge of regret tugged at her heart, and she pinched the bridge of her nose to fight tears. She had every reason in the world to be happy except one. She'd learned to live with far worse. She'd proved she could survive and fashion a decent life for herself, but she was tired of just surviving. Living without Adrian ate at her night and day. He had taught her so much in those few weeks. . . . She couldn't pack all that passion in a box and store it away again.

As the courtroom proceedings ended, Adrian stood and turned around. At sight of her, he produced a genuine smile and hurried forward. Faith had forgotten how easy it was for a lawyer to produce that kind of charm, but she'd learned to judge men by their actions and not their smiles. She'd hoped and prayed for two months now, and he hadn't called. She'd already let enough time pass her by. She knew she had to move on—but she had to give him this one last chance. She didn't smile as he took her hand.

"Faith! You didn't have to drive all the way back here to see this. I could have called you."

"But you wouldn't have." She withdrew her hand. She'd lived inside this man for over two weeks, knew when he was happy, knew when he was holding back. Knew he didn't want her here. She hid her tears. "I had Belinda ask Jim to keep tabs on the court date. I wanted to be very certain Tony didn't wiggle out of this one."

Placing a familiar hand at her back, Adrian guided her out. "They were so busy squealing on each other that the evidence I put together was scarcely necessary."

"They'll let you have your license back," she said politely. "I'm happy for you."

"Are you?" He looked down at her quizzically. She thought she saw sadness there, but they all made choices. The two weeks they'd spent together wasn't such a very long time. Perhaps he'd gone past it, as she hadn't. Perhaps, in time, she would get over it, too, find another life, another path.

It had taken her half a lifetime to find this path. She wouldn't lay herself out like a lovesick doormat, but that didn't mean she had to give up hope either. If there was no room in his life for her, fine. She would accept that and move on. But she wanted it laid out on the table, clear and irrefutable.

"You must be incredibly busy," she said carefully as they reached the chilly November sunshine outside the courthouse. "Belinda says you and the D.A. have patched your differences and you're working with him now."

The smile didn't reach his eyes as Adrian brushed a loose tendril of hair from her face, then ran his hand unconsciously up and down her arm. "I can't recover the four years that I lost, but I suppose I'm trying. How are you doing? Juan says you're selling his work as fast as he sends it."

"He's doing some incredible things lately. You must have taught him to focus his talents. The figurine reproductions are lovely and easy to sell; he's fortunate to have you to paint them, but it's the porcelain . . ." She gestured helplessly, in awe at the incredible talent she'd discovered. "They're art. It may take longer to sell, but some of it belongs in museums. I'm thinking of taking it on the road."

He beamed with pleasure even while wariness laced his words. "I'm glad it works for you, but if it's not selling readily, how can you make a decent living? I don't like the idea of you living in that flophouse."

She shrugged. He was trampling on uncomfortable territory. "I'm looking for a new place. The new singer worked out well for the band, so I'm giving up the bar, and your friends are such superb sales help, I'm thinking of expanding. I could target different markets with different locations."

"Are you in town for long?" he asked carefully, in the same tone he had used when they'd last said farewell.

That careful tone, more than anything, knocked hope from her heart. The Adrian she'd known had never been wary or cautious, but had flown full speed ahead into the wind. He was changing, but not the way she'd hoped.

"I'm planning on driving back tonight." She couldn't read his expression, but the person she'd become was unwilling to accept defeat without a fight. "Would you prefer it if I leave you alone?" she asked boldly. "I'd hoped . . . But I don't want to be a nuisance. I understand if you're not interested."

His jaw clenched, and the hand that had never quite stopped touching her dropped to his side.

"Never think I'm not interested, Faith," he said intensely, before halting to search for precise words in his best lawyer fashion. "But it could be years before I'll know if I can have my license back. I can't even afford a bed of my own right now. I doubt I'll ever be able to afford a family. And I know how you feel about having children. You deserve that family you've dreamed of. You're a beautiful woman with a wonderful future ahead of you. I don't want to be another wrong turn on your highway to happiness."

"I certainly wouldn't want to be accused of two wrong turns," she replied crisply, heart sinking at this confirmation of what she already knew. "I just wanted to be certain we understood each other. I still think you're an insufferable prick for thinking you know what I want better than I do, but it's best to realize that now and make the break clean."

"Like porcelain," he agreed sadly.

It was beautiful while it lasted, she agreed without saying it aloud, instead taking her leave hurriedly rather than let him see the tears pouring down her face. Or before she threw herself into his arms and sobbed like a baby.

December

Adrian held his breath as he slowly opened the kiln to reveal the cooled pieces inside. He prayed the slight modifications in size that occurred with porcelain glazing wouldn't affect the finished work too much.

Juan's fluorescent work lights weren't as good as sunshine, but it was almost midnight and he had no alternative. With the deftness of practice, Adrian unloaded the kiln, sorting the glazed pieces on the waiting rack.

With the eye of a skilled craftsman, he examined each piece for crazing or other flaws that would impede their value, but his heart beat faster as he neared the special one in the oven's center.

At last he'd unloaded the pots blocking the luminescent silver of the center piece. Reverently, he lifted it out, carrying the delicate, heart-shaped vase to the light to examine it thoroughly.

It worked. His fingers trembled as he smoothed them inside and out, searching for any imperfection. The color was exquisite, the pure moon-silver of clair de lune. Light flowed through the transparent thinness of the lip, and a shattered rainbow of color twinkled from the crystal burst on the base. The crystal would probably label the piece as commercial art instead of pure art, but he had no patience with labels. The crystal symbolized something far more important than the opinions of anyone but the person for whom the vase was designed.

He didn't know what she'd think when he sent it to her in Juan's next shipment. He knew she'd recognize the work, though. Faith had an excellent eye for detail, and she possessed the mate to this already.

Through the window he'd opened to let out the kiln's heat, he could hear the tinkle of Isabel's laughter, coupled with Juan's deeper chuckle and the babbling of an infant. They'd christened their firstborn after Faith, but they'd used her maiden name. Little Hope Martinez was the delight of her parents' lives.

Adrian felt a familiar arrow of pain as he heard the love and laughter spilling from the farmhouse. Poverty had tested Juan and Isabel's love much as the heat of the kiln tested the worth of a potter's art. Their love had emerged from the inferno sturdier and more unbreakable than before.

He didn't have their strength, he knew. Like unbaked clay,

he was drying out and crumbling. Pouring his love into this vase had held him together a little while longer.

And now it was done. Once he sent it to Faith, perhaps she'd understand. He'd never wanted to hurt her. The pain in her eyes that day at the courthouse had nearly crippled him.

The well of emotion dammed inside him threatened to burst as he set the vase down. He was grateful for the interruption of a sudden cloudburst of rain splattering against the tin roof. Rain this late in December didn't bode well.

Cleaning off his hands on a rag, wiping surreptitiously at the moisture in his eyes, Adrian stalked outside and glared into the starless sky. If the rain turned to ice or snow, Juan wouldn't deliver the shipment before Christmas. The vase wasn't on the shipment's invoice. It was a gift, and he needed Faith to have it.

Raindrops splashed his face as he stared upward, willing the clouds away. He had ten thousand nights like this ahead, ten thousand nights when he could stare into the empty sky and wonder where he'd gone wrong, wonder why it was his burden to love a woman enough to let her go so she might find happiness.

Droplets coursed down Adrian's cheeks, ultimately soaking into his shirt as his heart cried for its missing piece. Faith had turned his fury and misery and hatred into sanity and love. She'd poured honey on troubled waters, soothed his pain with just her presence. He didn't know how she'd done it, and he wanted to hate her for showing him what he couldn't have.

He'd thought it would kill him not to have his career back, not to have fine cars and nice houses, not to provide his family with the small luxuries they deserved. Instead it was killing him not to have what could have been his—had he broken his convictions and grabbed what she'd offered.

His career and freedom, or the responsibility of Faith's love. How dumb could one man be?

He'd made the choice for her. He'd never given her a chance to voice her opinion.

A snowflake struck his nose. A spot of white froze to the

ice forming on his soaked shirt. By morning the road out of here would be impassable.

Heart kick-starting into full throttle, Adrian raced to the kiln room. The vase sat there, radiating beauty in the harsh glare of the worklight. He had the power to give Faith the Christmas she deserved. She might not want him any longer, but he knew her heart better than his own. The vase would bring her happiness.

If he could do just one right thing at a time, he might dig his way out of this hole he lived in.

The trip to Knoxville usually took four hours in Juan's rusty pickup. By the time Adrian threw on dry clothes, wrapped the vase, added chains to the tires, and chugged behind crawling traffic over the mountain, it was well past dawn when he reached the city.

The snow had done no more than lay a frosting of white on trees and bushes, but salt trucks had churned the roads to gray slush, and traffic slid and spun as if it had been a blizzard. Adrian pulled into a Waffle House for a cup of coffee and to debate his next move. His sentimental midnight journey had become a complex logistical problem by dawn.

It was the day before Christmas. Would Faith open the store or did she have other plans? Should he call her? He didn't even know if she'd left that flophouse apartment yet. Juan had mentioned that she was moving.

If he just thought of it as a logistical problem, he might survive. He could deliver the gift and holiday greetings and see how she was doing. If she didn't seem interested in more, he'd move on. And keep moving on. The other side of the planet wouldn't be far enough. Maybe he could volunteer for outer space.

If he saw any sign of another lover, he'd probably slit his throat.

It was almost eight. He eased the truck back into the slush and steered for the fancy shopping center. He was still the ex-con who'd walked in on her months ago, but at least now he had some hope of having his record cleared. But he was still broke, and likely to stay that way. She deserved better, and he wanted her to have whatever she desired.

He just didn't want to know about it if it wasn't him.

Grunting at his own perversity, Adrian eased the truck into the nearly empty lot and rolled to the front of the shop, looking for a sign. She'd decorated the gallery windows with graceful ropes of live evergreen intertwined with cheap glittering gold roping, and he grinned at the combination. It looked festive and not in the least tacky. White fairy lights in the arrangement twinkled against the early morning gloom.

With disappointment, he read the sign announcing CLOSED UNTIL DECEMBER 26TH. She was losing high-volume, last minute Christmas sales, but giving herself and her employees a break.

That didn't seem right. Faith would work alone unless she had plans more important than the shop. The shelter?

The streets of the inner city were drier, and the traffic was fairly light. He pulled up in front of the shelter before nine.

The place had undergone a face-lift since his last visit. Windows sparkled in newly painted frames, and blinking lights offered a cheerful welcome around the door. He recognized the evergreen and gold motif of the roping and grinned again. The mixture of classy and common made sense to someone of Faith's open-minded view of the world.

He wished he'd thought to bring gifts as he entered to the music of children laughing. A tree gaily decorated in paper chains and cutout angels filled a corner of the hall, which also had been painted recently. Annie was doing wonders with this place—with Faith's help, he surmised, noticing a ceramic Santa Claus carrying a bag filled with real peppermint sticks.

Annie looked up in surprise at Adrian's entrance. She'd had her hair tinted and styled, and wore a thick oatmeal-colored sweater against the chill of the high-ceilinged room. She no longer looked worn or frantic, but he recognized the hostility she shot him. He'd never quite wormed his way into Annie's good graces after the kidnapping incident.

"What do you want?" she snapped ungraciously.

Adrian still grinned like a fool. Faith hadn't just left her mark on the shelter. She was rubbing off on shy Annie as well.

"I have a special delivery for Faith, but her shop is closed. I had some idea she might be here. Is that her causing the racket upstairs?" A burst of laughter and shouts of delight echoed through the floorboards.

"She'll be here later. That's Grizzly. Faith talked him into playing Santa Claus for the kids. He was too excited by the role to wait another day." Annie sat back in her chair and outwaited him.

He'd have to ask, but he couldn't hide his fascination with what Faith had wrought in the lives around her. He wished he'd been here to share her triumph in talking the old drunk into a useful role, or her joy in bringing light to a place known for its lack of it. Faith Hope. Her parents had named her well.

"I take it Tony didn't file an injunction against her trust fund, then." She must have put the fear of hell into him. "The shelter looks good."

Annie shrugged. "Our fund-raising is improving. We used her last donation for the down payment on another building, but all the rest is hard work. She doesn't have the fund anymore."

Adrian frowned. "Why didn't she tell me? Tony doesn't deserve a penny of that money. I would have fought—"

Annie waved away his protest. "She dissolved it voluntarily, with the help of her divorce lawyer. She had it in her cracked brain that Tony's kids deserved the bulk of it. She's tied it up so the Shaws can't empty it, but otherwise it's more or less gone."

Adrian absorbed this information without comment. He didn't have any argument with Faith's choice. It was her money, and she could use it as she wished. The remark about the divorce lawyer had him stirring uneasily, though. "Her divorce final?" he asked gruffly, not knowing any better way to come at it.

"Not that it's any of your business, but yeah. Tony didn't have a leg to stand on." Annie smiled gloatingly. "I went with her when she signed the papers. I wanted to celebrate with champagne, but she brushed it off as if she'd just written a

check for a new dress. I admire her fiercely." The threat behind that was unmistakable.

Adrian acknowledged her protectiveness with a nod. Faith
brought that out in people, but she didn't need or want it. He
understood that now.

"The world needs more people like Faith," he agreed, heart
racing erratically as his determination grew with every roadblock thrown in his way. "I brought her something for Christmas. Is she still in her old apartment?"

"She's moving," Annie stated flatly. "She didn't think this
was a good place to—" She cut herself off. "Anyway, I don't
know if she's at the old place or the new. She'll be here later, if
you want to leave it."

Drawing in a deep breath, Adrian remembered the loneliness of snowflakes and the warmth of laughter and the flash
of naked admiration he'd once seen in Faith's eyes, and he
gathered the courage to crawl.

"Please, if you would, give me her new address, and I'll
check both places." Faith had called him an arrogant ass and
an insufferable prick, and she was dead-on on both counts,
but he was prepared to eat humble pie and beg on his knees
right now. She could throw him out on his face, but he had to
see her one more time.

Annie narrowed her eyes and thought about it.

"I only want what's best for her," he promised. "It's
Christmas, Annie. Please."

"I'm probably making the worst mistake of my life," she
grumbled, reaching into her desk.

"If this is the only mistake you make, you're a saint," he
said fervently as she handed over a piece of notepaper with
the address scribbled on it. He scanned it quickly, committing
it to memory so nothing could part him from it.

"If Faith lets you through the door, she's the saint," Annie
corrected dryly. "Or a bloody fool."

"If she lets me through the door, she's both."

As Adrian turned to walk out, a pigtailed toddler ran
squealing down the hall, and terror and excitement exploded

in his chest. Faith would want children. He ought to turn around right now and head for the hills.

With the prize of Faith's happiness firmly in mind, he climbed into the derelict old truck and steered it onto the highway in the direction Annie had given him.

❧ THIRTY-EIGHT ❦

Sitting on the kitchen floor, wrapping the final package for the men at the shelter, Faith looked up in surprise at the sound of her doorbell. She glanced at the oven clock—it wasn't even ten in the morning on the day before Christmas. She wasn't officially moved in yet. Who in the world could it be?

Rising, she brushed snippets of ribbon and paper from her red cashmere sweater and tucked a straying hank of hair behind her ear.

This wasn't the inner city, and she didn't need a peephole, she decided as she reached for the knob. She refused to live in fear and paranoia. She had a sturdy storm door between her and the visitor, should she need it.

At the sight of Adrian on the other side of the glass, she grabbed the door frame for support.

She drank in every inch of him, the windblown raven hair, the tense, harsh line of his jaw, the glitter of silver at his ear, the way his eyes glowed with dark fires as his gaze swept over her. Suddenly nervous, she focused on the muscles straining against his flannel shirt—he wasn't wearing a coat.

She opened the door and wordlessly gestured for him to enter. His gaze never left her as he crossed the threshold carrying a cardboard box.

"You're more beautiful than I remembered," he whispered hoarsely. "You look radiant enough to light entire rows of Christmas trees."

His words could have melted stone, and she wasn't made of stone. She wanted to weep with joy, but she'd learned her lessons well. Pretty words couldn't mend the bridges he had burned.

He smelled of damp flannel and spicy aftershave and of the man she remembered much too clearly, naked and sweating beside her in bed. She closed her eyes as her head spun at the image. Desire clawed at her insides.

"Are you all right?"

His hand instinctively cupped her elbow, and she opened her eyes to read the concern etching his brow, the concern she knew was genuine and made her want to weep for all the months of missing it.

"I'm fine. I just never thought to see you . . ." She gestured helplessly and looked around for someplace to put him. The carpet was littered with boxes and odds and ends the guys had moved on their days off, but the only significant piece of furniture was the newly delivered mattress set in the bedroom. She didn't think she should offer him a seat there. "I can fix you some coffee," she said tentatively, "but we'll have to sit on the floor."

"It's a nice neighborhood," he said approvingly, not releasing her arm. She felt as if he were gobbling her up.

Nervously, she rubbed her hands up and down her arms and turned toward the kitchen. She wanted to be free and dependent on no man, but she loved him so much she thought she'd die of wanting him.

"The government has a fund for first time home buyers. Since Tony bought our house through the corporation, I apparently qualified." She chattered as she searched for mugs and measured coffee into the machine. "The loan required perfect credit. The truck loan hurt me, but some head honcho agreed the truck was worth more than the loan, so it was okay." He probably didn't want to hear any of this, but she was terrified of why he'd come here. Her hopes couldn't bear any more dashing.

He skirted around the stacks of cheerfully wrapped packages on the gleaming vinyl floor and gazed out the wide windows to the backyard. "Nice yard, room enough for a garden.

The fence ought to keep the dogs and kids out. Or in. You should like it here."

Adrian wasn't very good at hiding his feelings. He didn't sound happy for her. The mention of kids startled her, but she figured he was being pragmatic.

He'd set his box on the counter, and she eyed it speculatively. Juan had promised her a shipment, but this was the wrong size.

"Dolores sent me a Christmas card," she said politely. "She said you'd taken the pictures of her in the red cheerleading outfit, but you made her look as fat as Mrs. Claus."

He laughed shortly. "I wouldn't wish Dolores on any man, not even Santa. She thinks she wants to be a social worker. Can you believe it? It will cost fortunes to send her to school so she can be poor for the rest of her life. The girl has no sense, just like Belinda."

"She'll be all right, just like Belinda," she corrected, pouring the coffee and coming up behind him to hand it over. She didn't want to sound sharp. She wanted to touch him, wished she had the right to ease his anxiety, but she didn't. "Happiness comes from the heart, not from the pocket."

"Fat lot you know," he grumbled, absently taking the mug and sipping without looking at her. "Go ahead, open the package. I've already made a fool of myself by coming here. I might as well complete the job."

Tears stung her eyes at his gruffness because she knew it came from some inner conflict and not from anger at her. She ought to take a bite out of his shoulder and wake him up. Instead she obediently reached for the box.

"You've always been a fool, Quinn," she chided. "But when it can be found, your heart is in the right place, too. Your mother raised all her children well, and you're no exception." She used scissors to slice the packing tape.

He swung around and leaned against the wall, sipping his coffee as he watched her. Against her pretty terra cotta kitchen, he looked masculine and dangerous, but he exuded pain and warmth, and she desperately wanted to hug him and make him smile again. Why had he come here?

"Hearts are fairly unreliable, worthless bits of tissue," he scoffed. "They don't put a roof over our heads or food in our stomachs."

"No, that's why we have brains, and if yours is smart enough to deflate your massive ego on occasion, it can figure out how to feed you." She lifted the bubble-wrapped contents from the box. Juan had sent her a present, she guessed with a twinge of disappointment. "But your brain hasn't learned to listen to your heart often enough."

"Oh, it listens," he said reluctantly. "It just doesn't believe."

Faith was the one no longer listening. Her fingers trembled as the wrapping fell away, revealing the stunningly impossible porcelain within. "Clair de lune?" she whispered in disbelief. Then, as the final piece of plastic came off and she held the heart-shaped piece in her hands, she gave a tear-filled cry of joy.

"It's yours to do with as you will. You can heave it at my head if you like." Adrian remained frozen against the window, watching her warily.

"My God," she whispered worshipfully. "*You* made this. This isn't Juan's. He's good, but . . ." She swung around, clutching the precious vase to her chest, her eyes widening in comprehension. "You made the other! You're my lost artist!"

Adrian shrugged uncomfortably and looked down at his coffee. "I wanted to see if I could replicate clair de lune. It was a challenge."

She wanted to hit him, throw something at him, smack some sense into that damnably thick—brilliant—head of his. She could only clutch his gift more fiercely to her heart while tears gathered in her eyes. "You're a gifted genius," she cried incoherently. That wasn't what she wanted to say, but how could she tell him what he already knew?

Something bright and appreciative flashed across his expression as he lifted his head and their gazes met, but that didn't change his opinion.

"Creative genius doesn't pay the bills," he argued. "I just wanted to show you—" He flung up his hands in disgust, splashing coffee across his cuff. "Oh, hell, I don't know what

I wanted to show you. I've been out of my mind for months, maybe years, for all I know. You're the only one who can make me see sense."

His glare defied her to contradict him. She loved the man so much she could read him like a book when he opened up like this. Her heart did a silly Snoopy dance inside her rib cage as she clung to his offering of love, such as it was. For a lawyer, he seemed to have lost his magical gift for words.

She lifted the vase to study the burst of crystal before she melted beneath his heated gaze and forgot all the lessons she'd learned. They had problems so deep they would need far more than pretty words to cross them, and more rode on this than he understood. She might as well dash all her foolish hopes at once.

Very gently, almost reluctantly, she set the vase down, brushing loving fingers over the impossibly beautiful surface. But the man waiting for her reply was more important than this piece of genius. She wanted to throw caution to the winds, fling herself into his arms and plead with him to stay despite all his scruples. She would promise him the moon and stupidly try to give it to him because that was the way her heart worked.

This time there was more at stake than her dumb heart.

Relinquishing the vase, she crossed her arms and met Adrian's anxious gaze. She loved that he didn't try to hide his uncertainty. He could be macho man when protecting those he loved, but he suffered just as anyone else did, and wasn't afraid to show it.

"I love you," she stated simply, searching his face for understanding. He twitched and quickly shuttered a flash of hope, waiting for the "but" that would surely follow. Smart man.

"I know it's a silly thing to say," she admitted. "We never properly dated, and we were only together a few weeks, and I was certain it was just desperation on both our parts." She threw an apprehensive glance to the vase, seeking reassurance that she hadn't misunderstood his intent. The brilliant porcelain sparkled and winked with promise in the sunlight, and she drew a deep breath for strength. "But whatever we had together, it doesn't go away, and I can't stop thinking about you. I'll never stop thinking about you."

He relaxed fractionally, still looking for the "but," the reason this wouldn't work, as he had every right to do. They had huge barriers to cross, as they'd already proved.

"I thought I could drive you out of my head if I worked on that vase," he admitted, not moving toward her. "But everything I did reminded me of you. I could capture the translucent beauty of your skin, but I decided clair de lune didn't suit it. I wanted to throw out the glaze and develop another, one with the golden glow of sunshine. You're driving me *insane*," he said, before his jaw locked tight.

Faith smiled at his frustration, but if he thought sexual frustration drove him insane, wait until she hit him with the rest. His pretty words couldn't even begin to overcome that.

Adrian didn't give her the opportunity to break her news. Instead he dragged her into his arms and held her so tightly she thought he'd crack her ribs. She breathed deeply of his familiar scent, clutched the soft flannel of his shirt, and did her best to burrow through his hard chest and into the heart thumping against her ear.

"I have thanked God at least a thousand times for sending the miracle of you to prove I hadn't been forgotten," he said hoarsely. "I've tried to believe it was best not to tamper with miracles, but I'm afraid you've taught me how human I really am. I want to hold that miracle in my arms for a lifetime. Give me a chance, Faith."

She couldn't move, could hardly breathe, at such an admission from the grimly practical Adrian Quinn Raphael.

His arms tightened around her. "I don't know how to show you what I feel. You can even buy a damned *house* without me. You don't need anything I have to offer. Worse, I can't offer you anything but a lifetime of crises. I don't want to lay that burden on you, but dammit, Faith, I love you, and I can't see how I'll exist without you."

Tears spilled down her cheeks and she shook her head in desperation. They could so easily destroy each other like this. She had one too many experiences in self-destruction. She wanted this perfectly clear now, and to hell with him and his male pride.

She shoved away, wiping the tears from her cheeks. He looked bewildered but let her go without protest. "I can't change you. You have to want to change. If you still think you need money to control life, we don't have a chance."

He looked grim, but accepting. "I'm working on it. It's not easy, but give me credit for trying. I send the family money but don't tell them what to do with it. I like working with clay, and if there is any chance . . ." He gestured in despair. "But nothing I do matters anymore. Not without you."

Shaking, she caught her elbows for support and offered him the knife he could use to sever the thread between them. "I'm pregnant," she said flatly. "I know how you feel about not having children unless you can support them, but I want this baby, and I won't give it up for you or anyone else. I can take care of it without your damned money."

Shock and joy and panic flitted across Adrian's stark features in swift succession. Again his glib lawyer's tongue failed him while he struggled to absorb her blow without staggering.

Apparently without any font of wisdom to offer, he dropped his avid gaze to the region between her hips. "You're not showing," he declared idiotically, before running his hand over the back of his neck and returning his confused gaze upward.

Faith wished she had a Polaroid to capture this priceless moment. She waited expectantly. She'd said all she could. He was the one who had to offer proof that he'd changed. He needed to understand that love was worth more than money, that happiness came from who he was and not what profession he practiced, before he could trust her to share his burdens and not be one.

"I . . . We . . ." He stammered helplessly, then with the total ruthlessness of his mighty ego, Adrian grinned, dragged her into his arms again and murmured, "Thank God," before stifling all protest with a kiss.

Outrage melted into laughter at his utter disregard for anything but getting what he wanted, any way he could have it. Joyously, Faith flung her arms around the neck she ought to wring, and surrendered willingly as he swept her off the floor. She didn't even have to show him where the mattress was. He found it perfectly well on his own.

Propping his head on one hand, letting the other trail downward between Faith's breasts until it circled the slightly convex surface of her abdomen, Adrian looked for all the world like some self-satisfied pasha with his crown jewels. The smug smile hadn't disappeared from his face since she'd broken the news. That certainly hadn't been the reaction she'd been expecting.

"I thought you'd be angry," she said warily. She was still weak and panting from his physical expression of joy and love, but she'd worried for so long, she couldn't believe his brain had accepted all the problems involved with this new development.

He drew a dreamy circle around her navel before spreading his palm over the area he'd marked and meeting her gaze with a fierce smile. "Mine. Civilization and logic cannot compete with primitive possession. Half that creature growing inside you is mine, and I will do whatever it takes to be part of his or her life. If you really love me, you'll not deny me this."

He said it without a shred of doubt. Self-confident ass. Faith pummeled his shoulder until she'd laid him flat on his back. Straddling him, she pinned his shoulders to the pillow. She knew full well he could flip her off without wasting a drop of sweat, but he lay there expectantly, waiting for her take on the situation. She could argue until she was blue in the face, and he'd listen with that same air of interest, and still stick to his own agenda.

"I love you, even if you are a stubborn oaf," she agreed, "but that doesn't change the hurdles ahead. I just bought a house because you were too stupid to see beyond your own blind idiocy. I have a business here I don't want to give up. Maybe I can expand to Charlotte someday, but not right now.

How do you intend to get past your immense macho ego to be part of any child's life when you're living a mountain range away?"

He planted his talented hands around her hips and slid his fingers caressingly along the soft skin of her buttocks. Faith shivered at the sensation, but she didn't retreat. Adrian's dark eyes danced with delight at her challenge.

"Life is my goal these days. I can do anything," he boasted. "I can make porcelain or sell it. I fry a mean hamburger. Someday, I'll have that license back, and I can write wills from the back of pickup trucks. I can build your new stores and write the papers to incorporate them. I have discovered I'm a man of many talents."

He swung Faith back to the mattress and climbed on top of her, trapping her thighs between his while he smothered her breasts in kisses. When she was writhing beneath him, he sat up again with a triumphant smirk. "I even know how to change baby diapers. What I do isn't as important as how I live." The smirk slipped for a minute as he watched her. "You will have to learn to do without nannies and country clubs."

"I don't need nannies, but what about your family?" she asked breathlessly. "I set aside some of the trust fund for their education, but that doesn't—"

"You *what*?" he shouted in outrage. "For *my* family? I'm perfectly capable—"

She had his number now. Reaching high, she tickled his armpits, reducing his machismo to chortling protests as he rolled away in retreat. She climbed back on top again. "*My* family now," she crowed triumphantly. "*My* child, *my* thick-skulled genius of a—" She halted, momentarily nonplussed. She narrowed her eyes and glared at him. "You are planning on marrying me, aren't you? Possession may be nine-tenths of the law, but I believe in proper legalities."

"Oh, yeah, but I'm tying you up so tight it will require both our signatures before you can run away from me, *mi corazón*. We fight to the finish, which brings us back to the subject you are avoiding. What is this about *my* family?"

"It isn't much." She gasped as he gently tweaked her nipples and warm butter seemed to melt through her middle. How did he expect her to think, much less argue, like this? "I just calculated your salary times the four years lost and put that amount aside for your family. It isn't a lot, but the lawyers agreed it was perfectly reasonable, since Tony's sons got the rest."

Adrian growled and frowned and flipped her over again, but Faith didn't give him time to put together a measured argument. She'd never fare well in a war of words with this man, but she had other advantages. Digging her fingers into the muscled lengths of his arms, she lifted her head to lap at his nipples, and with a cry of surrender, he gave up the battle until a more convenient time.

Read on for a special sneak peek at the next
irresistible romance

by Patricia Rice

Coming in Fall 2001

❧ ONE ❧

I am a rotten person.

Biting her lip, Cleo Alyssum painstakingly printed this fact into her journal. She thought the whole idea of a journal of emotions about as silly as it got, but if the counselor wanted honesty, that's what he would get.

She would do anything to transform herself into the kind of mother Matty needed. *Anything.*

Of course, that's how she'd got into this situation in the first place. Sitting back in her desk chair, she gazed out the sagging windowpanes of the old house she was restoring. She missed Matty so desperately her teeth ached, but she had to do what was best for him. The schools in this rural coastal area couldn't offer the programs he needed, and Maya could.

She'd tried suburban life with her sister, but she just couldn't hack it. Trouble found her too easily in crowds. Out here on the island she could get her head together without too many people in her face.

She'd spent the last few years learning to restore old buildings, turning decrepit dumps into useful, viable business places and homes, and she loved the satisfaction of seeing the visible results of her hard work. Pity the difference she was supposed to be making in herself wasn't as obvious.

The opportunity to buy a small town hardware store

had opened up just as she'd run out of buildings to restore, and at the time it had seemed ideal. She knew the business inside and out, loved the isolation of the Carolina coast, and when she'd found this run-down island farmhouse for an unbelievable price, she'd known she'd found a home. The beach cottage down by the shore might be beyond hope, but she wasn't ready to give up on that quite yet. Maya and the kids might visit more often if she could fix it up. In the meantime she was diligently turning the main house into the home she'd never known. She hoped.

If she could only convince her federal supervisor she was a fine, upstanding citizen, she'd be free and clear soon, and just about living normally for the first time in her life.

With a job without hassles from any boss and a home where she could lock the doors against the world, she thought she finally had a chance of living a civilized life. She wasn't doing this for the feds, though. Matty deserved a sane mother, and she was doing her best—if the process didn't kill her first. At least now when he was with her she could give him her entire attention, and he seemed to be blossoming into a new kid with the change. Even Maya had noted how much happier he was.

Cleo ran her fingers through her stubby hair and returned to staring at the almost empty page of the notebook. She didn't think she was capable of verbalizing all her conflicting emotions about her sister. Maya could have written an entire essay on how Cleo felt about her. Cleo would rather hammer nails.

If she compared her mothering skills to Perfect Maya's, she was destined for failure.

The muffled noise of a car engine diverted her attention. A fresh breeze off the ocean blew through the windows in the back of the house, but the only things coming through the floor-to-ceiling front windows were flies. Thickets of spindly pines, palmettos, and wax myrtle prevented her from seeing the driveway entrance or the rough shell road beyond.

She didn't encourage visitors and wasn't expecting anyone. A lost tourist would turn around soon enough.

She returned to the blank page of her journal and printed: *People are pains in the a . . .* She crossed out the *a* and substituted *butts.*

She crinkled her nose at the result. One word probably wasn't any more polite than the other.

She could write in cursive instead of printing, but her letters were so small and turned in on themselves as to be illegible even to her. Maybe that was the trick—write illegibly so the counselor couldn't read this crap.

The smooth hum of the car's powerful engine hesitated, and Cleo waited for the music of it backing up and turning around. Someone took good care of this machine. She couldn't hear a single piston out of sync.

She rolled her eyes as the obtuse visitor gunned the engine and roared past the four-foot blinking NO TRESPASSING sign. One would think a message that large would be taken seriously, but tourists determined to reach a secluded beach were nearly unstoppable.

"Nearly" was the operative word here.

Biting her bottom lip again, Cleo reread her two-line entry. She had to go into town and open the store shortly. She didn't have time for detailed expositions. It looked to her like a few good strong sentences ought to be sufficient.

Adding *Men are the root of all evil* struck her as funny, but she supposed a male counselor wouldn't appreciate it. She left it there anyway. The counselor had said he wanted honesty. Of course, she was probably sabotaging all her efforts. She'd had enough therapy to acknowledge her self-destructive tendencies. Now, if she'd only *apply* that knowledge. . . .

She lifted her pen and waited for the car engine to reach the next turn in the half-mile long lane. The sound of waves crashing in the distance almost drowned out the wicked screech of the mechanical witch she had installed as a second method to foil trespassers. Still, she heard the car tires squeal as they braked. The battery-operated strobe light was particularly effective at keeping teenagers from turning this into a lover's lane at night. During the day, well. . . .

She struggled and capped the pen. That was enough introspection for one day. The counselor ought to know she was a mucked-up mess. She shouldn't have to lay it out in terms a first grader could understand. Another thought occurred to her, and she grabbed the pen again.

Baring my soul is not my style.

There. That ought to be letting it out enough for one day.

Her head shot up as the car engine drew closer, evidently bypassing the scowling witch. Stupid bastard. What was she supposed to do, dump a load of pig turds on him to get the message across? That might work if they were driving a convertible.

They usually were.

She despised the arrogant, self-confident yuppie asses who thought the whole world was their oyster. Didn't PRIVATE PROPERTY mean anything to them?

Apparently not. The car engine zoomed right past the pop-up sign she'd rigged in the middle of the lane. Forgetting to turn off the system before she'd left for work, she'd driven around the sign one too many times herself, and the dirt bypass was clearly visible. She'd plant a palmetto there tomorrow.

Slamming the notebook into her desk drawer, she picked up her purse and donned her glasses. She hadn't quite perfected the mechanism to shut the swinging post barrier to the beach. She hated the idea of erecting a fence across there. The moron would simply have to drown if he insisted on using her beach. A bad undertow past the rocks made this a dangerous strip for swimming, but she supposed the NO SWIMMING signs wouldn't stop this nematode either.

Maybe she could rig a siren to a motion detector. There wasn't any law out here for it to summon, but tourists wouldn't know that.

Pulling out her truck keys, she almost didn't hear the purr of the engine turning into her drive, but the shriek of a hidden peacock warned of the intrusion.

Damn. Did the jerk think the house deserted? Admittedly, she hadn't bothered painting the weathered gray boards and the sagging shutters, but she kind of thought them picturesque. And it wasn't as if she hadn't littered the place with warning signs. If the town council insisted on encouraging film crews to work here, she'd be prepared to keep them out. She hadn't traveled an entire continent to have that California lifestyle follow her.

She waited as the barking guard dog yapped through its entire routine. A real dog would scare the peacocks, but the tape recording was usually effective. Amazing how many people were frightened of barking dogs. The mailman had quit delivering to the door after he'd heard it.

She sighed as the driver shut off the car engine instead of turning around. Determined suckers. Only

Maya and Axell ever got this far past her guardians. She could slip out the back way, but curiosity riveted her to the window. She knew she was far enough back not to be seen, but she still had a partial view of the walk and porch. She couldn't wait to see how her intrepid guest reacted to her burglar alarm system.

She chewed on a hangnail as a pair of long-legged, crisply ironed khakis appeared beneath the porch over-hang. A man. She should have known. Men had to prove themselves by showing no fear. It didn't seem to matter if they showed no intelligence while they were at it.

She admired the lean torso decked in a tight black polo appearing next. She was sick of looking at fat slugs with pooching white bellies and hairy, sunken chests cluttering the view from the beach. At least this ape strode tall and straight and . . .

My, my. She stopped chewing her finger to relish the loose-limbed swing of wide shoulders and a corded throat topped by a long, angular face with more char-acter than prettiness. He was all length—arms, legs, nose, neck—but they all fit together in a casual sort of package. He had his hands in his pockets as he gazed up at her mildly eccentric porch, so she couldn't see his fin-gers, but she'd bet they were a piano teacher's dream.

Tousled sable hair fell across a tanned brow, and she was almost sorry she'd left the security system on. If he was selling insurance, she wouldn't mind listening to his pitch just to hear what came out of a package like that.

The aviator sunglasses were a downright sexy trim for this parcel.

"You are under alert!" The loudspeaker blared as soon as the intruder hit the first porch step. She'd used

charm as he could summon. Maybe this was a young relative of the old witch the kids had warned him about. "I'm looking for Cleo Alyssum."

"She's not here."

She said that so promptly Jared figured this had to be her. Well, well. Curiouser and curiouser.

He produced a business card from his pocket with his hotel phone number scratched on the back. "I've been told Miss Alyssum is owner of the beach property back of here, and I'm interested in leasing it. I'm prepared to make a generous offer." From the look of this run-down sprawling plantation-era farmhouse, she could use the cash.

She took the card and dropped it in her shirt pocket. "She doesn't like neighbors." Turning around, she shut and locked the peeling white door, and did something that reeled the skeleton upward like a collapsing party favor.

"Your car's blocking my drive," she said curtly as he moved aside to let her pass. "And you're trespassing, in case you didn't notice."

Not a smile, not a dimple, not a look of interest crossed her stoic features. Jared shrugged and ambled back toward his Jag. Women usually liked him, and he couldn't see that he'd done anything to tick this one off. NO TRESPASSING signs applied to salesmen, not legitimate visitors, as far as he could see. Surely she hadn't really thought to scare him off?

"Do you have some idea when Miss Alyssum might return?" He played along with her gag and cast her a sideways look to see if anything registered in her expression. She had a short, finely-honed aquiline nose with a sprinkle of freckles across it, and a mouth drawn too tight to reveal any trace of humor. He wouldn't call it a friendly face by any means. He could cut timbers with the sharp edge of her voice.

"She won't be interested. As I said, you're trespassing. I'd advise you to turn around before the police arrive." She headed for a beat-up black Chevy pickup truck, opened the door, then waited for him to move his car.

She didn't even show an interest in his antique Jag. Damn. That car drew more comments than honeysuckle drew bees. Was she blind?

There had to be some way around her. He'd never accepted "no" as an answer in his life. Not that many people told him no in the first place. He wasn't an unreasonable man. She had a run-down beach shack going to waste. He wanted to put it to good use. He couldn't see the problem.

"I can afford whatever price Miss Alyssum thinks the property is worth. I'll buy it if she'd rather not lease it. Just pass the message along, will you?" He leaned against his car door and watched her climb into her truck without replying. Well, damn.

Maybe she *was* a witch, but she had all his incorrigible hormones humming. He sighed as she cranked the truck to life without looking back. He'd better move the Jag or she'd drive over it.

Spinning his tires in the soft sand, he edged out of her way and let her fly off down the lane. He wondered if signs would pop out of the road and witches fly from the trees as she left, or if they were rigged to greet only incoming visitors.

He sure did like the way her mind worked. Wonder if she could rig up some of those spooks for him once he figured out how to obtain the beach house?

Bumping the Jag over a timber barrier, he drove down

toward the beach to inspect the house he'd only seen from a distance. The real estate agents had said there was nothing available out here in the middle of nowhere, but a friend of a friend in LA had told him about this island. The film business was a small world.

This place should be ideal. He could feel it in his bones. None of his friends or family would go out of their way to reach this remote spot. Surely, once he cleared his head, he would be able to think again. Surrounded by all this peace and quiet, he'd cruise right past the roadblock in his mind that had prevented his coming up with any fresh ideas lately.

A witchy landlady would be a distraction, but one distraction against the many his places in New York and Miami offered seemed a fair trade. His fingers itched for the computer keys already, just thinking about the sand and the waves and the peace.

Driving with one hand, he idly swatted at something tickling his ankle. He'd have to remember insect repellant. Beaches were notorious for bugs.

The house ought to be just beyond the curve in the road ahead, if he'd calculated correctly. He didn't know the name of the scrub brush blocking his view, but it grew in heavy thickets neither man nor beast would dare enter. He'd have plenty of privacy.

Especially with the witch's mechanical guardians blocking the way.

Before he could grin at the thought, an eerie high-pitched shriek shattered his eardrums, and an object the size of his mother's frozen Thanksgiving turkeys smashed into his windshield, scattering brilliant blue-green plumage across the glass, obstructing his view with an iridescent psychedelic hallucination.

Frantically swiping at the irritating tickle crawling up

his leg, cursing the Technicolor windshield, he slammed the brakes. The car's rear end resisted stopping and the tires swerved wildly in the soft sand.

Crawling. Up his leg.

Clinging desperately to the wheel for control, Jared glanced downward.

A shiny black snake's tail whipped his leather moccasins. The head had disappeared up his pants leg.

Clutching the spinning steering wheel while cursing frantically, Jared lost control as the car veered sideways on the soft shoulder.

The low-slung chassis hit the ditch at the side of the road, sailed upward, and landed, roof down, in the wax myrtle thicket.

Don't miss the wonderful novel by Patricia Rice

IMPOSSIBLE DREAMS

Maya Alyssum's impossible dream is to open a school where kids can find unconditional love and acceptance, the very things she never had as a child. The town council of Wadeville, North Carolina, is determined to stop her until the day Axell Holm walks into her life. He's the kind of uptight authority figure she loves to hate. . .and hates to love.

Axell knows trouble when he sees it. But he needs the ethereal schoolteacher and the magic she works on his motherless daughter. He's willing to face the wrath of his hometown to get what he wants, but he's unprepared for his reaction to this strange and wonderful woman who turns his ordered life upside down, making him believe in dreams again. . . .

Published by Ivy Books.
Available at bookstores everywhere.

VOLCANO
by Patricia Rice

After landing in gorgeous St. Lucia on business, Penelope Albright receives the shock of her life: She is accused of smuggling drugs. Then a sexy stranger appears, claiming to be her husband, and "kidnaps" her before trouble begins. Or so she thinks. Trouble and Charlie Smith have met. He needs a wife—temporarily—to help him keep a low profile while snooping into the mysterious disappearance of his partner. And like it or not, Penny is already involved.

Published by Fawcett Books.
Available at bookstores everywhere.

BLUE CLOUDS
by Patricia Rice

Around the small California town where Pippa Cochran has fled to escape an abusive boyfriend, Seth Wyatt is called the Grim Reaper—and not just because he is a bestselling author of horror novels. He's an imposing presence, battling more inner demons than even an indefatigable woman like Pippa can handle. Yet, while in his employ, she can't resist the emotional pull of his damaged son or the chance to hide in the fortress he calls a home.

Then Pippa's amazing gifts begin to alter their world in ways none of them could have imagined. But soon something goes wrong. Dangerous "accidents" occur, threatening to destroy the tremulous new love that Pippa and Seth have dared to discover.

Published by Fawcett Books.
Available at bookstores everywhere.

GARDEN OF DREAMS
by Patricia Rice

JD Marshall is a computer programming genius on the run to protect his company, his teenage son, and his life. When JD's truck flips over near the tiny backwoods town of Madrid, Kentucky, Miss Nina Toon comes to his rescue and offers him and his son shelter.

The lovely and lovelorn Nina, a high school teacher with very little experience with men, finds herself intrigued by the gorgeous, longhaired, motorcycle-riding computer nerd sleeping downstairs. Opening her home and her heart and her most precious dreams to JD, Nina decides to take a chance on love. But it will be the biggest gamble of her life. . . .

Published by Fawcett Books.
Available at bookstores everywhere.